I0523420

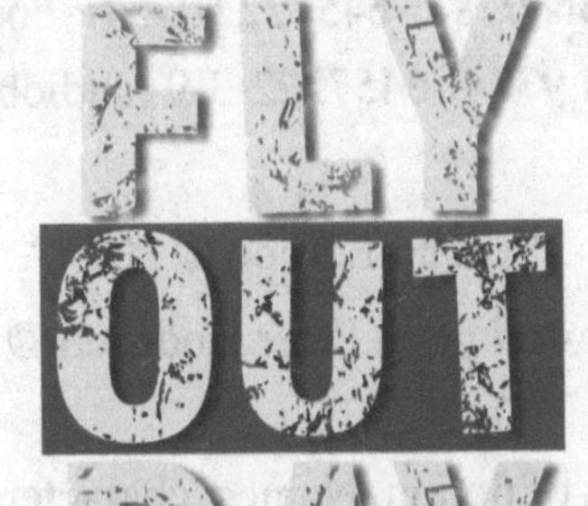

FLY
OUT
DAY

FLY OUT DAY

"I could not put this book down! I read it cover-to-cover in less than a day, I loved the way it was written and was jam packed full of action..."
- Rebecca B. (Goodreads review)

This novel was a labour of love that spanned more than twelve years, three continents, multiple career changes, several relationships and even a pandemic. It has been a *long* road filled with speed bumps and procrastination but here it is:

Fly Out Day; an Australian tale of mateship, mining, old flames, new sparks, guilt, anger and the inconvenience of the dead rising on fly-out day.

As seen in *The Kalgoorlie Miner's* Lifestyle feature article, heard on *ABC Radio's Pilbara Breakfast* morning show and talked about throughout the Western Australian FIFO mining community.

RISE & SHINE

Somewhere near the Gibson Desert
Remote drilling lease 113, Drill Rig No. 2
2000km from Perth, Western Australia

I wake up mid-flight and falling through the air, I've been thrown from my top bunk. My body crosses the room fast and crashes hard into the bunks on the opposite side of the offsider's sleeping quarters.

"Fuarrr…"

I'm winded mid-obscenity by the bunk bed's bulky frame, it strikes me in the back, causing fiery pain to fork its way across my skin. My body contorts in agony.

"Uh, oh, Jesus!" I stagger to my feet.

The room is pitch black and it's hotter than hell. Duffle bags, linen, and other random crap clutter the floor beneath me; I reach over for the light switch on the wall.

Click, click.

Click.

Nothing.

I reach above my head to touch the ceiling light itself to find that its plastic cover is broken, I push my fingers into it and feel the fragments of the shattered light bulb. A thin ribbon of light cuts through the darkness like a knife, it's coming from a crack in the room's only door. The beam of orange light illuminates dust particles as they float by. I try to clear the knee-deep clutter that's obstructing the exit, my body aches and I'm fighting to stand upright. I swear the floor is on an incline. The large plastic cover of the air conditioning unit is awkward to move in the tight, sloping space but I manage to get the area around the door free, only to find it buckled in its frame. I struggle with it for a few seconds before giving it a few swift kicks, it flies open and a wall of heat and unyielding brightness greets me.

I cover my eyes and blindly step out of the doorway, expecting the milk crate step below to catch my foot, but it's not there. I fall to the linoleum floor below and wind myself again, I groan in frustration at another unexpected fall. I mean, come on; I haven't even opened my eyes fully yet. It's going to be a great day, I think to myself.

I push myself up off the sandy linoleum floor and sit looking back up at the doorway and cock my head in confusion.

"That's a lot higher than it should be."

The caravan's doorway to the offsider's quarters is almost a metre higher off the ground than it should be. The annex is only half attached, the pop riveted tracks securing it to the outer wall have been ripped out. Tears in the annex's tarpaulin walls allow wind and red dust to swirl around freely inside the enclosure. I swat the irritating fine red dust away from my face, coughing.

"What the fuck is going on here?"

I get to my feet and look toward the front of the caravan, which is angled up even higher than the rear, it's floating at least two metres off the ground. The whole trailer is banking away from the annex that I'm standing in now, I look under the chassis and see something wedged deep under the front of the caravan. My groggy mind struggles to compute what it's seeing.

A strong smell strikes my nostrils. Exhaust fumes. I smell, a hot engine, coolant, and melting plastic. I hear the hissing of what sounds like a punctured radiator. Someone's crashed into the caravan! Who drove into the caravan? Is it Russell? I'm the only one here, what if he's injured? Help is miles away; it's fly-out day.

I run outside of the annex in a panic, barefoot and only in my boxers, the red-hot dirt welcomes my soft white feet aggressively, but there's no time to acknowledge the burning sensation. My heart and mind are racing. I round the outer corner of the annex and see the rear of a Toyota Hilux sticking out from under the caravan. The ute looks like it's taken one hell of a beating. The windows are smashed, the side panels are dented in and the drop-down sides and tailgate are buckled; the tray is empty aside from the fixed toolbox bolted to the deck.

"What the fuck?!" I run over to the passenger side door and catch sight of the bloody handprints streaking their way down its sides.

"What the fuck? What happened here?"

The support vehicle, a once-new mine spec Toyota Hilux dual cab four-wheel drive ute, is windscreen-deep under the front end of the caravan; twisted metal binds the two vehicles together. Two green jerry cans lay ruptured in the dirt spewing out fuel. I disregard it, and try to open the Hilux's door but it's jarred shut. I look through the shattered window and see Steve, one of the cross-shift offsiders, slumped over the steering wheel. His body is bloodied and motionless.

"Fuck!"

I grab at the door but it's completely fucked. The roof and ROPS are buckled badly on the passenger side and getting this door open will be nigh on impossible, this ute must've rolled or something. The driver's side door is hard up against the annex wall, access looks limited, so I start to wrestle with the passenger door. I lean into the cab through the shattered window and try to open the door from the inside. There's blood everywhere, my eyes dart around the cab's interior and I spot Russell's flight bag in the footwell.

Why is Russell's bag here? Was Russ in the car too? Wait, Steve was flying out today, what's he doing back at camp? Questions are piling up but the answers seem distant.

A loud crack and a shower of sparks interrupt my thoughts and force me to jump back from the Hilux. The power cables running down the side of the caravan are badly damaged, one cable is completely severed and its insulation is blackened and smouldering; the live cable sparks sporadically.

"Shit!" I spin around to see that the generator powering the caravans is still humming away dutifully. "Why hasn't it shut itself off yet? The breakers should have flipped by now. Fuck, they won't flip!" I panic, "The breaker switch!"

In the weeks prior, the generator breakers would flip at the drop of a hat, killing the power to the caravans. A simple act of multitasking, like putting on a load of washing and microwaving a meat pie simultaneously, was enough to trip them. Which is quite annoying, as no power meant no air conditioning and here, in the Australian outback, where it's forty plus degrees plus ev-ery-day, no air conditioning is catastrophic. Refrigerated air came third on my list of remote camp survival necessities, after Wi-Fi and beer but just before food. Now you'd think that a faulty breaker is an easy fix, just replace it, right? Well, we were out of spares, and patience, so we bypassed a few things and even duct-taped a small screw under the switch to stop it from tripping. Electrical safety at its finest.

The generator is too far away. Steve needs my help now. I make a beeline for the long toolbox in the back of the ute tray and open it. I grab the large aluminium pipe wrench and smash the hook jaw between the door and its frame. I start reefing on it to pry the door open, the ute rocks from side to side as I swing off of the wrench's long handle, but I struggle to get a good footing in the slippery, flammable slurry of fuel and red dirt.

Pssszzz... Crack!

I flinch as the power cable sparks violently against the caravan's outer wall. I've gotta get Steve out of the ute. Now. I throw all of my weight into prying the door open and manage to crack it open a few inches. It's not enough, I strain hard against the long aluminium arm of the wrench, pulling and pulling. The door swings open and

I fall into the mud, which now coats my bare legs and arse. The rocking of the ute causes the caravan to slide and grind its way down the bonnet of the Hilux and onto its roo bar. I hear a loud rush of air escaping, something just punctured one of the ute's tyres. Steve stirs within the cab, coughing and struggling to breathe.

"Steve, you're alive!?"

"Ru…" he stutters, coughing hard, "Run."

"Steve, we have to get you out of 'ere, man. Come on."

I'm up from the mud and inside the ute, kneeling on the passenger seat and reaching out for Steve's arm over the clutter inside the cab, but I can't reach him. I start throwing things out of the cab to get closer to him: an esky, Russell's flight bag, a box of rig parts, a backpack.

"Dan, leave me, bro."

"Get fucked, Steve. I'm getting you out of here! Now, move!" I reach for his arm, but he pulls away.

"Cunt!" I yell, "Quit being a fuckin' idiot and..."

I notice a large open wound oozing dark-coloured blood from Steve's forearm. I reach for him again when he swings out at me; his clenched fist connects with the left side of my face and hot pain pulsates from my cheek.

"What the fuck, cunt?!" I spit angrily. I make a fist with my right hand but I hesitate, because Steve's a big boy, a Māori lad from Christchurch. He's six foot two, built like a brick shithouse and could easily bench two of me. So, naturally, I reconsider hitting him back; copping another punch like that would likely knock me out. Steve is hunched over the steering wheel, and breathing heavily, I can see deep cuts and scratches all over his wide back and arms.

Surely, these cuts aren't just from the crash? What

could have made that hole in his forearm? It looks like an animal bit him?

Steve starts violently bucking back and forth in the driver's seat, smashing his head against the steering wheel, then the window, then the headrest and then the steering wheel, again and again. I crawl backwards and out from the cab, shocked; Steve's body convulses aggressively and he yells marbled words between painful cries. I just watch, speechless, as his body jerks and lashes out wildly within the cab when a strange smell breaks my trance. A familiar smell. Gas.

The sound I mistook earlier for air rushing from a tyre is, in fact, gas leaking from one of the two 90kg propane tanks mounted to the front of the caravan. The feed hoses to the caravan are damaged and a chunk of steel has pierced the side of one of the tanks, a pin-prick hole whooshes loudly.

"Fuck!"

I mentally list everything I can see: the pierced propane cylinder and the damaged hoses mounted to the front of the caravan, the ruptured jerry cans of unleaded fuel, the diesel leaking from the ute's fuel tank, the sparking electrical cables and, of course, Steve—caught in the middle of it all.

The chaos unravels in slow motion. The severed electrical cable sparks against the caravan's wall, igniting the gas cloud hissing from the cylinder, a roar rips through the air as one of the propane cylinders explodes.

BOOM!

The explosion knocks me off my feet and back into the mud, gasping as the fireball rips the oxygen out of my lungs. Shrapnel rains down in every direction as a cloud of fire and smoke plumes upwards; the heat is extraordinary. I quickly get to my knees and scurry away through the diesel-soaked mud. The mud covering my body from my first slip is now caked dry, half-baked onto my skin. I look back over my shoulder at the caravan and, surprisingly, it and the ute are still mostly intact. Small pieces of burning debris litter the dirt. I see something moving under the caravan, it's a gas hose, and it's whipping around like a snake with its head cut off.

"Oh, shit! The other tank, I... I'll close the"—I look to the top of the remaining gas cylinder to see the metal anti-tamper cage around its valve is mangled and padlocked shut—"Bloody hell!"

Steve starts screaming and thrashing about in the cab; he's still alive. The small hose clip restraining the whipping gas hose breaks and drops down from the caravan and into the mud. Nearby flames ignite the propane. The now longer, madder and fire-breathing hose lashes out, striking furiously at its surroundings. Its blue and orange flamed tongue licks at the flammable slurry of fuel beneath the Hilux. I stand and run for the fire extinguishers near the other caravan, it's only eight metres away, and I cross the length in the blink of an eye. The hot red dirt burns my bare feet with each stride as I try to dodge the metal shrapnel scattered across the ground. I get to the extinguisher and rip off its plastic sleeve, I pull the pin and spin back toward the imminent inferno, but there is no slow-motion explosion this time. Only fire.

The fuel-soaked slurry beneath the ute ignites, and tall, orange flames engulf the vehicle and a wall of thick black smoke billows skyward. The fire thunders like an angry beast as it spreads to the caravan, and, as loud as the flames are, I can still hear the screams inside the Hilux. Steve's screams. I hurry toward the blaze, crouched low and with intent. The heat is tremendous. I get as close as I can and aim the fire extinguisher at the base of the fire, a pressurised white cloud spews forth. Thank fuck, it works. I'm too far away though, it's not doing anything. The fire's heat is too intense and I can't get any closer. I'm half naked, for fuck's sake, and my boxers are still wet with the fuel-soaked mud.

The propane tank's pressure relief valve shoots a jet of fire six metres high as the flames from below boil its contents. Its valve opens and closes intermittently. I stand up and throw the now-empty extinguisher behind me. The relief valve flame thrower fires more and more rapidly, it's going to fail. I retreat backwards away from the increasing heat when I hear Steve's screams get louder and more desperate inside the cab. Fuck. He's being roasted alive.

The propane cylinder succumbs to the heat and ruptures, sending a third and final fireball ripping through the camp. The blast wave throws me backwards and I hit my head on the fire extinguisher behind me as I fall, knocking me unconscious.

I'm at the Fremantle house, my former home. A modest three-bedroom, single-storey home from the 1980s on a 900m2 block, with its updated rendered outer brick walls, lush green lawns and red stencil-patterned driveway, its street appeal looks neat and modern. An enclosed backyard with Colorbond fencing boasts a covered wooden decked patio, an outdoor kitchen complete with a wood-fired pizza oven, an inset gas barbeque grill and a small sunken coal fire pit too. The backsplash of the outdoor kitchen is painted blood orange and the countertop is made up of small tiles that my wife, Maria, had hand-painted tiny avocados and brightly coloured flowers onto. It was built this way specifically to remind Maria of her childhood home back in South America. It's almost a perfect replica of her father's outdoor kitchen. Although he is proudly Chilean, he loved the Spanish and Mediterranean approach to outdoor entertaining and dining.

An oversized hammock is strung up between an outer veranda post and a tall palm tree, this is one of my favourite spots to chill out in the evening and on weekends. Our home is only a short distance from the local dog beach, a few doors down from the local park at the entrance to our cul-de-sac and a tipsy stumble away from Freo's humming entertainment precinct.

Our house was built in the late eighties, it's a little small but it's ours, not the bank's, and we've made it our home. We didn't need a big flashy new house with all the bells and whistles that other FIFO workers buy, no, we settled for an established home in a great beach-side location. Plus, we had each other, our beautiful new addition to the family, Bella, our firstborn daughter and our giant dumb puppy, Bones, an Australian cattle dog and Siberian Husky mix, commonly called an Ausky. We are happy and we are untouchable in that house.

I'm on the deck in the backyard with eleven-month-old Bella lying against my thighs as we lazily swing in a colourful, oversized hammock. Bones is in the back corner of the lawned yard, sitting in his clam shell paddle pool, panting with his tongue hanging out of his head. The tri-colour Ausky pup has his ice blue-coloured eyes trained on the resident magpie that's walking along the top of the fence, taunting him. It must be summer because the dog is in his plastic pool and Bella is only wearing her nappy and nothing else. She hated wearing clothes and was very comfortable in her own skin, just like her mother, Maria, a stunning tan-skinned kindergarten teacher from South America. We gently sway from side to side in the hammock as I play with Bella. Her tiny hands are wrapped around each of my index fingers as I trace invisible circles in the air with her little hands and then boop her on the nose occasionally.

"Boop, I gotcha. Oh! Boop, gotcha again," she laughs adorably. Her chubby cheeks glow red with joy.

I look over to the hills hoist clothesline in the centre of the yard, where Maria is hanging out the washing. I laugh to myself quietly as I notice that she has to stand on a milk crate to reach the clothesline, she's not the tallest of people, that's for sure. She's wearing a long, red sundress, the one that hugs her figure and highlights her every curve. I love that dress. It's one of her favourite dresses too, only because she knows what it does to me. It is one of her many not-so-secret weapons of distraction, persuasion and seduction. Maria glances over at me and notices me fondling her with my eyes. She has my attention and she knows it, so Maria starts to exaggerate her every movement. She turns her back to me and slowly bends over to get an item out of the basket and then slowly reaches up to peg it to the clothesline. She rolls her hips as she stretches up onto her tippy toes, she glances back to see if I'm enjoying her performance. Latinas do like knowing they're desired, they crave it.

My eyes are glued to her hypnotic figure as she reaches down straight-legged for another item of clothing. She picks out one of her sexier articles from the basket. It's a small black lacy number, the bottoms from one of her many lingerie sets. She holds it delicately between two fingers as she slowly traces the outline of her smooth tanned thigh with it. She runs it behind her upper thigh and over her firm, toned butt cheeks, bringing some of her dress up purposefully as she does so, exposing her bare derrière just enough to show me that she's not wearing any underwear. I feel a warmth wash over me. I close my eyes and tilt my head backwards in a muted celebration of fuck yes.

Bella disappears from my lap all of a sudden, I turn in a panic to find her, only to see that she's inside, laying on her play mat. My brief moment of panic passes and I go back to just staring at Maria as she continues to touch herself and play with her dress, it's a well-rehearsed dance of seduction. I must be dreaming. She places one leg on the milk crate and slowly pulls her dress up her thigh, enticing me over with a sultry gaze, her delicate hand disappears under her dress. I adjust my boardies and sit up in the hammock. I don't know if it's her, or the sun, but I'm getting hot, I look up to the sun as it gets much brighter—blindingly so. I can't even look at it anymore, or Maria, the brightness stings my eyes. I turn away, but the burning sensation increases.

Everything goes white. I can't see, or move; the heat intensifies. It's like fire, I fall out of the hammock and onto the deck. The deck becomes sand. I curl into a kneeling ball and my back sizzles from the heat.

I yell out.

FAR FROM HOME

I'm lying face-up on the searing hot sand. It was a dream! I sit upright and feel a throbbing pain at the back of my head. I bring my hand up to my skull and find a large lump and a small gash. Something must have knocked me out. I turn and, through blurry eyes, see the fire extinguisher on its side with my dried blood on the base of the bottle. I touch my wound tenderly as I try to remember my dream but I only get flashes. Bella, when she was small. Maria. The milk crate. That bloody red dress. It was a memory, from many years ago. A pained, nostalgic smile creases its way across my face before my current reality materialises in front of me. I'm sitting in the middle of a remote exploration drilling rig's campsite, I'm in my boxers staring at the carnage caused by a kamikaze ute, two gas explosions and I'm surrounded by charred parts of a caravan that's been torn to pieces.

I lock on to the scorched shell of the burnt-out ute.

"Steve!" I jump to my feet and run towards him but stars fill my vision and I stumble immediately. Horrible smells pollute the air as I stagger toward the ute, I cover my mouth and nose and frantically look into the Hilux. Steve is a blackened, smouldering corpse. Pink meat and yellowy fat sizzle out from the deep cracks in his overcooked flesh. The skin from his arms and legs has melted to the chair and the inside of the driver's side door. I look up at Steve's face.

"Fuck!" Stomach acid burns my throat and I gag.

The top part of Steve's head is gone, from his eyes up. A piece of scrap metal is embedded in the back seat of the cab, it has the top section of Steve's missing skull and scalp sitting on it. My knees weaken and vomit forces its way out of me. I grab at the side of the burnt-out ute's passenger door on the way down.

"Ahh, fuck!" I rip my hand off of it, it's still very hot.

I hold up my reddened hand to look at it when a stretching, cracking type sound draws my attention back into the cab. The overcooked skin of Steve's swollen stomach splits open and steaming offal spills out into the footwell. I throw up again.

I pull myself together and whip on a Hawaiian shirt and some shorts that were in the annex and extinguish the last of the flames around the caravan and ute. I gag frequently as wafts of the sickly-sweet infusion of burnt hair, hot fat and melted rubber blow past me. I place a scrap length of the annex tarpaulin over the burnt-out vehicle, partly out of respect to Steve, but mostly to try to stop the smell of his corpse fingering my gag reflex. The front of the caravan is peeled open like a tin of baked beans and ninety per cent of the kitchen and annex are gone. Luckily, the offsider's quarters only lost a part of its roof and wasn't touched by the fire; meaning I can salvage all of my belongings. The fire didn't spread too far in the camp either, it didn't even ignite the scrub and grasses surrounding us. Fortunately, the contractor who cleared the pad for this site went a little overboard with his dozer, clearing an extra ten-metre-wide strip either side of our camp.

'I gave ya's a little extra' I remember him saying, chuckling, downplaying his unnecessary clearance of scrub. Russell, my senior driller, offered 'I guess we don't have to use the town's airstrip anymore, you gave us one of our own!' The pair laughed, disregarding the potential ramifications of clearing an excessive amount of native bushland on a mining lease from the local Aboriginal community.

I take a moment to catch my breath under the cool breeze of the air conditioning in the common room of the guest caravan on the other side of the camp, away from the strong smells and wreckage. After six failed attempts to use the satellite phone to call the client and several others, I throw the device onto the couch. 'No signal' flashes with each call attempt. It's now 4pm and thirty-eight degrees Celsius outside, I stand in front of the air conditioner and let the refrigerated air soothe the tender flesh on my back; eighteen degrees of heavenly bliss.

The guest caravan is the deluxe twin of the now destroyed company caravan, it has a large common room at one end with two dining booths, a big flat-screen TV, a bookshelf and a tall beer fridge in the corner. A massive black communications cabinet dominates the furthest corner; it houses the radio chargers, satellite phones and internet equipment. This caravan has two self-contained en-suite bedrooms too, each fitted with brand-new air conditioners, a TV, a bar fridge, a closet and a private toilet and shower, the latter being an absolute luxury out here.

The company caravan had three sections: the laundry, the kitchen and the offsiders' quarters. The laundry room was a cramped, narrow space that had a dryer and washing machine, a trough with a clogged sink and a tiny, filthy shower stall crammed into it. I could barely turn around in there, so I don't know how Steve, Russell or any of the other larger-built boys managed to. There is no toilet in this caravan. We have a long drop toilet about 200m away from camp as our 'official' toilet, but most of the boys, myself included, just take a shovel and a toilet roll for a walk into the scrub to take a shit. Not many of us can bear the heat inside the makeshift tin sheet outhouse, let alone stomach the hot fumes breathing up from below as we squeeze a brown out.

The kitchen section of the caravan was much cleaner and more spacious than the laundry. It had three large freezers and a double-door fridge along one wall, a gas stove and oven along another and cupboards and countertops occupied the remaining usable space. A concertina door separated the kitchen from the driller's quarters in the corner. It was a small room with a double bunk bed, one bunk for the dayshift driller and one for the night shift driller. But since the guest caravan had arrived, the drillers had upgraded themselves to the newer rooms. The former driller's quarters had become a dumping ground for dry goods, boxes of rig parts and new PPE.

The offsiders' quarters, my sleeping quarters, were nothing short of a nightmare. It's a small room with two sets of bunks that were separated by a narrow aisle. An inadequately sized wardrobe stood against the back wall between the bunks. Two of the bunks were for dayshift and two bunks were for nightshift. The room was forever cluttered with belongings and dirty uniforms; it was borderline uninhabitable. The sleeping arrangements weren't that much better either, it didn't matter which bunk I slept in, or whose shift I was on, there was always a downside. Always.

For example, if I chose the top bunk, I would have the air conditioner blowing cool air on me all night long, saving me from otherwise hot and sleepless nights. But, as we all know, hot air rises. So too does every fart and noxious odour emitted from the offsider on the bottom bunk. So, I'd get the relief of cool air but I'd also choke on the pink-eye-inducing fumes from below. Now, if I chose the bottom bunk I would have a proper spring coil mattress, as opposed to the thin foam mattresses of the top bunks, but I wouldn't feel any real relief from the air conditioning. The heat was constant and sleeping comfortably was almost impossible. Another downside to the lower bunk is that if my half-asleep top bunk buddy needed to piss in the middle of the night, he may just crush my arm or leg with his feet as he tries to get down. Or say my top bunk buddy gets half a carton of beer into him the night before fly-out day and pisses himself in the night. Guess who gets a free golden shower wake-up call from above? Me!

Even if I managed to find some glorious, comfortable,

non-piss-soaked bunk with air conditioning privileges, it would all be worthless if the other guy on my shift snored like a chainsaw. That room was a special kind of hell; I may just set fire to it again now and blame the propane fire.

"Load, you bastard!" I absolutely hate waiting for the work laptop to boot up, "Come on, you piece of shit."

Patience is not one of my strong suits.

Five seconds pass.

"Aww, mate! Fuckin' load! I'm going to fu—"

The login screen appears.

"Oh, hey. It loaded," I smile and log in to the work emails. The 'no internet connection' box pops up on the screen, "Great."

Luckily, the work emails had been downloaded the day before. There's one unread email titled 'Kinky Kate's Weekly Update'.

"Ha, that Kate," I mutter to myself.

Kate is the office eye candy back in Perth, a gym junky who rocks the hot librarian look, think Mia Khalifa but white, and with defined traps. Kate's long brown hair was often in a high ponytail, and a pair of black-rimmed glasses that framed her big hazel-coloured, fuck-me eyes. Her cleavage is only ever half-contained inside an open white shirt which must have reinforced buttons or something because if she took one breath in too deep, her bust would test every one of those buttons. She is always flirting with the boys yet always maintains that she had a boyfriend.

One Christmas party, at a riverside pub in Fremantle, she got quite intoxicated and started pole dancing around a light post in front of the entire company. Naturally, in her drunken state, she slipped off the pole and landed on her back on a table with her legs splayed wide open. She was wearing a very short skirt and a pair of black leather underwear that had a zip running from the front all the way round to the back.

On that day she was dubbed 'Kinky Kate' and she ran with it, claiming the title like an award.

I open the email.

Hey Boys,

I hope all is well. Are you getting excited about the end-of-year celebrations? I know I am! Sorry, I missed last week's update, it's been chaotic down here in the office trying to find labour hire to cover ALL of the guys on sick leave. Half the state is coming down with this virus! Rig 2 is the only one running a full crew, well when Matt's crew flies back in and if Dan's feeling better yet. Hope you're okay Dan xox

Rig News:
- 6 out of 7 rigs are down/ on standby.
- 83% of our FIFO staff are on sick leave.
  60% of Metro staff too.
- Rig orders are delayed due to contractors, not us!
Safety News:
- 107 days incident-free.
- Please ensure vehicle and plant prestart inspections are performed at the beginning of EVERY shift guys, the client is very strict on this.

-ALL STAFF RETURNING TO PERTH ON BREAK MUST SEE THE COMPANY NURSE FOR VACCINATION DECLARATIONS BEFORE FLYING OUT! NO JAB, NO FLY PEOPLE!

Monthly Bonuses:
- Most metres drilled (in 1 month): 1817m, Rig 2
- Most metres drilled (in 1 shift): 111m, Rig 2.
- Cleanest site inspections: Rig 2

Well done Rig 2!!! You have been the only crew drilling for the last 3 weeks but I won't take this from you ;)

GOSSIP TIME!

So, this infection (or 'Boaty Bug' as Channel 5 is calling it) has got everyone! The News is saying most of the state has it and it's getting pretty bad, guys. People are dying and those who aren't sick have started to panic buy and run amuck, Woolies and Coles are completely out of toilet roll and non-perishables, it's getting very Doomsday Preppers down here, boys. Commercial flights in and out of WA have been stopped but don't worry, our charter flights won't be affected.

They're talking about a state of emergency? People are getting scared, and acting silly and now the army has started helping the police with checkpoints and crowd control. You should have seen Armadale on the News last week, riots, fires and massive street fights! A normal day in Armadale, hey Russell? Hehe

They reckon there's a vaccine and have started distributing it but a lot of people aren't trusting it. You should see everyone in the city, wearing those white dust masks. It's just the flu, jeez people. You boys are lucky you're far away from all this drama. No schools or universities are open and the trains and buses are stopping tonight. It's cray-cray down here!

On that note, please feel free to use the satellite phones to keep in touch with your families, boys. I know it's hard being away with all this going on. It's not as bad as I make it sound, you know how I like a bit of drama.

Anyway boys, shift change is in a couple of days for most of you so stay focused, stay safe and enjoy your RnR AND don't let the Boaty Bugs bite hehe

- Kinky Kate xx

Kate never really sent a professional email in her life, but the information was always there.

"Huh, Perth's gone to shit then?" I sigh, "Terrific."

My thoughts stray to Bella and Maria. I haven't spoken to them in two weeks. The last I heard, Maria had pulled Bella out of school when the infection first reared its ugly head in Perth. But that's all I had heard. Maria had a sixth sense when it came to things like this, her 'Latina spidey senses', as she called it. I hope they are okay, so much has happened in the couple months, I can't keep up.

In early October, an asylum seeker vessel was intercepted off the coast of Broome by the Australian Border Patrol. On board were eleven men, seven women and five children; twenty-three in total. At the time, no one gave it too much attention, it was just another boat full of refugees. They would get processed, a quick health check and then sent back to their home country, or settled somewhere here if their asylum claims proved true. It only made the five o'clock News when the media caught wind that the children on board the vessel were sick, very sick. Nothing tugs on the public's heartstrings like photos of sick refugee children sitting on the deck of a leaky boat with their hand's cable-tied together. The public was outraged.

Petitions, Facebook pages and marches were organised overnight, demanding that the children be moved to better facilities and have access to the best medical facilities possible. Asylum seekers, or 'boat people', have been a very touchy subject in Australia since harsh new border security laws were implemented in mid-2017.

Amid the increasing hostilities between the Western world and a few extremist organisations, the world over, ignorance and media-fuelled fear shifted Australia's thinking. Muslims, Islamic extremists, terrorists and refugees were all the same, weren't they? And with this gross generalisation, the path was paved for a rising political party, Australian Pride, to come to power.

Australian Pride wielded this misinformation and ran wild with propaganda and fear-mongering campaigns pushing cruel slogans like 'Fuck off, we're full' and coining chants like, 'Ban the Burka, Ban the boats, Australian Pride keeps us afloat!'. Which got every opinionated bogan and his dog to the voting booth to vote for them. The Party gained momentum quickly and filled a lot of key seats, various new Acts and Laws were fast-tracked and passed, tightening Australia's borders, vilifying minorities and simultaneously pissing off every human rights group worldwide.

It was the photo of young Pasindu, a four-year-old Sri Lankan boy, and Sadie, a five-year-old Iranian girl, which captured the hearts of the real Australians. The now famous photo was of the two children sitting on the concrete floor of a processing centre holding cell, Sadie was lovingly consoling a sleeping, and sickly, Pasindu in her arms while holding a firm expression with tears welling in her eyes. As if holding back her sadness to stay strong for this boy, whom she now claimed responsibility for. Both of the children were as sick as dogs and extremely malnourished from their journey across the Timor Sea. The pair became a beacon of innocence, strength and unconditional love.

So, with the eyes of the world on Australia and pressure from the general public building, arrangements were made for the refugees to be transported to a private medical facility for treatment. But by this time, all twenty-three refugees, as well as several frontline staff, had succumbed to an unknown illness.

A recently built facility just outside of Perth would house them until a more permanent solution could be found. The facility was part of a new minimum security prison work farm that was still partially under construction; it was a perfect compromise. Every move the Australian authorities made was under scrutiny and when Pasindu died from his illness, there was a media frenzy. The chaos amplified the night after Pasindu's death when a group of human rights activists freed eight of the eleven refugee men. Initially, the activists had aimed to free them all but with an increased security presence, and the group's poor execution of their breakout attempt, the group's efforts were hindered. Unknowingly, the activists had unleashed a highly contagious virus into the beating heart of one of Australia's fastest-growing cities, Perth, current population: 2.2 million.

The eight men scattered in every direction. Churches, farmers and fellow nationals of the escapees tried to shelter the men as best they could but the authorities acted fast to apprehend them, only taking three days to find all of the men. However, the damage had already been done and people were getting sick. It was spreading fast. The authorities didn't release the exact locations of where each of the men were found but outbreak hotspots started popping up and it became pretty obvious.

Ellenbrook.
Toodyay.
Northam.
Joondalup.
Fremantle.
And as far down as Bunbury.

The public was assured the illness was nothing like the 'swine flu' or 'bird flu' scares in the years prior, yet, anyone who had helped the escapees was quarantined. Their houses were covered in airtight plastic tents and their neighbours relocated to nearby hotels for isolated observation. Physical contact spread the virus rapidly, husbands gave it to their wives, mothers to their babies and ignorant co-workers to their work mates.

The 'Boaty Bug' virus proved difficult to treat—and even harder to predict. It initially presented like a common cold: mild sniffles and headaches, nothing alarming. But soon came hyper-reactivity to light and sound; simple environments became unbearable. Painful sinus pressure, a raw throat and an unquenchable thirst followed. And this was only the first twenty-four hours. After that, things took a sharp turn. Patients lost the ability to speak, impulse control collapsed and basic bodily functions began to fail. Fever dreams bled into vivid waking hallucinations, trapping patients in loops of fear and confusion. In the final stages, body temperatures spiked, heart rates soared and uncontrollable hyperventilation set in.

Within hours, sufferers succumbed to cardiac arrest, fatal aneurysms or both.

Researchers started leaking information that the virus wasn't biologically possible, that it couldn't have occurred naturally, suggesting that it was synthetic. Media hype fuelled the chaos too, people didn't know what was fact, fiction or clickbait. Conspiracies about the outbreak being a terrorist attack or some kind of military test began to circulate and people were going feral.

The emergency services and medical sectors were preparing for the worst, while the commercial sector, especially retail and supermarkets, were battling spikes in shoplifting, panic buying and outright brawling in stores over rolls of toilet paper. People looted Bunnings, strolled out of Spudshed and Woolworths with trolleys full of unpaid goods and petrol stations had to hire armed security.

Social distancing was implemented immediately, and public transport, ticketed events and social gatherings were heavily limited or cancelled completely. Twenty-two of the refugees died from the virus within one week of their arrival to Australia. Only Sadie remained. The public's contact with the infected escapees resulted in three hundred and thirty people contracting the mystery virus, one hundred and ninety-five of whom had died, but that number was surely much higher.

A vaccine was rushed to human trials, the thinking was 'beat it before it beats us'. It wasn't even clear if the virus had been fully identified before they were pumping out a compulsory mystery concoction of 'vaccine'. Sadie received the first dose and the results looked promising, it fought the symptoms almost instantly. When the news of its success got out, the public demanded it. Immediately.

There's nothing like a few thousand mothers and fathers breaching lockdowns to rally on the streets of Perth to force a trial vaccine—with some not yet understood side effects—into mass production.

Sadie was the first to be vaccinated.
The first to die.
And the first to come back.

She turned within six hours and all hell broke loose.

An untested synthetic antibody and a mutated-canine-sourced adenovirus vector formed the biological core of the vaccine. This pairing was engineered to accelerate the immune system's ability to identify and attack the 'Boaty Bug' virus. It looked promising on paper, and that was all it took to get the green light—but once it was administered to a living patient, it bonded with the virus cells and created an entirely new enemy. It accelerated existing symptoms and caused adverse reactions that made recipients extremely difficult to manage. An overstimulation of the amygdala triggered permanent states of fight-or-flight, or 'limbic lockdown', and disruptions to key neural receptors in the brain spawned rage-seizures and psychotic episodes.

Once the dose had fully bonded with a host, mutations continued on a cellular level. The body started producing necrosis-resistant properties; structures capable of sustaining dying tissues. These corrupted tissues and pathways severed the brain's ability to interpret pain signals and remapped its hunger centre; jamming it into overdrive.

The vaccine injected rage, erased cognition, built its host a suit of armour—oblivious to pain—and created a bipedal, hungry-hungry honey badger. One bite was as good as getting the jab, except there was no lollipop or cool superhero band-aid afterwards.

The vaccine didn't put out the fire—it poured fuel all over it.

FOR BELLA'S SAKE

I slap the laptop shut and try to make a call with the satellite phone. I punch in Maria's phone number but the call doesn't connect, let alone ring. Something isn't right. I grab my backpack and pull out my mobile phone. I have seven missed calls, two voice messages and four text message notifications. Almost all of them were from Maria, excluding the two voice messages from dad.

Maria only contacts me for two reasons nowadays: when Bella has begged her to let her talk to me, her father, or when Maria decides it's 'abuse-the-fuck-out-of-Dan-for-no-reason' o'clock. I open the messages and read them quickly, my eyes jump ahead faster than my brain can keep up. Maria's messages were the length of novellas and none of it was good news. I run hot with worry; my hands begin to vibrate with nerves so I put the phone down on the bench and sink into the booth seat behind me. The first attachment I opened was a screenshot of an automated text message that was sent to Maria's phone, it was from the Department of Fire and Emergency Services. The words 'Biological/ Infectious Threat' and 'Civil Unrest' grab my attention but the list of public safety recommendations to follow terrifies me.

Barricade your homes and stay indoors.
Stockpile a month of food, water and medical supplies.
Be prepared to defend your homes.

Shit had gotten real in Perth.

The way Maria had typed her messages was unnerving. There was a sense of urgency, her sentences were short and direct, and there were spelling mistakes and grammatical errors everywhere. Her heart was behind these messages, not her head. Maria never made these kinds of mistakes in her messages anymore. Since we separated, Maria would edit, re-write and spellcheck every message she'd send me because nothing would infuriate her more than me correcting her English mid-argument. I took joy in correcting her mistakes in the heat of the moment, obviously. It was like I scored points for every correction I made and, admittedly, I spellchecked each message I sent to her, too.

Because I didn't like having my English being corrected either, especially by someone whose first language was Spanish, not English.

It's the petty things in life that matter, right?

Of all the information in Maria's messages, it's her last message that scares me the most.

Mi amor, come home. We are scared and we need you here. Please. For Bella's sake. Te amamos mucho
- Maria y Bella xx

In the time since I had moved out of our family home, Maria hasn't once called me 'mi amor' and she has only ever mouthed the words 'I love you' after we drunkenly made love one evening a while ago. Things were bad and she was scared. My thoughts stray back to that drunken night for an instant. Huh, I remember it like it was only yesterday. In reality, it was seven months ago.

After a few too many glasses of wine, we had gotten into a pretty heated argument about my responsibilities to the family and her unrealistic expectations of me, we were at each other's throats. Names were called, past actions called upon and threats were made. During a pause between harsh words and Maria's frenzied slapping attack, anger grew to passion. Yelling turned into a heated embrace.

I had a fist full of her hair and she had her nails dug into my back. Our mouths aggressively locked onto one another. Tongues chased tongues and teeth bit lips, the jolts of pain only increased our desires. We suddenly craved each other. We stripped our clothes from one another and we very quickly became entangled on the kitchen floor. Fiery, drunken, Latina make-up sex. It's a hell of a thing. As we laid, staring at each other's familiar, yet somehow forgotten faces, she mouthed, 'Te amo, amor' to me and I kissed her forehead. For a moment, everything was ok again. We slept together in our old bed, but in the morning, Maria said it would be best if I left.

So, I did, and that was the last time we were together. Maria is a strong and incredibly stubborn woman, so for her to ask for help the way that she did, something must be wrong.

I sit with my head in my hands, trying to piece together the events of the day. Steve crashing into the caravan. His injuries. The caravan blowing up. The email from Kate. This 'Boaty Bug' bullshit. The messages from Maria. I pick my phone up again. It's 4.25pm and it's Thursday.

"What?" My mind halts for a second.

"Bullshit. I've lost 2 days?" I ask myself aloud.

A few days ago, a bad ham and salad roll, some dehydration and a sprinkle of heat stroke caused me to pass out while I was cleaning core samples at the rig. Russell, my senior driller, ordered me to end my shift and go and sleep it off, so I did. I grabbed some food, drove back to the caravan and then, exhausted and unwell, I fell into a deep sleep. That was Tuesday.

"I didn't sleep for two days? Did I?"

Maybe the twenty-two consecutive twelve-hour shifts baking under the Australian sun had taken its toll? But I knew it was fly-out day? I stop questioning how long I'd slept for and focus on my situation. The camp is fucked and no one is around. Where are the boys? Where's the other crew? It doesn't matter anyway, this shit's fucked.

"I've gotta get home."

I spend the next couple of hours salvaging gear, putting out spot fires and packing. I grab my gear from the offsiders' quarters and I plug in my phone, satellite phone, handheld radios and laptop to charge, all of them were practically dead. I pillage from the guest caravan fridges and I manage to pack enough food and water for three to four days; I always pack more than I need for these road trips. A flat tyre too many or a vehicle suffering the cursed 'limp mode' could turn any short trip into a very long one. I hop up into the old water truck and drive out toward the rig. Hoping that the other Hilux is there.

The access track to the rig is a tight, winding, boggy pain in the arse. It will take the best part of an hour to get to the rig in the water truck, which is an old workhorse from the eighties that had very stiff suspension. Every bump and jolt from the track's washouts and ruts rattle up my spine and toss me around the cab. Perfect conditions for the tender wounds across my body. I arrive at the rig and I'm pleased to see the other Hilux parked near the lighting plant. I park the truck and head over to the ute, my heart sinks as I see a yellow 'Out of Service' tag hanging from the driver's side door handle.

"Get fucked, no. What's wrong with it now?"

I flip the tag over and read the information section on the back, expecting to see the usual 'batteries dead' or 'cunts fucked!' written in the blank box. Thankfully, the tag only reads:

Not to be driven by fuckheads,
that means you, Matt.
Love Russell x

Matt is Rig 4's senior driller, he's a special kind of stupid and we are stuck with him until the other rigs are fully manned. Matt's an agro, gym-junkie, egomaniac who is definitely on the juice or meth. The fuckwit even has a 'NO PAIN, NO GAIN' tattoo across his knuckles. All brawn, no brains. Act first, think later. The type of person that shouldn't be allowed on a remote rig, and yet, his breed frequently infects the drilling industry with their old-school macho bullshit. The rest of Rig 4's crew are just different shaped versions of Matt, they had the same mentalities and, simply put, are just shitty people. Except for Corey, he is like Steve, a 150kg wall of bulging Māori power with the heart of a gentle giant, he isn't fazed by anything or anyone, he is just here to work, to pay off his debt and to try to get custody of his two daughters, just a genuine bloke.

The Rig 2 and Rig 4 crews did not gel well at all, this is mostly because of Rig 4's lack of respect for everything: their crew members, the other shift, the rig, the tools and the vehicles. Matt's crew had rolled two vehicles by racing to and from the rig, they have melted rod strings to the bottom of 700m deep holes and had the highest turnover rate for offsiders. How do they keep their jobs, you ask? They got metres, and metres mean dollars and that's all that mattered to the company.

I rip the service tag off the driver's side door and complete my prestart. I leave the vehicle idling while I get some equipment out of the humpy. I grab a small tool bag, the solar-powered universal charger, three jerry cans of diesel and some reading material for the trip, some old-as-fuck Picture, Hustler and ZOO magazines. The essentials. By the time I get back to the caravan from the rig and finish packing everything into the ute, it's 9pm. I toy with the idea of leaving now but I decide a decent sleep and an early start will be best. I walk into the guest caravan common room and sit down to watch something on the TV before bed, I grab the TV remote.

"No satellite phone, no internet, no kitchen, no..." I turn the television on but the screen is just static, "TV signal, no fucker is around. What the actual fuck."

I throw the TV remote to the ground and make my way to one of the rooms in the guest caravan. I take off the random XXL Hawaiian shirt and shorts and hop straight into the shower. The water stings as it hits my singed skin, which isn't as bad as I thought it was, I've had worse cases of sunburn. Smoky brown swirls of dirt and muck circle the shower drain; the filth of the day washes off of me. I towel myself dry and lie on the bed directly under the air conditioner naked. It feels amazing.

"Goodnight, Dan," I say to myself.

It's eerie how quiet it is. No one's outside playing music or drinking secret beers or on the satellite phone with their wives. It was just me in the camp. It's never just me in the camp.

"I'm the only one here... Hmmm."

A filthy thought crosses my mind, I turn my head to the side and look at my backpack. A Picture magazine is sticking out of the unzipped pocket, and its pages flicker in the breeze of the air conditioning. I glimpse a breast here, a bare arse there and, oh, two breasts now. Privacy is not a frequent luxury in a remote exploration camp, so any moment alone was usually spent abusing yourself. I grab the adult magazine and seize this opportunity.

Fap. Fap. Fap. Fap.

WARBALLA BOUND

My phone's alarm wakes me with a start; I grab it clumsily and squint at its screen with blurry eyes. It's 3.30am. I leave the alarm sounding and put the phone back on the bedside table, wanting to go back to sleep but knowing I have to move.

"Warning, warning…" I muffle into my pillow, still half asleep, "Enthusiasm levels, dangerously low."

I force myself upright and I reach for my phone again to cancel the alarm and check for messages, but there's still no service. I put it back down and jump into the shower. I stand tall with my face directly under the showerhead, trying to wake myself up. I turn around in the shower stall and as the water hits my back I'm instantly reminded of my tender flesh; I'm wide awake now.

I gather my things from the caravan and throw them into the Hilux. I decide to lock up the caravan and the spare key lockbox, just in case opportunistic locals make an unexpected visit. I get to Russell's room and before I lock it, I peer inside. Tucked in the corner is his 'boredom bag' stuffed beside the wardrobe. I smile.

Russell is the biggest man-child I have ever met. He is over 6ft tall, built like a Viking and has a long, wiry ginger beard—which is meant to distract people from his bald, shiny, dome of a skull. If you saw him at the pub, you'd think he was some brutish, bush bogan type—the type that went roo shooting, drank cheap rum and started fights with random dickheads. Well, he is, but he's so much more than that, too. It was only after my third month on his rig that I started to see the funny, cheerful larrikin that he actually is; and that was six long years ago. Since then, we've shared many a laugh and played countless pranks on each other around the rig. Russell is a giant, ginger toddler with a love for all things that go bang. In his 'boredom bag', Russell usually had rocket motors, fireworks, small amounts of explosives and a box or two of ammunition for his rifle. Everything inside that bag was against every company policy and very illegal, especially out here on the rig.

Russell's justification for the bag's contents was summed up in six words, 'But, what if I get bored?'. Whenever we shut down the rig to service it, or when we'd drilled enough metres for the day, Russell would bring out his boredom bag and we'd set off rockets, blow up dead roos or fire a few rounds at empty mud buckets with his rifle. Being as remote as we are had its perks, at times.

I stare at the bag for a moment and something tells me to take it. I grab the bag, fetch the super-secret, definitely illegal rig rifle from behind the wardrobe and I stash it all in the Hilux.

We had taken the rifle with us to town plenty of times before, so I couldn't see the harm in taking it now. I'll be travelling alone after all. I run through a mental checklist and take one last look at the tattered camp. It's eerily peaceful. I look up at the night sky, and there's not a cloud in sight, the full moon shines brightly down on the camp. The endless expanse of desert stretches off into the distance as a warmth lingers in the air. I stare at the caravan and the scrap of now-melted tarpaulin encasing Steve inside the burnt-out ute.

"I'll be back soon, I'm sorry I couldn't save ya, mate."

I jump in the Hilux and start the five-hour drive to Warballa, the closest community to us with a serviceable airstrip and access to the Great Central Road.

Warballa, here I come!

I still don't have anything in the way of a plan; all I know is that I'm going home, even if I have to drive the two thousand odd kilometres to get there. Well, that's not all that I know. I know that Steve drove back to camp alone in the only other Hilux and that no one had followed him. I know that no one, near or far, tried calling us up over the radio about the smoke, and that plume would have been visible for miles. I know that Steve is very dead. I know that Bella and Maria are scared shitless. I know that Russell is going to be pissed when he finds out I took his 'boredom bag' and I know that I'm going to have a lot of explaining to do when I get to Warballa.

The first leg of the Warballa drive always feels like it is never going to end, the darkness makes judging distance difficult and the road is fucking shithouse. It's a sandy, boggy, narrow goat track that snakes its way into South Australia and then doubles back on itself into Western Australia. This part of the track is known as 'stake country' because of the dead tree stumps that line each side hiding beneath the red sand, they camouflage themselves amongst the green, bushy new growth waiting to puncture a tyre at any given moment. It's a nightmare. When we first mobilised the rig to this site, we had six punctures within a two-hundred-metre stretch of track. I do not want to be changing a tyre this early in the day.

Just before the turnoff to Warballa, I notice two deep, distinctive trenches off to the right of the track. Someone had cut the corner off of the main road at speed, and it looks like they may have even rolled it. A fire extinguisher, a spare tyre and a heap of random shit are strewn all over the scrub. They made one hell of a mess. I spot a toolbox with our company logo on it; it was from one of our company vehicles. Steve! I stop the vehicle.

"Why were you in such a hurry, Steve? What the hell happened in Warbo?" The twin wheel ruts split into four and then disappear before a flattened section of scrub. The four tracks reappear a few metres after and continue onto the track—he must've rolled the ute. That'd explain the buckled roof, "Fuckin' hell, Steve."

I can only shake my head as I pull onto the gravelled main road and continue toward Warballa. I grab my phone and press shuffle on the music playlist titled, 'The Hymen List', the Red Hot Chili Peppers 'Snow' plays through the speakers.

I remember when Maria and I were on our first road trip together back in Canada, we were off to a new ski resort to sample their terrain and I handed her my phone to DJ. After shuffling through my music, she blurted out,

"What the hell is this? Why is this playlist called 'The Hymen List'?"

"Oh," I laughed, "That's my playlist for new songs people have shown me. Some are current chart toppers, some are classics and some are random as. I'm breaking them in, getting a feel for them," I pause, hoping Maria grasps the far-fetched link, "Do you get it? Breaking them in? My first time? Hymen?"

Maria stares at me blankly.

I begin with, "Well, when a man loves a virgin, he has to—" Maria gets it and her face scrunches up, "You're fucked!" she interrupts, "The Hymen List, really? How did you get me to like you, again?" she asks.

"Umm, I'm pretty sure you just like my accent?"

"Ha! You call that noise an accent?".

A playful back-and-forth of Crocodile Dundee and Sofia Vergara impersonations ate up the rest of that drive. They were good times on those road trips.

On long and lonely drives through the vast desert scrub, boredom strikes pretty quickly, even with music playing, and my thoughts wander. I try not to think about the madness of yesterday or what's happening back in Perth. So, I dig deep into the rabbit hole of distraction and the strangest things start to arouse my curiosity. Like, how did the first humans figure out sex? How did they know that this act is how you make a smaller human? *Did* they know? Did they get the right hole the first time around? Did they know you needed a man and a woman?

Questions like this make hundreds of kilometres of shitty gravel roads disappear in the blink of an eye. Once my shower thoughts subside, I decide it's karaoke time to try and stay alert. Usually, I'd be butchering the classics like the B-52's 'Love Shack' but no, today I will sing my own mind-numbing version of '99 bottles of beer on the wall' and it goes a little something like this:

219 kilometres to go, 219 K-M's

My lead foot's down, I'm driving to town,

218 kilometres to go!

I continue singing until the 199th kilometre when I see something in the road ahead. I back off the accelerator and kill the music. The haze of the low morning sun rising over the gravel road makes it hard to see, but something is definitely there.

"Allo, allo. What's all this then?"

Something moves in the distance, a large shape rises from the road and its silhouette stretches out from the orange horizon. And then another. And another. There are at least three of them and maybe more still huddled on the ground. But a cluster of trees cast long shadows over the road, hiding the shapes' true identity. I roll over the rise in the road and the spotlights illuminate the figures, their tall skinny legs and top-heavy forms are distinctive, long thick necks lazily sweep in my direction.

"Oh, it's just you guys."

Beep. Beep. Beep, Beep, Beep.

"Fuckin' camels," I jab the horn again, "Get off the road, ya dopey bastards!" I yell at the windscreen.

Five feral camels are startled to their feet, the blaring horn and flashing headlights force action, and they skulk off into the scrub like majestic, hairy drunkards. I pass the camels slowly before I speed up again, I turn the music back up and drive on.

A feral camel can quickly ruin your day out here; those things are more lethal and more abundant than kangaroos. I didn't even know Australia had feral camels until I started working out here. I mean, I knew we had camels in a few places for tourism, like Broome and even Kalamunda, but I was dumbfounded when I was told we had more than half a million of these dopey beasts roaming around central Australia. They destroy native vegetation and crops and are very deadly to road users; a couple of deaths a year are owed to camel vs. car accidents. Some of their flocks, or caravans, can have as many as a hundred camels in them. The excitement of the lumbering road-dwelling camels passes and I look out to the horizon toward Warballa and notice something ominous up ahead.

"That's a shit tonne of black smoke. What the hell are the locals burning now?"

Thick, black fingers of smoke tower up into the sky, someone's either set a car alight or the burn-offs at the rubbish tip have blown into the scrub again. Warballa, affectionately known as 'Warbo', is a small, remote community of about sixty people. Ninety per cent of whom are indigenous and commonly referred to by the mining contractors as T.O.'s, traditional owners.

The township of Warballa has a small airstrip, a fuel depot, a rubbish tip, a mechanic's workshop and a general store, all of which are run by one family; the Darby's. A father and son's outfit and a bloody reliable bunch of blokes, that's for sure. They are the only white people who live in the town permanently, it's not the most desirable spot on the map. As I get closer to town, a wall of smoke forces me to slow down to under 40km/hr. I have to lean up to the windscreen to see, and I still can't see a bloody thing. The smoke stings my eyes, so I roll up my window and shut the air conditioning vents. I reach for my two-way radio to try to call up the Darby boys.

"LV2 to the Darby's, LV2 to the Darby's. Do you have a copy, boys?" A moment passes and no one answers, "LV2 to the Darby's. You boys got a copy?"

I try calling them several times, but I get nothing. With no answer from the Darby's and with my eyes stinging from the smoke, my frustration peaks and I throw the radio into the passenger's side footwell.

"Answer ya fucking radio, boys!"

The smoke screen partially clears and I speed up again. The radio crackles. Someone's finally answering. I reach for the radio in the footwell but it's just out of my reach, I pull on its coiled cord but it only stretches. The handset's trapped under the passenger seat. I glance at the road to check that it's clear and then I lean across the centre console to fetch the radio, my head drops below the dash and I can no longer see the road.

"Come onnnnn. Come on!"

My left hand tries to untangle the radio cord in a hurry as I ghost-steer the ute with my right hand. I unintentionally push the accelerator down harder as I stretch across the cab. I grip the last coil of the cord and give it a final tug and the handpiece springs back up at me, "Hahaa... Got ya!".

I snap back into my seat and look ahead. A tall aboriginal man is standing in the middle of the road, just metres in front of the Hilux. I panic, but I don't brake. I don't swerve either. I don't do anything. I just sit there like a stunned mullet as I drive into the man at 80km/hr. The roo bar hits him at stomach height and the upper part of his torso slaps against the bonnet. His face and his chest cavity explode, spraying blood and viscera everywhere. The windscreen is crimson with gore. The whole ute bounces and jerks to the right as the body drops out of sight and violently rolls under the vehicle. I grip the steering wheel tightly and slam on the brakes. What have I done?! I jump out of the vehicle and run back down the road towards the man. Pink and brown strips of flesh litter the gravel road.

"Aw, Fuck!" I gag.

An entire arm lies mangled in the dirt, its hand twitches, as if it's trying to click its fingers. I walk past the severed arm, giving it a wide berth, and continue toward where I think the body is. There's nothing there. I walk further down the road. Still nothing.

The smoke becomes thick again, but not so thick that a body can just up and disappear. I have no idea where the man is and he didn't just vanish into thin air. I couldn't have hit him that hard, surely. I walk back toward the vehicle and stop by the arm. I crouch down next to it to investigate, it's missing chunks of flesh from the forearm and bicep, the wounds look like the ones on Steve's arm.

"What the hell could have done this? Maybe one of the feral dogs from town attacked him?".

I squint through the smoke screen but see no sign of the surely dead bloke, the smoke stings my eyes and burns my throat. I don't have time to play hide and seek with this guy! I pace back and forth for a moment while deciding what to do.

"I've got to go, I'll let the community liaison know

what's happened. Sorry, man."

I go back to the Hilux and pop my head in the cab, and, thankfully, there are no warning lights or any other signs of mechanical failure on the dash. I walk to the front of the ute to check the damage there. Aside from the dent in the bonnet, and the bloody slop covering my windscreen, the Hilux is okay. I grab a couple of rags and wipe most of the gore off the windscreen, it's a gruesome task and I gag multiple times. The smell of hot blood baking on the ute's bonnet becomes too much so I retreat to the cab and let the wipers finish the job. I feel ill, but I have to keep moving, so I push on to Warballa.

Accidents involving cars and locals on this highway were pretty common. In fact, this isn't even the first person I've hit on this outback highway. It's my third. The first time, I unknowingly ran over two blokes who were sleeping in the centre of the road in the middle of the night. I was in the 8x8 MAN truck, I didn't know I had hit them until the community liaison officer and police came to pay me a visit. I couldn't eat for a week after finding out what I did.

It's the liaison officer's role to manage relations between the mining companies leasing the land and the local traditional owners occupying it.

The officer told me that even with spotlights and high beams, the chances of seeing a person lying on the road at night are slim. And the chances of safely stopping a heavy vehicle doing 80km/hr on a gravel road before hitting a sleeping human speedbump were even slimmer. It's a disturbing reality, but a reality nonetheless.

"Fuck me, I'm having a shit couple of days," I say to myself, "Well, not as bad as that armless bloke back there, but still, pretty average."

A large red sign with 'R E D U C E   S P E E D' in white lettering stands on the side of the road up ahead. Eight 44-gallon drums line the road's edge to mark the entrance to the community, 'W A R B A L L A' is spray painted in large yellow letters across the black drums. The smoke is still pretty thick, but the community is now visible and I slow down to a walking pace. This community always looks a little run-down but now it looks like a warzone. To my right, a house is on fire with a Pajero jutting out of its living room. To my left, a blood-smeared station wagon has all of its windows smashed and a person is hunched over in the rear bench seat. I lock my doors and reach into the back seat for the rifle, and place it in the passenger's seat next to me.

"What the fuck is going on here?"

The road is littered with dead dogs, as far as the eye can see, bloodied tufts of fur and lifeless four-legged bodies are strewn everywhere. Dogs outnumber humans three-to-one in Warballa and they roam freely around the town, eating and humping to pass the time. No one owned them and no one cared for them, they were just strays that multiplied and ran amok. I try to manoeuvre around each of the dead dogs but there are too many. I flinch as the sound of their small carcasses crunch and pop under the ute's tyres. I drive toward the supply yard, with its seven-foot-high steel fences, heavy gates and armed occupants, it is exactly where I want to be right now. And it's the first place Russell would go if shit hit the fan and the shit had well and truly hit the fan in Warballa.

NED BLOODY KELLY

I turn down a side street to bypass the carpet of dead canines littering the road. Which is a poor choice, as down in a roadside v-drain ahead, I see an obese aboriginal woman lying face down in the red gravel. Her clothes and skin have been torn off her. I roll slowly toward her in the ute and see that the back of her head is caved in, it's a sickly crater of bloody matted hair and crushed skull. I avert my eyes, but across the other side of the road, I see a body crumpled against a Colorbond fence; he's also covered in blood, his body twitches and jerks unnaturally. I look straight ahead and drive fast around the next corner, my heart is pounding in my chest. The wheels spin and loose gravel spits out behind the ute as I accelerate down another street. More people are scattered on the road, some are lifeless and some are on top of others, shaking them violently; I can't tell if they're mourning or attacking them. The screens of smoke mask their intentions. Maybe the dogs turned rabid and started attacking people?

Every blood-stained person looks like they've been mauled by something. I see a smaller body, a young boy's, maybe seven or eight at most, lying belly up on the bonnet of a white late 90's model Ford Falcon. A blood-spattered concrete block sits where the boy's head should be and two steel star pickets are sticking out of his concave chest. My face and lips start to tingle as saliva fills my mouth, the kind of tingling that precedes uncontrollable vomiting. I scrunch my eyes shut in disbelief. Rabid dogs didn't do this.

Something is very wrong.

I speed toward the supply yard, the community is in ruin. Every other weatherboard building is ablaze, the orange glow of flames radiates through the haze of the thick smoke. Vehicles are on their sides, their panels are bloodied and their windows smashed. I hear screams, some near, some far away. I hear the sounds of glass smashing and flames crackling as they consume homes, the air is heavy with nauseating fumes. I see figures move quickly through the smoke all around me but I try to ignore them. I double-check my rifle is still by my side, it is, but it's not loaded. I speed around the final bend in the road and almost slide out in the loose road base, but I manage to save it, I brake hard and skid to a stop. I scan the empty street and eyeball the perimeter fence of the supply yard, I made it, but I don't see anyone. I hear yelling, from a large group, maybe. Then I hear gunshots, I think. Each shot sounds like an angry dog's bark, more of a 'woaf' rather than a 'tshh' sound. I'm sure that the yard's entrance is on this side, but I'm disorientated as fuck. I roll forward slowly as gusts of hot wind swirl past, lifting the choking curtain of smoke.

"Get fucked," my jaw drops open.

A mass of bodies are heaped up against the tall, steel perimeter fence of the yard, half of the town is lining up against it. The crowd screams and claws at the fence in a frenzy. I see someone inside the yard, a large man wearing tattered blue overalls and a welder's face shield, a long beard is sticking out the bottom of it. And he's armed with what looks like a shotgun; he looks like Ned-fucking-Kelly.

I decide that now is a brilliant time to load the rifle, but I keep a close eye on old Ned as I handle the gun. He's on the move, the man marches toward one side of the fence and fires at it twice as he walks. I can't see what he's shooting at but he's pacing fast and firing off shots even faster. I'm idling outside of the yard's eastern fence, nervously watching the man in the yard. A cloud of smoke swirls by and the stench of burnt hair and molten rubber putrefies the air. It passes, and I see two men attacking the fence across the yard, running up and down its length, trying to get in. I place my loaded rifle beside me and watch, I grip the steering wheel tightly as I look on. I lean in closer to see better, and to my surprise, Mr Kelly walks right up to the fence and shoots twice at the men at point-blank range. The first round cuts straight through the head of the taller man and his brains scatter into the wind; wet pulp and bone rain down onto the pea gravel. The second shot rips a hole through the side of the shorter man's neck, causing his head to drop to one side as he collapses to the ground convulsing.

I lean closer to the windscreen. I can't believe my eyes; I lean too close—my chest accidentally presses the horn in the centre of the steering wheel. Beep!

The short, sharp honk alerts the gunman to my presence.

"Fuck, fuck, fuck," I panic and put the car in gear.

The gunman spins around with his shotgun braced snugly into his shoulder. He marches forward, aiming his shotgun at me. I fumble blindly with the gear stick in a panicked attempt to flee, and I stall the ute. I look up to see if he's still coming, he is, and he's looking down the shotgun's long barrel, sighting me in; when he suddenly lowers his weapon. He raises the welding helmet visor, as if he wants to eyeball me before shooting me dead. I swear I see him smile and even laugh.

Oh, God. I'm dead!

The gunman waves at me.

"What? He's fucking playing with me?!"

I start the car again and put it in reverse. I look back up at him and he's still waving at me, or is he waving me over? I look closer and notice his uniform showing through his unbuttoned overalls, it's my company's polo shirt. Holy shit, that beard, that long, glorious ginger beard.

"Russ? Russ!" I drive toward the fence and wind my window down. I call out to him, "Russell, is that you? Russ! What the fuck is going on?"

He yells something back at me but I can't hear him. Russell points at me and then points to the other side of the yard. He wants me to drive around to the other gates. I give him a thumbs up and boot the accelerator, the wheels spin in the loose gravel and I speed toward the gates. Russell throws something over the opposite fence and it explodes. A ball of fire grabs the mob's attention and they rush over to it as Russell crosses the yard and starts unlocking the gates.

I pull up and step out of the car to talk to him.

"Get back in the car!" he yells.

"What? What's going on?"

"Get back in the car, Dan, we can talk once you're inside!" Russell flings one side of the gate open, "Go, go, go!"

I drive in and stop just past the gates, unsure of what's happening. Russell locks the gates behind me.

"Reverse up to the gates! We can't let them get in here!"

I reverse the tailgate up against the gates and park, when Russell opens my ute door and hurries me out of the vehicle.

"Come on, let's get inside before more come."

"More what? Locals?" I ask,

"No, fuckhead, more of those pissed off black cunts throwing themselves at the fence," Russ gestures at the fence aggressively, "Mate, you have no idea how much I need you to get-the-fuck-inside, like, right now. Leave your shit in here, we'll get it after."

"Alright, alright. Fuck."

Once we're inside, we lock the security gates between the workshop and the admin offices. We run through the workshop and into the brick building, and towards the back offices. Russell dumps his welder's helmet on a table and plonks himself down into a black leather office chair, and he starts reloading his shotgun with shells from his pocket.

He casually looks up at me, "It's good to see ya, mate. Sorry about the rush. When did you get into Warbo?"

"Russ, what the fuck's going on? Why are the locals going fucking mental? There are bodies everywhere?!"

"You don't know?"

"Know what?"

"They're infected. The charter plane that Matt's shift

flew in on brought it with them. Whatever it is, it makes killing those psychos really fuckin' hard."

"Matt's shift? What, with that Boaty Bug virus?"

Russell looks at my cockeyed, "Boaty Bug what?"

"That virus, the one that the refugees brought with them?"

"Yeah, nah. This is something different, something new. Something to do with the vaccine, the boys were sent to get vaccines before flying out and, yeah."

"The vaccine didn't work?"

Russell laughs, "I don't think so, mate. The vaccine fucked them up, if you saw the boys, you'd understand."

"Fucked them up?" I feel like a dumb fucking parrot, mimicking select words.

Russell stares at me, looking pissed off that I don't know what he knows. He stuffs extra shells into his pocket from the ammunition box on the table and then leans the shotgun up against the wall.

"Okay, I'll lay it out for you. When Steve and I got here, to the yard, the Darby boys said that they hadn't heard anything from the plane in the last half hour. No call-ups, no approach info, nothing. The last that the Darbys had heard from the plane was that one of the boys were giving them trouble. I just thought Matt or Aaron had hit the bar before flying in and were getting rowdy again but it wasn't the case," Russell stands up and looks out the window through the blinds, scanning the fences, "We heard the plane overhead, it was close, real close. The sound of the engine was insane; something was wrong. We raced outside: me, Steve and the Darby sons. The plane was coming at us fast and low, so low that it clipped the radio antenna on the other side of the yard with its wing. It was nowhere near the landing strip and it was going to crash, right here in town. We watched the Cessna wobble and try to correct itself to land, but the landing gear wasn't even down. It skimmed across the footy oval and crashed straight into the side of a parked semi-trailer."

"Holy shit, did they survive the crash?"

"Kind of..." Russell takes several gulps from a water bottle, "We acted fast, Steve drove the ute out and I hopped in that red firefighting support truck. Grey smoke was pumping out of both plane engines and the semi-trailer was spewin' thick black smoke too. Whatever was inside of that trailer was flammable as fuck. A few locals got to the wreckage before us, they were trying to open the side access door to get people out of the plane. The nose of the plane was gone and the cockpit looked like a crushed paper cup. One of the wings had snapped in half and jet fuel was spilling out everywhere. I called the Darby boys over the radio and told them to bring as many extinguishers as they could and that's when the plane's entry door swung down," Russell stares blankly at the floor.

"Russ?"

He shakes his head, freeing himself from the memory's grip and then he looks me dead in the eye.

"It was like something from a horror film, Dan. That lanky pale fuck, Aaron, was covered in blood from head to toe. He looked like that Carrie girl, but without the prom queen tiara. He fell out of the doorway and hit the dirt, hard. Steve and two of the locals went to pick him up off the ground when Aaron went absolutely fucking ballistic. He grabbed one of the locals by the hair, wrenched his head back and started hammering his fist at his throat. Aaron crushed the guy's windpipe by the second blow but kept going, again and again. I just stood back, Steve took one look and ran off into the town."

Steve! Russell doesn't know he's back at camp, dead, how could he? Should I tell him? No.

"Wh… What?" I ask but Russell interrupts me.

"No, no. It gets worse. The local that Aaron attacked was suffocating and he grabbed at Aaron desperately. Some local fellas tried to pull Aaron off of him but then Aaron ripped the guy's crushed throat open, blood sprayed everywhere. Aaron was just clawing at the hole and trying to bite it, he was screaming like a meth-head, the cunt tore that poor guy apart. The other local guys ran off into the town yelling for help, and Aaron chased after them. That's the last I saw of him."

"That's fucked, did anyone else get off the plane?"

"After Aaron fucked off into the town, I went into the plane to see if any of the other boys were still alive. I can't describe it, mate. There was blood everywhere. The plane was in tatters. Three seats had been pulled up from the floor and thrown up against the cargo net at the back of the plane. I saw Corey tangled up in the netting, it looked like he was pinning the chairs against the net, trying to keep them there. He was dead as fuck but his eyes were still open, so wide and so intense, he looked scared out of his mind. His body jerked and I jumped. I called out and tried to climb into the plane but I couldn't get in, some panelling and the pilot's seats were blocking the entrance to the plane. Corey's body moved again but it wasn't him that was moving, something was behind him."

"What was behind the net?"

"I didn't see much, all I saw was a hand reaching out from between Corey's fat fucking legs, P-A-I-N was tattooed across the knuckles."

"Matt?! Matt was behind the net?" My thoughts swirl, "He must have started a fight or—"

Russell interrupts me again, "It doesn't matter. I think someone went into the plane after me, though? Because I swear I saw someone jump out of it as I got into the fire truck. I don't know, I got the hell out of there. Just in time too, I was half way across the oval when the plane blew up. Flaming shit went everywhere!"

"I guess that's why half of the town and most of the scrub is on fire then?"

"Pretty much, mate."

"So, what? The abos went wild because of that?"

"No, what Aaron did triggered them, but I think whatever was wrong with Aaron spread to the others. Anyway, after the plane blew up, I drove into town looking for Aaron and Steve."

"Did you find him?"

"Ha. A breadcrumb trail of fucked up people eventually led me to Aaron. The local guy that Aaron chased from the plane was the first body that I found, his eyes were gouged out and his jaw was smashed in. A woman was running around with her nose bitten off and her cheeks hanging off of her fucking face, man. He was biting cunts, Dan. I mean, who does that? Why?"

I shrug at him, not knowing how to respond.

Russell continues, "More bodies were lying in the gutter, I swear one of them looked like Steve but I heard yelling and shit in the next street and drove on. I got to

Aaron too late, a mob had gotten to him first. I didn't want to get too close, about nine locals were surrounding him and more were joining every second. The mob had him on the ground, they were kicking and stomping the hell out of him. Then I saw one fat fuck jump into the air and land two feet first on Aaron's face. He was dead for sure. I reversed out of there, so damn fast."

I stare at the ground. The plane crash. Aaron going on a killing spree. Corey and Matt tangled in the cargo hold. Russell seeing what he thought was Steve's body.

"Dan, it gets so much worse."

I look up at Russell.

"When I drove back through town toward the Darby yard, I took the same road that I drove in on. But the bodies that were on the ground were gone. The guy who looked like Steve, the bloke without his eyes; they disappeared. I saw someone cradling that woman with half of her face chewed off, too. I stopped the truck in the middle of the road and watched this guy wailing over her. It was so fucked up."

"Farkinell, Russ."

Russell begins to nod and then to rock back and forth, trying to gain momentum to say what he had to say next.

"She wasn't dead though, Dan. She started attacking him. The fat bitch was biting at the guy's chest and neck, she grabbed him by the back of the head and then smashed his face into the road. Three times. The guy was fucked, he tried to get a hold of the woman but after the fourth blow against the road, the dude went limp."

Russell swigs from his water bottle, "Then the bitch looked up at me, she dropped the guy she was mauling and tried to get to her feet. Bitch tried. By the time she had gotten one knee up to stand, she was chewing on the fire truck's bull bar. I ran her over, GTA style."

Russell is a gentle giant, but he's no stranger to doing what had to be done and dishing out a bit of violence.

"So, you came here?" I ask.

"Damn straight, this is the only secure place for miles. This place was built to keep feral locals out, it's ram-raid proof, plus, all of the food, fuel and communications gear is in here. Anyway, go get your stuff from the ute. We're holing up here for a while, mate."

"Okay, throw me the keys for the workshop gates and I'll go grab my things." Russell throws me the keys and just before I head out to the Hilux I turn to Russell and say,

"Oh, yeah. I brought your 'boredom bag' too, Russ, I don't know why, but…"

"Really? Aw, you legend, I've been cursing myself for leaving it at camp. Thanks, buddy."

"No worries, eh," I pause for a second before continuing, "Err, what happened to Steve? Was that his body in the street?"

"I think so, but he might have just been pretending to be dead."

"Why do you say that?"

"When I drove past the oval, I noticed that the support ute was gone; Steve had the only set of keys. Maybe he thought 'fuck this' and headed to Kal?"

Steve didn't head to Kalgoorlie; he went back to camp, and he will probably be there for some time.

"Yeah," I agree, "Steve's likely heading for Kalgoorlie, he's smart, he got the fuck out of dodge as soon as possible. Ha! You and I both know how much he loves those skimpy wenches on at the Exchange."

Russell accepts my version of Steve's escape and laughs, "He's probably balls deep in that Irish or Estonian skimpy right now, the filthy fucker."

"I bet that's exactly what he's doing," I add as I head out to the ute, knowing full well that Steve, and his balls, were dead, charred and melted to the driver's seat of a burnt-out ute.

YOU PASSED THE TEST

I get to the driver's side door of the ute when a nearby scurrying sound grabs my attention, it sounds like a dog digging in gravel. I look around only to see a few locals attacking the fence on the other side of the yard. The digging sound gets louder as I walk toward the back of the vehicle and I freeze. Two shirtless men are clawing at the compacted blue metal with their hands, trying to get beneath the gate.

"Fuck!" I quickly cover my mouth, hoping I don't attract any more attention to myself.

"Russ! Get the shotgun!" I urge, both men look up at me and scream, they're angered by my presence, and start to burrow faster and deeper.

"Fuck. Fuck. Fuck. Russ! Get out here!"

I don't know if he can hear me inside the building but these two bastards will be on our side of the fence in less than a minute. I grab the closest thing to me, a shovel that's leaning against the fence, and start shovelling loose dirt at the men but it doesn't slow them down in the slightest.

"Fuck, Dan. Think!"

A calm mind would have remembered the rifle sitting in the cab, but no, I'm panicked and the thought doesn't even cross my mind. The hard ground makes my shovelling efforts look futile compared to the headway that the shirtless digging twins are making.

"Fuck," a stray thought jumps at me. They can't dig if they don't have any hands to dig with. I start spearing the shovel into their busy hands. I miss the first few times and only graze their hands but I keep trying.

"Russ!" desperation fills my voice.

I launch the shovel down hard and fast, several fingers come off their hands but I'm aiming for their wrists. Their hands move far too quickly but I bring the shovel down as hard as I can and sever one of their hands off at the wrist.

"Yeah, try and dig with your bloody stump, ya dud cunt! One down, three to go."

Losing a hand doesn't slow him down at all. So, I hack off his other hand, he reels backwards for a second but then returns to digging with his bloodied stumps. The other man pushes past his stumpy mate and tries to wriggle his body under the fence, so I start pounding at the base of his skull with the back of the shovel. His head and shoulders are through the gap under the gate now but he's struggling to squeeze the rest of his body under the fence. Perfect.

"Aw, mate. You're fucked now."

The man chomps and rips at the dirt as he struggles, I start spearing the shovel at the back of his neck until he stops digging. I didn't think a shovel was sharp enough to cut through flesh, muscle and spine but look at me go. His body goes limp but the now detached head still lives, I kick it away and watch it roll down the fence line. The man with bloody stumps for hands starts pulling the headless body out of the way when Russell finally appears. He rushes up to the gate, pushes the barrel of his shotgun through it and blows the man's head off; hot, meaty pulp splatters across the blue metal floor of the yard. I look up to Russell, out of breath and grateful, and he returns an expression that I roughly interpret as, 'what-the-actual-fuck-Dan?'.

"What?"

Russell steps back toward the driver's side door and points into the cab, "The rifle is right fucking there and you chose a shovel? Over a rifle?!"

Wow. I don't even try to explain myself.

"Grab your stuff, now, we have to get back in—"

The sound of hurried footsteps across the workshop's tin roof stops Russell mid-sentence. We both look up as something leaps off of the building. Russell only manages to raise his shotgun hip height before the weight of a man takes him down to the ground. I jump back, surprised by the new aerial assault tactics that the crazed locals have employed.

"Get fucked," I blurt in disbelief.

A large, muscular man is on top of Russell, punching and elbowing him in the head and neck. Russ tucks his arms tight against his head and digs his chin into his neck to try to protect himself.

Where the fuck did this guy come from? Wait, that red shirt with *TapOut* scrolled across the back of it.

"That's... That's Matt! Oi!"

The 'roided up, meth head driller from Rig 4 yells and whoops like a mad hyena as he tries to get at Russell's face. Russell starts bucking and thrusting his hips upwards, attempting to toss the infected bastard aside, but Matt remains on his chest and pins him to the ground.

Matt throws an arm around the back of Russell's head and pulls him in close against his chest. I jump up and start swinging the shovel at Matt. I strike his lower back, upper back, lower back, and then the back of his head. Matt releases Russell from the headlock and stops for a moment. A dazed Russell tries to focus on Matt's burnt and bloodied bulky form as he drops his guard and attempts to reason with him.

"Matt, mate, stop. What the fuck are you doing? Get off of me, now." Russell grabs Matt by the scruff of his red shirt, "Now, cunt!"

Matt just smirks and belts out some godawful noise before he buries his head and gnashing teeth into Russell's neck.

"Oi!!" I yell, "Get the fuck off him."

I try to wrestle Matt off of him but I can't move him. Matt is one solid bloke, his suit of pharmaceutically enhanced muscles acts as armour. I pace backwards and get a run-up to tackle him off of Russ, but I'm thrown off of him and land beside Russell's shotgun.

The gun! Why didn't I grab it sooner?!

Without hesitation, I grab the shotgun, rack it and aim it high at Matt's menacing face.

"Oi, carrrnt!"

Matt spins around to the sound of my voice and I pull the trigger, fire spews out from the barrel of the shotgun and, in slow motion, I watch the shell cut through the air and force its way into Matt's arrogant face, his facial features and flesh fold in on themselves and disappear into his skull before his teeth, bone and brain matter explode out of the backside of his head. I kick Matt in the chest with the heel of my boot just as Russell bucks. Matt's lifeless body collapses next to Russell and starts to jerk and convulse in the fetal position. It kind of looks like Matt is trying to hump Russell.

"Ha! Trust Matt to take a shot in the mouth like that and grab at ya for more, hey Russ?" I rub my tender shoulder from the recoil of the shotgun as I watch Matt's body air hump the space between him and Russell.

"I think he wants a post-romp-cuddle too, mate," I look over to Russell, laughing, "Russ?!"

Russell is lying on his back in the dirt with his hands cupped firmly around his throat, blood trickles through his fingers and covers his shirt. A cold, vibrating sensation surges through my body.

"Russ?!"

He struggles to speak, "Inside… get me… inside."

I drop the shotgun and grab Russell by his feet and start to drag him inside. There's no way I can lift him and I wasn't going to waste any time trying. I get him to the workshop entrance.

"Russ, you're going to have to try and stand, mate. I can't drag you through the workshop gates."

Russell nods. I lift him from behind, looping my arms under his armpits. I struggle to stay upright, he's heavy and his blood is everywhere; it's so thick and slippery on the concrete floor of the workshop. We both strain as we get him to his feet. He manages to brace himself against a workbench with one arm as he cups his bloodied neck with the other.

"The gun," Russell nods, gesturing behind me.

"Aww shit. Yeah, I'll get it. Try get yourself to the back room," I open the gate and help him inside.

"The gun, Dan," Russell sputters.

"Okay, okay." I race back outside and grab the shotgun. I daren't look up or around, I just grab the gun and run back inside. I run through the gate, swing it shut behind me and lock it. I hang off the gate relieved, and try to catch my breath for a moment. The noise of the mob at the fence and the stink of the burning Warballa offends my senses. I try to wipe the warm, slippery blood that's coating my hands and arms off onto some rags.

I turn toward the back offices to see a wide, undulating wave of blood smearing its way down the right-hand wall. It continues down the entire length of the corridor.

"Jesus Christ," I follow it with quickening footsteps until the crimson trail ends at the back office's closed door.

"Russ? Mate, are you in there?" I try the door handle, it's slick with blood, and it's locked, "Russ, open the door."

I start to rattle the knob and push on the door.

"Dan. Leave me."

"Like fuck, Russell. Come on, man, open the door," I start knocking loudly on the door, and I kick at its base.

"I'm not… Letting you in… Go. Now," Russell finishes his sentence with a gurgling cough.

I look through the corridor window into the office. The cheap blinds are half-closed but I can just see Russell in the back corner. He's in a bad way, sitting slumped over in one of the office chairs.

"Open." I kick the door with each word, "The. Fucking," Frustration fuels each blow, "Door, cunt. Russell!"

"You're not getting in here, mate," Russell coughs, it sounds wet and coarse, "I'm not letting you see me turn into one of those things." He sounds strangely calm.

I launch my entire weight against the door and it swings open. I lurch forward and just stop myself from hitting the ground, I stand quickly and give Russell the well-earned 'what-the-actual-fuck?' stance.

You know the one: arms open, leaning back slightly, your chin tucked into your neck. A confused, borderline pissed off expression is painted across your face as you glare wide-eyed at the irritating cunt in front of you.

It's kinda like the one Russell gave me at the gate, but with more feeling, and emphasis on the irritating cunt part.

"Care to explain yourself, Russ?" I ask.

He looks up at me and smirks, "You passed the test."

Back on the rig, whenever I did something wrong or had forgotten to do something entirely, Russell, being the senior driller, noticed pretty quickly and, of course, piped up about it. I'd always offer the same response, time and time again, 'You passed the test'. As if I had intentionally forgotten something to see if he was paying attention. It was a cheeky way to acknowledge what I had done, or had not done, and it made light of the situation at the same time, usually lessening a punishment. Russell took to this idea quickly and he started leaving actual 'tests' of his own all over the place, like loosening straps on trucks or spinning core trays around the wrong way. If I didn't notice these little things, in turn, failing his test, I'd end up owing him a six-pack or having to lick the rod grease brush.

"Ha-fucking-ha, Russ."

He smiles weakly and then coughs bloody spittle over himself. I cross the small room to grab a handful of rags off the filing cabinet in the corner.

"Here, move your hand. Hold this against your neck," Russell moves his shaking hands and I see the extent of his injury: a gaping, ravaged hole of torn muscle and flesh. I can't even look at it. I press the rags into his wound and put his hand back on his neck, it squelches audibly.

"It doesn't hurt anymore, Dan."

I stand back and look at Russell. He must be in shock, he's pale and strangely docile. He's holding something in his hand, a small square laminated card, he stares at it with great focus as his eyebrows undulate between emotions. Anger. Heartache. Love. Sorrow.

"I know what's coming, mate, and," he starts coughing, "I won't become one of those things."

Russell's arms begin to shake, he brings his bloody hand down from his neck and rests it between his thighs, trying to hide the shaking rather than stopping it. I reach out toward Russ to keep the rags from falling out of the cavernous wound in his neck.

"You need to keep pressure on the…" Russell shrugs away from me, I flinch and he cuts me off.

"You know, I've spent more time out here in this fucking desert than with my own family?" I step back from Russell and he continues, "Nineteen years I've been doing this, Dan. Nineteen fucking years." Russell pulls the bloodied rags from his neck and lets them fall from his grip;

they slop onto the floor. "I missed the birth of my baby girl, countless anniversaries, birthdays, school plays, my uncle's funeral"—Russell squeezes his eyes shut, trying to crush the pain out of his tears to try and force them back.

"That's FIFO, man. We do this shit so we have the money to give our families everything they could ever want or need," I try to justify the fly-in, fly-out lifestyle, "And exploration pays the best by far."

I step closer and look down into Russell's hands, it's a photo of his wife, Amy, holding their baby girl, Ava. Small colourful letters scroll across the baby's tummy in an arch spelling '1 week old'. Amy's smile glows as she looks down at Ava in the photo. Russell admires it, running his thumbs across their faces, tracing their every feature. A tear rolls down his swollen face.

"My family needed me there with them, just like your Bella and your Maria needed you. We failed them, Dan. This FIFO life has torn families apart for years. I mean, look at half of the boys' histories, divorce, cheating, bitches running off with their kids. Even your marriage copped it, mate. Enough is enough."

There's a painful truth in his words but now isn't the time to dwell on it.

"We're going back to them, right now, Russ. We'll drive if we have to, I'll get the first aid kit and" —Russell swings his fist at the wall and cuts me off again.

"Too little, too late, Dan. Take this," he tries handing me the photo, "You have to get to them for me. I'm not going anywhere."

"Bullshit, get your arse up, Russ!" I demand, a bit pissed off that he's giving up so easily.

"Lift me then, buttercup," Russell half laughs, "Look, mate, I don't know how long it takes to turn but I know I'm done for, you've gotta do something for me."

"What?"

"You saw Matt, right? What he became?"

I look up at the ceiling dismissing what he's trying to put across, "Yeah, but he was a fuckin' dog, an addict. Fuck that cunt!"

"I'm not becoming that, I can't. I won't," he stares intently at the photo, "I don't mince my words, Dan."

"Yeah, I know."

"You have to shoot me, mate."

I laugh a single 'ha', not knowing how else to respond.

Russ goes on, "It's the only way to stop me from turning, you saw what this vaccine-virus shit did to everyone in town. Put me down like a dog. It's the only way to *keep* me down."

"Wait, you're not serious?"

"A plane crash didn't kill them. Losing limbs didn't kill"—A long, wet coughing fit stops Russell mid-sentence.

I hand him the bottle of water he was drinking earlier. He takes several gulps and red stained water trickles out of his neck wound, "Hell, you chopped off one's hands, and his head, and he still kept coming."

Fuck, he's right, but still, I can't just shoot him dead. I can't. I just can't.

"Russell. I… I…" I can't even bring myself to say the words.

"You can and you will," Russell looks at the photo again, "Tell Amy I love her and tell my daughter—" Russell keels over and his body starts to shake.

His eyes burst open. He lashes out and forces the photo

into my hands and then he kicks me away, falling back into his chair and rolling back into the wall.

"Russ?! Mate?"

Russell bolts upright out of the chair, like a soldier called to attention, every muscle in his body tenses as he falls backwards into the wall as stiff as a board and then he goes wild, thrashing about between the filing cabinet and the wall. I quickly grab his shotgun and corner myself against the door. Russell starts attacking the wall and the cabinet. Whipping papers and stationery everywhere. He screams and yells like a stuck pig, as blood spatters out of his mouth and his neck wound. He flips a small table and the box of shotgun shells flies across the room and spills open at my feet. I glance down at it and then straight back up at Russell. I slowly slide down the back wall to reach for the scattered shells. My eyes stay trained on Russell, he's tangled up in the aluminium venetian blinds like a spastic cat. I load the first shell. Click. Russell doesn't flinch. I load the second shell just as he stops thrashing about.

Click.

Russell's head snaps around like a fat kid hearing a bag of crisps being opened. He stares at me through wide, grey and bloodshot eyes, and then he charges at me. Russell rips the blinds off of the wall with him and runs at me at such speed I barely have time to react, but I pull up the shotgun, squeeze the trigger and shoot him in the chest as I dive to safety. Russell crashes into the wall beside me and then to the floor, I scuttle away but keep the shotgun pointed at him. I rack the shotgun. Ch-chk. Russell's head flicks up at the sound of me reloading and our eyes meet, we stare at each other for a moment, silent and still. The good mate and solid father that was Russell is no more. The whites of his eyes are now cloudy grey with blackened veins forking across them. Bright bursts of fresh blood flower at the ends of the poisoned blood vessels. Russell's chest heaves as he takes fast, shallow breaths. I look at his arms, similar blackened veins are covering his clammy and discoloured skin, too.

The infection, this vaccine-tainted virus, whatever it is, has consumed him entirely. Russell breaks the standoff with a stomach-turning screech and lunges toward me. I close my eyes and pull the trigger, fulfilling Russell's final request.

I grab the box of ammunition and get out of that room as fast I can. A high-pitched ring screams inside my skull after firing the shotgun in such a small room. I run out of the building, leaving Russell and the photo of his family in a sticky pool of blood on the floor. Every second between the back office and the door of the ute is a blur, I don't even register bludgeoning the two zombies that surprise me in the yard. A shotgun stock to the face of one and an elbow to the throat of the other put them both on the ground. I shoot the chains securing the gates and I jump in the ute. I reverse through the gates and over several infected locals digging under the gate. I spin the ute around in the middle of the road and speed toward the southern exit out of Warballa.

Kalgoorlie, here I come!

THE FIFO CURSE

I'm thirty kilometres southwest of Warballa when I stop on the side of the road and succumb to the angry, unrelenting sobbing that only overwhelm a man a few times in his life. I had lost a great friend, I had taken a husband and a father away from his family and I had left him all alone. He's dead and it's my fault. All of it. I should have killed those two fuckers clawing under the fence faster. I should've just grabbed the fucking rifle. I should have handled it myself. Matt couldn't have killed Russell if he had never come outside and if Matt had tried to get into the workshop, we would have just shot him through the gate.

I lose myself in this self-destructive should-have loop for some time. With both hands on the steering wheel, I breathe heavily into my lap, exhausted. My face is wet with tears and hot with emotion. I try to breathe deeply and slowly, to calm myself down. I inhale a long, deep breath.

"Calm down, Dan," I release a long breath and slowly inhale another, "You're okay. Russell asked you to help him." I repeat my breathing exercise, "You helped him. The *thing* you killed wasn't Russell," I reassure myself.

"You heard Russ, I've gotta get back to my girls. I've gotta get home." I grab the rear vision mirror and angle it toward myself to assess the tired human looking back at me. He is spattered with blood and beads of dirty sweat stain his forehead. His eyes are puffy and bloodshot, and his short brown hair and beard are matted with dried blood and dustings of crushed blue metal and red pea gravel.

"Clean that shit off of your face, mate, we've gotta get a move on," I tell the reflection.

I jump out of the Hilux ute and whip my shirt off, throwing the blood-stained article into the gravel drain. I reach into the back seat and pull my bag close to fetch a small bottle of antibacterial hand soap from its side pocket. I lather up and wash my hands and face vigorously, I splash my face with water and dry it with a clean singlet, sliding it on afterwards.

During my escape from Warballa, my belongings had been thrown around the cab of the ute, I quickly tidy it and restack some of my bags. I restrain the bigger bags with seatbelts and then start picking up all of the loose shotgun shells that had spilled out of the open box in the passenger side footwell. I throw them back in their box and put it inside of Russell's boredom bag. I grab the shotgun and the rifle and lean them against the rear door. I stare at them.

"Fuck it."

I pick up the shotgun and I start feeding shells into it, better to be safe than sorry. I don't know much about shotguns, but I was pretty sure they had ammunition limiters; this shotgun did not. He must have removed the plug that limited the shell capacity, how delightful. The weapon holds eight shells.

"Darby, you dodgy bastard," I laugh.

I make sure the safety is on as I delicately place it on the passenger seat. I grab the rifle more confidently. I have played with this rifle many times and, since Russell had put a new scope on it, we have been practising a lot more on shift shooting at empty Milo tins. I check the magazine, which is fully loaded, and place it alongside the shotgun. I stand back and admire the tidied cab and, having satiated my need for organisation, I jump behind the steering wheel. I choose the perfect song to start the next leg of the journey and I slap the accelerator down as 'Hit The Road Jack' by Ray Charles plays.

I glance at the in-dash clock and its neon green display shows 12.12pm. It's at least another six-hour drive until the next stop before Kalgoorlie, Laverton, and that's *if* I get a clear run on the highway. I'll need to fuel up when I get to Laverton. too. Fuck, I might even have to stop for the night. I have no idea what the road ahead is like but if Warballa is anything to go by, I'm going to need a shit-tonne more luck and a hell of a lot more bullets. I turn the stereo up and drive.

The kilometres tick over and time passes quickly. My thoughts stray back to Warballa and snapshots of each horrible scene scroll past like clockwork. The bodies. The locals. Matt attacking Russell. The blood. The streets full of dead dogs. The smoke. Russell's gaping wounds.

Screams and the sounds of gunfire clatter through my head alongside Russell's words, 'We failed them, Dan.' His words repeat over and over again. 'Take this.' A vision of him handing me the photo of his wife and baby girl plays in my head. The image burns itself in like a sunspot.

"Fuck, Russell's family. My promise!" A flash of his family photo swimming in a pool of blood, blinds me. I slam on the brakes and skid to a stop in the middle of the road. I squeeze my eyes shut, trying to block out the flashes. And the guilt. I promised him I'd save his girls. But I need to get to Bella and Maria first. They need me home. They've needed me home for years.

In the early stages of my FIFO career, Maria started resenting my job and me, her new husband, who was away more than he was by her side. She had grown tired of coming home to an empty house every night after a long day at work or studying. Her overseas teaching qualifications weren't recognised here, so she had to upgrade them to get a better-paying job here in Australia. She was adjusting to a new country, a new chapter of our relationship and her husband's new job that came with a lot of time apart. The loneliness that consumes every FIFO worker's partner started to eat away at her. To make matters worse, I didn't have consistency with my shift patterns. I was bouncing between four weeks away with two weeks home or two weeks away and only one week home. This made it even harder to plan getaways and celebrations to make up for ones I had missed because of work.

Sure, when I was home, we'd go to unique cabin stays, buy cool stuff and do extravagant things, like adrenaline experiences, but Maria didn't need things like this. No, Maria cherished the everyday moments and was quite content with the routine of a normal family life. All she ever wanted was to be together, be it hiking through a national park or drinking a few beers by the beach. Or the occasional lazy day smoking a joint or two, making pillow forts and watching cartoons, that was by far her favourite. But even in these moments, I could never fully switch off, all I knew was work and it showed. Maria loathed my inability to enjoy the moment. Answering an email or work call during our time together was relationship suicide.

My mind was always ticking away. It had to be. I was away from civilisation for up to a month at a time and I only had one week at home to address things from the month prior and to tend to anything pressing in the coming weeks. I tried to divide my energies between Maria, a social life, my family and work obligations. As well as dentist appointments, mowing the lawn, enjoying a sleep-in and then packing for my next swing away. It wasn't easy. It was exhausting for the both of us. Our marriage was under a great deal of pressure and then, just to up the difficulty level, Maria fell pregnant. And that's when she decided that I was going to quit the fly-in, fly-out lifestyle and get a local position in town. And I did. I made the effort to change my 'work, work, work' thinking and four months before Bella was born, I started working in the yard in Perth. I was home every night and things couldn't have been better. But that dream only lasted ten months.

An economic boom had flooded the mining industry with countless new drilling contracts, and my boss wanted me back on the rigs, asap.

In my eyes, it was perfect timing, Bella was six months old, Maria was a happy and healthy mamacita and we could definitely use the extra money. Having a kid is far from cheap and yard hours and rates couldn't support us for much longer, I had to do it.

In Maria's eyes, though, I was jumping at the first chance to leave her and our newborn, Bella, to get away from the crying babies and city commutes to work each day. This is when everything started to go downhill. I had been working away for years and had adjusted to the 'FIFO life', and the salary that came with it. It was hard to swap that lifestyle for a nine-to-five-Monday-to-Friday gig earning half of what I used to. I saw it as a step backwards. So, I jumped right back into the FIFO trap and its better salary, but a wonderful new onslaught of misery came with juggling working away and a young family. The weight of the responsibilities that I was failing to meet grew over the months, and then years, and things started to crumble. Then came the fighting over the phone. The fighting through text. The resentment of a pissed off Latina. The fighting in person. Being labelled as an absent father, an absent husband and the absent best friend that my wife so sorely needed. I failed her. For years. I'm failing her now. I'm failing Bella too. I need to get back to them.

"Farrrk!" Frustration burns across my face.

I start twisting the steering wheel's grip in my hands. The rubber squeaks under the force of my Chinese burn attack. I suddenly realise that I'm holding my breath. How long had I been holding my breath? I exhale sharply and release my hands from the wheel. Pins and needles sting my hands, and I rub them together to regain sensation.

I lose myself in my past too often. Focusing on it like

an obsession, thinking that if I focus on it hard enough, I can change something, anything—everything! It eats away at my present like a swarm of locusts does a crop. I need to get my mind off of things so I check the time.

"It's 3pm already? Shit…" my stomach grumbles.

"I suppose I'd better grab a feed."

The last meal I'd had was a quick breakfast back at camp. I reach into my esky and pull out a sandwich and three muesli bars. I eat them quickly and scull my entire bottle of water.

"Aww, that's the spot," I immediately feel better, energised even, "Huh, maybe I was just hangry?"

I look at the fuel gauge and the red needle is sitting just below the 'E' symbol. The orange fuel bowser symbol flashes.

"I guess you're thirsty too?"

I pull over and hop out to fetch a jerry can from the tray when something odd stops me in my tracks.

"Jesus!" I jump back but freeze mid-start. My heart beats ten times faster and I turn my back to the ute.

"Be calm. Act calm," I look back at the rear of the ute. Nope, not calm. Far from calm, "Breathe Dan, fuck."

I take a deep breath and close my eyes. Suddenly, I hear Russell's voice inside my head, telling me the same thing he told me on my first day on his rig: 'Fake it 'til you make it, Dan. Just act like you know what you're doing and you'll be surprised by how far it gets you in life.'

"Russ is right, just act casual. Act like it's not real. It's not real." I open my eyes and turn around with the newfound confidence and bluff my way forward.

"Thought you'd hitch a ride, eh?" I ask.

I crouch down at the rear of the ute and cock my head

as I examine the decapitated head that is happily gnawing away on the tow ball. Its hollow black eyes dart back and forth between me and the Hilux's bumper, it chomps excitedly on the steel, my presence agitating it instantly. Long black hair flows from its scalp down to the gravel road, it would easily be shoulder-length hair if it had any shoulders for a reference point. The hair is matted with dried blood, red dirt and gore. The thing's jaw is contorted and definitely broken, its mouth hangs loose and agape. The tow bar fills its toothy, wet maw and the 50mm tow ball looks to be lodged deep in the back of her mouth. Well, I assume it's a her, judging by the long hair, smeared glittery eye makeup and a notable deep-throating ability, I mean to take an entire tow hitch without gagging? Lady's got skill.

I look down the road behind me, "How long have you been hitchhiking for, friend?" I ponder for a moment, "I must have picked you up when I rammed through those gates back in Warballa."

I brush her matted hair from her face. Her skin is brown, like coffee or chocolate, and strangely smooth; she's a young woman, maybe in her early twenties, she had looked after herself and made an effort to look nice.

"I bet you were the prettiest thing in town, eh?" I look at the other side of her face, which is swollen and lacerated.

I cringe, "You've had prettier days, though. Fuck."

The decapitated head continues to gnaw on the steel, her teeth scraping and clanking against it. I reach out and touch the back of her head. Her flesh is hot to the touch. If she was still human, I'd say she had a fever, but she wasn't human. Not anymore.

"You're burning up," I stand up from my crouch, "Stay here, I'll get you some medicine."

I reach into the back of the tray and grab the mattock clipped to the headboard. I wedge the wide flat end of the mattock between her face and the rear bumper. I pause and sigh, I push hard on the mattock's handle and the head slides off the hitch and drops to the ground.

I never thought, not in a million years, that I could so casually lever a dead chick's head off my tow ball and barely bat an eyelid, yet, here I am. My mind is proving to be a powerful thing under these circumstances.

I almost empathise with the girl, but I can't think of her as human anymore, she has become a thing. For all I know, it's a prop head, it isn't real, so why act like it is? I put the mattock back in the tray and leave the head on the ground. I add a couple jerry cans of diesel to the ute's tank and get moving.

I glance in my side mirror as I drive off and see the head still chomping at the dirt.

Poor girl.

TALES OF LAVERTON

I'm unusually quiet after my encounter with the severed head. I don't know if I'm in shock, numb or broken. I drive along the gravel highway to Laverton with ease, not fully registering my surroundings; autopilot has engaged. I think this fake-it-til-I-make-it approach might have to be my default for a while. I might make it through this after all.

I fly by a few smaller communities and roadhouses along the way. It's unclear whether they have fallen to the infected or if they were completely untouched by it. The boarded-up buildings and rubbish-lined verges were standard features on a normal day. As was the odd dishevelled person shuffling about or lying in a ditch. I don't know. I don't care. I just lead-foot past it all and continue along the Great Central Road. I get to the long rising curve in the road that marks the upcoming town of Laverton.

I park on the gravel shoulder of the highway. I step outside of the Hilux and stand between the door and the cab. I take in the unexpected beauty of the evening sky. It's 7.45pm and brilliant oranges and purples ignite the sky. The sun sets slowly behind a band of dark, stretching clouds as prisms of blue, red and yellow dance across the horizon. I hear the screeching of pink and grey galahs and sulphur-crested cockatoos chattering in distant trees. The town below lies in darkness, absent of streetlights and vehicle movement.

The outback boasts an amazing sunset, it's a forever-changing and awesome spectacle. Tonight's sunset is especially hypnotic, a much-needed silver lining to an otherwise shitty day. I can't look away, so much so that I don't notice the figure approaching me slowly. Timid footsteps crunch in the gravel behind me. My eyes dart to the corners of their sockets. Something strains to speak behind me, clearing its throat. I spin around with my fist raised, ready to slam it into the creature's face, only to have a smooth stick strike the left side of my face. I stumble backwards.

"Hey, now. Calm down, son. Is that how you greet an old man?" the voice says. I quickly find my footing and raise my arm to charge at the old man.

"Uh, uh," the old man lowers the cane that he struck me with and raises a silver revolver lazily, yet with intent. I catch a glimpse of it and halt, the old man warns me again,

"I said, calm down, son."

No one's ever pointed a gun at me at close range before. I can't think, all I see is the gun. It's shiny and looks heavy; the barrel is long, almost comically so, but I'm not laughing. My eyes quickly flick to the shotgun sitting in the passenger seat of the Hilux but I know that if I reach for it, the old man would put a bullet in me. I raise my arms in surrender and stare at him.

He's seventy years old, at least, and looks like a weather-beaten Australian version of 'Doc' Emmett Brown from *Back to the Future*. He has long, thin grey hair fizzing out from beneath his worn Akubra, and white stubble covers his tanned neck and jowls. A stockman's jacket hangs loosely over his slender form, and a tattered flannelette shirt is tucked into his dirty, faded jeans. They bunch up at the bottom as they sit over his equally hard-worn black steel-toed work boots. His hunched frame leans against his walking stick, which apparently doubles as a club. I rub the tender side of my face where the old man struck me.

"The town's gone mad, you know? It's been four days since I've seen anyone normal," the old man raises his revolver a little higher and looks at me quizzically.

"You are normal, right, son?"

"Yeah, mate. I'm normal," I laugh, "Well, I'm not infected anyway." He seems to perk up at my answer.

"Ha, I was beginning to think that maybe I was the only one left. I'm Pat."

"Good to meet ya, mate, I'm Dan," I lower my right arm and reach out to shake his hand.

Pat glances at me sideways, sizing me up as my hand hangs in wait. A long moment passes before he nods and tucks the revolver into the belt of his pants, and he shakes my hand firmly, "Alright then."

I relax, dropping my hands by my side. Pat grasps the top of his walking stick with both hands and jabs it into the dirt. He rocks it back and forth and then smacks his lips together.

"Do you have any water? I ran out this morning, and I'll be damned if I'm going to try to fetch it from town."

"Uh, yeah," I lean into the passenger seat from the driver's door and grab a fresh bottle, "Here," I hand it to him, "How bad is it in town?"

Pat quickly gulps down several mouthfuls.

"Ahhh," he wipes his mouth, "It's not beer, but it'll do."

He looks down at Laverton below, "She's gone to shit, son, the whole place."

"Shit, eh?"

"Yes, it went down the clacker years ago with that flaming mining boom and now we have these bloody half-dead bastards running amok," Pat shakes his head.

I half laugh, "When did the infection hit here? Are there any other survivors?"

Pat sighs and takes off his hat so he can wipe sweat from his brow, "Do you think we can sit in the ute, mate? I'm buggered."

"Um, yeah. Let me move some of my shit," I move a few things into the backseat but place my ammo and guns next to me in the driver's side footwell.

"Hop in. Pat? Was it?"

"Thanks, Dan. Yes, Pat's the name."

We get into the ute and close the doors, Pat places his walking stick and backpack between his legs as he sits. He reaches out and turns the air conditioning knob to its highest setting.

"Ah, that's heaven," Pat leans closer to the vent, "I never used to feel the heat, you know, it's only in the last couple of years that the summers have really started to affect me."

"It's staying hotter for longer and the rains are few

and far between, the seasons are shifting, they reckon."

"Hmmm, definitely," Pat adds, his eyes are closed and his face is centimetres from the air conditioning vent.

"So, what's it like in town, Pat? I'm needing to get some fuel and—"

"Son," Pat interrupts, he leans back into his seat and opens his eyes, "Forget it. I've been watching the town for the last couple of days, staying out of sight as best I could. Every time I thought I had a way into town to get my car, another one of those zombie bastards shows up. They're not too smart, but they can sense us. They know the difference between us and the infected."

"Wait, what do you mean sense us?" I ask.

"I've seen it, I don't know if they can smell us or what, but they know when we're around and if they alert the others, they flock to you like hungry seagulls to a chip." Pat drinks from his bottle and goes on, "There are different types too, have you noticed?"

"Types of what? Infected?"

Pat sighs as if I'm blind to something painfully obvious.

"Different types of zombies, son. There's no better word for them. They're dead yet alive. Human yet not."

I return a blank look.

"Well, what do you call them?" Pat asks defensively.

"I, Uh." I don't get to finish my thought, Pat continues.

"The *zombies* that have turned within a day or two are more agile and violent. They're tricky. Cunning even. Then there's the zombie who turned three to four days ago, they're just as mean, but much slower, and they are starting to rot. You can outrun one, sure. I've done it. But they can still kill you if they swarm," he takes a moment to scan the landscape as the last light of the day begins to fade, "And anyone who had that bloody vaccine, well, you can spot those ones a mile off, you know?"

I think back to Matt in the compound, I have some idea.

"How do you know all this, Pat?"

"I observe, son. I stay out of sight and commit everything to memory. I've done it for years. I keep an eye on the people who call this place home and on those who are just passing through. I can read people and I like to think I'm pretty good at it too. It's predicting people that's hardest," he gulps from his water bottle and then raises his finger as if remembering something.

"There's one more type, Dan. Type of zombie, I mean. I've only ever seen one but it is by far the scariest," Pat stares off into the distance. "Some people in this world simply don't deserve to draw breath, son, they shouldn't be allowed to breathe the same air as you and I." He gestures to him and me, "I don't know whether the infection corrupts the person or whether the person infects the infection but," I listen intently, "Evil is as real as night and day, and it can poison anything, son, including this virus madness," Pat motions to the darkened land beyond the bonnet.

"What on earth do you mean, Pat? I don't follow."

"There was a man who used to call Laverton home, well, he wasn't a man by any means of the word. He was a scoundrel. No better than the dog shit under your boot. Bruno Hughes, was his name," Pat's expression changes, his face wrinkles in disgust as the name leaves his mouth, as if he could taste it. Pat turns to face me, "This animal was as wild as he was brutish. He'd pummel a man for looking at him twice and fight up to four guys at a time, for a laugh.

I've seen it many times. I once saw him walk up to a dog in the street, pick it up by its hind legs and bash its head in with a brick because it barked at him."

"He killed it for barking?"

"Son, it gets so much worse. No man, or even a group of men, would stand up to Bruno. He was a wall of muscle and ego. He had no regard for anything, or anyone, and had no comprehension of morals; you know, right and wrong. He thought himself untouchable, which was true, to some extent. Anyway, a couple of months ago, Bruno's brother, Clay, had died. And Clay's thirteen-year-old daughter was put into Bruno's care, as her mother was in jail. The girl, Summer, was a very bright and well-loved little girl." Pat smiles talking about her, "She was always volunteering here and there, starting fundraisers or food drives and she made friends with everyone. She was always smiling. Always," Pat's chin quivers at the thought of her.

"What... What happened?" I dare ask.

Pat leans his head back, trying to keep his welling-up tears at bay, "Uh. Urgh," Pat clears his throat, "She'd been living with Bruno less than a month when things changed. Little Summer stopped smiling. She became withdrawn. Flinchy. People started noticing bruises on her arms and legs. It was obvious Bruno was abusing her, obvious to everyone, but no one acted; myself included. One day, Summer complained about her wrist at school and her teacher took her to the walk-in clinic. It was the town nurse who discovered the extent of it all, though. There were bruises, burns and cuts all over her. And small fractures in her wrists and fingers, which X-rays later showed, but it was the *other* injuries, the ones below the waistline that violated every law known to man. The internal bleeding was..." rage burns in Pat's eyes and his hands tremble.

"No," I hazard.

"Yes, son. That evil, disgusting cunt took lil' Summer and ra... he rap..." Pat couldn't bring himself to say a beautiful name like Summer, and follow it with the vicious word that defined the vilest act someone could commit against another human—let alone a child.

Pat leans forward and scrunches his eyes shut. I go to place my hand on his back, but retract it hesitantly.

As quickly as he had started to tear up, he stops.

"Sorry about that, son. Anyway, the nurse who examined young Summer, made one phone call to the police and they were on their way to arrest Bruno." Pat laughs, "Little did the coppers know, the nurse, Sarah, was already marching across town with a scalpel clenched in her hand, the Irish lass had some justice of her own to deal out. The police, three car loads of them, had already arrested Bruno by the time Sarah arrived, but that didn't stop her from pushing her way through the officers and plunging that scalpel into Bruno's skull"

"Ha! Did she kill him?"

"Nope. Just gave him a headache. He had a thick skull, it seems, some kind of hybrid Abo-Māori-scalpel-proof skull, he's a half-cast or something."

"Damn."

"So, do you understand what I meant by evil now, son?"

"I sure do," the tale of Bruno Hughes sours my mouth.

"Good, this next part will make more sense then. Once the town's people found out why Bruno was arrested and why the town nurse had stabbed him in the head, a mob quickly formed. They wanted Bruno's blood; they wanted his head on a fucking stake and his cock fed to hungry dogs. The coppers had to get him to Perth, to a more secure location, to protect him! Can you imagine?"

"I would have let the mob take him."

"So would I, son," he says nodding, "He was kept in the holding cells with a few folks that were a part of some refugee breakout, activists or something. Anyway, Bruno was jabbed the night before his transport and then his transfer date was leaked. The whole town was waiting at the police station's gates that day, some people had rocks, others had star pickets or cricket bats, and a few farmers even brought their rifles. I was there too, with my revolver, he wasn't leaving town alive. We knew it. Bruno knew it. The police knew it."

"Holy shit, really?"

"They dragged Bruno out in a full set of ankle and wrist cuffs. He looked as sick as a dog, but four coppers still struggled to keep him upright as he wrestled against his restraints. The mob went wild, screaming and taunting him, rocks started flying and people were tearing at the fences. The police were shitting themselves, they fired shots into the air to try to disperse the crowd but the farmers fired warning shots of their own right back at them; each side stood their ground. The cops weren't doing anything wrong; we weren't trying to hurt them. They were just standing in the way of true justice. Now, I don't know what took Bruno down, maybe a rock or a bullet or just the exertion of fighting against the coppers, but he went down and the crowd roared in celebration."

"He didn't stay down long, did he?"

"No, son. Officers surrounded his body to protect him and started dragging him to the transfer van. That's when the mob rushed the fence. I couldn't see what was happening for a while. But then the screaming started. Shots were fired, many times, and people scattered, then I could see into the yard again. Bruno stood there covered in blood, he had been shot several times in the chest, but it didn't seem to affect him. The coppers were dead, or dying, at his feet. Bruno looked down at his hands and admired them, at what they had just done. He touched the smoking holes in his chest. I'll never forget the menacing smirk. Like he realised he had become what everyone had thought him to be—a monster."

"Wait, he was infected? But in control, what?"

"He was in control, yes. The madness of the virus and Bruno's ruthlessness fused together," Pat answered.

"So, Bruno is the last kind of zombie? A bulletproof nightmare?" I offer.

"Yes, son. I've seen many people turn since then, but no one changed like Bruno did. "

"Fuckinell," I had seen one of these creatures before, in the shape of Rig 4's driller, Matt.

"But don't you worry, son, he may have escaped the virus, but it would have taken heaven and earth to prevent Bruno Hughes from getting what was coming to him. I followed the bastard through town, through all of the bodies that he left in the street and while he was tearing open some bloke with his bare hands, I managed to sneak up behind him. I put two bullets in the back of his head," he says with an accomplished grin.

"I can vouch for your sneaking abilities, Pat. That's a

God-given talent right there. You're pretty quick with that cane too," we share a little laugh and talk for another twenty minutes.

The sun sits well below the horizon now, it's getting darker by the minute as the thin slit of orange light disappears from the horizon. If it wasn't for the small fires still burning in the town, it would be pitch black. Pat sits with his chin tucked into his chest, drifting in and out of sleep, he must have needed the rest after his last few days. I sit in silence for some time before I speak.

"Pat, what are the chances of getting some diesel from town? I'll be running on fumes soon enough."

Pat, with his eyes still closed, thinks for a moment.

"I doubt the pumps in town even work, son. No power means no pumps. There is a backup generator for the petrol station, but by the time you get into town, break into the servo, start the generator and put the nozzle in the fuel tank, half of Laverton's undead welcoming committee would be on top of you."

"Hmmm, that's me fucked then."

Pat opens his eyes and sits upright, "Well, hold on now, son. There is another option, you see that dark patch over there?" Pat points to the eastern outskirts of the town.

"Everything's a dark patch, Pat."

"Come on, now," he says with a hint of frustration, "Do you see that red blinking light over there?"

"Yeah, just. The one that's kind of floating there?"

"That light is at the top of an old water well borer's drill mast, it's sitting in the town's dump. Dennis, one of the council boys, has a stash of 44-gallon drums full of diesel hidden there. Eighteen drums at least."

"Really? Brilliant."

"I can show you the back way into the dump, too. It's a narrow little track but it saves you the hassle of going through town."

"Thanks, Pat. You have no idea how badly I need to get back to Perth. Back to my little girl. We could go and get your four wheel drive, too."

Pat nods, "Sure, I can show you the way in, but nothing in life's free, son."

"Oh, of course. Um, I don't have any money or"—Pat interrupts— "What good is money out here now, Dan?" he laughs, "I've lived a long and happy life with relatively little money. Sometimes money holds the least value. Especially in situations like these." He opens his arms, gesturing to our surroundings and then looks back at me with a serious expression across his face.

Shit, what does he want? My guns? My food? My Hilux?

"You're probably thinking I want your car or your guns, right? No. I don't need any of that," Pat stifles a smile and then continues, "I've loved many women in my life, Dan. And yet, in all my years, I've never kissed another man," his eyes lock with mine and he places a hand on my thigh, "I'm not much to look at, I know, but I'll help you, if you'll help me. What do you say, Dan, will you help me cross this off my bucket list?" Pat wets his lips.

Fucking what?!

"Uhh… I…" sheer panic flushes my face bright red.

Pat turns his body to face me properly. He leans over the centre console, closes his eyes and puckers his lips.

Is this actually fucking happening to me right now?

Pat just sits there, his wrinkled pursed lips waiting.

"Don't keep me waiting, son."

I sigh. I need that diesel. I look around, desperately looking for an out. I hesitantly wet my lips. My face scrunches up into a hideous pre-kiss pucker. I start to close my eyes and inch closer when I see Pat's one eye open and his lips twitching into a smirk. Then a smile. One of his eye's creases open further. His smile widens and then he bursts out laughing. He falls back into his seat in hysterics.

He points at me, mimicking my terrified pre-kiss facial expression, "You should see your face, son!" he rocks in his seat, laughing uncontrollably and holding his stomach, "Oh, my sides!" he laughs.

I half smile back at him, "You bastard."

This fucking guy, this old man and his jokes; this cunny funt. I'm torn between wanting to hit him and wanting to push him out of the Hilux and drive off.

Pat brings his hands to his face, "Oh, my cheeks, I haven't laughed like this in weeks, son."

My face is hot with embarrassment. I actively avoid eye contact with him and look out the window ahead, when something catches my eye. Just past the headlight's beams; something moves low and fast across the road.

"Pat. What's that, over there?"

Wiping tears from his eyes, he replies, "What's what, you gullible fool. I'm pretty convincing, aren't I?" he boasts with a gleeful smile.

"Look, over there. By that road marker on the right," I direct him.

Pat chuckles intermittently, "I don't see anything, son," he wipes delighted tears from his eyes, "So, would you have kissed an old man for some fuel, you hussy?"

He starts laughing again.

"No, shut up you weird, horny, old man," I try to say without smiling, urging seriousness to show its face.

"Aw, did I upset you, princess? Come here, let Uncle Pat kiss you better," Pat reaches out for me in jest, making kissy, kissy sounds.

I fend him off playfully with my elbow when we both see something, several things actually, scurry across the road in a group. We freeze mid-tussle.

"Pat, what was…"

Distant growls interrupt my question and answer it simultaneously. Pat's smile disappears. We remain still and silent. The growling intensifies and barks echo all around us.

"Bastards!" Pat spits,

"What the hell is that?"

"I thought these damned things left town. Damn," Pat grabs his revolver.

"Damn what? What's out there?"

Something launches itself at my driver's door window. Its teeth and paws violently scratch against the ute. Drool and tufts of bloody fur smear across the glass.

"What the fuck!"

Pat chimes in, "That's Horse, we've gotta move, now!"

DOG PIN BOWLING

"What the fuck is 'Horse', Pat?! That ain't no horse."

"Kill the lights, son. Now!" Pat demands.

"I can't. The ute's mine spec, the headlights are always on."

"Bloody safety bullshit!"

Another beast slams itself against Pat's door. Then another. One more lunges itself at my door.

"Fuck this, hold on!" I throw the ute in reverse and boot the accelerator. Pat struggles to brace himself against the dash as we surge backwards, blindly steering into the night.

"Yep, we're stuffed, son," Pat comments.

I flick on the spotlights to see what is trying to attack us. A pack of wild dogs, spanning the width of the road, is chasing the ute. There must be more than twenty of them bounding toward us. I whip my head over my shoulder, looking back to try to see where I'm going as I reverse up the road.

"I can't see shit back there!"

"Just keep going, son!" Pat squawks, struggling with his seatbelt.

Smack. Smack.

Smack. Smack. Smack.

"Fucking road markers!" My blind steering has us heading for the gravel shoulder. I jerk the steering wheel and straighten back up onto the road and away from the metal reflective road markers. I position the Hilux over the painted centre road line and focus on that. I look over to Pat, who's leaning out the window with his revolver.

Who is this guy?

"Keep 'er steady, son," Pat fires his revolver into the dogs, a kelpie's head explodes and its body rolls beneath the rest of the chasing pack.

Bang! Another round slams into the chest of a German Shepherd, and it barrel rolls off into the bushes.

Bang! Bang! One bullet hits the tarmac and ricochets off into nowhere, but the second bullet shatters the front leg of a large Doberman. Its leg folds like a plastic straw under the animal's weight and sends it into a face-arse-face-arse somersault.

"Down she goes!" Pat commentates.

We start gaining some distance between us and the dogs, so Pat sits back in his seat and starts reloading what he'd spent back into the revolver.

"Why are these dogs chasing us, Pat?! They look rabid as fuck!"

"They've been eating infected corpses, likely, the infection affects them differently. It doesn't seem to slow them down, does it?"

Something larger than all the other dogs begins to cut up through the centre of the pack. Snapping at the others and tossing aside any smaller dog that gets in its way.

"What the fuck is that?" Pat looks up as he slaps his reloaded revolver cylinder shut.

"Ah, here comes Horse."

"Horse?!" I repeat.

"Yes. He's one of the townie's dogs, a massive Irish Wolfhound, I believe. He was in the lock-up at the back of the cop station for attacking a sheep or something, he was meant to be put down last week." Pat shrugs, "He must've got out. We might need something a bit bigger to take him down," Pat says, eyeing off my shotgun.

"I have a better idea." I brake hard and screech to a halt, and then smash the gear stick into first and floor it. We launch forward at the fast-approaching wall of fur and teeth. Horse is ahead of the pack by a few lengths and is closing the gap fast.

"This is going to be messy," I tighten my grip around the steering wheel and brace for impact.

A split second before Horse's face meets the ute's steel roo bar, he dives off to the right, and I miss him entirely. The same can't be said for the rest of the pack, though. The vehicle shudders from the force of row after row of rabid dogs meeting their gruesome fate. Loud thuds, yelps and the sounds of bones cracking, pierce the air. The dogs at the tail end of the pack try to get out of the way and one silly mutt tries to jump over us. A retriever, he tries to leap over the bonnet but his back legs hit the top of the roo bar and they break instantly. The mutt howls as he slides up the windscreen and over the cab and then rolls off onto the road.

A much smaller dog, a staffy, attempts the same feat, but as it jumps, it half somersaults into the air. Its head dips below the height of the bonnet and goes through a gap between the roo bars, as its arse continues to sail overhead and, with a sickening yelp, the staffy's thick neck snaps like a twig.

"Fuckinell!" I wince.

We mow down the rest of the pack and I whip up the handbrake and turn hard, spinning us 180 degrees. A damaged spotlight hangs by its cables, and a beam of light swirls erratically between the road and the night's sky in a kind of figure-eight pattern. I kill the spotlights and look out at the road ahead of us. A thick, twitching carpet of bloodied fur and fucked up canines blankets the road.

I turn to Pat, "Do you think that's all of them?"

"No, son. Look," Pat points straight ahead.

Horse walks towards us, stepping over the broken and yelping remains of his pack. Two other dogs sheepishly follow behind him, both look injured, but an obligation to their alpha drives them forward. Horse glares at us, a low growl rumbles in his throat as his hackles raise; he drops his head and his lips curl.

"Go on, get! Ya filthy mongrels!" Pat fires a shot at Horse's feet, pelting tarmac at the dog's face, but Horse doesn't flinch. His growl deepens, "Bold bastard, isn't he?"

Pat steadies his gun at Horse and he pulls the hammer back again. Horse barks at the two dogs behind him and they disappear into the scrub on the road's shoulder. Horse lingers briefly before he trails in behind them.

"Huh. That was unexpected. Alright, son, all this racket will have attracted some of the town folk. Head up to that track over that hill there. We'll wait them out and head into the town later."

We skirt around the carpet of dead and dying dogs and drive away from Laverton. Pat scans the scrub for Horse and his buddies, but can't see anything in the darkness. We double back towards the town down an old gravel access track, which is particularly challenging because Pat insisted that I remove a fuse to avoid advertising our position with the ute's bright headlights. Luckily, intermittent breaks in the cloud cover above allow the moon's light to guide us. I park on a high ridge facing the town and turn the ute off.

"We'll stay here for a couple of hours, Dan. We'll roll into the scrap yard once we're sure everything's settled down, and we'll get you some fuel and get me my car."

"Yeah, mate. Sounds like a plan. I might even try to squeeze in a nap, if that's okay?"

"That's fine, son. Rest up."

I recline the seat back and close my eyes. Pat continues to talk to me, as if I'm listening, knowing full well that I'm not. I only catch snippets of what he's saying. I hear the name Natalie, that she's a Spanish backpacker. Olive skin and crazy hair. That's all that I catch. Pat speaks fondly of her. I fall into a deep sleep, yet still manage to dream. Which seems like a blessing at first, but soon proves to be a curse. I'm tormented by images of Steve burning alive and of Matt tearing Russell apart. Bella is there too, Bruno Hughes is chasing her. It's so real, so vivid.

"Wake up, son, you're having a nightmare," Pat shakes me awake, "Everything's okay, wake up!"

I wake wide-eyed and gasping. My eyes find Pat's and hold his stare. I try to catch my breath, "Phfwoaah…That was a shit time." I shake my head trying to rid myself of the horrors that had assaulted me in my dream.

"Son, you need to let go of my arm now," Pat politely requests as he slowly looks down at his arm. I had unknowingly lashed out when Pat woke me and grabbed his forearm.

"Shit. Sorry, Pat." I let go and retract my hand.

Pat rubs his forearm, "Must've been some dream, son. Don't worry. You'll get back to her, your Bella."

I must've mumbled, or yelled, her name as I dreamt.

"Sorry, again. Yeah, it was some dream, alright. Is it time?"

Pat sees the worry in my eyes but moves past it, "Yes, son. You see that old caravan?" he points down toward the town's dump, "If you park behind that, we can get you all the diesel you want, but you have to do one small favour for me."

"I'm not kissing you, Pat," I interrupt.

Pat smirks, "I'm out of your league anyway, son. No, I need you to come with me to see someone in Kalgoorlie. The Spanish girl, Natalie, to make sure she's alright."

"Natalie?" I ask, not remembering the name.

"The backpacker? The young girl I told you about?"

"Oh, yeah," I lie, having fallen asleep during his, well, *our* conversation, "Sorry, where is she again?"

"She is working at a small Alumco laydown yard just outside of Kalgoorlie. It's here," Pat pulls something out of his shirt pocket and shows me a hand-drawn map, "Natalie drew this for me so I could visit her."

I pull out my phone and take a photo, "There we go." I check the photo and zoom in, "Clear as crystal, I'll come with you, Pat, it's the least I can do. Plus, it's on the way."

"Thank you, son. Now, she's quite a looker, so don't cream your pants when you see her, alright?"

I laugh, "I'll try my hardest not to, Pat"

"I have something that I have to give to her, I've been holding on to it for some time, but let's get the diesel first."

We roll down the washed-out gravel track and coast into the junkyard. We park behind the old caravan and leave the ute idling at Pat's request.

"Don't worry, son. No one will jack our ride, everyone's dead, and I'm fairly certain zombies can't drive."

"Ahuh. 'jack our ride' eh? Are you a gangster, too, Pat? Patty Smalls? Tu-Pat Shakur, maybe?" I jest.

Pat smirks and distorts one of his old, leathery hands into a gang sign and holds it out in front of his chest, "You know it, my doggie homeboy."

I shake my head at him, "You're a strange unit, mate."

I go to grab my shotgun, but Pat stops me.

"That shotgun is too big, son. Do you have anything smaller? You want something that you can hold one-handed, something you can use in close quarters. Trust me."

"Okay? I'll see what else I've got."

"Good, I'll go up ahead and check if the coast is clear."

Pat tucks his cane into the footwell and closes his door.

"I'll catch up," I put the shotgun back in the car and grab Russell's boredom bag. I unzip it and see a sawn-off shotgun sitting on top of a pile of other goodies.

"Where the fuck did you get this, Russell?" I pick up the sawn-off and snap open the barrel, it's empty. I grab the box of shotgun ammunition from the bag and, to my surprise, the shells that I had taken from the Darby office fit snugly in the barrel, "Oh yes!"

I look deeper in the bag and find a makeshift shoulder holster fashioned out of an old belt, some stubby holders taped together and a bunch of cable ties. Russell was resourceful, I'll give him that. I put the holster on and adjust the belt to fit me comfortably across the chest. The sawn-off slides into the stubby holders securely. I jiggle my torso, like a stripper showing off her new tits, to test the holster and it holds, "This will do nicely."

I pull out the two empty jerry cans from the tray of the ute and meet Pat by the side of the caravan. He's peering around it, scoping out the junkyard. We squat silently for a few minutes before Pat sneaks across the yard and crouches by a tall pyramid of old tyres. It's eerily quiet, like the calm before the storm, the bright moon lights up most of the yard but many places are still completely dark. Long black shadows stretch out from mountains of scrap metal and white goods. A mischievous breeze blows through the yard every now and then, scaring the absolute shit out of me. It rustles a bush here. And makes a caravan door creak open there. It entices a broken windmill to squeal loudly back to life behind me. You know, the typical nerve-rattling-arsehole-tightening type shit that wind does in creepy and tense situations like these.

"Fucking wind," I mutter.

I scan the yard too, keeping an eye on Pat and for anything that may try to surprise him from behind. I touch the sawn-off shotgun that's secured across my chest for comfort.

"Psst," Pat calls my attention from across the yard and waves me over. I crouch-walk over to Pat and squat next to him beside the pyramid of tyres.

"Where are these 44's, Pat?" I whisper.

"They're just there, by that sea container. Under that tarp," Pat points to the darkest section of the junkyard.

"Joy. How do you want to do this?"

"You fill your jerry cans and I'll stand watch. The drum pump should just be sitting on top of one of the 44s. You ready, son?"

"As ready as I'll ever be," we start crossing the yard, in a hunched-over, stealth-like, fast-walking fashion.

"Now, we've gotta be real quiet, son, so try not to make too much"—as if jinxing us immediately, my boot catches a piece of metal sticking out of the ground, and I trip. I lunge forward and send one of the jerry cans flying. Fuck. It sails through the air and crashes against the side of an open sea container door. Needless to say, the sound it makes is far from fucking quiet.

"Son of a..." I spit under my breath.

Pat and I both freeze. Our eyes bounce from shadow to shadow scanning for anything reacting to the sound. We squat with weapons drawn and scan the yard for a good five minutes, before Pat turns and gives me that 'really?' look and whispers, "One job, you had one job, son. Just be quiet, that's it."

"Shut up, man. It was an accident."

I nudge him with my elbow.

"You're lucky you're pretty, Dan. Come on, let's get this done."

We fill the jerry cans without incident, and I walk back up and put them in the Hilux while Pat stands guard by the 44s. I hop in the driver's seat and spy the in-dash display, the orange fuel light blinks at me, "Fuck!".

Sweating and slightly exhausted from hand-pumping

and hauling full jerry cans through the yard, genius strikes. Fuck lugging those jerry cans back and forth, I'll just pull up beside the drums. I pop the handbrake and roll down toward Pat and the diesel drums. I throw Pat a thumbs up and park up.

"Hmm. Smart thinking, son," Pat whispers.

I fill the third jerry can and then feed the hose into the ute's fuel tank and start hand pumping again. Both of our heads are on a swivel, searching and scouring our surroundings for something that's probably not even there. I rock the drum to see how much is left, it's about half empty.

"Come on, son. I'm getting antsy in my pantsy over here," Pat admits.

"I'll finish off this drum and that'll be us. We're almost there." I start pumping faster, but the hand pump starts to squeak loudly. Eeee. Ee. Eeee. Ee. Eeee. Ee

"Slow it down, Dan. If throwing jerry cans all over the place didn't attract anything, that sure will," Pat instructs.

"Okay, okay," I mumble, slightly embarrassed. I pump slower, "There's only a quarter left, almost done."

The wind cuts through the yard, whistling and moaning its way through car bodies and scrap metal heaps. Swirls of dust and sand whip up all around us. We didn't notice the clouds thickening above us, but it's starting to block the ever-helpful moonlight that was illuminating the yard. It's getting very dark, very quickly.

"I think a storm's a brewing, Dan. Let's get a wriggle on."

Slow down. Speed up. Which is it, Pat?!

"That's full enough," I stop pumping and pull the hose out from the fuel tank.

The wind is well and truly picking up now, it howls

through the yard at speed. Loose debris floats through the air and light sheets of tin clatter.

"Oooh, listen to that wind, son. It's angry, it sounds like it's growling at us," Pat says, raising his voice over the sound of the wind.

I click the fuel cap door shut and pause for a second to listen. The wind howls and coos around us. But wait. A low droning sound continues in the breaks between the harmonic gusts. A gravelly gurgling noise.

"Holy shit, it kinda does sound like it's growling at us."

I look around to see if I can pinpoint where or what the wind is coursing through to make such a sound. I walk away from the ute to try to hone in it as the noise gets louder.

"Ooh, it's really growling now, Pat."

"Uh, son."

"It sounds like it's coming from up..." I cock my head upwards, toward the towering pile of old fridges and freezers. I can't quite see the top of it, so I step backwards.

"Son..." Pat says in a firmer tone.

A beam of moonlight creeps its way up the side of the pile of white goods, and the sound intensifies. So much so, that it no longer sounds like growling, it *is* growling. The moon's light reaches the peak of the white goods mountain and illuminates the source of the growling.

Pat and I let out a synchronised, "Fuck."

The persistent, four-legged, son-of-bitch called Horse, stands proudly atop the white goods mountain's summit.

DIESEL, DOGS & THE UNDEAD

"Son, keep your eyes on him. His two friends won't be far away," Pat cocks his pistol, "I'll go find 'em, you stay by the ute."

I nod and slowly step back towards the Hilux, and pull the sawn-off shotgun from its holster. I stare up at Horse and he stares right back at me. A continuous growl rumbles through his clenched snarl.

"Yeah, I see you, ya hairy fuck," I mutter. Only a few tense moments pass before I call out to Pat, "Oi, have you found his mates yet?"

"Not yet, son." Pat paces slowly away from me.

"Stay close, eh? We don't want these sly shits getting between us."

Pat waves me off with his other hand like 'yeah, yeah'.

I back up into the side of the ute door and see the rifle in the back seat, and a thought springs to mind. I could definitely nail that prick from here with the rifle. I slowly swap the sawn-off into my left hand and reach through the open window, fumbling for the rifle with my free hand in the darkness. Horse watches me like a hawk, his head tilts to the side as he tries to figure out what I'm up to.

"Aw, bud. You have no idea what's coming."

My hand finds the barrel of the rifle and I grin. I very slowly holster my shotgun and start to pull the rifle out of the window by the barrel, when Horse's growl ceases. I freeze, somehow, that half-dead, mangy mutt puts two-and-two together, and he raises his head and howls.

Aroooo-a-a-oooo!

We hear barking in the distance responding to Horse's call, he whips his head backwards and howls again.

Aroooooooo!

I shoulder the rifle and take aim, I close one eye and sight him in. Horse drops his head and his hackles raise along the full length of his spine. A lunar glow shines through his wiry outer coat, turning the grey matted hair a silvery white. The backlit silhouette of the formerly domesticated dog now makes him look like some kind of supernatural dire wolf.

I steady my aim.

"Gotchya," I prematurely celebrate.

The clouds above the junkyard move fast and swallow up the moon's light, the peak of the white goods mountain darkens just as I finger the trigger and fire.

A swing and a miss.

"Fucker!" Horse disappears over the back side of the peak.

"Pat, get back to the ute!" I yell out.

Horse runs off toward the other side of the junkyard and I fire another round aimlessly into the night.

"Dan, quick, bring that rifle here! One of the other two mutts is over here. Behind that old tow truck, just there. I can hear it."

"Pat, I lost Horse. Get back here. Get back to the car!"

"Shhhh… Listen. Here they come. Get ready," Pat raises his cocked revolver.

I move across the yard over to the side of the caravan, and I brace myself against it, to cover Pat. We hear a dog growling, and the sounds of its paws shuffling in the gravel on the other side of the tow truck. I'm twenty metres from the tow truck. Pat is closer by ten metres. A short distance down from the tow truck is the town-side entrance to the junkyard. This might be our way out, if Pat would just get the fuck back to the ute. My heart races and my eyes dart around the yard. I'm aiming the rifle toward the dog behind the truck, but I'm more concerned about where Horse went.

It sounds like the dog is dragging something; its growls seem laboured with effort rather than intimidation. And there's another growl that doesn't exactly sound canine, or even beastly, it is more of a moan than anything else.

Maybe it's the wind playing tricks with us? Or maybe the dog is hurt? This could work in our favour.

A dog's arses scoots out past the front of the tow truck, it's a red heeler, and it's dragging something big. She jerks and tugs against the weight of whatever it is she has clamped in her mouth. She seems very eager to show us.

"What the fuck could it possibly be dragging?" the mutt drags its new chew toy into view, "Oh".

Pat laughs, "Clever bitch."

"Get. Fucked," I add.

She's dragging something alright; the fat, hairy shin of

an obese, flano-shirt-wearing-zombie fuck. I look over at Pat, who looks just as dumbfounded as I am. Pat quickly and silently mouths 'don't shoot' to me, shaking his head in disapproval. I take my finger off the trigger.

"What? Why?" I argue in hushed tones.

He loudly whispers back, "You'll attract more."

And the two shots I just fired wouldn't have?

Pat pulls a ball peen hammer out from his jacket pocket and, without hesitation, crosses the yard and brings the hammer down hard on the dog's skull. It dies instantly. Pat springs up and swings the hammer straight into the zombie's thick neck. It stumbles backwards, stunned by the blow, and Pat lunges forward again and slams the hammer into the side of the fat bastard's head. Right in the temple. He swings at the same spot again and again until he drops to the ground. Pat steps back and takes in big gulps of air. He is mildly winded from his efforts and braces one arm on his knee to catch his breath. I look on in disbelief. He walks past the tow truck and looks down the town-side driveway into Laverton.

Pat sighs heavily, "Clever bitch."

He pockets his hammer and swaps it for his pistol. He starts firing down the driveway into the town, one shot after another.

"Pat!" I jump out from behind the caravan and race toward him. He spends every round in his revolver as he steps back into the yard. I run over to Pat, and when I get to his side, I see why he's shooting into the town. A large group of infected are slowly shuffling out of the mining accommodation village and up toward us.

"Don't be shy, son! Them or us," Pat urges, reloading

his gun. I start shooting into the crowd too. They're dropping like flies, but more are coming. The sound of gunfire draws them out like moths to a flame. They know we're here now, there goes the stealth element of our plan.

"I'm empty!" I yell.

I quickly get behind Pat as I reload the rifle.

"Son, check this out," Pat points at the town, "Look. To the left of the pack. Near the ground, by their feet."

Horse's second bitch—a slightly overweight staffy—weaves through the crowd of infected, barking at them and nipping at their heels. I squint hard, trying to figure out what she's doing.

"Is... Is she?"

Pat finishes my thought, "She's bloody herding them. The zombies. She's herding them right up here and into the yard." Pat and I look at each other and echo, "Clever bitch."

"How many are there?" I ask.

"Your guess is as good as mine, son."

"Errr… There are three in this group at the bottom of the driveway and there's—" Pat interrupts, "Five in the rear. You get the ones at the back and I'll get the bitch and her friends at the bottom of the driveway."

Pat and I walk down the sloped gravel driveway side by side, firing into each group.

"Two down!" Pat calls.

I sight one of the larger fellas at the rear of my group and I send a round through the side of his face. Pink shit sprays out of his skull and he collapses to the ground.

"One down," I call out, as I expel the empty shell. I quickly line up the frizzy-haired woman in the tattered dress limping her way toward us and fire again. Her nose and upper jaw buckle into her face, and her limp body and unkempt head of hair hit the dirt.

"Make that two down, Pat!"

Pat paces ahead of me, "I see your two and raise you…" Pat shoots the lead zombie of his group, and the bullet punches straight through its forehead, spraying bone and gore out the back of its head.

"…Three!" Pat boasts.

"Actually," Pat aims at one of my three remaining zombies and fires, "Make that four!" he laughs.

"Oi, they're mine!" I argue, smiling, "Get that dog, ya cocky bastard!"

I fire into my group and hit the tall, gangly-looking bloke in the side of the neck, chunks of flesh and muscle explode out of him. His head slumps to the right, but he keeps shuffling toward the junkyard.

"Shit!" I fire again and put him down. "Pat, you killed that dog yet?" I yell out.

I spot a random shuffler making its way towards the driveway and end him with two shots, one hits his chin and the other goes through his eye.

"Son, I uh… Well, the little bitch," Pat scratches the back of his head, "She ran back into town."

"One job, Pat!" I jest, "Let's seize this opportunity and get the fuck out of here, eh?"

"Agreed," we turn and jog back towards the Hilux, scanning the darkness for movement as we do, "Keep your eyes peeled for Horse, I don't want him surprising us."

"Way ahead of you, Pat."

The night sky moves wildly above us, the wind howls and rumbling thunder rolls in. Little to no light pierces through the thick blanket of clouds now, and the only light is that of the many fires still burning in the town. I look back at the town only to see a new wave of infected bastards being herded our way. This group is much larger and moving a lot faster than the last.

"Pat…"

Pat turns back toward the town and sees the massing undead shuffling their way towards us. He only offers two words, "Well, then."

"I might need a little more than that, Pat!" I bait, glancing back and forth between him and the horde.

"I think we save the ammunition, get in the car, drive off and then you can plant a kiss right here to say thank you?" Pat turns his head and points to the side of his cheek.

I shake my head at Pat and counteroffer, "Save bullets, get in the ute, *withhold* kisses from Pat and get the fuck out of here. Cool, let's go with my plan."

We head toward the Hilux as Pat takes one last look at the town, his eyes fix on something in the approaching zombie pack.

"What is it, Pat?" I walk over and stand by his side.

"Look, who's staring me down. Over there, in front of the crowd. It's Horse's little bitch."

"Come on Pat, leave her. Let's just get out of here," I try to reason with him.

"What? And let her live? I don't think so, son. She threw zombies at me! At us! It's personal."

"Come on, she didn't throw…" I don't finish that sentence, Pat continues, speaking over me.

"Anyway, by killing her, Horse loses his last loyal little helper and seeing as Horse isn't around for me to kill," he looks around exaggeratedly, "I guess I'll just have to shoot his bitch instead. Yes. That's fair, let's do that."

"Make it quick, Pat," I don't argue with him, "I'll keep an eye out."

"Good, lad." Pat smiles widely, like a child who just got his way. He puts his fingers in his mouth and wolf whistles for Horse's bitch, "Here, pussy, pussy, pussy!" Pat calls, slapping one hand against his thigh, "I've got a big bone with your name on it!"

The dog's ears prick upwards.

Pat whistles again.

"I don't have all night, ya hairy bitch. Come and get it!"

The dog stands its ground, growling and barking at Pat from a distance. Unsure whether to attack or not. I look over to Pat and hear him muttering to himself.

"Come here, you lil' mongrel. I've got your bone right here," he raises his pistol and shoots at the ground right in front of the dog, coarse dirt and gravel spray up at her. She doesn't like that one bit, her hackles raise, and she barks wildly. She starts sprinting toward him. I give Pat a side-eye and then shoulder my rifle, but Pat reaches out with his hand and dips my barrel.

"No, no. Trust me, son. I've got this," his eyes glisten with confidence, "Stand back, this is going to look pret-ty cool," he dips his Akubra and widens his stance.

I take several steps away from him, raising my rifle just in case. The dog bounds towards Pat at great speed, growling and barking as she gains on him.

My heartbeat thuds in my chest.

"Wait for it..." Pat mutters to himself, calculating the dog's approach to time his counter-attack.

She's fifty metres away.

"Wait for it…" he crouches down to entice her, slowly curling his index finger toward himself, beckoning her enthusiastically.

Twenty metres away.

She's coming up the driveway.

"Almost there…"

Pat cocks his pistol and extends his arm.

Five metres away.

"Perfect!"

Pat lowers his pistol.

Dafuq?

Pat throws out his left hand with fingers splayed as if he is going to try to grab the dog by its face.

My heart almost stops.

I take aim, but it's too late, there is only a metre or so between Pat and the dog. *What if I hit Pat?* All I can do is watch as the dog launches itself into the air with its teeth snapping ferociously.

Pat just sits there.

Only centimetres are between his outstretched arm and the dog's nose. *What the actual fuck is this man doing?!*

Finally, Pat makes his move and jumps to the side at the last second. He fires a round into the dog's chest. Its jaws barely miss Pat's outstretched hand as it slips behind her and grabs for her collar tightly. The inertia of the pup's powerful leap carries the dog past Pat and, with the collar in hand, Pat heaves back with all his might and snaps the bitch's neck.

"Whoa, holy shit, Pat! Well done," I cheer.

"The job's not done yet, son," Pat spits through gritted

teeth. The dog's body lay limp in the dirt, but her head and, more importantly, her mouth are still very much alive. They snap and chomp at Pat as he pins her down with one arm. He brings the barrel of his pistol to the back of her head and stares down at the furry pain-in-the-arse, and just before he pulls the trigger, he stops.

"Wait a second, I know this dog. This is the Richardson's pup," Pat remarks.

"What?" I ask, puzzled at its significance.

Pat checks the purple collar on the dog, and the cursive embroidered text reads: ' T h e   R i c h a r d s o n ' s '.

"Well, I'll be. This is Heather and Charlotte's pooch, they live just up that road there, they have the Scottish flag and one of those rainbow flags hanging in their front window," Pat explains.

"Ahuh, that's fascinating," sarcasm peppers my words, I point over toward the town, "Well, down this road here, is a hungry pack of undead fuckers that are thirsty for our hides, so, let's hurry this up a little, yeah?" I insist.

"Okay, okay. Don't get your knickers in a twist. She only obeys Scottish commands, you know, or is it Gaelic?"

"Cool story, bro. Kill her in Gaelic so we can go then, I don't want to be here when Horse comes back," I press.

"Will do, son," he kneels down close to the dog's ear and says, "Cluich marbh," Pat leans back and shoots the mutt in the side of the head, "Now, fuirich!"

"Finally, Pat. Jeez. What was that cloo-ish-marb-foo-reach nonsense?"

Pat stands up and brushes himself off, "If I remembered it correctly, I told her to 'play dead' and then to 'stay'; hopefully, I pronounced it right. Young Heather taught me those commands years ago. I think it's right?" Pat smiles back at me, all chuffed with himself.

"Alright, bilingual Barry, let's go. Gaelic class is over," I walk off ahead toward the ute.

"Ooh, okay, princess. No need to get uppity," Pat retorts, "Maybe a kiss from Uncle Pat will make my princess smile?"

I stifle a laugh and turn around, "You are one creepy, troubled man, Pat."

"Is that why you love me?" Pat asks, laughing.

"What? No," I fire back.

Lightning cracks loudly above us and scares the absolute shit out of us.

"Yep, time to get a wriggle on, son."

He didn't have to tell me twice. I move quickly to the Hilux and Pat follows closely behind me.

Fat raindrops start to fall as the lightning above intensifies, it's going off like a strobe light at a rave. The insane brightness and the complete darkness that follows each flash make it hard to see, my depth perception is battling hard.

Pat stumbles and falls into the back of me, "Sorry, son."

I help him up to his feet, "No worries, Pat, I can't see shit either."

He rights himself and grabs onto the tail of my shirt to follow me, like a baby elephant gripping its mother's tail. A massive lightning flash ignites above us and booms like fucking artillery and curtains of rain begin to fall.

"The ute is just over there, come on."

I quickly pop the bonnet to replace the headlight fuse and then climb into the driver's side. Pat opens his door to get in, but he starts kicking the mud off of his boots and pants first. I take the gun holster off from around my chest and wedge it down beside my seat. I shut the door and click my seat belt in. I place two hands on the wheel and look out the windscreen into the headlights' beams.

"Errr… Pat. Get in the car."

"Hold on there, son. I'm just—"

"Pat, get in!"

Hating to be rushed, as well as interrupted, Pat stops and looks up at me with hard eyes, only to see me reacting to something in front of the ute.

He turns, "What are you... Oh."

Pat half-asks and half-answers his own question as he, too, sees what I'm staring at.

PAT vs. HORSE vs. DAN

Horse stands defiantly in front of the ute's headlights, sporting his signature raised hackles, pissed off snarling expression that he wears so well.

"Get in, Pat. I'll just run him down with the ute," I offer.

"Hmmm… You missed him with ute last time, though?"

"…Yeah, but…"

"No," Pat steps away from the door and closes it, "It's time to put this bastard down, for good. Stay here, son, I'll be quick."

"Wait, no!" I fling open my door and throw my legs out of the cab to stop Pat, but I'm abruptly hung up by my seatbelt, "Ugh! Aw, come on!"

I quickly try to unclip the belt. Nope, not happening. I scoot back into my chair to loosen it, it doesn't budge. I try to slide the entire seat back but the ROPs prevent that and the belt only tightens across my chest.

127

"Dafuq?!" I struggle to free myself, my frustration and haste to escape only thwart my attempts. This naturally makes me battle even harder against the belt. I continue to tango with my shiny, black belt of a dance partner as Pat paces toward Horse.

"Aww get fucked, cunt!" I spit.

My eyes flick back and forth between Pat and the safety buckle. Four seconds pass, the limit of my patience it seems, and I start contemplating shooting my way out of the buckle. I reach for my gun when a faint, familiar voice echoes into the back of my mind, 'Breathe, babe'. Ah, the verbal prompt I had heard many times before to calm and prevent me from doing something dumb, it's the echo of my former voice of reason, Maria.

In moments of anger, overreaction or minor everyday inconveniences—when my temper would start to get away from me—Maria's voice could pierce through the foggy emotional haze and soothe my racing mind in an instant. Her voice, the very same voice she'd use to soothe Bella in her crib, put me into a kind of trance, like a snake charmer does a cobra. I could fight against it, yes, but with her repetitive and soft hypnotic tone, she'd easily calm her bearded, ill-tempered cobra. I could be inches away from confronting some clown who squeezed Maria's arse in a bar or who just cut me off in traffic and Maria would simply place her hand on my shoulder or thigh and reel me back to reality. She could centre me like no other. Kind of like Wolverine's girlfriend, Kayla, in *X-men Origins: Wolverine*. In fact, exactly like that. At times, I wondered if Maria had these same powers of persuasion but if she did, she would have convinced me to quit this FIFO shit a long time ago, and I would be at home with her and Bella right now.

Her voice replays in my head now as I close my eyes and exhale. I press the release button on the seatbelt's buckle and it clicks open.

"Ha ha! I'm free!" I grab the sawn-off shotgun and race out of the car. I yell out to Pat, "Pat, get in the car."

He's gone.

"Pat?" Panic mode engages, "Pat?! Where the fuck? Pat!" I raise my sawn-off, ready for anything, as I try to spot him through the darkness and pelting rain, "Pat!?"

Lightning cracks above, its flash lights up the junkyard and I see Pat's hunched form heading toward the mountain of white goods. I chase after him and close the gap between us in an instant.

"Oh, thank fuck, there you are."

"Shhh, son. I got him cornered," Pat's crouched down in the mud with his revolver drawn and his eyes locked with Horse, who's backed up against a wall of fridges and washing machines.

"Son, I need you to take a few steps back and keep your head on a swivel. It's not just Horse in here with us, remember? Those shuffling freaks will be on us anytime now," Pat reminds me.

"Just shoot him and let's go. Hell, I'll shoot him," I slip my finger down onto the trigger of the sawn-off.

"No, Dan. He's mine. Just keep an eye out for those bastards coming up from the town."

I huff and hesitantly comply.

The rain is absolutely belting down now. Horse and Pat are locked in their standoff. And I'm standing here drenched from head to toe playing in the mud by myself on 'zombie watch'. What a lovely way to spend the evening.

Pat entices Horse, "Come on, boy, I've got a treat for you. It's the same treat I gave your little bitch girlfriend not too long ago, and she loved it."

Horse does a wet-dog shake and growls. He spreads his stance and lowers his head, preparing to attack.

"I think he understood you, Pat," I call out over the pouring rain, "Just shoot the cunt."

Pat ignores my remark, so I dutifully return to scanning the yard. The intermittent lightning flashes both help and hinder my attempts to keep watch. Yes, each flash lights up the yard, but each flash comes from a different place. The shadows dance and stretch across the muddy ground of the yard. One flash sends them away from me and then another flash sends the shadows rushing back toward me. It's distracting as fuck and it is not helping my nerves. My hands are trembling with adrenaline for fuck's sake.

I look back at Pat, he's still playing with Horse. I take a few steps away from them to check down a corridor that leads off toward town. It's walled with scrap metal and appliances, an upended dinghy stands against some fridges and blocks my view. In the absence of the lightning flashes, the thick cloud cover makes it hard to see more than fifteen metres. I walk further away from Pat and Horse to peer around the dinghy and down the narrow corridor of mud and metal. Sure enough, there's some shuffling zomb-cunt squelching his way up the muddy track.

"For fuck's sake," I drop my head, disheartened.

"Oi, Pat! Hurry it up, we've got compan—"

CRACK! BOOM!

A brilliant bolt of white-hot lightning strikes the top of white goods mountain and ignites the air around it; obliterating its peak. The explosion sends superheated scrap metal shards in every direction. The loud fiery spectacle grabs the immediate attention of both Pat and me, but not Horse. He makes his move and gallops through the mud with vicious intent. By the time Pat realises this, it's too late. Horse had closed the gap.

A snapping maw of teeth and rage descends on Pat, whose quick reflexes are disadvantaged by the mud and his own disbelief; he slips backwards. Horse's jaws clamp shut around Pat's shoulder, hard. A painful wail leaves Pat as Horse forces him into the muddy ground, tearing at his jacket. My body jerks at the ready for either fight or flight, but my brain? It freezes, becoming stunned and useless. Pat thrashes about beneath the monstrous hound as it buries its snout into his chest. Horse quickly shreds the little clothing standing between his teeth and Pat's flesh. I can only watch as Horse rips at and tears fleshy red strips of meat off of Pat's slender frame. I remain frozen as Pat's head whips back and forth in agony as he battles against Horse's ferocity. It's all happening so fast, yet so horrifically slow. Pat reaches for his pistol in the mud, it lies only centimetres away from his hand when Horse pushes off of Pat's chest and goes for his hand. Horse savages Pat's hand with everything he has. My mind screams, 'no, no, no,' and then the words finally escape from my mouth, "Noo!".

My fists clench and my back tenses, my feet start moving, but something grabs my arm.

The zombie from the corridor has joined the chat.

"Carrrnt!" My elbow explodes backwards like a cannon into the zombie's rotting, swollen face and it falls backwards into the mud. Before it even realises it's on the floor, I lean over him, weapon drawn, and blast his hideous face through the back of his skull. Adrenaline and rage course through me now, I yell and kick the absolute shit out of the downed zombie. My uncensored display distracts Horse, he whips his head up to look at me for an instant, and Pat fires off a shot. I sprint toward him. He fires again, that's two shots straight into Horse's chest. The hound's head reels back briefly and then whips forward to lock eyes with Pat. The two share an intense glare: one's eyes exude a primal brutality, while the other's project a stubborn and unmoving determination.

Pat smirks and pulls the hammer back on his pistol, Horse's lips curl back, exposing the blackened pinks of his gums before he launches at Pat. Luckily, Pat gets off one last shot just before Horse's mouth closes fast around the entirety of his weathered old face. Horse's toothy, vice-like jaw clamps tightly around Pat's head and starts thrashing side to side viciously, attempting to snap Pat's neck. Horse snaps and tears at Pat's face and throat as I barrel into him like a freight train wrapped in Hi-vis. I loop one arm under him and grab the scruff of his neck with the other as I jump over him. Horse releases Pat's head suddenly and I use my momentum to hurl Horse off of Pat and into a nearby fridge. He yelps—like an absolute bitch—as he crumples up against it. I don't give Horse a second to react and I jump on top of him. I pin down the back of his head with my left hand and drive the sawn-off's barrel between his shoulder blades with the other. I fire. Horse's body goes limp and everything below the neck is paralysed. Only his mouth continues to snap away, his eyes are wild and as black as the night. I make sure he doesn't move by dropping a nearby bar fridge on top of him to make sure he stays put.

"You stay right fucking there, cunt. I'm not done with you yet," I wipe the mud from my face and rush over to Pat.

"Pat, mate, are you alright?"

Mud and blood cover his face, and large chunks of flesh dangle from his cheekbones and jaw. I look down at his bloodied chest, which is so much worse, and I look up at Pat quickly.

"Fuck. Errr, it's not that bad, it's just. Err," I stammer.

"Dan," Pat chokes on his words as blood and fleshy pulp fill his throat, "Son, you gotta get out of here."

"Yeah, nah. Come on, I'll get you in the ute and we'll get you sorted, all fixed up, you know?" I speak fast, "And err… We can," I struggle to string a sentence together. I've never seen so much blood.

Pat goes to wipe the blood from his eyes with his mangled hand, and it trembles uncontrollably. He can barely hold it in front of his face, so I take his hands and place them by his side.

"I've got it, Pat. Just errr… breathe and…"

"Son, shush for a moment,"

"You're going to be fine…" I hush my hole and stare wide-eyed at him, I'm surprised by how calm he is. I take a second glance at his injuries. His arms shake by his side as raindrops hit the exposed gore that was once his chest. The deep lacerations on his neck and face pulsate, spurting thick blood from their depths; his grisly wounds make my stomach feel weak.

"Fuckinell," my gag reflex is borderline. I lean over him to stop the rain from hitting his face and pooling in his eyes.

"Son, promise me," Pat starts.

"Promise you what?"

"Promise me you'll get back to your Bella," his crippled hand reaches out for mine. I put my hand in his and he grips it with both hands, he winces with effort. His words lisp as they pass through his torn lips.

"Get home to your girl... Your girls," he corrects, "But please, I need you to find Natalie and give her this letter."

Who the fuck is Natalie?

That thought must have printed itself on my forehead because Pat feels like he has to prompt me.

"Son. Natalie? The Spanish girl, outside of Kalgoorlie?" he persists, trying to jog my memory, "She's my—"

I interrupt, "The crazy-haired girl? The backpacker?"

"Yes, son. Natalie. Here," Pat reaches for his jacket's inner pocket, but his hand falls by his side.

"No, no. Don't move, I'll get it." My fingers probe his jacket pocket and I find a folded envelope, the letter.

I hold it in front of him and Pat clenches his hands around mine again, "Make sure she gets this," he holds my stare for a moment, nodding as he adds, "Good lad."

"What is this? What's inside?"

"Ev... Everything," he splutters, blood pools in the back of his throat and he starts coughing.

"What? Where the hell would I even find her?"

"The address is on the back, use your map. It's a yard. Secure. Remote. She wouldn't have left there by choice."

Pat instructs, before a smirk creases across his face.

"She'll like you," he adds, winking. "You'll like her too."

"I... I don't understand. Why do I need to find her? How do you know she's even alive, Pat?"

Pat stifles a laugh, "If she's anything like her father..."

I don't quite understand his cryptic, nonsensical chatter, so I refocus on what's right in front of me: an old man, dying in the mud.

"Come on, Pat, I've got to get you out of here, to a hospital or, shit, anywhere but here," I try to lift him to his feet by his jacket and heave.

"Huaarrgh...Stop!" he grunts.

Fuck. I can't move him.

"Son, son. Son. Stop," Pat breathes heavily, "Listen. That lightning strike. The explosion. It will have attracted everything for miles. You've got to go, son. Get to my Natalie and get to your Bella," I shake my head and go to pick him up again, and he twists in agony.

"Son, look at me," he pauses, trembling. I look over his mangled form again, I wince and squeeze my eyes shut.

"Fuck," my chin sinks into my chest.

"Dan. Get out of here, but kill that fuckin' cunt first," he turns his head to the side and violently points at Horse.

"Oh, I'm going to, Pat, after I get you out of..."

"Princess, stop," he reaches out and grabs a hold of my hand once more, pulling himself up towards me.

"Don't let me turn, son," his chin quivers as he nods, prompting me to understand what he's saying.

A flashback to Russell in the offices at Warbo blindsides me, my stomach feels hollow. This is almost the exact same scene; a man—a friend—asking me to help his girl as he bleeds out, begging me not to let him turn; to end his suffering as quickly as possible.

"Wait. No. Pat. I can't," I argue, fighting the growing lump in my throat, "You're going to be fine, I..."

Pat takes a deep, laboured breath and holds it briefly. He lowers himself down into the mud and stares up into the sky, a smirk creases across his face, "Son, I…"

Pat's grip loosens around my hand, and he dies right there in the mud. I stare in disbelief and the world around me falls mute.

"Pat? Mate, come on," I try to gently shake the life back into him, "Pat?!" I shake him harder, his body is limp and heavy. Pat is gone, and the only thing left of the cheeky old timer is his body. I kneel beside him in the bloodied mud of the junkyard's floor, soaking wet and numb. I stare at Pat, willing his soul to come back, for the light in his eyes to return. I met him less than six hours ago, and now he is dead.

Just like Russell.

Just like Steve.

A long moment passes before the world starts to filter back in. The sound of the rain beating down against the corrugated sheets of scrap tin. The licks of heat from the burning dump around me. The smell of smoke, mud and rotting meat stings my nostrils. Then, my ears prick back to the sound of Horse barking. My despair instantly turns to anger, a blind and numbing thing that I battle to keep at bay as I cross Pat's arms across his chest and close his partially open eyes. I take his revolver from his side and the ammunition from his pocket. I stand up and stare down at him as I check the revolver's cylinder, it has one unspent round left. I nod and close the cylinder. I lean over Pat and pull the hammer back, I aim the weapon at his forehead and my hand tremors before I speak.

"See you soon, old man…Try, er, watch over me, eh? I need all the help I can get…you're a strange, old bastard, Pat," I swallow the massive lump in my throat and try bargaining with him one last time, "If you come back, I'll give you that kiss you wanted?" I smile for a moment, but it fades quickly, a strange emotionlessness washes over me.

"I'm sorry, mate," and I squeeze the trigger.

I close my eyes and tilt my head all the way back, letting the heavy raindrops hit my face. Horse's barking gets my attention again. I drop my head to the side and slowly open my eyes to see him snapping his jaws in the mud. I walk over to Horse, who's still pinned under the bar fridge, and I crouch down beside him. He starts thrashing his head from side to side, barking and growling with all his might. I hold up Pat's pistol in front of my face and admire it for what it was about to do. I dump the spent shells out, reload the cylinder and snap it shut. I press the gun barrel into the bridge of Horse's snout and push it deep into the mud. Horse tries to bite his way out of it, but it's futile. Bubbles rise up through the shallow pool of mud and I contemplate trying to drown Horse in the red sandy slop. With hollow eyes I watch him struggle, savouring his agony. I push the barrel harder into Horse's snout and it sinks deeper into the mud. I get down low and enlighten dear Horse of his fate and I speak very clearly into his ear.

"You're going to die here tonight, cunt."

Horse stares up at me as muffled growls bubble out of the mud, determined to fight to the last second.

Dogs can understand up to a thousand human words, apparently, and I really hope it's true, but, even if it's not, I think Horse will understand very fucking soon.

"This is a gift from me to you. I hope you like it."

I lean away from Horse as I blast a hole through his fucking snout; mud and shit splatter everywhere. I slip Pat's gun into my jacket pocket and stand tall. Horse goes ballistic, he snaps and whips his head back and forth, trying to lift it out of the mud. He tries to bark, only to have teeth and part of his tongue fall out of his mouth. His bottom jaw is half-missing and only attached by one length of muscle.

"How does that feel, ya dumb dog cunt?!" I spit, the calm veil masking my rage slips away.

"You are fucked now, Sonny-Jim!" I reach down and grab Horse by the remainder of his face and look him in the eyes, "I really hope you feel this."

I drop his muzzle and grab Horse by the back of the head and rip him out front under the bar fridge.

"Pffwoah, you're a heavy fuck, aren't ya? Come on then, come with me," I drag him through the mud and aimlessly walk through the yard.

"What are we going to do with you, Horse?" I swing his limp body into a fridge, "Ooh, what's that over there?" I hurl the snarling mutt against an oven as I walk toward the corridor leading into town, he barks and gurgles as I drag him about. My aimless search finds purpose when I see the aluminium boat in the corridor ahead of us.

"How about in here?" I throw Horse into the open hull of a standing dinghy and it slaps down into the mud. Horse lay inside it, crumpled between the bench seats. A loose fuel pod detaches from its mounts in the back of the boat and starts to leak fuel.

I laugh to myself, "Perfect."

I grab the fuel pod and, to my delight, it's very full. I twist off the cap and throw it between the seats with Horse, fuel starts pouring out of it and pools around Horse's head. I spot a small red case beneath the bench seat, I reach in and grab it. I unclasp the lid's black plastic clips.

"Oh, hell yes! A flare gun. Ha, Ha! And it's loaded!" I celebrate. Lightning cracks overhead and reveals a lone zombie squelching his way through the mud toward me.

"Nope. Busy, mate." I draw the sawn-off and shoot it in the face, his body drops against the wall of scrap metal and settles right beside two 9kg gas bottles. 'Half full' and '3/4 full' are written in permanent marker on the sides of each bottle. Lightbulb!

I drag the two bottles over to the dinghy, crack the taps open and place them in the boat with Horse.

"Here, hold these for a second."

I peer past the boat and see the large group of undead fuckers from town are coming up to join me and my little send off for Horse, they're only ten metres away.

"Fuck. Oh well, the more the merrier, I suppose."

I put some distance between myself and the boat and, for some reason, I start humming 'Amazing Grace'.

"This is for you, Pat." I close one eye, breathe deeply and aim at Horse and the dinghy full of fuel and open gas bottles, "Catchya, cunts," I fire.

I completely fucking miss, "For fuck's sake."

The flare flies right over the boat and bounces off a fridge door, sending the orange ball of fire straight into the tattered chest cavity of one of the zombies.

"Ha! What a shot."

The flare ignites the guy's chest and sets his clothing

on fire, he falls backwards into the horde. The group is now only a few metres away from Horse. I throw the flare gun aside and I pull out Pat's revolver.

"Let's try this again," I clear my throat, "This one's for Pat, you bastards!" I shoot into the boat and boy, oh boy, did I hit my target this time. The round pierces through the gas bottle and a massive flame spews out from its side and into the pool of unleaded fuel.

FUCK – ING – BOOM!

The dog, formerly known as Horse, is cremated in an instant, and the resulting fireball ignites the second gas bottle, causing it to rocket out of the dinghy. It spins out like a firework and strikes one of the zombies in the forehead like a territorial magpie swooping at school kids in the Spring. The flaming bottle spirals off his head and deeper into the zombie pack and explodes, zombie meat flies everywhere. A crazed, Jack-Nicholson-esque smirk of accomplishment creases across my face as I watch the pack burn. I walk back to the ute and jump in. I'm briefly halted by the sight of Pat's cane leaning against the inside of the passenger side door but I ignore it for now.

"It's time to get the fuck out of dodge. Kalgoorlie, here I come," I buckle up and bulldoze my way out of the junkyard, leaving a trail of buckled and burning corpses behind me.

The storm rolls on through the night as I drive toward Kalgoorlie, different coloured lightning bolts dance their way across the night's sky in electric blues and vibrant purples. Brilliant white bolts fork their way through the dark and pregnant clouds, reaching for the earth below. Curtains of heavy rain fall around me; the spectacle adds a hint of awe to the wide and haunting landscape. Beneath the electrical ballet, here on the ground, scattered vehicles and discarded luggage clutter the highway. Cars are upturned on the sandy banked shoulders of the road, and several multi-car crashes block many sections of the two-lane highway. Progress is slow because I can only see as far as my headlight's dulled and bloodied beams allow. Navigating the wrecks and the growing number of bodies soon becomes frustrating. Of course it does, I'm in a hurry, but I guess these poor bastards were in a rush too.

So many people had tried to flee their own nightmare only to find a new one in their escape. I can't even imagine the chaos. I notice that the cars are facing both directions; some were Perth-bound, but most were inland-bound. Each end of the highway thought that the other end was somehow free from this bullshit. Brutal.

The carpark of stationary vehicles starts to clear up a couple of hours down the road and the storm itself appears to dissipate. The rumbles of thunder and sheets of rain are now distant and faint. The tension of weaving between bodies and horrific accidents eases, too, and my body begins to focus on itself; its exhaustion, its fading supply of adrenaline. I shudder in my seat as the cool air from the air conditioner blows over my saturated clothing. I look down and notice the white-knuckled-death grip I have on the steering wheel. I release my grip and feel the muscles in my hands, forearms and shoulders relax, the brief relief is immediately followed by a burning ache.

"Oh, sweet baby Jesus." I roll my shoulders to try to release the discomfort, knots of muscle roll and crunch between my shoulder blades.

I consider pulling over to change my clothes and stretch, and after a quick debate between me, myself and I, we quickly come to the unanimous decision that that's a brilliant fucking idea. I pull the ute into a somewhat dry and, more importantly, empty roadside gravel rest spot.

I slide myself out of the cab onto the pea-gravel ground and begin a lengthy series of stretches featuring what must have sounded like a tone-deaf elderly man reciting 'A-E-I-O-U'. Each vowel is assigned to a specific type of stretch. I stiffen each leg separately as I scarecrow walk away from the ute, "Ayyy". I stretch my arms above my head, "Eeeyeah". I hold my arms out as I lean side to side, "Ayeeee". I start swinging my arms from side to side to twist my back, "Oh!" I hear multiple pops. I finally straighten my legs and reach down for my toes and exhale, "Yeww...wah", I stand back up and become very lightheaded, "Farkinell," I lean against the ute.

The humid, yet slightly cool, early morning air smells of wet road and dirt, I inhale deeply. It's just after 3.30am and I can already see the sun's glow creeping over the horizon, daylight is coming. I wonder what will try to kill me on this new and exciting day. I open the rear passenger door and reach into my bag for a towel and some clean clothes. After wrestling my limbs out of my wet clothing, I throw on a clean set of work clothes and towel-dry my hair and face.

"Ah, I feel like a new man."

I throw the towel over my soaking wet driver's seat and slink back into the cab. I drive up to the carpark's exit and go to pull out onto the bitumen, I stop and stare at the road ahead of me. The mind is willing, but the body is fucked. Fatigue is a swift mistress. My eyelids are suddenly as heavy as concrete and my neck is as strong as a wet noodle. I can barely keep my head up.

"Yeah, nah. It's time for a nanna nap," I tell myself.

I pop the ute in reverse and drive back into the carpark. I roll over the concrete sections of kerb to make my way down a side track amongst some trees. I power the ute backwards up and over some sandy banks and park hard up against a tree. I do this so my door can't be opened from the outside and so the ute is hidden from anything that may come along the highway. The fluoro yellow high visibility strips down the side of the Hilux will stand out like dog's balls in any oncoming headlights. I lock the doors, load the revolver and shotguns and set my alarm. I pick up my phone and stare at the screen, the 'no service' message blinks in the top corner, reminding me that I still can't reach anyone and no one can reach me. A sadness causes my body to sag.

Bella. Maria. Are they okay? Are they together?

I open up my phone and see Maria's last panicked message and the failed replies I tried to send after it. I drop my phone into my lap and lean back into my seat, defeated. I close my eyes and whisper to some unknown force.

"Please let them be safe, let them be okay." I hope someone or something hears my wish. I drift off to sleep.

THE HOUSE OF SAND & VENOM

"Shit, shit, shit! Fucking shit!"

I don't know how I fucked this up, but I did. I'm running as fast as I can, but it's not fast enough. The sand on this boggy dune track is too deep. Something is chasing me and a storm is raging on around me. The sky above is as black as night and I'm seeing everything through some kind of greyscale filter. Lightning cracks and thunder booms violently. I quickly look behind me.

"FUCK!"

Five zombies are hot on my tail and are gaining ground, their cries and howls are shrill and primitive. It's terrifying. A glance back confirms that their screams are not the scariest thing, it's their running, their 'you-owe-me-money-cunt-get-back-ere-you-dog' Midland traino pursuit special running. Their eyes are wild and they're locked onto me.

I need to run faster!

"Move. Faster. Cunts. Move!" I urge my legs, punching my thighs out of frustration as I high-knee it through the sand. Praying that the physical prompt gets the results I need, but no such luck strikes, my legs remain non-compliant.

I'm running up a sandy four-wheel drive track that's walled in by thick scrubland, large bushy trees sway wildly in a turbulent headwind that's fighting against me. The deep red sand slows my getaway as sheets of heavy rain beats down on me like lead. I'm gulping breaths of humid air and I'm sopping wet, the desert rain hisses as it thuds down into the hot sand around me.

How did I even get here? Where's the Hilux?

Something hits my foot and ends that thought.

One of my pursuers dives for me, but misses, his outstretched arms slaps at the heels of my feet as he tumbles into the dirt. His clumsy attempt ends up tripping the two others trailing closely behind him. Now's my chance! I throw myself off the track and leap into the cover of the bushes.

"Go, go, go!"

I bob left and right, dodging tree limb after tree limb, hoping that I'm distancing myself from my half-dead, flesh-hungry fan club. Nope, my ears prick at the sound of branches snapping behind me; they're still coming. The group's laboured grunting grows louder and louder as their steps get closer. I push harder into the dense bushes and brave the barrage of face-slapping branches when I suddenly burst out into a clearing. I stop dead and stare in awe as I stand at the base of a colossal dune.

"Whoa."

The dune towers thirty storeys high into the darkened

sky above, long wave-like ripples snake their way up the dune's face all the way up to its summit, the wind courses through the channels like an invisible serpent. I glance behind me, no zombies, not yet, I start legging it up the steep dune. I struggle to power up the intense slope and fall forward into the dune, the sheer gradient reduces me to an upright version of an army crawl. The rain is still bucketing down, but the dune is somehow dry. It seems to get deeper the higher I climb, when, like a glitch in a video game, the dry sand turns to a muddy slop.

A zombie bursts out from the bushes like a rabid-hi-vis-clad-undead version of the Tasmanian Devil, you know, that old animated character from Saturday morning cartoons. The fetid piece of zombie shit stands there, its chest heaves in and out as he hunts for any sign of me. His face twitches and then his head snaps up in my direction. His psychotic eyes widen as he grins widely.

"Shit."

An excited cry bellows from the creature and it makes a frantic start up the dune. My body jolts into action and I order myself, "Climb, cunt. Climb!"

My limbs become a blur of get-me-the-fuck-out-of-here as I practically swim up the dune as fast as I can. Three more decaying zombie hunters fly out from the tree line and start their ascent up the dune too, just behind the Tasmanian Devil's undead doppelgänger.

"Fuck!" I look up toward the summit, and I have to squint as fat raindrops pummel my face; the colossal dune's peak may as well be a million miles away. I dip my head to the side in disappointment when a flickering in the distance catches my eye. A bright light shines at me, the flash from nearby lightning reflects off of the object. I bring my hand up to my face and peek through my fingers to see it properly.

It's a door.

Fifteen metres above me is the top of a doorframe wedged upright in the dune. I drop my hand, and the grey haze filter that was cloaking my surroundings fades. A splash of colour returns to the landscape, but seemingly only around the mysterious doorway. There's a silver plaque fixed to the top corner of the door frame. I strain my eyes trying to focus on it. The number fourteen is etched into it, written in a black cursive font.

"It can't be..."

A freak gust of wind slashes its way across the dune face, picking up millions of tiny grains of dry sand as it whips past. The gust persists for ten seconds and exposes the entirety of the door. The shifted, now somehow dry, sand, however, buries me up to my hips. I pull my legs out of the sand and study the doorway; which I can only imagine is a mirage at this point.

With its Jarrah timber frame and dark cherry-red glossed, hardwood door, it could only be one door, the front door of my family home. 14 Coddiwomple Place.

"That's my door!"

The cries from the zombie pack below startle me as they race up toward me. They're only metres away. I scramble for the top, my limbs slap wildly at the dune as I battle upwards. But for every two steps I climb up, the deep slope reclaims one for itself. My eyes flick back to check on the zombie pack's progress.

"Of course, they're right fucking behind me!"

It appears they aren't experiencing the same two-steps-forward-one-step-backward handicap that I am. I battle upwards, as they climb over each other to get to me, competing like greyhounds chasing a stuffed white rabbit around a track. I get to the door and slam my weight against it to open it, but it's stuck. I try again, nothing happens.

"Story of my life!" I spit in frustration.

These fuckers are almost at my feet, so I kick sand at them to buy me a second or two. I try the door again with no reward. One of the zombies surges ahead of the pack and crawls toward me, it fights hard against the deep sand and his fellow pack members. He scurries up the slope and lashes out at me, missing me by centimetres. He barks like a frustrated mutt, and he scurries up a second time, but I smash my size eleven boot into his face. Most of his teeth snap off and his nose folds to the side like origami, he flops backwards into the pack. I launch my shoulder into the door once more and it flies open, I swing off the stainless-steel doorknob as I fall inside. I slam the door shut behind me and throw my weight against it to deadbolt it shut. I face the door and brace myself against it as hard thuds shake it from the other side; they're trying to get in. I lean my head against the door and close my eyes, exhausted and wringing wet. I mumble inaudibly, wishing them away when a soft voice pierces through the mayhem.

"Will you be joining us for breakfast, amor?"

I push myself away from the door and look at my hands. I calmly run my fingers down the grain of the wood and take a step back from it. I'm convinced my eyes are deceiving me.

Am I really inside my house?

"The zombie pack!" I lunge forward and grip the doorknob, thinking that they must still be out there and ready to burst through the door at any moment. I lean to the side of the door to peer out through the narrow glass panel of the entranceway and into my front yard. The limestone path, the one I'd poured with my dad years earlier, stretches away from the entrance and out alongside the thick, green lawn before curving its way to the right toward my red and white stone-stencilled driveway. I look up at the sky; it's a bluebird day with no storm in sight. I look back out at the lawn, there's no pack of crazed zombies to speak of, it's just my front yard with a few of Bella's toys scattered across it, each of which are getting wet under the lawn's sprinklers.

I rub my eyes with balled fists, "This can't be real."

"Amor? Are you just going to stand in the doorway? Come eat with your daughter and me," the voice interrupts.

I stand up and turn, my eyes travel along the wall slowly, noting each of the family photos that hang there. I skim over all of the travel souvenirs that fill the tall antique cabinet that stands against the milkwood beige coloured wall. A tattered, old, brown leather recliner sitting across from the cabinet halts my gaze momentarily. I smile, it's my favourite chair, but I could have sworn Maria got rid of it? Never mind. My eyes cross to the kitchen counter where a pan of sizzling bacon and a bowl of steaming scrambled eggs sit side by side, a smaller plate of freshly smashed avocado and a half loaf of bread lay open by the toaster. My mouth waters and my nose awakens to the aromas of the breakfast feast when I see who is speaking to me.

"Maria?"

Maria sits at the round breakfast table in the corner of the room with her back to me. Her long black hair drapes over the wooden back of the dining room chair. The low morning sun radiates through the kitchen window and Maria's hair shines; her bronzed shoulders glow in the orange light. Maria's wearing that red sun dress again, eating her avocado on toast as she sits in her morning spot. Maria loves that chair, well, not the chair itself, but its location. It's where she starts her morning ritual of 'charging her energies for the day'. Bella, Bones the dog, or even me, for that matter, could not charm our way into that seat if we tried. It was Maria's spot and she defended it well. A barrage of pinching and strategic pokes would descend upon any who dare attempt to sit there.

Bella sits to Maria's right, her shoulder-length hair is just as black and as shiny as her mother's. A yellow sunflower headband keeps the hair out of her face as she colours in some drawings next to her breakfast bowl. Bella looks so grown up; her naturally good posture always amazes me. She swings her feet loosely beneath her chair as she hums some random tune. I step toward them and realise my boots and clothes are now clean and dry. I'm dressed in my fly-out gear, the cleanest uniform I own. I smile, chuffed that I'm no longer wringing wet and that I won't be trekking mud across the hardwood floors—a trespass like that would annoy Maria way too much this early in the day.

"Your bacon will go cold, amor," Maria politely reminds me.

Bella looks up from her drawing and pure delight fills her little face, "Daddy, come see what I drew!" Bella pleads excitedly.

"Of course, sweetie, I'll be right—"

I take two steps forward and something stops me

abruptly; my forehead bounces back, stopping me dead in my tracks. I try again. I have full use of my body, yet I can't get past the doormat. I bring my hands up and feel some kind of barrier—an invisible wall—stopping me.

"Babe, what's… What's going on?"

I start tapping on the invisible wall. It doesn't feel like anything I've ever encountered before, it's not glass. I bang again, and a hollow thud echoes from it. It's not Perspex. It's not cold or warm. It's not smooth or rough. I bang on it again and again. It's. Nothing. Yet. It's. Still. Fucking. There. Each pound on the 'wall' releases a blueish light that ripples throughout its entire surface.

"What the fuck!"

I must have triggered some kind of booby trap with that last blow because the room darkens and the refreshing morning air grows stale, the colour and warmth drain from the room. I can feel that the grey filter coming back.

From behind the invisible barrier, I look over at Maria and Bella, who are frozen like statues. I can only see Bella's face as the room, and everything in it, becomes an inky grey. Her cheerful face changes, it becomes hollow and vacant, and her smile becomes a tight, thin line as she drops her textas on the table.

"Bella?" I call out.

Her arms drop by her sides and she stares blankly at the wall across from her. Maria's arm slowly rises to the side of Bella's cheek, she slowly caresses our daughter's motionless face.

"There, there, mi niña," Maria comforts Bella.

I start to panic, "Babe, I know what's coming, so we really need to…"

"Shhh… Danito," Maria continues to comfort Bella, she strokes Bella's long dark hair, "we don't need to do anything. We will be fine all by ourselves, won't we, sweetheart?"

Bella nods compliantly, her face is still and devoid of expression. Maria turns her head to the side so she can just see me standing in the doorway in the corner of her eye. Her chin is raised high and hovers over her shoulder, she sits poised, like an indifferent queen displeased by one of her once loyal subjects.

"Amor, I assure you, *we* will be fine. We are always fine. *We* have each other."

I butt in, "Babe, we…"

Maria's one visible eye bursts open and angrily darts in my direction, "*We?!*"

I move along the invisible barrier to see more of Maria's face. I stride to the right as she just stares at me sideways through the long, thick eyelashes of her half-open eye.

"*We*, Bella and I, will be fine, amor. You haven't been a part of our *we* for quite some time, now. While you work away, you miss our birthdays, our celebrations and our anniversaries. We don't have you by our sides, so we had to learn to live without you, and learn we did."

A pang in my chest and guts jolts me. Maria knows exactly how to get a rise out of me and I react predictably.

"Are you kidding me?! *We* wouldn't have this house if I didn't work away, we wouldn't have any of this. We wouldn't be able to go on holiday three times a year to go see your fucking family if I didn't"—Maria slaps her hand on the table—"You! You don't get to use the word 'family'. A family stays together. A family is together every night and every morning, not once a month. There is no family with this FIFO bullshit of yours. There's just you with your work and me, with my niña." Maria turns away and leans over to comfort Bella. Young Bella turns and looks up at her mother. I remain behind the barrier, muted and furious.

I try using every pet name, and then obscenity, to try to get their attention, but nothing works. Maybe they can't hear me? I begin pounding on the wall when the room darkens further. Maria and Bella remain seated, staring at each other like mannequins. Tears well up in their eyes, Maria cups our daughter's face, and wipes away a tear as it falls down Bella's cheek.

"We don't need him, do we, sweetie?" Maria prompts. Frustration and anger swirl violently inside of me. I need to get past this wall, now! I headbutt the wall and stare at the hardwood floor, urging my brain to find a solution.

"Fuck it, I'll go around!"

I frisk the invisible surface of the wall with my hands, searching for a hole or a weakness of some kind. I cross the entire room and find no such flaw and end up at the outer brick wall of the room.

"Fuck!"

I start following the brick wall back toward the front door, "Yes, the window!" I grab the window's latch and try to open it. The latch breaks off in my hand.

"Are you fucking kidding me? Carrrrnt!"

I punch the window three times in protest and watch cracks expand to every corner of the pane before they retract back into the centre of the glass, making it whole again. I race over to the front door and rip it open. A wall of red-tinged, grey sand pours in through it, almost knocking me over. I quickly step backwards as the sand spills into the room.

"Aw, fuck!" I'm standing in thigh-deep sand. I look up from my legs and out of the doorway at the sea of sand dunes stretching out into a seemingly endless desert. The bright blue sky and lush green lawn are no more; desolation and darkness claim it all.

"Babe!" I yank my legs out of the deep sand and plough my way toward the invisible wall, "Maria! We have to go now. We can fight later, I need to get you both somewhere safe. Now!" Maria's eyes remain locked with Bella's and my plea falls on deaf ears.

"Babe!" I hammer at the wall again, each strike marrying to my words, "We. Have. To. Go. Now!"

I check the doorway behind me, fearing that my zombie friends from earlier may return, thankfully, the only thing making its way through the door is more sand. Bella turns in her chair and stares through me, her lips and chin quiver. She slams her eyes shut, trying not to cry, my heart breaks.

"Oh, sweetie, everything's going to be"—The kitchen window explodes inwards and shattered glass sprays across the kitchen. Glass covers the table and the floor under Maria's and Bella's feet with razor-sharp fragments.

"Girls, you have to get up and you have to hide or something! I can't get through this fucking wall, Maria, take Bella and…"

A series of wailing howls and screams drowns me out.

"They're coming! Girls, get up, go!"

Bella buries her face in her hands and sobs. Maria reaches out and rubs her back as she weeps, and she starts shaking her head in disappointment and looks over at me.

"You're not a man, Danito, a real man can protect his family. I guess we're fucked now, huh?" Maria's words sting like acid.

"Daddy, why weren't you here?! You're never here!" Bella adds, her face is swollen and red, her cheeks are wet with tears.

Their words cut deep and course through me like venom.

"I… I…" I stutter, I have no words or excuses to offer, I begin to hyperventilate, not knowing what to do.

Zombies pour in through the kitchen window into a pile on the floor as more and more flood in over the top of them. Another group rush in from the back hallway as *another* group smashes their way in through a side window on the opposite side of the room. I turn to check the door behind me, which is still pinned wide open by all of the sand, but there are no zombies. I turn back to Maria and Bella, horrified.

"No. No. No."

The entire room is wall-to-wall with zombies, they stand shoulder-to-shoulder forming a crowd of unmoving upright corpses that encircle the dining room table; I can't even see the girls anymore.

"Girls? Maria? Bella?!" I call out, the zombies don't react to my voice, they just stand there panting heavily when I hear a faint call over the horde.

"Daddy?"

Oh, my God, Bella!

"Honey, I need you to close your eyes, okay? Don't open them," I instruct.

Bella calls for me again, but louder, "Daddy?"

The fifty-strong zombie pack shudders. Bella's sweet

voice triggers something in them, their sunken heads rise and their hands twitch. Some form fists and others stretch out their dead, ghoulish fingers; exposing their sharp and bloodied fingernails.

"Shhhh… Bella, you have to be quiet. Can you still see your mother?" I try to talk as quietly as I can.

Bella must still have her eyes open, I hear her little breaths quicken before she lets out a desperate, "Daddy!?"

The entire pack jerks forward and descends on Bella and her mother in that instant.

"No!" I yell.

The howls of the zombies and my family's screams erupt on the other side of the wall, I bang violently on it, yelling and pleading. I look down at the sand around my legs to hunt for something to hit the wall with. I'm wrist deep when I find a boulder, I grab it and hammer it against the wall. The frenzied pack ravages at each other trying to get at the girls. I can't bear to watch, I squeeze my eyes shut as I raise the boulder with two hands high above my head and I drive it into the wall with everything I have. A deafening crack reverberates through the wall as the boulder strikes, and a brilliant white light fills the room and then dissipates. A light pulses from a thin slit in the invisible wall.

"I broke it. I broke the wall!"

The light is so bright that I have to turn away from it. I try to cover my eyes when something grabs me by the shoulders. I open my eyes to see the decaying face of some zombie fuck only inches away from mine. Its fingernails dig deep into my flesh, and my collarbone creaks under the force of its grip. Its matted, blood-stained eyebrows crease as its soulless black eyes glare into mine. Its disgusting, putrid mouth opens unnaturally wide—wider than it should be able to—and an offensive odour stings my nostrils.

I try to lift my hands to attack when its rotting, jagged-toothed maw launches at me, and snaps shut around my face.

A THING OF NIGHTMARES

"Fuck, fuck, fuck!" I swat erratically, slapping the rear-view mirror and sun visor. My knees dance desperately beneath the steering wheel as I fight off the imaginary zombie attack. I open my eyes to find myself sitting in the driver's seat of the ute, I pat myself down and try to orientate myself. I'm okay, it was a dream. It was just a dream.

"Fucking nightmares!" I spit.

I punch the steering wheel and then assess my surroundings. It's nighttime. I'm in the Hilux. I'm not injured. The storm is still rolling by outside, I think, it's too dark to be certain. I cup my hands to my face like a hood over my eyes and press up against the glass to see outside.

A flash of lightning lights up a figure standing on the other side of the window. I yell and reach for the rifle beside me. I quickly glance between the window and the gun and another flash lights up the figure, this time I get a better look at him, or should I say, it.

"For fuck's sake," I exhale in relief.

The lightning flash reveals a harmless knot in the trunk of the tree that I have parked beside.

"Bastard," I mutter. I release my grip on the rifle, "This fatigue is fucking cooking me."

I relax into my seat and something grabs me, hard. I bolt upright in my seat and see a muddy hand wrapped around my forearm. I flinch and spin to the left to see who grabbed me. The frizzy grey hair, the exposed ribcage, the bullet hole in his forehead.

It's… It's Pat.

"Pwincess…" rancid, black ooze spills from his mouth as he speaks and it smells like absolute shit. I turn away and try to peel Pat's hand off of me, but his fingers just snap off in my hands. Pat springs from his seat and attacks me.

My eyes burst open again, this time for real. I'm in the Hilux, again, but it's daytime and I'm sweating bullets. I whip my head around doing multiple scans of the car and everything around me. I pull my gun close to me for comfort.

"What the fucking fuck? Really?!" Frustration takes over and I begin punching the dash and steering wheel.

"Another. Fuckin'. Dream. Get. Fucked!"

After my temper tantrum inside the ute, I hop out of the vehicle for some fresh air. I open the rear door and get my toothbrush and toothpaste from the duffle bag in the back seat. I walk around the Hilux brushing my teeth when I catch a glimpse of myself in the wing mirror.

"Jesus," I inspect my reflection more closely, "You can't half tell I've had a rough few days, look at this mug."

I'm sporting a just-woke-up-after-a-night-of-hard-drinking hairdo, I have some new dark bags under my eyes and a face that's spattered with blood and mud. I could almost pass for one of those undead bastards if I wanted to.

"I think I'd better wash up a little before I go anywhere, I'm likely to get shot looking like this," I say into the mirror.

I make myself presentable, for who, I don't know, and I jump back into the Hilux and start 'er up. I grab the road map book and rummage through last night's clothes to find Pat's letter to Natalie. The envelope is covered in muddy, somewhat bloody, fingerprints but the address on the back is still legible. Usually, I'd just type in the address into my maps app and I'd be on my way, but no; I don't have the luxury of a posh lady's English accent prompting each instruction. Today, a tattered five-year-old road map book would have to do. I figure it's about a three to five-hour push through to Kalgoorlie, depending on how bad the roads are, and how many zombies want to come outside and play with me.

"Alright, alright, alright. In the famous words of Big Lez, 'Let's fuck this bum'ole!'" I hit the accelerator and motor toward K-Town.

The kilometres tick by on the odometer and my mind jumps back and forth between the fucked-up events of last night and the cruel dreams that tormented me this morning. My body twitches randomly at the recall of each memory. I try to shake off the involuntary reminders by singing random tunes and blaring music loudly, but still, they remain.

Images of Pat dying in the mud, excerpts of Maria's venomous words and the helpless screams of Bella. I sigh deeply, it's Maria's words that play on my mind the most. Although it was only a dream, I have heard those words before: 'You're not a man', 'You don't get to use the word family'. Maria knew how to crush me and, if that failed, she would turn my own daughter against me by planting seeds of doubt like: 'We don't need him, do we, sweetie?'

It'd been almost two years since the separation, and since I had heard such bitter things, but damn, those words still sting like running barefoot through a double gee patch.

The separation was a confusing time, it was filled with heartache, guilt and so much anger. As I look back on it, I've realised that the only real issue was time. Too little time spent together and too much time spent apart, I simply wasn't there enough for my girls. And Maria, although a very strong and independent woman, needed frequent reassurance that she was loved, desired and that she was a great mother. Which she absolutely was, or should I say is, but when I didn't give her the attention and reassurance she needed, Maria would lash out. When lashing out didn't get the desired attention she so desperately craved, time after time, she had to find it from another source and, sadly, found it in another man.

She always said that I pushed her to cheat on me, and I believed it for a little while, too. I later realised that she was just a selfish, insecure child in a woman's body. There was a four-month period of vicious name-calling, threats to flee the country with my daughter and social media posts trying to break one another. But it was poor Bella that suffered the most, and young Bella called us both out on it. So, we decided to control our bullshit for her sake. It worked, for the most part. Fast forward to my recent interactions with Maria, which have been a lot more civil as we actively try to give Bella the 'family' she deserves. We keep our petty shit to text messages or snide coded comments, but it's no walk in the park. Maria and I were so close and so intimate. She was my best friend and we were so in tune mentally and, of course, sexually; we were like two filthy pieces of a Kama Sutra jigsaw puzzle. A perfect fit. But distance, contempt and anger tore us apart, it ate away at our once solid foundations. It's proving to be a monumental task to try to repair it.

I used to wonder why I thought of the sexual aspect of our relationship so fondly and vividly after the separation until about a year ago, when a lovely country pub barmaid, named Shelley, offered me a nugget of wisdom.

"Darlin', you had a hot lil' foreign gal rocking your world day and night for the longest time. She distracted you from the reality of being stuck on a rig, surrounded by blokes and a desert full of sand and flies. Of course, it lives in your head rent-free! Sex and Maria were the light at the end of the tunnel. It's the only enjoyable thing you did outside of work, and then, before you knew it, it was time to fly in again. She was your escape, your release," I remember her doing a mid-air, hand job action that resembled wanking off a firework, "And you're not the type to hit up the brothels with the likes of Adzy or Steve, so there was only you and Maria. And now, you're single. Your silver lining, your 'release' is gone. So, you can either try your luck with one of my Irish barmaids or," she then annoyingly and very loudly sang, "It's just you and your hand toniiiight!"

Shelley was incredibly astute when it came to picking

apart someone's problems, and pointing a lost soul in the right direction. A skill she had no doubt finely tuned in her many years hopping between country pubs and her next adventure. Shelley was right on the money, too, I could sum up my month's routine in one sentence. Work for three weeks, fuck for one week and repeat. No wonder it was always on my mind, it was the only thing I did that wasn't working on the rig.

In the months after the separation, I had tried the ole 'to get over one girl, you have to get under another' trick, which my dad had insisted on numerous times, but it didn't seem to cure me. And the new world of dating profiles and apps was a strange and seedy place. The only women that seemed to pop up on those apps were either obese, single mums with four kids and drug addictions or confused polyamorous teens with daddy issues and an inclination to go ass-to-mouth on the first date.

Don't get me wrong, I waded through that dating swamp and met some normal women, and I even got under a few of them. I had a blast, but it was short-lived, something wasn't right. Fucking wasn't quite the same as having sex with someone who knows you inside and out. At the end of the day, whether the date ended up in a hotel room or with me scrolling through porn on my phone, Maria's words would creep back into my head and haunt me.

You're not a man.
This is not a family.
You're never here for us.
It's just you and your work.

164

Maria's words, and our failed marriage, play on my mind for a few hundred kilometres or so. Navigating the mazes of wrecked cars and crowds of wandering zombies manages to push it all to the back of my mind though.

I'm still sixty kilometres outside of the large mining town and the highway heading into town is chockers with vehicular carnage. I pull off the main highway and park beneath some trees to organise myself and to plan out my next move. Kalgoorlie lay ahead in the distance, and it's a familiar horizon; pillars of thick black smoke reach high into the sky and cast an eerie haze over the landscape. The dash's exterior temperature display reads forty-four degrees Celsius. I wipe the sweat from my brow and flick open the map book to look for a back road or trail to bypass the highway of bullshit ahead of me. I see a goat track running parallel to the highway along a disused railway line. I finger the map along the intended route and find that it pops out behind where this compound is meant to be and where Natalie should be.

"Fuck yeah, everything's coming up Milhouse."

I drive along the highway for another twenty kilometres before I turn off onto the dirt track. I engage the 4WD and ease up the narrow winding side tracks toward the main track, which follows the railway line to the compound. All the while wondering whether the compound is still standing and if Natalie is even there.

Then it hits me, what if she is there? Alive and well? What am I going to say? How will I give her the letter without scaring her or getting shot at or shooed away?

I look at myself in the rear-view mirror again. Even if a zombie apocalypse wasn't in full swing, I wouldn't accept a letter from me, not looking like this. My car alone would scare the hell out of her, it's still covered in splattered zombie and pieces of dog. Ah, she's probably long gone by now, there's no need to waste time thinking about it.

Unless… What if she's attractive?

I smell my breath and check the mirror again, critiquing my features. What if she's all alone at this compound, scared and in need? I straighten my collar and shake the sand out of my hair. What if she needs me to rescue her, a classic D.I.D., a Damsel in Distress? I hit a boulder in the track and the sudden jerk rips the steering wheel out of my hands.

"Idiot, eyes on the road, Danito!" I laugh at myself, shaking my head at my stupidity, "Who am I kidding?"

I reach the top of one of the highest rises along the range that I've been winding through for the last hour and park at its peak, where I have a pretty good view of Kalgoorlie and its surroundings. I pull out a pair of digital binoculars that Russell had left in the glove box and scan the area.

The town of Kalgoorlie looks fucked. Cars are burnt-out in the streets, buildings have been reduced to piles of rubble—or are still on fire—and bodies are strewn all over the place, and some bodies are walking around aimlessly. Kalgoorlie CBD is relatively clear, as if someone had started to tidy up. Cars and rubble have been bulldozed into side streets and dead bodies are stacked in piles at three of the intersections near the town centre.

"Maybe the army is in town?"

I scan the town further.

South Kalgoorlie and Boulder are behind the wall of smoke, but I can't imagine they're in any better state than the city centre itself. I swing the binoculars back into town.

"Damn, there are more zombies here than I thought," I spot a group of zombies shuffling their way up a side road, then I spot another group and another.

"Fuck, they're everywhere."

I spot a few larger groups and they all seem to be heading toward Boulder, almost drawn to it.

"Well, at least they're heading away from downtown. I might be able to get some supplies and some more diesel. Hell, I might even find a bottle-O and score a few cartons of piss!" I smile at the thought.

I swing the binoculars away from the mess of Kalgoorlie and shift my focus to the dirt track ahead of me. It snakes its way down the range and swings around a large granite hill. I see some transmission lines leading into the range from the highway, but the power lines don't continue through it.

"Me thinks the compound is on the other side of that hill."

An unexpected rush of excitement puts a spring in my step. I jump in the Hilux and roll down the bumpy, disused track towards the compound. I exaggerate each bump and knock that the track throws at me and start singing 'Chitty Chitty Bang Bang' as I cruise down it. Paying homage to one of my favourite scenes in *Ace Ventura: When Nature Calls* where Ace drives with Greenwall to the Consulate and takes that unnecessary but hilarious shortcut.

Two hundred metres of winding track remain to the compound when a loud cracking sound rings out.

"Fuck! What was that?" I stop the vehicle and pop my head out of the window, thinking the noise came from under the vehicle when I hear it again.

It's quickly followed by another two cracks.

"That's gunfire! It's gotta be close too."

I grab the binoculars, my rifle and holster the sawn-off shotgun to jog up the track. As it rises up the side of the granite hill, I hear the sound of an engine and loud crashes of metal on metal.

"What the fuck's goin' on up 'ere?!"

I slow to a half jog as I reach the top of the track and crouch low to sneak forwards over the rise, a fenced structure in the valley comes into view.

"There it is, that must be the compound."

THE COMPOUND

The compound lies in a valley below. A chain link fence surrounds its outer perimeter, and three metres inside of that stands a taller, heavy-gauge steel security fence. Inside the fencing are two demountable buildings and a workshop made out of three shipping containers laid out in a U-shape. A domed tarp enclosure is erected between them. At the back of the property stands a water tower and a laydown with a random assortment of generators and machine parts. At the front of the compound, the Kalgoorlie side entrance, sits a large white LPG tank on skids with two long rows of fuel drums stored alongside it. The front entrance has a ten-metre-long reinforced, automated gate for heavy vehicle access. A smaller set of gates allows light vehicle access at the rear toward the old railway line.

A main driveway dissects the yard in two, running from the front gate to the back gate. Concrete road dividers are staggered in several rows down the middle, preventing vehicular access into the yard entirely. A telehandler, forklift and an old work ute sit under the domed workshop area. Picnic table-sized boulders are dotted around the entire exterior of the outer fence, they are spaced just short of two metres apart and are surely a ram-raid deterrent. A mess of different-sized tyre tracks inside and outside of the yard suggests that the boulders and concrete dividers are recent additions to the compound's security measures.

Above the compound, I squat behind a large log at the edge of the hillside track, and I whip out my binoculars to assess the scene below. Two vehicles are outside the front gate, the first is a red Nissan Patrol, which is ramming the gate violently. A guy is hanging out of the passenger side door and firing a handgun into the compound.

"Holy shit, someone's trying to get into the compound!"

The second vehicle is an older, white coloured Land Cruiser; it's parked further back from the red Patrol. Two men stand beside it, firing rifles into the compound, providing covering fire for the Patrol.

"Fuck me! Who are they firing at?!"

I scan the camp's interior with the binoculars and spot someone hiding behind a concrete road divider in the middle of the compound, "Fuck, he's pinned down."

I adjust the zoom on the binoculars to get a closer look at the bloke in the compound.

"Wait a minute, that's a chick."

A slender frame with a lot of frizzy brown hair is crouching low behind the divider. She is blindly firing at the guys in the red Patrol over the top of her concrete shield,

I see several firearms lying at her feet in the gravel. Outside of the fence, two bodies are on the ground, she must have killed them earlier, but she's still outnumbered and looks to be alone.

"Fuck these cunts!"

I drop my binoculars and grab my rifle. I lay down at the furthest end of the log for cover and take a potshot at the open door of the white Land Cruiser. The round goes straight through the door and into the guy standing behind it. He drops to the ground, grabbing at his leg. I fire again and it hits him in the chest; last night's target practice in the junkyard has improved my aim significantly. The older, potbellied guy takes cover behind the Land Cruiser, so I focus my efforts on the two clowns in the red Patrol ramming the gates. I aim for the driver through the windshield and fire, but I only manage to put two holes in the bonnet. I'm not too good with moving targets, it seems. Steam hisses out from the engine bay, my two shots weren't a complete waste. The woman in the compound takes her opportunity and runs ahead to one of the demountable buildings for cover.

"Smart thinking, girl," I fire again into the Patrol's windscreen to give her some extra time, "Come on!"

I push myself up off the ground and take a knee to get a better shot. I just hope that the guys below still can't see me. I take another shot at the driver and unintentionally put a bullet straight through a guy's neck as he hangs out of the passenger side door.

"Ha ha, fuck, flukes count!"

The red Patrol stops suddenly, and the driver reaches across to help his mate, when the woman fires three shots through the windshield and kills the driver. I look back into the compound with the binoculars to see her firing from behind a demountable building. Her rifle sounds a whole lot more powerful than mine; each shot echoes off the valley's high rock walls. I watch the woman as she fires two more rounds into the Patrol's windscreen, finishing off the guy that I had shot in the neck.

"Savage!"

A round ricochets off the granite boulder behind me.

"Shit!" I drop behind the log for cover.

The man standing behind the white Land Cruiser has spotted me. I stay low as three more shots fly my way. The woman must have been keeping count of the fat man's shots because as soon as he stops to reload, I hear a smaller calibre weapon firing rapidly. I pop my head up from behind the log and see the tanned woman marching toward the fence. She fires relentlessly into the Land Cruiser with a handgun as she drags the heavier rifle behind her. The man scurries back into the driver's seat and launches the vehicle backwards, attempting to flee. The woman empties her handgun into the vehicle as it speeds off, and I join the party and start emptying the rest of my clip into it, too. The Land Cruiser retreats wildly in reverse and slides out of control on the gravel road and into a pile of scrap metal, which flips the vehicle onto its side. I try to reload as quickly as I can and keep my eyes trained on the Land Cruiser, just in case the man emerges from the wreck.

"Come on, come on. Get in the fuckin' slot."

I struggle to load the rifle as the back door of the flipped vehicle opens, and the man crawls out; he's bloodied and weak-kneed. He stumbles for a moment but is quick to his feet and starts running down the road back towards

Kalgoorlie. He's definitely out of range now, and the valley wall is obstructing my view. I look down to see the woman raise her rifle and fire at the fleeing man. She jumps on the spot and lets out an excited 'woo!'. She must have hit him.

I let out a, "Yeah! Haha!" and throw my arms up in celebration, only to see the woman's rifle swing in my direction—she fires.

"Ooh, shit!"

I hit the deck again as the round bounces off of the rock wall behind me. I drop my gun and throw my arms up in surrender, trying to show her that I'm not a threat.

"I'm here to help! Don't shoot! I'm on your side!"

My voice carries deep into the valley as I cautiously stand up. The woman dips her weapon and then ducks behind a concrete divider.

"Aw, thank fuck. I'm coming down!"

I don't know if she heard me, but I see her run into the middle of the yard to grab the rest of her stuff and then run into one of the demountable buildings. I grab my shit from the dirt and run back down the goat track toward the Hilux and jump in. I roll along the track at a turtle's pace, trying not to frighten the woman into shooting me in the face. The track winds down the side of the rocky hill and brings me to the rear gate of the compound. I'm about twenty metres away from the outer gate when I see her standing behind a telegraph pole with her rifle drawn. I artfully steer with my knees and push both arms out the window, my hands are open in surrender as I roll towards her.

"Stop! Stop right there!" the woman calls out from within the compound.

Her accent sounds Spanish; this has to be Natalie.

"Turn around and leave this place, now! Or I'll shoot you," she instructs.

"Please, wait. I'm here to help, that's why I helped you shoot those guys at the—"

"No, shut up. How do I know you're not one of them, trying to trick me, huh?" She shoots at the ground beside the Hilux, "Go!"

"Shit, wait! I know Pat! Pat told me to find you!" I offer, "You're Natalie, right?"

The woman pauses and drops her guard slightly.

"How do you know that name?"

"Pat sent me here, he was going to come, too, but..." I stop myself from finishing that sentence and start another, "I have a letter for you, from Pat. Can I give it to you?"

I turn the ignition off and slowly reach for the letter on the dash, I grab it and hold the envelope out of the window.

"I'm going to open the door, now, okay?"

Natalie raises her rifle, "Who are you, random man?"

"I'm a friend of Pat's, he sent me here to deliver this letter. I'm Dan," I slowly step out of the vehicle.

Natalie isn't buying my story at all.

"Okay, Dan, do you have weapons?"

"Yes. I have a rifle and a few other things in the cab here, but I'm not carrying any of them on me."

I stand upright and slowly twirl as I walk toward her to show that I have nothing behind me.

"Ahuh? What's that then?" Natalie gestures towards the stubby holder holster and the sawn-off shotgun hanging across my chest.

I freeze, "Sorry, sorry!" I slowly undo the belt buckle and lower the holster to the dirt. I raise my arms again.

"Slide the letter under the fence and leave."

"Of course," I nod and approach the fence.

As I get closer to her, I'm struck by how beautiful she is. The hot wind plays with her dark frizzy hair and the sun penetrates the outer layers, making it glow a goldish brown. I'm immediately drawn to her intense expression, which flutters between a fierce glare and an almost confused curiosity. The twitching of her full eyebrows marks the transition between the two.

The sheer size of her rifle hides the majority of her face, so my gaze wanders along her slender wrists and down the length of her arms; her tanned caramel skin glistens under the heat of the sun. I map the entirety of her tall, slim frame, all the way down to her full hips, strong thighs and down to her ankles. She is fucking stunning.

I smile.

Oh shit, I smiled.

I look back up at Natalie, shit. I make eye contact but look away too quickly, now I look guilty of something.

My brain screams, fuuuuuuuck.

Natalie's chin sucks in slightly and her eyebrows rise, making her forehead wrinkle; she smirks.

This is surely a non-verbal confirmation that she is fully aware that I was checking her out.

Fuck. Fuckity. Fuck, fuck, fuck.

Thankfully, she appears to be mildly entertained by my embarrassment, I didn't offend her enough to make her finger the rifle's trigger. I stare at the dirt in front of my feet as I continue toward the gate, trying to hide my reddening face.

"You fucking idiot," I mutter to myself.

Natalie slinks between the two heavier internal gates and approaches the chain link fence gates.

"That's close enough, *Dan*," she grins briefly, but continues in a much sterner tone and instructs me, "Now, pass me the letter between the gates."

"It's all yours."

I step forward and slide the letter between the chain link gates and Natalie takes it from me, and I take several quick steps backwards. The muzzle of Natalie's rifle rests inside one of the diamond-shaped chain links in the fence, it's aimed at my chest as she inspects the letter. She flips the envelope back and forth, analysing it intently.

"It's his handwriting…" she mouths softly, "And it's unopened. You didn't read it?"

"Uh, no. That's your letter. I was only given it last night."

Natalie's eyebrows furrow and her nose wrinkles angrily, "Did he give you this letter or did you take it from him?"

"No, he gave it to me last night. I swear."

"Why is there blood and mud all over it then, uh? Did you kill him for it? Or take it from his dead body? Answer me, Dan?!" Natalie places her finger on the rifle's trigger.

"No, not at all," I insist. I try to think of how I can prove that I knew Pat and didn't just find and search his body.

"Err, Pat, he's an old guy, at least seventy, uh…" I struggle to recollect any of Pat's distinguishing features because my most recent memory is of him bloodied and dying in the mud. I scrunch my eyes closed, trying to block out that image.

"Uh, he's quick with his walking stick, he wears an Akubra hat and an old stockman's jacket. He has a weird sense of humour and… And he kept calling me princess."

I laugh nervously, hoping my answers are acceptable.

Natalie pulls the barrel of her rifle out of the fence and lowers it by her side, "He called you princess?"

"Yeah, he even tried to make me kiss him once, too," I anxiously overshare.

"Really?" Natalie bursts out laughing, "He must have liked you then, uh?" Her hearty laugh echoes through the compound, "Did you?"

I smile, "Did I what?"

"Come on, Dan, did you kiss him?" Natalie asks, her widening smile exposes her perfectly white teeth.

"No!" I shake my hands in protest, "Well, almost. But no, I didn't kiss Pat." I go bright red, embarrassed by the memory and ashamed of the first impression I'm making on Natalie.

"Ahuh, I'm sure you didn't, Dan," she nods slowly, unconvinced, "Where is he anyway?"

I pause for a moment and try to think up something fast.

"He, uh, didn't want to leave town. He said he had everything that he needed in Laverton and that he was happy there, he said there are fewer mining bastards there than here in Kalgoorlie."

"I see," she takes a moment to respond, "He's so stubborn, but if he trusted you enough to send you here, then you must be okay. Grab your things, I think you've earned yourself a beer."

"Oh, thank fuck."

"You're not staying, but bring your bags and your guns inside, just in case we have any more uninvited visitors. And Dan, I'll be holding on to your guns while you're inside my compound."

"Yep. Fair enough."

I go back to the Hilux and gather my things. I stash Pat's revolver in the glove box and hide a few of Russell's toys—homemade explosives to be exact—under the passenger seat as a back-up. I place one of the charges in my backpack though, something tells me I might need it and I trust that feeling. I spot a bottle of red wine at the bottom of Russell's bag, and I place it in my backpack. It'll make a good peace offering if the opportunity presents itself.

Natalie waits patiently by the fence. She holds her rifle loosely, but keeps it pointed in my general direction. She looks more closely at my bloodied and beaten Hilux in disgust and calls out to me.

"What is that all over your car, Dan?"

"Uh, I had to drive through some infected dogs and some crazy people, it wasn't pretty."

Natalie's face grimaces as her grip tightens on her rifle. I approach the fence with my bags and stop at the pre-designated 'close enough' marker and drop them. I wait for Natalie's next prompt.

"Hand me your guns first, Dan. You'll get them back when you leave here."

"Yeah... Okay," reluctance tickles the back of my throat.

"Hand the rifle to me stock first and then place that bag," Natalie points to the backpack containing my sawn-off, my ammunition and the homemade charges, "At the gates and step back."

I hesitantly comply. Natalie slings my rifle over her shoulder, along with hers, and picks up my backpack of goodies. She pulls a handgun out from its concealed spot in the small of her back, and she points it at the ground.

"If you try anything stupid, Dan, you'll join those men

at the front gates. Do you understand?"

"Crystal clear, Natalie. Can I put my hands down now?"

"Yes, just keep them in sight."

Natalie opens up the chain link fence gates and lets me in. We pass through both gates and lock them behind us and walk towards the demountable buildings. I look through the yard at the front gates and see the Patrol's engine steaming.

"Should we move that Patrol and the dead guys? It might attract unwanted attention."

"You can help me clean that up later. Do you wish to shower and clean yourself up?"

Apparently, my roadside spruce up this morning isn't up to Natalie's standards, so I sniff my shirt. I half laugh, now self-conscious of just how much I may stink.

"Is that your polite way of telling me I need a shower?"

"Yes and no," she returns with a smile.

Pat was right, I like this girl already.

PAT'S LETTER

I step into the first demountable, which is the accommodation and kitchen amenities building of the compound, I'm surprised by the open-plan space. The kitchen and dining area has some cafe-style tables and a common area that takes up most of the left-hand side of the building. Modern fixtures fill the common space: a pool table, a gaming area, with several different consoles and monitors, and a massive wall-mounted TV. A few bean bag chairs and a couch are close by, for movie nights, I guess, and a wall of shelves filled with DVDs stands nearby. Along the wall to my right are three separate rooms lined in a row. The greatest feature is the glorious air conditioner humming away on the nearest wall, three other units on opposite walls help to cool the space.

"This is a very nice setup you have here. How many of you live here?" I ask, trying to make small talk.

"Just me now," she quickly changes the topic, "The bathroom is the last room at the end, take your time in there, but keep your shower short. I only have a limited supply in the water tank."

"Okay. Thanks again for inviting me in."

"Don't make me regret it, uh?"

Natalie places my rifle and backpack in the room closest to the front door and into a heavy-duty lockable cabinet. She doesn't lock it though. I make a note of it.

I step into the bathroom and the overwhelming urge to poop grabs me by the guts. I whip my pants down and slap my arse on the toilet immediately. I hastily twist the dial for the timed exhaust fan and it squeals to life. Thank fuck it's so loud, as it helps muffle the sound of my insides painting themselves all over the porcelain bowl.

A poo-nami erupts out of me and, as I sit and strain my way through the waves of chocolate thunder violently surging out of me, several thoughts cross my mind.

When did I use an actual toilet last?
I hope Natalie can't hear this, fuck, or smell this!
When did I last poo?

I flush the foul toilet gravy away and give the toilet bowl a good scrub. I go to the basin to wash up and glance in the mirror, I'm filthy as sin and look absolutely buggered. No wonder Natalie suggested I take a shower. I grab my toiletries bag and meticulously brush, floss and rinse with mouthwash before I start assessing the years that I had added to my face in the last few days. I lean closer to the mirror and catch a whiff of a strong, earthy aroma that triggers memories of a winter season that I spent working at a Canadian ski resort. Almost every ski bum, hospo staff party and accommodation building on the hill had some slight tang of this sweet, dank scent to them. It was the smell of good times, new friends and uncontrollable laughter.

My nose tells me to open the mirrored door of the cabinet in front of me. I open its white plastic door and on the top shelf, next to some old cardboard air freshener trees, I see a small mason jar with 'ole smoky' embossed across the front of it. Inside the glass jar sit three fat buds of marijuana.

"Oh, sweet Mary Jane, it's been a long time," I mouth quietly. I crack the lid and inhale deeply through my nose, "Holy shit, that's strong. Mmmm."

I sniff the jar again and nostalgia grips me by the balls for a short, sweet moment. I'm transported back to chairlift joints while snowboarding in British Columbia, stoned summer hikes through Banff National Park and rainy winter days pulling bongs on the marina at a hidden-away fishing resort on Vancouver Island. I exhale and reseal the jar's lid and place it back in the cupboard.

I undress and hop into the shower, the hot water cascades over my tired and beaten body and washes away the nightmares of the last few days. I grab my Old Spice shower gel and lather it all over my arms and across my chest. With each lather of soap, I discover countless new bruises, cuts and grazes, much to my discomfort. I quickly scrub every inch of my body vigorously to try to keep to Natalie's time restrictions. I look down at my feet and see the red-stained, dirty water streaming off of me, it startles me. Is that blood? Is it Pat's? Mine? Or maybe, Horse's?

A zombie's? Or a combination of them all?

I realise that I have left my shampoo back at the rig, so I decide to use a little bit of Natalie's. I peruse her collection and pick the *Moroccan Coconut Oil Caramel Xplosion Hair Conditioner* for its scent alone. It is a big step up from my no-name brand anti-dandruff shampoo, to say the least. I lather it all over my head, rinse it off and then turn off the shower. I towel myself dry and slide into some clean jeans, my long-sleeved Frankie's Pizza shirt and slip on my trusty pair of thongs. I look in the mirror at the new and improved Dan, I nod and deem myself worthy of being within smelling distance of a girl like Natalie. I collect my toiletries and dirty clothes and return to the common area.

"That shower was bloody amazing, thank you, Nat…"

Natalie is sitting over at the white fold-out table by the air conditioner with her fingers pressed to her lips. She is reading Pat's letter, "Natalie?"

Her eyes dart from side to side rapidly, speed reading their way through the contents of the letter as her face becomes red and her eyes tear up.

"Are… Are you okay, Nata—"

Without looking up from the letter, Natalie silences me with an index finger at the end of her outstretched arm, instructing me to shut up. I stand compliant and muted in the bathroom doorway as Natalie continues reading. She drops her arm and puts down the first page and picks up the next double-sided handwritten piece of paper; two more unread pages lay on the table in front of her. I figure she may be there for a while, so I try to sneak across the room and over to the couch, which will be out of eyesight and earshot.

Flip. Flop.

Flip.

Flop.

I wince at the loud, wet slapping sound that my thongs are making against the linoleum floor as I walk. I quickly slip them off and tiptoe over to the couch barefoot. I sink into the comfortable cushions of the four-seater couch and pull out my phone. I pretend to play with it meaningfully, even though I have no internet or reception.

She stands up quickly and, on the way to the fridge, she tells me, "I, uh, need to shower, so you will need to wait outside. Here, take a beer, and I'll come to get you when I'm out." Natalie kicks my thongs over to me and hands me a beer, her red eyes meet mine for an instant before she looks away quickly.

"Are you okay? Did you get some bad news or..."

"These are happy tears, unexpected ones, but happy nevertheless." She forces a smile and ushers me outside, she pulls the door closed behind her and locks it. I leave the comfort of the air-conditioned demountable and brave the heat of the afternoon sun. I step onto the gravel in my thongs, crack open the XXXX Gold stubby and take a long swig from the ice-cold bottle.

"Ah, 'tis the nectar of the Gods!"

The golden lager flows willingly down my gullet and into my stomach, "Ah, that's the ticket," I smack my lips loudly. It has been some time since my last beer. Alcohol was a luxury on swing, mostly because the majority of our drilling contracts were in 'dry zones' where alcohol is strictly prohibited and illegal. That's not to say alcohol didn't find its way onto the rig, but those who danced with that devil, danced alone, luckily, the fines and termination of employment deterred most.

I wander over to the front gates of the compound to have a nosey at the damage the red Patrol had done to it during its ram-raiding efforts. The gate itself held up rather well, but the Patrol is destroyed. The engine bay is shredded and the hot engine still ticks and creaks, the smell of hot radiator coolant is strong as steam hisses out of its bullet hole-riddled core. It's no longer driveable.

Inside the Patrol's cabin sit two very dead men, the driver is slumped over the steering wheel and the other man hangs awkwardly out of the passenger side door. His blood drips down his limp arm and into a dark red pool of coagulating gore in the dirt. The two men are dressed in mine-spec Hi-Vis uniforms, patches on their shirt sleeves identify them as drill and blast contractors for the mine just outside of town. Hopefully, that's the last we see of those guys. I peer around the Patrol and try to look over the rise in the driveway, expecting to see the guy that Natalie had shot, but I see nothing, heat waves rising from the hot gravel warp my view. I notice something on the driver's side door of the Patrol: two large red letters, 'A' and 'P', are poorly painted onto the door with a circle surrounding the two letters, it's a crude attempt at the Australian Pride political party's logo.

"That's a bit fuckin' strange."

I take another swig of my beer and savour the flavour, not thinking too much about the logo, and take in my surroundings. The late afternoon sun beats down on me and sweat beads already speckle my sun-kissed face, a gust of wind whips up and peppers my face with the searing desert sand.

Twenty minutes or so pass as I loiter around the compound, I'm spinning my empty bottle in my hand when Natalie invites me back in from the doorway of the demountable.

"Dan, come on inside. Are you hungry? I'll make us something."

Fuck yes rings out in my head, but I offer a more acceptable response, "Natalie, mate, I'm starving. Let me help you whip something up," I walk towards Natalie as she counters my offer.

"Can you even cook? Maybe you will have another beer and I'll tell you if I need your help?"

"That's fine too," I accept.

Natalie lets me in and sits me on the couch, she fetches me another beer, all the while assuring me that she has everything under control. I'm pleasantly surprised by her hospitality, and I'm slightly relieved that I don't have to do anything in this moment. I enjoy this unexpected glimpse of normality, but a hint of unease lingers at the back of my mind. I eyeball the front room where my belongings are being stored.

Natalie throws on a random Spotify playlist and dutifully gathers some ingredients as easy-listening tropical beats play from a Bluetooth speaker in the background.

"So, Natalie, if you don't mind me asking, what did Pat write to you?" I probe.

Natalie stops chopping lettuce briefly and offers a compromise instead.

"How about this, you tell me five things about yourself and I'll tell you what Pat wrote to me?"

I agree to her terms once again, "Sure."

"Um, let's see," I rummage through my thoughts and try to pull out the most interesting aspects of my life so far, I count out the facts on my hand as I go.

"I'm Australian, born and bred, but my family are all from across the pond, England. I can snowboard, just," Natalie nods her head as she listens and continues to chop vegetables, "I have a daughter, her name's Bella. She's almost eight years old now, and I have a dog called Bones, or sometimes Huesitos, which is Spanish for 'little bones' or 'skinny', he's almost nine years old now."

Natalie looks back at me with an exaggerated amusement, as if to sarcastically say, 'Oh, really? Wow, I don't know any Spanish'. Maybe translating for *her* was unnecessary and hovering dangerously close to man-splaining.

I continue, "That's four things... I don't know. Oh, I have had more jobs than I care to count, like, fifty. After all, variety is the spice of life."

Natalie runs over the facts in her head and then glances over at me, "So, you have a daughter and a dog, but no wife? I see that you wear no ring?"

I look down at my left hand and see the faint tan line where my wedding band used to sit.

"Yeah, nah. The Mrs and I split up a while back. It turns out, working away for a month at a time and only being home for six days every two months doesn't quite keep a marriage strong, who would have thought, huh?"

I take a long swig from my beer.

"Hm. How old is your daughter again, Bella, is it?"

"Yes, Bella. She will be eight in a couple of months, she's growing up so fast."

"Do you have a picture of her?"

"I sure do," I open my phone and scroll through my albums, "Here. This is us on Australia Day at the beach. It's my favourite photo from when she was younger."

I walk my phone over to Natalie and show her the photo. Bella is sitting on my shoulders in her frilly pink, yellow polka-dotted bathing suit with her hands wrapped around my forehead, leaning back as she giggles about something I don't quite remember.

"Oh, my goodness, she's adorable. I'm guessing she doesn't get her tan from your side of the family?"

"No. That's definitely from her mother's side; she's from South America, Chile."

"You look very happy in this picture, Dan."

"I was," I smile at the photo for a lingering moment.

I scroll through my photos to show Natalie a more recent photo of Bella. A photo of Bella from her jiu-jitsu class in her Gi receiving an award.

"Oh, yes. She's beautiful, Dan. And a fighter?"

"Yes, she's beautiful, and stubborn as all buggery, too."

I lock my phone and throw it onto the couch, "Well, I have fulfilled my end of the deal, so what did dear old Pat have to say in his letter?"

"Ah, yes. A deal is a deal, Mr Dan," Natalie dries her hands with a tea towel and continues, "Since I can remember, my mother spoke of a kind man that she met many years ago, before I was even born, his name was Patrick. They had met by chance at some Canadian cowboy carnival in Alberta—"

I interject, "Was it the Calgary Stampede?"

"Yes! That's it. Well, they got along so well that they

travelled around for a year or so, through Canada, Alaska and the USA. My mother told me stories of their adventures almost every day as I was growing up, two best friends laughing and exploring a strange country together. Hearing their stories made me want to travel and adventure too, as soon as possible! But after each story, my mother would add 'but then Patrick had to go back home, to Australia, to work' and she always looked a little sad after telling their happy stories. I never understood this, until today."

Natalie throws the vegetables on the boil and starts seasoning up a pretty impressive steak and some chicken breast, and then she continues.

"When I was a child, my mother and father were the best parents I could have asked for, my mother was loving and affectionate and my father, although a little distant, was the first man I loved. He taught me everything, from brushing my teeth to changing the oil on my motorised scooter. My parents married young and had me almost right away."

"The horny buggers," I add, jokingly.

Natalie gives me a stern look and points the kitchen knife at me, she squints her eyes and smirks slightly.

"My mother always wanted a family, but in her younger years, she became very ill and was told that she couldn't bear children, so when I came along, my mother was over the moon. I was her miracle," Natalie smiles, "Before I went to sleep each night she'd whisper 'Mi regalita', which is Spanish for 'her little gift', you know?"

I lean against the countertop in the kitchen listening to Natalie's story, impatiently thinking, what does this have to do with Pat's letter?

"In my teenage years, I was very, how do you say? Troublesome?" Natalie half laughs, "I gave my father a hard time and one day during an argument, he said that I was not his child, his biological child. And that my mother was already pregnant before they had met, and that now that I was older, I wasn't his responsibility."

"Oh, wow…" I can't think of anything else to say.

"We reconciled shortly after that, but I asked my mother many times who my real father was and she always said, 'Marco, is your father! He raised you and he loves you like a daughter. No more of these questions!' I never really got an answer out of her, even after my father, Marco, died, which was three years ago."

"I'm sorry to hear that, Natalie."

She acknowledges me with a slow nod, mouthing 'thank you' quietly. She clears her throat and continues.

"A few months after my father had passed, my mother insisted that I get out of Spain and see the world, she recommended that I spend a year in Australia. She and Patrick had been in touch over the years through letters and more recently through emails and Patrick said he could easily find me a job near him and organise a place for me to stay. I remember thinking wow, I get to meet my mother's best friend and hear all about their adventures from Patrick himself! So, I came as soon as I could. I met Patrick, and he insisted that I call him Pat. He was a lot older than I imagined, sixteen years older than my mother, but he was so kind and so funny, I could see why my mother spoke so highly of him."

Natalie stops for a long moment and then goes to the fridge to grab another beer for herself and for me. She pops the tops and hands me my beer.

"Cheers," she toasts.

We tap bottles and I say, "Salud, Natalie."

She smiles and then downs half of the beer.

"Impressive," I comment.

Natalie winks and burps, "Thank you, Dan."

I laugh at her flattering display.

"Now, fast forward to this afternoon, when you come to me with a letter from my mother's dear Patrick and the first page of his letter reads 'If this page is the first thing you see, my dear Natalie, I am most likely dead…'"

My face instantly runs hot, and I jerk upright.

Natalie catches my reaction in the corner of her eye, but keeps cooking the steaks.

"The next pages tell me of how deeply Pat loved my mother and how he wanted nothing more than to be her happiness and her everything. He wrote of how my mother's father reacted when she brought him home to Valencia to announce their intent to wed and my mother's miracle pregnancy. He wrote of how he was beaten by my grandfather and his brothers and how he was forbidden to see my mother ever again. And how he was dropped off at the airport the very next day. He wrote of how sorry he was for missing seeing me grow up and how he wished every day that he was still with my mother and me, his family. He finished the letter by saying how much of a blessing it was to meet me as a woman and how much I reminded him of my mother and of the happiest times of his life. Pat is my biological father, Dan. That's what the letter said."

I'm unable to move, I sit rigid at the counter and

panicked thoughts course through my mind. My eyes flick to the front room where my weapons are.

"Dan," Natalie turns to me with watery eyes, "Where is he? What happened to my father?"

CONFESSIONS

My heart is pounding, I can feel it in my stomach as I try to organise my thoughts. I push my beer away and reach out to clasp my hands around Natalie's. She resists at first but quickly starts to sob.

"Natalie," I choose my words very carefully as I notice the large kitchen knife by Natalie's right hand, "Pat and I were getting fuel in Laverton when we were attacked."

Natalie's body tenses as she digs her chin into her collarbone, hiding her tears.

"We were surrounded by those infected things in an old junkyard. We were cornered and running out of options. Pat and I charged a group of"—I can't bring myself to mention Horse and what he did to Pat—"Those things. And we killed most of them. Well, Pat did. He was an unbelievable shot, but it was dark and raining. We didn't see one of them coming from behind us and Pat was bitten."

Natalie sobs a little harder, so I stand in front of her and place my hand on her shoulder.

"We got out of there as fast as we could, but Pat insisted that I stop and let him out. He handed me your letter and got out of the ute. But as soon as he stood out, he collapsed onto the ground," I lie.

Flashes of Pat's last moments blind me again and I scrunch my eyes shut.

"He didn't want to turn into one of those things and he wasn't able to do it himself, so he asked me to… Help… him. And to make sure I got this letter to you."

I pull away from Natalie and gently raise her chin with my fingertip, I stare into her beautifully bloodshot eyes.

"He put his gun in my hand and made me promise that I wouldn't let him turn into one of those things." I pause for a moment, "Do you understand what I'm saying, Natalie? What he asked me to do?"

Natalie closes her eyes and slowly nods, knowing that I pulled the trigger and ended her father's life.

"I'm so sorry that you lost your dad, Natalie. He was a wonderful man, and because of him, you and I are still alive."

Natalie places her hand on the kitchen knife, but then retracts it. She hugs me tightly, she exhales loudly and inhales just as deeply. Strangely, she begins to laugh. She leans closer and sniffs my neck and then the side of my head; she laughs knowingly.

I pull away from her, puzzled, "What? Do I still smell?"

Natalie laughs as she answers, "Yes, you smell like my coconut and caramel conditioner!"

I turn a guilty shade of red and laugh.

"Yeah, I left my shampoo at camp and,"—Natalie

sniffs me again—"You smell like such a pretty man! Like a princess!" Her teary laughter breaks the tension.

Natalie walks past me to go to the bathroom and wash her face. I take the opportunity to go and spray myself with some of my cologne to mask the 'pretty man' smell. When Natalie returns to the kitchen, she seems a little shy, as if regretting showing me a vulnerable side. I try to distract her with idle chit-chat as she finishes cooking.

We sit at the dining table across from each other and I stare at the mouth-watering feast placed in front of me; a thick, medium-rare steak dusted with black pepper sits steaming on my plate with some boiled root vegetables and a salad on the side. Natalie's plate has a large chicken breast peppered with chilli flakes sitting on top of a small bed of salad. My mouth tingles with anticipation.

"This looks amazing, thank you, Chef Natalie."

"It is no bother. You'd better enjoy it, it's the last steak."

"Then enjoy it, I will."

There's something to be said about a home-cooked meal after an ordeal like the last few days and it shows. I inhale the first half of the meal in the blink of an eye, but I have to slow down to match Natalie's eating pace. I notice that her beer is empty, which reminds me about the bottle of wine that I stashed in my bag.

"How rude of me, would you like a glass of wine?"

"Wine? I do not have any wine here. You have wine with you?"

"Of course," I push my chair back and stand up to fetch the bottle.

"Hmmm. What kind is it?" Her interest piques.

"It's a Californian red blend."

"I haven't had wine in weeks," Natalie smiles, "How about you get us another beer each and we'll save the wine for after dinner?"

"Sounds like a plan to me."

We finish our meals and sip our beers quietly as our food digests, both of our plates are picked clean. Our bellies are full and cold beers are in hand, island beats play in the background, and I smile at how amazing the evening is becoming.

"So, Natalie, how have you survived out here with everything that's happening?"

"Can't you tell? I'm a strong and independent woman. Smarter and braver than most Aussie men, you know?" Natalie cheekily responds.

I laugh, "That response seems rehearsed. I guess you've had a lot of people ask you, 'what's a girl like you, doing out here in a place like this?'"

"Yes, well, being in a mining town populated entirely by large hairy men, with their even larger egos, brings a certain set of challenges with it. Like having to sidestep horny boys and their terrible pick-up lines. But I'm a big girl, I can handle myself." Natalie winks at me as she swigs from her beer.

"Well, your little display in the compound today certainly gave off a 'don't fuck with this girl' vibe, and I bet you've probably heard every pick-up line under the sun. Every man and their dog must've tried it on with you."

"Why do you say that?"

"You're stunning, confident, and you can obviously handle a bit of banter; the girls of Kalgoorlie stand no chance up against you."

I swig nervously from my bottle, hoping I didn't overstep a line. Knowing that I could easily wander into overstaying my welcome at any moment.

Natalie smiles before she answers, "I am all of these things, yes, and yes, many men have tried to talk their way into these shorts," Natalie leans back on her chair and pulls on the loose waist of her denim shorts, "But only the lucky ones get that privilege."

Natalie is now four beers in, and her confidence and sass levels are increasing with every bottle.

I offer a toast, "To the lucky ones," and we clink our bottles and our eyes meet.

Natalie adds, "To the few and far between."

We swig from our bottles, sharing a lingering gaze.

"What's the worst pick-up line you've ever heard?"

"Oh, there have been some really bad ones, but I forget them as soon as I hear them," I stand up and head towards the fridge, hoping to find something specific. "I bet you haven't heard this line before," I start rooting through the fridge looking for my mystery prop.

"What are you looking for, Dan?" Natalie asks, craning her neck curiously. I halt her investigations with a, "Shh… You'll find out soon enough. Patience is a virtue, young Natalie."

She strangely obeys.

"Yes! Ha-HA."

I conceal my pick-up line prop and saunter back to the dining table. I stand beside Natalie and offer her my open hand, inviting her to take it, and follow my lead.

"Say we are in a club, some kind of classy lounge…"

Natalie places her hand in mine, it's soft and warm and small calluses dot the inside of her palm. I gently pull her to her feet and continue to set the scene for my pick-up line.

"We've been catching each other's eye from across the room for most of the evening, we are both sitting alone and I've been waiting for a signal, a wink or a smile, but, of course, you've been waiting for me to come to you."

I slowly walk her over to the four-seater lounge and offer her a seat.

"I've just approached you at the bar and offered you an espresso martini and my hand, I haven't spoken a word to you yet, but you figure, 'he's a bit cute, he has a nice smile, let's see where this goes'."

Natalie interjects, "Dan, I hate espresso martinis, make it a rum and lemonade with two lime wedges."

Perfect woman checklist: Likes rum. Tick!

"Haha, okay, so…" I sit down beside her, not too close but definitely not too far, "I stare into your eyes and I say 'close your eyes and hold out your hand, gorgeous'. You let your curiosity get the better of you, and you lend me your hand and cautiously close your eyes."

I take Natalie's hand and place something inside of it, I roll her fingers closed over the top of it and release her hand and lean back onto the couch.

"You begin to roll this unknown object in your hand, squeezing it, trying to figure out what it is; it's cold, firm, a weird round shape."

Natalie giggles, rolling the object in her hand.

"What did you put in my hand? What is this?"

"As you open your eyes…" I lead.

Natalie opens her eyes slowly.

"You gaze into your open palm to see a small green thing and you ask, 'What is this?'"

I let the suspense build for a moment and stand silently.

"Well, I know what it is. Why did you give me this?"

I smile and reply, "That there is my lime, my pick-up lime." A tremendous smirk sneaks its way across my face, amused by the glory of my pick-up lime pun.

Natalie smiles and shakes her head, "Well, Mr Dan, congratulations. I have never heard that one before."

She laughs, holding the lime in her fingertips.

I burst out laughing, "It's a good one, right?"

Natalie downplays how impressed she truly is.

"It is unique, I'll give you that, but does it ever work?"

"Every. Single. Time." I pause, "No, not at all, but it always gets a chuckle."

I place my beer on the coffee table and relax into the lounge again while Natalie plays with the lime.

"How have *you* survived this long, Dan?" she laughs.

"Luck mostly, it's all I've got going for me. Like finding Pat. If it wasn't for Pat, I wouldn't have survived Laverton and even if I did survive, there's no way I would have found you here. Actually, if I did make it to Kalgoorlie, I probably would have run into people like your gate friends in town."

I ponder that thought for a moment.

"Anyway, aside from your independence, wits and rifle skills, how did you end up here, Natalie?"

"There were four of us here at the beginning, my boss, myself and two backpackers, but when the backpackers heard about what was happening in Perth, they packed up their campervan and headed inland. I miss them terribly, but once they left, it was just Colin and me."

"Who's Colin?" I probe, hoping he's not her partner.

"He was my boss, a very kind man."

Natalie picks at the label on her beer bottle.

"May I ask what happened to him or...?"

She takes a deep breath and answers, "Today wasn't the first time those men have come to the gates. The first time they came, they pretended to be injured and Colin went out to help. That's when they beat him and then shot him. I only buried him yesterday."

"Fuck, I'm sorry to hear that, Natalie."

"Thank you, Dan. Tell me, what will you do when you get back to your daughter and dog?"

"Umm, I haven't really thought that far. Hopefully, they are still at the house, safe and sound, and if they are, I'll probably take them to my uncle's farm and lay low for as long as we can. Surely, the army or government has a contingency plan for outbreaks like this, but who knows?"

I shrug dismissively and then begin dwelling on the uncertainty surrounding Bella and my plans to get home when Natalie reaches over and places her hand on my forearm.

"I'm positive they are fine, Dan. You'll see them very soon, and Bella will welcome you home with many hugs and kisses." Her warm hand squeezes my arm reassuringly.

Natalie pulls herself up from the lounge and heads over to the fridge, "Let's play a game or something, Dan. It's been a long day."

I turn to acknowledge her and catch sight of her bending over into the fridge. Her long, tanned legs are perfectly straight as she dips low into the fridge. The curves of her arse cheeks peek out from the bottom of her cut-off jean shorts.

Fuck me, she is stunning. I look off into some random distant part of the room, not wanting to be caught ogling her again, and I quickly answer.

"Sure, what sort of games do you have in mind?"

"Let's play a card game, do you know how to play Texas Hold'em or anything?"

"Oooh, I haven't played cards in ages," I admit.

"I can teach you, or we can play Cards Against Humanity or 21 questions, maybe?"

"How about we smoke a jay and play Would You Rather?"

Natalie throws me a suspicious look.

"Do *you* have weed, Mr Dan?"

"Well, no, but when I was in the bathroom, I did get a whiff of something rather fragrant. Do *you* have weed?"

"Uh-huh, have you been snooping?"

"Me? Nooo," I smile mischievously, "I just have a really good nose."

"You're quite cheeky, aren't you?"

"Sometimes. So, what do you say?"

"I say yes, you're lucky that I rolled one earlier this morning, I'll go get it," Natalie places our beers on the coffee table, and she happily wanders off to get the joint.

"I did say; luck is the only thing I have going for me."

Natalie returns with the joint and sits herself down beside me. She lights it and takes the first couple of tokes before handing it to me. I take a long, slow pull and hold the smoke in my lungs.

"Mmm. This takes me back," I exhale, "I hope I don't have any drug tests in the next couple of weeks."

"I think there are more urgent matters, now, like which game shall we play," Natalie reaches out for the joint.

We pass it back and forth until the room is hazy with smoke. We decide on games pretty quickly to prevent our buzz translating into just zzz's. Rounds of Jenga, Mancala, Battleships and Connect4 keep us engaged enough to combat the sleepy enemy that hides in this indica-dominant bud. Once we get over that speedbump, our conversation flows like cheap wine from a goonbag hanging from a Hills Hoist at a university party.

Each of us tactfully probed into the other's lives, finding out what makes the other tick and what has kept us sane since the start of this infection bullshit. Our mutual interest in each other's lives quickly conjures up some interesting observations about adult life and some out-there hypotheticals; a natural conversational evolution where two stoned souls are concerned.

Between the banter and anecdotes, I discover how wonderful Natalie's laugh is, and I try to make her laugh with every chance I get. Her laugh is as contagious as it is beautiful, and her involuntary half-laugh-half-snorts trigger laughing fits from both of us. These bouts of cheek-burning laughter are soon followed by lingering stares that ignite something different inside of me. The music continues to roll on in the background as I go to finish my beer.

"Oh, tragedy. My beer's gone warm."

We had been so absorbed in each other's stories that we hadn't touched our beers in at least an hour, "Shall I pour us a glass of wine?" I ask.

Natalie smiles, "Of course, but please bring me my phone. I want to change the music."

I return with the wine bottle, two glasses and Natalie's phone. I begin pouring a glass of red for each of us as Natalie swipes and taps her way through her smartphone searching for songs.

I offer a toast, "To my wonderful host," I hand her a glass and Natalie counters, "To my cheeky guest, lucky he's cute."

I smile as we drink and my thoughts stray as I watch her full lips gently press against the rim of her glass as she sips.

"Mmm. Dan, this wine is good," she sips again.

"It's perfect, right?"

We fall silent for a long moment, enjoying the break in conversation as Natalie's song choice plays over the speakers; it's a rhythmic Spanish number. I watch Natalie as she closes her eyes to feel the music.

A moment later, an idea comes to Natalie and a smile lights up her face. She takes a quick sip of her wine and places her glass on the table. Natalie jumps to her feet and stands before me with her delicate hand held out, asking for mine, "Dance with me, Mr Dan."

AND WE DANCED

"Lead the way, Miss Natalie."

Part of me hopes that she doesn't want to dance properly, as my two left feet may embarrass me and injure her. She turns up the speaker's volume and takes my hand, pulling me to my feet, and then she lets go and twirls off into the middle of the living room floor.

My head spins a little as I stand, and my legs feel a little less reliable than normal. Oh man, am I high. Come on, battle through it!

The tempo of the song increases and Natalie takes my hand again, her energy leaps out of her as she jumps and swings herself around me. She sings along to the Spanish lyrics of the song as she swings her head back and forth to the rhythm. Her energy is flooring. I'm a little more reserved with my dancing, but I do jump in and throw myself around to the music, too. We do-si-do around each other playfully as we dance, the sweetness of her perfume and hair is hypnotic as she swirls by. Or am I smelling my own hair?

We laugh uncontrollably as we swing each other around the room, the combination of the beer, weed and her touch is intoxicating. The energetic fiesta of dancing and laughter peaks after a few songs and we both stand, a little out of breath, as we sip from our glasses. Natalie picks up her phone and shuffles through her music again, and a much slower acoustic track plays. I'm standing in the middle of the living room as Natalie walks across to me with her two hands held out low and open-palmed. She takes my hands and places them on her hips. Natalie brings her arms up over my head, interlocks her fingers, and rests her loosely gripped hands against the nape of my neck.

A wave of warmth washes over me as we slowly sway from side to side. Natalie pulls me closer and places her head on my chest. I wrap my hands around her waist and my heart begins to race.

Natalie speaks softly into my chest, "Thank you, Dan."

"For what, Natalie?" I'm puzzled by her gratitude.

"Thank you for today. For getting my father's letter to me. For helping me get rid of those men and thank you for tonight. I didn't know just how much I needed it."

She finishes her sentence and squeezes me tightly.

"Gorgeous, meeting you has made my entire week. You're funny, fiery and incredibly sweet. Thank you for not shooting me at the gate or sending me on my way."

I kiss the top of her head, and Natalie squeezes me once more before looking up at me. We stare for a moment and then my eyes sink to her full lips. I see her eyes dip to my lips too, she catches me wetting them with the tip of my tongue and she inhales deeply. I raise my hand and place it on her cheek, and I slowly lean in. Natalie's mouth opens in anticipation and she pulls me in, closing the distance between our soft, wet lips.

Natalie's warm tongue finds its way into my mouth and our tongues tease and chase each other as we synchronise technique; the taste of wine and sweet saliva dances on our tongues. I bury my hand into her light and frizzy hair and massage her scalp with rigid fingers as our embrace intensifies. Natalie grabs my hips and pulls herself into me and we lose ourselves in the moment.

The bulge in my jeans grows as Natalie presses her frame against mine, she notices my hardening member as she straddles my thigh and moans into my mouth. I gently entangle my fingers in her hair and make a fist, the sensation causes Natalie's head to crane backwards, exposing her neck. I kiss my way across her cheek and down to her slender neck. Natalie digs her nails into my back and balls up a part of my shirt in her hand and starts pulling at it and rolling it up my back.

"You won't be needing this," she informs me.

"Then you surely won't be needing this," I slowly slide her loose-fitting pink shirt up over her head and we take in each other's bodies. I reach out and slide a finger through each of the belt loops of her jean shorts above her hips.

"Come here."

I pull her close and hold her there as our tongues slide their way deeper into each other's mouths. Our hands blindly map each other's bodies. My left hand cups the back of Natalie's head as my right hand glides across the smooth skin of her lower back and hips. Natalie rolls her hips upwards as I near her shapely arse, I slide my hand into her shorts and squeeze her, firm rounded cheeks. She rolls forward onto her tippy toes and pulls herself up a few inches closer to my mouth. My hand to sinks further into her shorts and I curl my hand up underneath her. The inseam of her shorts rubs against the back of my hand as I feel the heat radiating through her lingerie. My fingertips slide along the warm, silky liquid that wets her lacy underwear and upper thighs. Natalie's body shakes as I massage her through her thin underwear. She bites my chest and neck as she reaches down and grabs the bulge in my pants. I pull my hand out from the back of her shorts and slide it down the front. Natalie has sneakily undone the top button of her shorts as I teased her from behind, it seems. My hand glides over a small patch of groomed pubic hair and my thick fingers slide between her plump slippery lips.

Natalie inhales sharply; she can no longer juggle kissing me and the sensation of my hand inside her shorts, so she kisses and sucks her way across my neck and chest. I roll her enlarged clitoris between my fingers and Natalie moans into my neck, she pulls my arm deeper into her shorts and I slide two fingers inside of her.

"Mmmm... Not yet," Natalie pushes herself away from me, "I want you in my mouth."

Before I can even respond, Natalie drops to her knees and begins stripping me of my belt and jeans. I stand before her wearing only cotton boxers. She looks up at me from her knees and smiles as she rubs my hardened cock through my boxers. She then traces the contour of it with her open mouth, running her teeth gently across its length. My penis throbs, begging to be released from its cotton prison. Natalie pulls down my boxers and grabs me. She squeezes and pulls on my hardening member, making sure it's as hard as she needs it to be before her soft, wet lips begin kissing the tip.

Natalie's small wet kisses soon become wide-mouthed, tongue-filled sucks as she inches more and more of me into her small, talented mouth. She grips the base of my shaft with her right hand and grabs the back of my thigh with the other, she pulls me closer and forces me deeper into her mouth. Her velvet tongue and cheeks consume the entirety of my cock. She starts pushing my thigh away from her and then pulling me back toward her rhythmically, encouraging me to thrust into her as she fucks me with her mouth. Natalie sucks, pulls and forces me into her mouth. Alternating between long sensual draws and mind-blowing rapid bouts of blurred oral gawk-gawk-gawk domination. She looks up at me and winks, knowing full well that everything she is doing is driving me wild. I pull myself out of her mouth and pull her up to her feet and kiss her deeply before I insist we take this into her room and onto her bed.

We blindly navigate our way toward the bedroom as Natalie slips off her jorts and as I remove her bra, we bump into every piece of furniture along the way, laughing at each new object we pinball off of. We reach the foot of her bed and I throw her onto it, I mount her immediately. I brace myself above her as she lay beneath me. The light from the doorway behind us illuminates every soft caramel curve of her stunning form. Her breasts rise and fall with each breath she takes and her chocolate brown nipples harden as the cool air from the bedroom's air conditioner greets them.

"You are absolutely stunning, Natalie."

I run a hand through her curly mess of hair. Natalie

stares up into my eyes and encourages me with a wide smile and a consenting nod; I melt into her.

I kiss her deeply before I slide myself down her frame to fill my mouth with one of her breasts. I suck and caress the entirety of it and then press both of her breasts together and messily kiss both of her nipples at once, her body twists beneath me. Her subtle moans and sharp breaths fuel an inferno inside of me and it's now my highest priority to see how loud I can make her moan.

My mouth continues to tease and explore my way down to her stomach and then to her waistline. I run my tongue along the inside of the elastic waist of her lingerie from hip to hip. I kiss one inner thigh before returning across her panty line to kiss the other thigh. I push her legs apart and slowly inch closer to the growing wet patch in her lingerie, she looks down at me over her breasts to see my face hovering centimetres above her crotch. We maintain eye contact as I breathe hot air onto her and lick her wet lingerie with a wide, fat tongue, building the anticipation of what's to come. I run my fingers from the tops of her knees and down her inner thighs and back up again, her hips rolling in frustration.

I pull her lingerie to the side and relieve her of her frustration. My warm, wet mouth descends on her, my flat tongue makes long passes up and down the length of her opening and full lips. I lap up every sweet drop of her abundant nectar as I explore each fold of her skin and every inch of sensitive pink flesh. My tongue swirls across her clit and then slides back down to her tiny opening, I push my tongue into her and she grabs the back of my head. I grip the underside of her knees as I bend Natalie to my will. I push her knees up to her chest and then to each side, trying to find which angle and what position drives her wild the most. I whip off her now-drenched and obstructive underwear to see all of her.

Natalie tries to say something, but she struggles to find her words, so I return to filling her with my tongue and filling my mouth with her. Two of my fingers glide into her as I flood her clit with deep sucks and slurps. I dose her with soft rhythmic licks as I massage her from the inside, Natalie arches her back and moans in pure ecstasy. Her body is becoming more and more sensitive to the passes of my tongue and the pressure of my fingers inside of her. She's going to come and the thought of this alone drives me wild.

Natalie's other hand swings down from above and grabs me by the back of my head, she grips a handful of my short brown hair and pulls my face into her as she rolls herself into my mouth. She's going to come, very fucking soon.

Suddenly, Natalie commando rolls herself on top of me so she is now sitting on my face, grinding my head into the mattress as her powerful thighs pin me down. I glance up from my new position, past her flat stomach and up to her supple breasts. I slide my hand out from between us to grab a handful of her toned arse cheeks, I roll one shoulder out from under her to fondle her chest. She rolls her hips into my face like waves crashing against a cliff. I slide hand down from her arse and ease my thumb inside of her from behind. I grip her like I'm eating a fat burger, she moans loudly in approval and simultaneously rips my other hand off of her breasts and clamps it around her throat.

"I'm coming, Dan. Don't stop!" she pleads.

Her hand squeezes mine, urging me to tighten my grip

around her throat. I comply immediately. Her thighs squeeze firmly against my ears as she grabs my outstretched forearm with both of her hands, I grip her throat tightly as I feel her entire vagina throb and slicken with excitement. My thick, wet tongue is pressed flat against her clit as she rides herself to climax. Her whole body shakes and her warm juices fill my mouth.

After an instant of inaudible pleasure, I release my grip around her neck, she inhales loudly and collapses to the side of me. Her body twitches with the aftershocks of her orgasm. Natalie holds a hand to her forehead as she tries to speak, but I give her no such chance.

I roll on top of her and brush the hair out of her flushed red face, and kiss her deeply. I push her legs apart and slide between them. Natalie reaches down and grips my penis and pulls it toward her. She guides it to her dripping, still pulsating opening, and releases her grip; allowing me to push myself inside of her. I slide into her a couple of inches and then ease back a little, I push into her again, harder and completely. She inhales sharply. Our bodies entangle as I fill her and our hips begin to roll and buck as we fuck each other senseless. Natalie's nails dig deep into my back, it appears she's an absolute banshee when it comes to fucking and the sting of each new claw mark makes me thrust into her harder; which is exactly what she wants.

I ease out of her to change position. I roll one of Natalie's legs across her body and push that knee high up into her chest, she's incredibly flexible. I pull her other leg straight out beneath me and sit on top of it, Natalie is now lying belly down.

The curves of her arse and thighs are phenomenal. I

slap her bare rump loudly and Natalie winces from the unexpected sensation. She arches her back and pushes her hips back at me, I catch a glimpse of the wet, pink glistening flesh between her thighs. As she lies on her side, I slide myself into her again and she buries her head into her pillows. I thrust long and hard into her. I pin her two hands on to the small of her back with one hand and grab a handful of her hair with her other. I pull her hair back firmly. Her neck and back arch, and I feel her pussy tighten even more as Natalie moan.

I think I have found the perfect balance of pain and pleasure. I slide in and out of her hard and fast, she rips one of her hands free to push a pillow into her face. She screams into it. I consider slowing down, but then she throws her hand outwards and braces it against the wall. Natalie starts pushing herself back into each of my thrusts. It's fucking mind-blowing. Natalie's rhythm soon surpasses mine and I find myself struggling to keep up with the sheer pace and energy that she is throwing back at me.

All of a sudden, she twists on to her back and a hand comes flying around and slaps me across the face, hard.

I stop abruptly, "What the fu—" I sputter.

"Shut up, get in that chair!"

Natalie bucks me off of her and quickly sits me in the recliner in the corner of her room. She pulls my knees forward, scooting my arse to the edge of the seat and then spreads my legs wide. She pushes my torso back in the chair and then she steps up onto the chair, her feet on either side of my hips. She grips the back of my neck and then sinks down into a squat to mount me, she guides my penis into her once more.

"I want you to come with me, Dan. I'm so close to coming again. Will you come with me?"

I don't respond with words, merely a 'hmmph' at the sentence that just left her mouth.

Natalie rolls her hips and her body in ways that I have never experienced before. She grabs my hands and slaps them against her breasts. Her facial expressions contort between physical exertion and absolute bliss. Her brows furrow as her mouth opens wide and muted. She drives herself into me, squeezing my cock with every vaginal muscle she has. Her forehead tightens and her mouth stretches into an exhilarated smile as she slides up the length of my cock. I feel a surge of pleasure building inside of me as I watch Natalie manipulate me into the exact place she wants me to be, on the brink of coming.

"Don't stop," I urge.

An even bigger smile explodes across her face. Natalie immediately adopts a new speed and rhythm, her hips become a blur as she fucks me senseless.

Short moans pulse out of her, "Ah. Ah. Ah. Ah."

I grab her by the hips and rock her forcibly back and forth. I feel Natalie's slippery, warm muscles contract around my hardened member, she strangles it with all her might.

"I'm coming!" She announces.

Her words tip me over the edge, "Me too!"

I explode into her as she milks every last drop out of me with long draws of her hips and our bodies shake involuntarily. We embrace each other tightly as we continue to throb into one another. Natalie moans with each pulse of my cock, knowing full well that rope after rope of my ejaculate is filling her. We didn't even consider protection, but we couldn't care less about it right now. We are lost in this moment, and in each other. Anything outside of right here and right now, is none of our fucking concern.

Moments after, Natalie slides herself off of me and pulls me onto the bed. She rolls onto her side and I crawl in behind her, she pulls my arm over her and I spoon her from behind. We lay naked on top of her bed covers with our chests still rising and falling heavily. The alcohol-buzz and weed-high collide with the sweet post-romp flood of endorphins and we drift off to sleep for a few hours.

We enjoy the gift of each other's bodies once more in the dead of night and again in the early hours of the morning. We had awoken hungry beasts in each of us and they demanded satisfaction.

There's nothing like the sexual appetite and warmth of a gorgeous, wild-haired woman to make you forget about the zombie apocalypse raging on just outside the bedroom door.

THE EYE IN THE SKY

I stir from my deep and restful slumber and blindly reach behind me, searching the blankets for Natalie's naked form. I only find her warmth on the mattress. She is gone, I don't think too much about it. The scent of weed and sex still lingers in the room. I twist and roll around the bed, stretching and cracking various joints as I smirk and mutter into the pillow.

"Good night. Great night."

Natalie breezes through the door with two cups of coffee in hand and a smile on her face. My Frankie's Pizza shirt is the only thing she has on.

"Good morning, Mr Dan."

I un-pretzel myself from my stretching routine and prop myself upright against the wall.

"And a good morning to you too, Natalie, was it?" I laugh, "I'm joking, obviously. G'morning, gorgeous."

Natalie smirks and comes back with,

"I'm surprised you have the energy to run your mouth, Ben, was it?" A thought crosses Natalie's mind as she looks down at the coffee in her hands, "You're very lucky that you're in my bed, otherwise you may have worn this cup of coffee," she threatens playfully.

I roll off the bed and stand before Natalie, "I guess I'll just shut my mouth then," I kiss her softly on the lips and go to take one of the coffees from her when she pulls my cup away from me.

"Hmm, disarming me, are you?" Natalie asks.

I take a cup of coffee out of her hand, "Absolutely."

And I scurry back to the safety of her bed. Natalie shakes her head and slides into her spot on the bed, positioning herself up against the wall next to me. I pull my arm out from between us and drape it over her shoulders.

"I have to say, Nat, last night was... Something else."

I squeeze her shoulder gently. Natalie closes her eyes as she sips from her mug, "Yes, it was, Dan," she leans over and kisses my neck and then returns to her spot, relaxing against the wall.

"Although, later in the night, I could tell that you were torn between one feeling and another, or one place or another. Maybe regretting something?"

I become embarrassed and retract my arm slightly, twitching at her comment. I had been torn. Torn between enjoying my time with her, feeling guilty about Pat's death and feeling ashamed for indulging myself when I should be racing home to my daughter.

Natalie places her warm hand upon mine and says, "Dan, don't misunderstand me, last night was one of the most exciting things I've experienced in a long time. I could just tell that, in some moments, you were between emotions, like you were choosing between guilt and joy. I don't know." She pecks me on the cheek, not knowing what else to say, "Maybe I'm just being weird, it's been a long time since anyone has shared this bed with me."

Natalie recoils and crosses her legs. She cups her mug with both hands as she sips—unaware of how accurate her intuitions were. I lean over and kiss her temple. After a moment of silence, Natalie searches for something to say.

"Do you want to see something cool, Mr Dan?" Natalie springs from the bed, "Wait here," she skips out of the room and into the living area.

I place my mug on the bedside table and peer out of the door, trying to see what she is up to. I can just see her through the gap between the door and its frame and I see her rifling through a large suitcase on the living room floor.

"What are you doing out there, Natalie?" I ask.

"Shhh. You be patient," she whips back.

I lean over the side of the bed to see more. Natalie is squatting on the balls of her feet as she rummages through the suitcase, I'm privy to the sight of her shapely arse peeking out from the bottom of my black Frankie's Pizza shirt. Insert praise Jesus hand emoji. Natalie snaps upright with a large, bulky object and makes her way to the front door. I fall off the bed in a panic, thinking she might have caught me ogling her again.

"Stop looking at my ass, Dan," Natalie calls out as she heads outside.

"Damnit," I lay contorted and tangled in sheets on the ground, by the time I've gotten up and propped myself back up against the wall, Natalie has another smaller, black object in hand and skips toward me.

"What are you up to?" I ask again, Natalie hides an object behind her back and sits beside me.

"Colin, the compound owner, was a very smart man and a very dumb man. You see, Colin had a terrible habit of drunk driving into Kalgoorlie to get more beer after drinking all day. After his second D.U.I., he had to reconsider this behaviour or lose his license. So, rather than change his behaviour, or his drinking habits, he figured out a way to 'safely' drink and drive."

I laugh, "How do you safely drink and drive?"

"Like this."

Natalie pulls out a small black pelican case and sits it on her lap. She unclips some latches on the front of the heavy-duty carry case. She opens the case; a small computer screen is fixed to the inside of the case's lid and sitting inside a padded foam cutout is a chunky handheld remote controller that looks like an old Lynx gaming system, with a smartphone is clipped into the centre of it.

"What on earth is that?"

"One moment."

Natalie clicks a button on the bottom of the monitor screen and grabs the remote control with both hands.

"This is Colin's pride and joy."

Natalie pulls on the tip of a remote control's telescopic antenna and extends it fully, it's almost a metre and a half long. She leans in toward the monitor screen, trying to remember the sequence of buttons to turn it on, mouthing them silently to herself, "Aha!"

The monitor screen lights up and an image of white

corrugated sheet metal appears on the display.

"This is what Colin uses to 'safely' drink and drive."

Natalie's thumbs work two joysticks on the remote control and the image begins to move; it's a video recording, a live feed from outside the demountable.

"This is Colin's long-range drone, he uses it to see if the road between here and his favourite pub, The Exchange Hotel, is clear," Natalie smiles and turns her head to me, to see if I'm impressed.

"That's the coolest thing I've ever seen. How far does it go? What's its range?" My face beams with curiosity.

"This can go all the way to the super pit!" she boasts.

"Holy shit, this must have cost him a fortune."

"I believe it did, he only ever let me fly it when he was too drunk to. Most times, when I flew it to check the road for him, I'd lie to him and swear I saw a cop car hiding in an alleyway or something," she laughs.

"Sneaky girl."

I shuffle closer to Natalie and she slides the monitor between us. We hear the hum of the drone's propellers outside as it flies skywards and the monitor screen relays a crystal-clear image to us.

"I can't believe the quality of the footage. What kind of camera is mounted on that thing?"

"An expensive one! Check this out," Natalie manipulates a few buttons on the remote and the image magnifies, "It has amazing zoom." She clicks the buttons several times, zooming in on a street sign at least six hundred metres away. The sign reads;

Alumco property. No trespassing. Contact Colin B. prior to entry!

"This sign is at the bottom of the driveway," as Natalie zooms out and returns to the original frame, I see the entirety of the red gravel driveway leading from the compound all the way down to the tarmac road.

I see the buckled car wrecks from yesterday's attack, the patrol at the compound's front gates, the fat man's rolled Cruiser further back. Strangely, the body of the fat man whom Natalie shot as he ran away is not there, but I don't bother to comment. Natalie flies the drone at speed down the driveway and toward the centre of Kalgoorlie. As it glides over the outer suburbs, we see the extent of the chaos that has consumed the large mining town.

Abandoned cars litter the roads; some are burning and others are flipped onto their roofs. The infected fill most of the streets, they walk aimlessly through suburbia. Piles of burnt, or burning, bodies crowd some of the major intersections. I can't imagine what that must smell like. A few buildings have been completely levelled, as if dozers had been through them, and shop fronts bear the tell-tale signs of looting and vandalism.

Many of the side streets have makeshift barricades blocking access to them, wide windrows of rubble and car bodies form high walls. Hannan Street, Boulder Street and Maritana Street are lined with these walls, which all meet at the intersection outside of the Exchange Hotel. Thick, black smoke chokes most of the city centre and its neighbouring suburbs, so I don't see much more.

Five minutes of silence pass as we process the scene.

"The men who came here yesterday, they are the ones who are blocking the roads."

"Why? To try and keep the zombies out?"

"I don't think so, the infected are still on both sides of the blockades. I think they're using them to ambush people who try to enter Kalgoorlie. I've heard gunshots and car chases over the last few days. I've only flown the camera into town once since Kalgoorlie went into a lockdown, and I didn't like what I saw."

I hum to myself, unsure how to respond.

Thick smoke rising from burning buildings forces Natalie to pilot the drone higher, "I'm taking it up, the smoke is too thick, the last thing I want is to fly into a building or something."

A large commercial block is in flames, several shops are ablaze and I can see the carcass of a smouldering Bunnings warehouse; loose sheets of green corrugated metal hang from the twisted frame of the building. Only the first three letters of the store's front signage are legible, fire has destroyed the rest.

Natalie sees something on the screen.

"What the hell is that?" Natalie leans in.

"What's what?" I lean in too.

Natalie points her finger at the screen, "That."

I follow her finger and see something moving just beyond the smoke screen, something big.

"Here, I'll go higher," Natalie sends the drone upwards again and zooms in through the smoke.

The thick smoke from the burning Bunnings store keeps us guessing, but there's a lot of movement in the streets below, the drone's microphone picks up something and we hear familiar noises coming from the monitor's speakers.

"Does the volume go any higher? Turn it up," I ask. Natalie nods her head and clicks the side buttons of the monitor. The roar of engines crackles through the speaker. Diesel engines, motorbikes and something I can't quite put my finger on, but whatever it is, it's loud.

Natalie takes a sharp breath and her whole body tenses. "Oh, no. They're coming."

I place my hand on her thigh and lean even closer to the screen, "Who's coming?"

The smoke clears and we see everything.

"The men from the mine! The men who attacked us yesterday!" Natalie's voice fills with panic.

I stare at the screen in disbelief, "Fuck. Off."

"What, Dan? What is it?"

A CAT 793, a giant mining haul truck from the Super Pit, rolls through the streets of the North Kalgoorlie light industrial area. Its wheels are as high as a second-storey window and its width takes up the entirety of the road. The drone's camera shows a structure of some sort in the massive tray of the dump truck too. Natalie spots three mine-spec utes weaving in front of the monster truck and two guys on dirt bikes leading the group through town.

Natalie steadies the drone and zooms in on the cab of the big yellow dump truck and sees him, the man she shot in the back yesterday afternoon.

"It's him, the... the fat man I shot in the driveway," Natalie zooms in to confirm.

In the driver's seat of the dump truck is a fat, fifty-year-old, beer-bellied, HiVis-clad moron sporting a new sling on his left arm—Natalie struggles to keep the camera focussed on him—the man who had killed her former boss.

I try to see what is in the tray of the dump truck.

"What the fuck is that?" I cock my head trying to figure

out what it is, "It kind of looks like a…"

Natalie quickly spins the drone around and cuts me off,

"It doesn't matter what is in the back of that truck, if that gets here," Natalie stands up and points out the window, "Those fences will do nothing. We have to leave, now!"

A thousand scenarios play in my mind, but one sticks out like a baboon's red arse.

"Wait!" I prompt.

I rush out to my backpack that Natalie had confiscated when I arrived and I start rifling through it.

"No, they will be here in twenty minutes. We have to move, Dan. I'm coming with you to Perth."

I pull several items out of the bag.

"How about we leave them a little present?"

I open my bag and show her the explosive charge that Russell had built, "We'll hide this out on the road and blow them away! I've got more in the ute. They're not big enough to stop the dump truck, but we can definitely thin out the herd before they get to the gates." I hold out the charge in my hand and Natalie reaches out and takes it.

A weighty rectangular brick wrapped in black duct tape fills her hand. She inspects it and notices the semi-dismantled hand-held radio fixed to the front of the brick; she gives it a puzzling look.

"Is it big enough?" Natalie asks innocently.

I dodge the perfect 'that's what she said' setup and answer her straight, "That there is equivalent to a couple of grenades, gorgeous, it's plenty! My driller and I have launched whole car bodies into old pits with one of these. We'll use the radios to detonate them."

I hold up two tetra radios.

"We'll pay them back for what they did to your boss!"

Natalie's eyes dart between the charge, the Kalgoorlie facing window and the drone monitor's screen. She weighs up her options fast.

"Okay. I like your plan, but we will do it my way."

"Fuck. Yes!"

ROUND I:
THE GIMP & THE FAIRY

Natalie presses the 'return' button on the drone and leaves it to navigate its way back to the compound. In the few minutes it had taken to fly back, Natalie had formulated a plan, delegated our tasks and began preparing for the convoy's arrival. First priority: clothes!

Natalie quickly throws her things into the Hilux while I grab the other goodies that I stashed under the car seat: four more explosive charges and some radio detonators. We decide to place three of the charges on this side of the rise in the driveway, in a staggered diagonal formation, some distance away from the front gate. The fourth charge will be placed up on the back track, the track that I came in on. Just in case someone tries to surprise us from behind. Natalie also has the bright idea of sticking random nuts and bolts to the charges to create some extra shrapnel.

I like how this girl thinks.

I drive up the back access track and set the fourth charge first, burying it in the loose gravel close to where I had taken cover by the log yesterday; if our guests try to do the same, they'll be blown away. I drive back down and park inside the compound's gate. I run through the compound and out the front gate to set the driveway charges. I'm going to use the scattered debris from yesterday's attack to conceal the explosives in the driveway. then I'll set up the radio detonators behind a concrete road barrier in the centre of the compound, making sure that they are labelled and ready to go. Natalie is sprinting around the compound, dropping ammunition and secondary weapons in a few strategic locations, in case we are forced back somehow.

She has a lot more weapons than I thought, a gun cabinet full in fact. She has an automatic rifle, another hunting rifle, a shotgun and a lot of ammunition. She moves fast, Natalie has already packed everything of ours into the Hilux and fuelled it up before I get back from burying the charges.

"Time check," I call out.

"Err, I don't know, Dan. Not long!"

I run through a mental checklist;

    Charges: set.

    Hilux: packed.

    Weapons: ready.

"Alright, I think we're good."

I look over at Natalie, who's loading the bolt-action rifle; her skin beads with sweat from the heat of the morning sun as she confidently handles her weapon. Her wild hair is held back by a thin hair tie and her wardrobe choice is holding my attention hostage. Her dark green denim dungarees, black boots and red crop top combo screams sexy, freedom fighter pin-up girl.

"Well, that's hot as fuck," I volunteer audibly, "I think I meant to say that in my head."

I leave Natalie to her rifle and scan the compound for anything that I may have missed. The front gates are locked, the back two gates are dummy locked for our quick escape and the makeshift detonator rack is set. My eyes fall upon the drone sitting next to the demountable building and genius strikes. I grab the final charge and start to tinker with it and the drone. Natalie comes over to see what I'm up to.

"Dan, what are you doing?!" urgency niggles at her patience, "They could be here any minute!"

"I'm rigging the drone up as a bomber."

"What, why?"

"Okay, hear me out. These charges won't do shit to the dump truck from the ground, and it definitely won't kill your mate in the driver's seat. But if my plan works, we can use the drone to fly this charge over the dump truck and drop it right in front of his face. You see this here," I turn the drone on to its side and press a blue button labelled 'landing gear' on the remote repeatedly, four automated legs open and close at the drone's base.

"If I can attach the charge to these plastic legs, we can use it to drop a big old 'fuck you' right on top of your mate. We don't need to wait for him to get to our gates, we can get him out on the road or in town even," I explain.

"How will it go bang, though?"

"I'll use these barbeque igniters and radio parts. As soon as the charge hits anything, it'll depress this little red button, or these wired springs, and the completed circuit will make it go bang!" I look up and smile, impressed by my MacGyver-ing skills.

"Okay, hurry up. I want the drone in the air so we can see where they are!"

"Yes, boss."

I hastily finish turning the drone into a bomber and Natalie carefully sends the drone back up. She pilots it up the rear side of the range and when it reaches the peak of the cliff on our left, Natalie switches the drone to hover mode and zooms in on the advancing convoy.

"I think they've stopped," Natalie announces.

The monitor's live feed shows a large dust cloud consuming the halted convoy parked on the highway at the end of the gravel driveway. Natalie zooms in further to see what's happening as I peer over her shoulder.

"It looks like your mate with the sling is leading them, look," I point to the screen which depicts the portly, sling-wearing man barking orders down to his men. I reach over and finger the camera control joystick to pan left.

"What are you doing?" Natalie snaps.

"Look," each guy has a large rifle or military-type assault weapon. "Holy shit, they're armed to the teeth."

I continue panning across the crowd when something else grabs my attention, a fucking cannon mounted to the roof of one of the Land Cruisers, one of those belt-fed *Rambo* machine guns.

"They must have raided the army barracks near town to get that kind of firepower. Fuck me, we'll have to make sure we save a charge for that guy."

Natalie stares at me with uncertain, pleading eyes.

"We should leave here, or go up into the hills at least,

and blow them from up there. We don't have to be here."

"Gorgeous, if we run, they will follow us. But if we stay and fight? We can finish this here and now, it's your compound, not theirs. You've scared them off before and, together, we will scare them off again. We have the advantage; they don't know that we know they're coming. And they definitely won't be expecting our little booby traps. Look," I point to the two sheer cliff faces that wall the driveway of the compound.

"We have them in a bottleneck, they have to come from the front, the charges will be our biggest weapon and then they'll be exposed and rattled," I try to convince her.

"Dan, there are so many of them."

"Yes, they outnumber us, but we'll take out most of them with the charges. Anyone who survives the explosives surely won't survive you and your rifle or me with my bag of tricks."

Natalie nods and her enthusiasm builds, "Yeah, okay, Dan. You're right. This is my compound and those bastards aren't taking it from me."

"That's the spirit!"

There's movement on the monitor's screen. Natalie zooms out and refocuses. One of the vehicles, the one with the roof-mounted belt-fed machine gun, drives north, most likely heading for the goat track to sneak around the back. He'll take a while to get up that track, so we don't have to worry about him just yet.

Two motorbikes start ripping up the driveway toward the compound, long fingers of red dust stretching out behind them as they approach.

"They'll be here in less than a minute," Natalie says,

her eyebrows wrinkle with concern, but then barks, "Get behind the barriers and turn on those radios!"

The drone hovers above the nearby cliff like a watchful hawk as we crouch low behind the barriers, waiting for the motorbikes. The loud 4-stroke dirt bike engines scream as they power towards us, getting louder and louder as I peer intermittently over the barricade. Natalie sits with her back against it and rechecks her rifle. Our hearts race. Here they come. We look over the top of the barrier to track our soon-to-be-dead guests.

Two KTM motorbikes brake and slide to a halt on the rise of the gravel driveway. They straddle their stationary bikes and twist their throttles, revving their engines hard repeatedly. I look over the barrier again and laugh at the two riders standing in the distance. I think to myself, these two have definitely watched a few too many *Mad Max* movies.

"Nat, check out these two clowns."

The tallest of the two riders is wearing shiny black leather riding gear from head to toe with makeshift spikes and armour covering his shoulders, forearms and knees. His modified helmet is also black and features a wide row of long black rubber dreadlocks that flow out of the top and trail down the rider's back—a tribute to *The Predator* franchise, surely. He may have been going for the dystopian *Predator* look, but he missed the mark. He looks more like the Gimp from *Pulp Fiction* than an alien hunter-warrior.

The other rider, a heavy-set Māori fella, is sporting an open-faced moped helmet with a novelty Native American feathered headdress duct taped to it. A pair of speed dealer sunglasses sit tightly on his round face, which has a prominent tribal tattoo inked down the whole left side of his face. The rest of his outfit consists of a fluorescent yellow singlet, exposing some serious side boob action, and some blue Stubbie work shorts—that are way too tight and expose just as much meat as his singlet. A pair of pink, steel-capped boots and a large flamboyant pink-frilled tutu complete his outfit. When he turns to talk to his gimp mate, I spot a pair of shimmering glittered fairy wings flapping in the wind, its two purple straps cut into his bulging shoulders.

Natalie and I share a quick look of confusion before sinking back behind the barrier. She shoulders her weapon and I pick up the first of the radio detonators.

"What are they waiting for?" Natalie whispers to me.

"I don't know," we check the monitor and see what the others are up to, "None of the others have moved from the end of the driveway," I push one of the joysticks to turn the drone toward the goat track, "…And the guy in the Land Cruiser on the back track is still ages away, maybe they're waiting for him, trying to coordinate themselves?"

"I don't like it, Dan. Let's shoot these guys now."

Natalie goes to raise her rifle, but I reach out and grab her barrel to stop her, "No, no, not yet. They haven't seen us yet, we have the element of surprise."

I try to bargain with her, but she isn't having any of it.

"No." Natalie pulls the barrel away and steadies it on the concrete barricade.

"For fuck's sake."

I clench the radio tightly and pull my rifle closer to me and peer over the barrier. My eyes shift between the Predator Gimp, his mate, the Māori Fairy, the monitor and Natalie's impatient, and itchy, trigger finger.

The Fairy spots Natalie from the rise and points her out to the Gimp excitedly. Fuck.

"If you have a shot, take it, but I'd wait until they're a bit closer."

Natalie nods silently and leans into the butt of her large rifle. The two men chat for a moment before the Gimp reaches into the black bag that's hockey-strapped to the tail of his KTM motorbike.

"What are they grabbing, Dan? I can't see."

Natalie keeps the men in her sights as I pull out the binoculars, I zoom in on the two riders. The Gimp hands a small shotgun to the Fairy and pulls out a pistol for himself, which he slides into the holster hanging off his black leather costume. The Fairy secures his shotgun to a homemade bracket mount on his handlebars as the Gimp digs deeper into his bag and pulls out something bulky and strange-looking.

"It looks like these two only have a handgun and a shotgun, maybe."

"Huh, they'll be dead before they get close enough to use them," Natalie chirps.

"Wait, he's got something else in his hands now."

I squint hard into the binoculars, spinning the focus wheel to get a clearer image. The object in the Gimp's hand looks like a giant, poorly made soap-on-a-rope. A length of looped blue rope is attached to a ball of some sort, it's about the size of a rock melon, just not as smooth, it's quite lumpy. I dial in the focus more and piece together what I'm seeing. The creamy tan colour of the ball suggests that it's made of dried expanding foam. I can see grinder disc fragments, screws and drill bits jutting out of the ball.

I pull away from the binoculars, frowning.

"What the fuck is that?"

"What, what do you see, Dan?" Frustration eats at her.

"One sec."

The Gimp picks up the end of the long, black length of cable that's hanging out from the top of the ball. The cable is marked at increments with white lines. The Gimp looks up at the compound and then back at the cable. He shrugs his shoulders and pulls something from his pocket. The Gimp yells out to the Fairy and nods, the Fairy twists his throttle repeatedly and throws his head back laughing.

"They're making their move, get ready," I instruct.

"Where's the Land Cruiser, Dan?"

"Uhh," I check the monitor, "Still a few minutes away and"—I check on the vehicles and the yellow monster dump truck—"The others aren't moving, they're still at the bottom of the driveway." I look through the binoculars one last time and see the Gimp with a lighter, igniting the cable.

"Holy fuck, it's a fuse," I turn to Natalie wide-eyed, "It's a bomb or something. He just lit a fuse!"

Natalie fires a round at the duo in the driveway and startles the Fairy into stalling his motorbike.

"Stay on the Fairy. I'll handle this Gimp cunt!"

The Gimp loops the blue rope handle of his D.I.Y. bomb around his handlebars and twists his throttle hard, accelerating toward us on one wheel. I turn on the radio marked '#1' and rest my finger gently on the call button, waiting for the perfect moment.

The Gimp flies toward us, slapping his foot through the gears as he powers forward.

"Come on, you prick."

He approaches the marker for the first charge: a broken wing mirror from the Patrol.

"Seeee ya!!"

I squeeze the call button and the charge detonates just as the front wheel of the motorbike passes it. A loud crack echoes between the cliffs as an explosive cloud of red dust vaporises the Gimp and his bike. Fragments of KTM and black leather scatter into the air as the bulk of the bike's chassis slides across the pea gravel into the base of the cliff to the right. Chunks of meat begin to hit the ground with wet thuds. The Gimp's roped-ball bomb flies off harmlessly out of sight.

I jump to my feet, "Ha, Ha! It fucking worked."

Natalie calls out, "Dan, I can't see the pink tutu guy through the dust!"

I quickly ditch the radio marked '#1' and squat back down to check the monitor. I pick up my rifle and get ready for the other rider. The Fairy sits on his stalled motorbike with both hands on his helmet in complete shock, the explosion and pink-misting of his Gimp mate jar him.

A smaller explosion detonates in the distance, the Gimp's bomb-on-a-rope. It startles the Fairy into action, he starts his bike and barrels toward us, hell-bent on revenge.

"Natalie, you're up!" I call out.

The pink tutu emerges from a cloud of red dust with his head down and his left hand gripping the stock of the shotgun, he only fires one shot before Natalie puts a round through his chest. He slumps to the side and loosens his grip on the handlebars. Natalie fires a second shot into his open-faced helmet. His speed dealer sunglasses shatter as the bullet passes through his right eye. The Fairy buckles forward and the front wheel snaps to the side, front-flipping the motorbike into the air.

"Check the monitor!" Natalie yells.

I spy the screen and see the group at the end of the driveway scurrying around like ants, "They're coming!"

Two Land Cruisers race up the driveway as the dump truck starts and roars to life. I pan the drone left and catch the Cruiser with the machine gun on its roof snaking its way up the last couple hundred metres of the rear track.

"Here!" I call out to Natalie and throw her a radio marked '#4', the back track charge. "Hold that power button in to turn it on and when that Land Cruiser gets close to that bit of blue pipe"—I point to the spray-painted pipe marker sticking out of the ground near the edge of the cliff-side track—"Hold down the call button to blow it! I'll handle the two guys out front."

Natalie crosses the compound to get a better vantage point as I sit and wait, clutching my rifle tightly. The first Land Cruiser crests the rise in the driveway, I look down at the monitor screen and see the second Land Cruiser slowing, leaving a sizeable gap between the two.

"Damn, I was hoping to 'two-bird-one-stone' these fuckers," I reach down and turn on the last two radios.

I rest the barrel of my rifle on top of the barrier as I hold the radio labelled '#2' in my left hand, I watch closely as the first Cruiser approaches. Four men fill its interior, the two passengers in the back are hanging out of the rear windows, straddling the doors like cowboys with one leg on either side of it. One has a handgun and the other has a bolt-action rifle with a scope. The front seat passenger also has a rifle, but without a scope, he's resting its barrel on top of the wing mirror. I flick my eyes hillside to see if our sneaky backdoor friend has arrived yet, nope. I check on Natalie to see her keenly watching the hillside above us, brilliant. I fire a shot into the oncoming vehicle and the bullet shatters a roof-mounted LED light bar. The driver flinches and swerves right and into the path of the first explosion's crater, he quickly swerves left to correct it. His front wheels narrowly miss the crater, but one of the rear wheels does not. The deep crater consumes the rear tyre and violently kicks out the rear of the vehicle. The man riding the rear passenger side door struggles to stay on and grabs for the door's frame in front of him with his handgun hand. He slaps the weapon against the door's frame and it fires, shooting the man in the front passenger seat in the back of the head.

My grip on the radio tightens as they speed towards the marker for the second charge: an orange whip aerial.

I yell out "Ka-boom!" and squeeze the call button for the second charge. Nothing happens.

I click it several times.

It's a dud.

"Fuck!"

I drop the radio and grab for the third.

ROUND II:
WE'RE SURROUNDED

With its three remaining passengers, the speeding Land Cruiser passes over the second charge unhindered and barrels towards us. The two passengers start firing and stray bullets punch into the dirt and barricades around me.

"Get down!" I call out to Natalie.

She ducks down behind a metal skip bin beside her, but tries to keep her eyes on the road above us.

I peer around the side of the barricade, "Come on."

I nod my head encouragingly at the vehicle, urging it to veer right and toward the last charge. Like a ten-pin bowler convincing his ball to change course and hit the desired pins. The men in the vehicle hoot and holler as they fire wildly into the compound when they cross the marker; half of a hard hat, the final charge in the driveway. I squeeze the call button hard and the charge detonates. Thank fuck.

A fireball erupts beneath the Land Cruiser and sends the back of it skywards, the vehicle's nose buries itself deep into the loose gravel and flips sideways towards some nearby boulders. The man riding the rear door loses his grip again and as he attempts to grab at the vehicle's roof from the inside, he inadvertently shoots the man across from him in the stomach. The man with the gutshot is flung from the vehicle and cartwheels through the air. He hits the dirt awkwardly and breaks his back as he scorpions himself. The Cruiser completes its sideways roll and crumples against a pile of large boulders, crushing the friendly-firing, crack-shot rear passenger.

"Holy shit, that charge packed a punch!" I stand up and turn to Natalie, "Did you see that?!"

Natalie turns away from the cliff track, "I felt that in my chest, Dan. Wow."

I laugh to myself, looking at the new burning wrecks now littering the driveway when shots from above hit a diesel drum nearby. I duck instinctively and before my knees hit the dirt, Natalie returns three shots at the man on the road above us.

"Fuck me, kill that back-door-bill cunt!" I urge.

"On it!"

Natalie fires up at the hillside and clips the shoulder of the man squatting behind the log. I fire blindly at the hill above too, trying to distract the gunman long enough for Natalie to shoot him, but then the second Land Cruiser comes over the rise in the driveway and towards the front gates.

"Shit," with no more road charges at my disposal, I have to rely on my rifle.

"He's running away!" Natalie calls out.

I turn and look up to the hillside road and see the back of the man retreating out of sight, clutching his left arm.

"Keep that radio handy! You know he's coming back with that fucking machine gun!"

On the driveway, the Land Cruiser approaches more hesitantly, aware that the road may have more hidden explosives. He drives around the first crater and then turns hard and parks behind the mound of boulders that the first vehicle flipped into.

"Clever girl."

I'm slightly relieved that the men took cover and didn't try to ram the gates. The men exit the vehicle, but the smoke from the burning Cruiser obscures part of the road and I can't see them fully. I grab the ammo bag and scurry to the concrete barrier beside me. I raise my rifle as a man in a blue shirt sprints across the driveway towards a smaller pile of boulders on the other side. I fire two rounds at him, but only hit the dirt at his feet, missing him entirely. Another man attempts the same run, but trips over some debris. He sprawls out on the gravel road, and drops his assault rifle. The man tries to get to his feet but I shoot him twice in the side of his chest and he drops facedown into the dirt. Both men on either side of the road start yelling to each other, trying to organise their efforts. The third member of the party lies dead in the dirt. I only hear fragments of their conversation.

"They killed him, they… Raymond!"

"Hold 'em down… until… gets here!"

I see a shorter, round man by the Land Cruiser pick up a hand-held radio and yell into it.

"Keith… Keith… bring… down. Now!"

"Natalie, they've got radios! Something's coming!"

"Check the monitor!" she calls back.

I jump back to the previous barricade where I left the monitor and eyeball the screen and see the vehicle on the rear track coming to the top of the cliff edge above Natalie.

"The hill!" I yell out, I point aggressively at the range.

Bang! Bang!

Two shots ring out from the duo on the driveway in front of me and I dive behind the barricade. I pull out one of Nat's handguns and fire blindly back at them.

"Dan!" Natalie swings her rifle toward the driveway and empties an entire magazine at a man crouched by the four wheel drive near the boulders.

The vehicle with the mounted gun races to the cliff's edge above and slides to a stop. Natalie and I whip around to see a man aiming an automatic assault rifle out of the driver's side window. Another man pops out of a manhole and stands behind a roof-mounted heavy machine gun. He swings the weapon towards us and both men open fire.

"Get down!"

I drop behind a barricade, and Natalie crouches down beside the steel skip bin full of building rubble. Round after round slams into the dirt around us and bullets ricochet off the steel hull of the skip bin. The concrete road barriers are peppered with the rhythmic boom, boom, boom, boom of the heavy machine gunfire.

"Natalie! Are they near the charge?"

Natalie is crouching in a ball behind the low cover of the skip bin. The bombardment of bullets raining down on her eats away at the bin and the nearby concrete barriers, showering her with chunks of concrete. Natalie covers her ears and face. She looks up at me, helpless—the two men are focusing their fire on her and her alone.

"Your radio! Press the call button!"

I hold out my radio and wave it at her, hoping she understands. Natalie sees the radio and snaps into action, she reaches out for her radio in the dirt, but she's pinned down by the gunmen. She flinches at every bullet impact into the dirt. I fire my handgun aimlessly at the upper road, trying to buy her a window to get to the radio that's only inches away from her feet. She leans up against the skip bin and waits for her moment, when the booming of the large gun stops. He's jammed. I see the gunman struggle with the weapon. Natalie grabs the radio and scans the ridgeline. Several rounds from the driver pepper the interior of the skip bin, she ducks back down.

"Shit! Dan, I'm blowing the charge!"

"Now, do it now!"

Natalie squeezes her eyes shut just as the booming from the mounted gun resumes. She takes a quick breath and then presses the call button. The charge detonates impressively and launches the Cruiser sideways off the cliff. It tumbles violently down the cliff's steep face.

The man standing in the roof's manhole is crushed on the second roll down the cliff face, his lifeless body rag dolls for the rest of the fall. The vehicle comes to a sickening halt when it lands upside down on a bed of jagged rocks. Part of the cliff slides down and buries one side of the vehicle. I look over to Natalie as she slowly stands and looks up at the road. More loose boulders and earth slide down from the upper road and pile up against the side of the compound's outer fence. We hear yelling from inside the Cruiser's cab, someone is still alive, Natalie raises her rifle and opens fire.

"You piece of shit!" Natalie yells.

She starts firing at the vehicle.

"For fuck's sake. Natalie, wait!"

I run over to her and grab her shoulder, but she shrugs me off and continues putting holes into the vehicle.

Fuel trickles down the chassis toward the smoking engine. Natalie spies the loose red jerry cans protruding out of the smashed rear window and fires at them just before I pull her to the ground. The two men behind the rocks in the driveway start shooting at us. I take her by the hand and run back to the centre barricades. Natalie shakes uncontrollably. I sit her down in front of me and try to calm her down.

"Nat, Natalie. They're dead. We're fine. Look at me, look," I place my hand on either side of her face and stare into her wild eyes as she starts to tear up.

"I was so scared," Natalie starts, she's unable to control her breathing, "And... And... You were over there and the bullets were coming! That sound, that boom, boom, boom it, it..." I pull Natalie in and hug her tightly.

"Natalie, you did so well. Let's kill these last few guys, and then we'll drive to Fremantle and get you away from all of this. You'll get to meet my daughter, Bella's going to love you!" I run my fingers through her frizzy, concrete dust-filled hair, "She will go bonkers when she sees how crazy your hair is."

Natalie laughs, "Really?"

"Yes, really. Come on, let's kill your mate in that yellow fuckin' dump truck and be done with it."

Natalie nods and pulls herself up, wiping the tears from her cheeks, the concrete dust colours her tears a milky grey.

"Okay, Dan," she leans in and kisses me, her wet, tear-soaked lips press hard into mine.

Panicked yells come from the Land Cruiser beneath the cliff debris. The guy inside is still alive. We hear the hissing of fuel as it pools against the hot engine. A spark ignites the fuel and engulfs the vehicle in tall orange flames. The trapped man screams. We look on in horror as flames spew out from the cab. Natalie buries her head into my chest.

Bang!

Bang, bang!

The guy by the vehicle in the driveway starts firing into the burning Land Cruiser.

"Shoot him, Spud. Put him out of his misery!" he yells.

The man in the blue shirt, Spud, hesitates and doesn't fire a shot, but the man across the driveway fires several shots into the Land Cruiser and the screaming stops.

"You. You bastards!" Spud yells out from behind his rocky cover. "Norton! Norton! My brother, you just killed my fucking brother! Argh! You're fucking dead, you dog cunts! Dead!"

I call out, "We didn't shoot him, dickhead! Your mate just killed him!"

"Ooaah, nah! You're fucked, now."

Spud stands up and marches toward us with his rifle high, unleashing one shot after another.

"Fuck, Nat, stay down. I'll go over there and try to draw his fire."

Natalie fires a shot back at the gunman to cover me. I run low and fast toward the outer barricades. I overhear the rounder man by the four wheel drive yelling at his friend in the blue shirt to get back and stop being stupid, but I think

Spud has his heart set on stupid.

The man marches toward us, firing at random with his rifle. He walks straight down the centre of the driveway until he stands level with the flaming wreck, where his brother is. The body is hanging halfway out of the driver's side window and is still burning. Spud looks across at the upturned four wheel drive and wails. He grips his rifle tightly and unloads everything he has into the compound. As soon as we hear him run out of ammo, Natalie pops up to shoot him, but quickly squats back down as a bullet whistles past her head. The other man in the driveway is covering Spud. I fire a few rounds at the man by the vehicle and force him to take cover. I turn my rifle to Spud and see him throw his rifle into the dirt.

Is he surrendering?

"Natalie, cover that fat fuck in the corner! I'll watch Mr Blue Shirt."

Spud walks toward the burning Land Cruiser, his legs wobbling as he does, looking like they may buckle beneath him at any moment. He wails loudly as he nears the wreckage and sees the blackening torso of his brother hanging out of the cab. Spud tries to get closer to his brother, but the heat from the flames forces him backwards. He brings his hand up to protect his face and stands there sobbing. Natalie fires at the man by the four wheel drive again as he pops his head out to see what is happening.

"Stay on him, Nat," I call out.

"What is that man doing? Why aren't we shooting him?"

"He's grieving, Natalie, give him a sec."

Mr Blue Shirt looks over at me, his swollen, red face is wet with tears. His eyebrows furrow, wanting to be angry, but his sadness overpowers it. He just stands there crying. He pulls a handgun from the waist of his pants and I tighten my grip on the rifle. He holds his gun loosely by his side, tapping it nervously against his thigh.

Natalie fires another round at the fat man as he peers his head out, "He's getting restless, Dan."

I'm fixated on the broken man in the blue shirt as he crumbles to his knees in the dirt, he's crying loudly and yelling at the sky. I take my rifle and aim at the base of the man's skull and place my finger on the trigger. The man looks down into his lap at the handgun, letting the weight of it shift between in his hands. He clicks the safety off.

Natalie fires another round at the fat man.

"What are we doing, Dan?" Natalie demands.

Before I could answer her, Spud nods to himself and starts crawling on his hands and knees toward the blazing Land Cruiser.

"What the fuck?" I mouth to myself. I call out to Spud, "Mate, what are you doing?!"

He ignores me and pushes forward toward his brother, covering his face from the intensity of the car fire's heat with his arm. He crawls as close as he can and then starts crawling toward it on his belly.

"Dan, is he trying to save his brother? He's dead?" Natalie asks. I put my rifle down.

"I think he's trying to join his brother," I sigh, "I'd look away if I were you."

"What? Why?"

And just as those words left Natalie's mouth, Spud grabs the blackened hand of his dead brother, kisses it and then sprawls out onto his back and shoots himself in the head. All three of us stare at Spud, shocked.

Natalie snaps herself out of it first and takes a shot at the man down the driveway. The bullet explodes through his elbow and he falls back in agony.

"Snap out of it, Dan, bring me the monitor!" Natalie brings me back into reality.

"Uh, yes. Got it. Coming, dear."

I cross the yard and pick up the monitor.

"I don't think the fat man will be much of a problem anymore, I shot his elbow. Did you see that?"

"The elbow?! Fuck. Good work, Nat. Let's see where your mate in the dump truck is."

I shake the sand and spent ammunition out of the monitor box and look intently at the screen. The giant yellow monstrosity is just over the rise in the driveway and turning around. He's now facing back toward Kalgoorlie.

"He's leaving! We scared him off!" Natalie yells.

I manipulate the camera controls and focus on the dump truck's tray to finally get a good look at the strange structure filling it.

"It's probably a good thing that he's leaving. Look what's in the back of that dump truck."

I turn the screen to show Natalie.

"What is that?" she asks.

"That's our worst nightmare."

ROUND III:
THE MAN IN THE YELLOW MONSTER

The tray of the dump truck is rimmed with aluminium scaffolding that's bracing a metre-wide length of chain-link fencing and large coils of barbed wire. The fortification is angled inward, toward the centre of the tray, to prevent its captives from climbing out. The people inside the make-shift prison are shoulder to shoulder and crammed into it like sardines. Some of them are tangled up in the multiple rows of barbed wire that border the open edge of the dump truck's tray.

"Oh my God, are they prisoners? Is that where we are going to end up?" Natalie questions.

"No," I reply bluntly, "They're not people, well, not anymore. They're all infected. Look."

I toggle the joystick on the camera's controls to zoom in, grey flesh and limbless monsters fill the screen; fifty to sixty zombies at least. I zoom out quickly and the monitor screen shows the dump truck parked on the soft shoulder, halfway down the driveway.

"What's he doing? Why did he stop?"

"I don't know, maybe he's stuck?"

The familiar sound of a reversing alarm starts barking.

"Fuck," we both realise what's happening. "I think they're meant for us, he's going to dump them in here."

We look at each other, horrified.

"Grab your things, let's go!" Natalie commands.

"You don't have to tell me twice."

We stand up to head for the Hilux when a spray of bullets hits the demountable building closest to Natalie. We hit the dirt and take cover.

"Jesus, was that the fat man, Dan?"

"Yeah, but that sounds much bigger than the rifle he had before!"

I peek over the barrier to see where the fat man is shooting from. It takes a moment, but I see him lying on his belly in the dirt between the pile of boulders and his Land Cruiser. A large rifle barrel is sticking out from between two boulders, a small tripod is at the end of it, stabilising the muzzle.

"Holy shit, I think that's an M60!"

"What's an M60, Dan?"

A hail of automatic fire from the heavy machine gun answers that question for me.

"That! We need to move back, go to the last barrier at the back of the compound and grab everything!"

We move back to the second row of concrete barriers and take stock of what we have left. We are getting low on rifle ammunition. Fuck. We still have the handguns, two shotguns, an assault rifle, a few smoke bombs and, of course, our drone bomb. I pop my head over the barrier to see the rear of the yellow CAT 793 dump truck dominating the landscape. Both visually and audibly. Its roaring engine and incessant reversing alarm barks over the top of the bursts of automatic fire; it's a cacophony of chaos.

"It's so loud!" Natalie yells,

"I know, let's send in the drone bomb! Can you fly it?"

"Yes, what am I aiming for?"

"The driver's cab at the front, under the overhang of the tray. If you fly it in from the side, straight at the windows, the explosion should definitely kill him. Take the controller and get behind the last barricade. I'll distract the fat man on the ground."

"Okay, I'm opening the first gate, in case we have to leave quickly," Natalie says.

"Brilliant!"

Natalie runs to the rear barriers as I spend the last of my rifle's ammunition forcing the fat man to take cover. Luckily, Natalie left me one of her larger rifles as backup. I pick it up, and the weight of it, and its matte black finish, brings a smile to my face.

The massive dump truck comes to a stop twenty metres short of the first crater and its reversing alarm ceases. The crackling of a P.A. system comes to life and the nasal voice of a heavy-set man booms from two large speakers mounted on the tray of the dump truck.

"Attention. This is your captain speaking," the voice mocks, "I've always wanted to say that," he laughs into the microphone. His breathy cackle sounds like a disturbing mix of Seth Rogen's iconic stoner chuckle and the sadistic laugh of *Wolf Creek's* antagonist, Mick Taylor.

"Now, who's the bastard with all of the explosives? You've killed a handful of my best guys."

I look back at Natalie and whisper-yell, "Is the drone ready?" I point to the left-hand side of the canyon, "The cab is on that side, line up a clear shot and wait!"

Natalie gives me a thumbs up and ducks behind her concrete barrier to operate the drone.

"Ah, it must be you, ya fuckin' dickhead," the dump truck's speakers accuse.

"How the fuck can he see me? Where is he?"

I pop my head up and try to find him, but I only see the fat man on the ground. He's struggling to lift the M60 to a new position, onto a flat rock at shoulder height, his face is red and sweaty with effort. I lift the rifle onto the barricade and fire at him twice, the stock of Natalie's rifle belts my shoulder as a fire—this thing has got some fucking kick to it. The fat man ducks for cover and leaves his M60 on its side.

"I've got cameras around the whole truck, dickhead! I can see everything! 360° range of view, mate. I don't even need to leave my seat to see ya!" the voice taunts.

"Now, where's that Spanish slut hiding?"

Natalie's right arm flings up from behind the barrier and she flips him off.

"Oh, still as feisty as ever, hey, girly? That's nothing a good fuckin' won't fix."

I clench my rifle, my face distorts angrily.

"As soon as I get a hold of you, girly, I'll be fucking you day and night for a very, very long time." The man laughs disgustingly into the microphone, "I just hope your pussy holds out for a few months!"

I glare over the top of the concrete divider and see the cameras mounted under the dump truck's tray. I fire at one of them and it shatters into a thousand pieces.

"This must be the new boyfriend, nice try, moron, but I can still"—I interrupt the arrogant piece of shit by destroying the second rear camera.

"You were saying, cunt?!" I yell out.

The man sighs loudly into the microphone.

"Two things, dickhead," the voice starts, "One, you're going to regret being a trigger-happy smartarse and, two, I can't fucking hear ya from all the way up here, mate, so shut ya fucking mouth! Let me introduce myself, I'm Keith Turner, and I'll be taking that little brown slut off of your hands. Me and the boys have big plans for her. It's date night!"

I duck down and try to get Natalie's attention, "Nat, are you ready?!" Natalie's hand appears from behind the barrier with a thumbs up, "Nice, okay. Wait for my signal and then fly that drone right into his cocky fucking mouth."

"With pleasure!" Natalie calls out.

"Don't interrupt me again, cunt, you have a choice to make. Now, you can stay in there with that little slut or you can walk that brown bitch up to the front gate, hand her over to us and that will be the end of it for you. We will leave with the girl and you can go back to wherever the fuck you crawled out from. Choose quickly or I'm going to dump these zombie cunts in there with ya's while my 2IC, Brian, mows you both down with that M60." Keith pauses for a moment, "I'll let you think it over."

Natalie raises her head above the barrier and throws an

anxious look my way.

I shake my head at her, "I'm not handing you over, Nat. We're leaving here together."

She smiles back at me.

"Send him our answer by air, Nat!" I yell.

Natalie ducks behind the barrier and pilots the drone. I spring to my feet and heave the rifle up onto an empty fuel drum. I start firing round after round at the fat man, Brian.

"Does this answer your question, cunt?!"

Brian falls backwards behind the boulders, so I start firing at the colossal tyres of the yellow beast idling in the driveway.

"I see you've made your choice. Pfft. What a waste of good pussy," Keith's broadcast finishes and the reversing alarm starts again.

I watch the drone make a beeline for the dump truck's operator's cab. It flies low and fast along the top of the range, all it has to do is cross the open air between the cliff face and the driver's cab and this saga ends. I fire off the last two rounds of my magazine into the fat man's Cruiser and then duck behind the concrete divider. I watch the drone fly over the cliff face and into the open air of the valley, pleased that only metres stand between it and the cab.

Two shots ring out from the dump truck's cab, "Shit!" Natalie yells. "He's shooting at the drone, Dan!"

One of the drone's four propellers disintegrates and the drone banks steeply to one side.

"Fuck!"

Natalie thumbs the joysticks hard, trying to force the drone back on course. Keith, distracted by the incoming drone bomb, loses control of the yellow monster, he begins swerving and snaking backwards down the driveway.

"I can't fly it properly, Dan!" Natalie cries.

"Kamikaze it!! Fly straight into him!"

Natalie tries to steady the drone, but she over-corrects and flies it high above the driver's cabin and over the dump truck's tray.

"Shit, shit!" She tries to regain control of the drone.

"Go higher, go higher," I call, urging the drone to climb, but the drone dips too low and banks hard into the tray. One of the drone's propeller arms gets tangled in the barbed-wire coil. One end of the coil unclips from the fence and allows the tangled drone to climb upwards. The drone flies high, intent on untangling itself, when the barbed-wire coil becomes taut and swings the drone down like a hammer into the steel side of the tray. The explosive's barbeque lighter detonators trigger.

An explosion rips through the tray of the dump truck, turning a third of its zombie captives into red paint and blowing the fenced structure apart.

"You sly fuckin'..." Keith spits over the P.A. system, cutting himself off as he struggles to control the truck. I watch eagerly as the truck rocks and then swerves toward the fat man and his vehicle.

"Oooh, I think he's gonna..."

The dump truck powers backwards blindly on a collision course with Brian's Land Cruiser.

"Yep, he's going to..." I wince at the pending impact.

The giant tyre of the dump truck slams into the side of the Cruiser; crushing it, and Brian, into the cliff wall and kills him instantly. The tray of the yellow dump truck hits the canyon wall with an almighty thud and the engine stalls.

"We did it!" Natalie celebrates, jumping to her feet. She drops the drone's remote excitedly, "Yes!"

She jumps the barrier and runs over to me.

"Wait, wait. That wouldn't have killed him."

I grab Natalie by the shoulders and turn back toward the stalled dump truck. Keith's voice crackles out of the one remaining speaker.

"Nice try. You almost had me there, but..." —the dump truck comes back to life— "It'll take a little bit more than that to stop what's coming to you both!"

The truck lumbers forward onto the driveway and straightens up. The tray points toward the compound again, and the familiar sound of the reversing alarm resumes.

"Fuck, get the guns and unlock the last back gate, we're leaving now," the truck speeds backwards towards us, "Move, move, move!" I yell.

Natalie bounds over the concrete dividers, but on the last one, she slips on something on the loose gravel as she lands. Her ankle bends unnaturally and it makes a sickening crack as she falls to the ground.

"Ahh, Dan! My ankle!" Natalie cries.

"Fuck!" I race over to Natalie.

I jump over the same barrier and crush something into the gravel as I land. Another explosion booms in the valley.

I take cover behind the barricade with Natalie.

"Natalie! Are you okay?!"

"Yes, well, no. My ankle. What was that explosion?"

"I don't know, stay down, I'll check it out."

I pick myself up and look under my boot to see what I crushed. I see the radio marked '#2' broken in the gravel.

"Ha, ha! Would you look at that, better late than never,

eh?" I pick up the broken radio and kiss it, "You lil' beauty!"

The dump truck sits motionless in the driveway, its driver's side rear tyres are in tatters; strips of thick black rubber hang from the outer dual tyre, and its rims sit deep in a large crater. The inner tyre on the passenger side has taken some shrapnel too; it hisses loudly as air escapes from it. That truck is going nowhere fast.

I kneel to help Natalie with her ankle; she's frantically undoing her bootlaces.

"Natalie, stop, stop, stop," I place both of my hands around hers as she tries to remove her boot, "Keep the boot on, it'll help support it until we can have a proper look at it. Once we're far, far away from here."

Natalie's face is red and wet with tears as she fidgets.

"I'm not crying because it hurts," Natalie tries to assure me, "I'm crying because I'll slow you down now and… and I don't want to be left here."

"Natalie, all you have to do is get to the Hilux, it's just there. And I'm right here to help you, okay? Leave this stuff here, I'll come back for it. Let's get you into the ute."

Natalie nods, wiping the tears from her face. I throw Natalie's arm around my neck and limp her around the concrete barriers toward the back gates.

"Oh, you two fuckers have done it now," Keith taunts over the speaker.

I spin around to see the dump truck struggling to free itself from the crater. Its damaged rear tyres can't gain any traction and the back axle is digging into the road like an anchor.

"Come on, Nat, move that beautiful ass."

Natalie laughs as we hobble through the first set of gates.

259

I lean her against the chain-link fence so I can open the outer gates and drive the Hilux into the space between the two. I open the passenger door to help Natalie into her seat.

"There you go, sound the horn if there's any trouble. I'll be right back," I kiss her forehead and jog back into the compound.

"Please hurry, Dan!"

The dump truck rocks back and forth as it strains to free itself from the deep crater and the truck stalls.

"Ya fuckin' bastards! You're both dead, ya hear me, dead! I'll show you, fuckin' mongrels..."

Keith climbs down the cab's access ladder, awkwardly juggling his slinged arm and an army green duffle bag. He reaches the ground and walks towards the back of his dump truck. I quickly grab my handgun and take cover alongside the wall of the demountable building. Now's my chance to end this piece of shit.

The heavy-set man walks past his grounded beast and stares back at the shredded tyres and the crater it's stuck in. He swears angrily at it before casting his gaze toward the compound.

"You!" he points directly at me.

I fire two shots at him but miss completely. Keith dives behind the remaining rear tyres of the dump truck. I look into the compound and see the rifle Natalie had given me propped up against a concrete barricade.

"I need that rifle."

I look over to the dump truck and see Keith kneeling on the ground and elbow deep in his duffle bag.

"Oh, that can't be good."

I fire at him and to force him back behind the tyres, but

he manages to drag the duffle bag in with him.

Keith emerges from behind the tyres brandishing a grey Steyr AUG assault rifle, the Australian Forces' weapon of choice, one-handed. A thick, black utility belt swings from the hand poking out of the white sling of his injured arm. Keith lifts the assault rifle, smiling widely, and then opens fire at the compound.

"Fuckinell!"

I drop to the ground and scurry to the nearest barricade and kneel against it. I look over at Natalie, happy to see her slam the car door shut and fold herself into the footwell of the vehicle.

ROUND IV: SUDDEN DEATH

Bursts of automatic gunfire pin me down as Keith marches forward unchecked. I fire blindly at him over the concrete divider, but he returns fire tenfold. I crouch down as low as I can as bullets smash into the barrier, chunks of concrete explode everywhere. I grunt and groan, fighting between the urge to run and the need to stay behind cover. I look at the next row of barriers and see the barrel of Natalie's rifle standing tall.

"That's my ticket outta here."

I brace my heel against the concrete divider, preparing to sprint over to the next divider as soon as Keith stops to reload. The rifle fire stops.

"Go! Go! Go!" I prompt myself.

I power forward and jump over the concrete hurdle, grab the rifle by its barrel and roll into the dirt. I don't hear any shots ring out, so I push forward the next barrier.

My heart is pounding in my chest as I charge over the last barrier. I make it. I slap the rifle's bolt back and forth and shoulder it just as Keith shoulders his weapon too. I fire at him as he unleashes two bursts of automatic fire and we both duck for cover.

"Dan! Come on, let's go!" Natalie yells from the partially open passenger door. Her call is met with a flurry of bullets.

"Stay down!" I urge, "I'll be there in a sec!"

I reload the handgun and fire blindly over the barrier again, my body tenses, anticipating return fire but nothing happens. It's a trap, I convince myself; I stay low and wait. I hear Keith yelling something and he starts firing. But nothing enters the compound, I peer cautiously over the barrier. I bob my head up and down from my concrete cover, trying to see him.

"I feel like a fuckin' meerkat out here."

Keith is shooting at two zombies as they run at him across the driveway. He shoots up at another zombie as it leaps from the tray of the yellow dump truck. It screams all the way down and then goes silent as it hits the ground with a heavy thud.

The detonation of the drone bomb in the dump truck's tray had severely damaged the makeshift jail and excited its zombie cargo. They claw at the twisted reels of barbed wire and climb over the hot, wet piles of eviscerated corpses. Several zombies climb over the entangled ones and use them as a meat bridge. They jump from the tray and into the action on the ground.

I watch intently, hoping the zombies overwhelm Keith. The escaping infected fall clumsily out of the tray, some seem to leap from it, whatever the case, each escapee breaks its arms or legs as it hits the hard red earth below them.

Keith hastily executes a handful of zombies that lay buckled and writhing in the dirt before he drops his rifle and runs towards the compound's front gates. He struggles to free something from his heavy black utility belt.

"What the fuck is he doing?"

I stand tall and fire at him as he runs for the gates. He zigs and zags side to side as he barrels forward. This guy must've been a rugby player or something because he can sure move for a guy his size. Keith pulls something from his belt and then overarm throws it like a cricketer at the front gates. The round object sails high as he plucks another metallic avocado from the belt and piffs that towards the propane tank and fuel drums. He lobs one more at the demountable building and then doubles back towards the pile of boulders in the driveway and takes cover.

The first metal avocado lands at the foot of the heavy front gate and explodes. The steel frame buckles and the gate bounces off its track and falls into the compound. It gets hung up and it leans over at an angle.

The second avocado, clearly a grenade, blows up between the fuel drums and sends two barrels flying sky high. The blast sends a destructive shockwave down the fence line and several flaming drums roll beneath the propane tank.

The third grenade explodes beneath the demountable building, the corrugated sheeting from the outer walls is shredded and fibreglass insulation scatters everywhere.

"Dan? Dan?!" Natalie cracks open the passenger door.

I throw my hand up, "I'm fine, I'm okay. He has

grenades! The front gate is gone and the fuel barrels are about to go up in flames!"

"Dan, look. He's running back to his dump truck."

Keith is at the bottom of the access ladder to the dump truck's cabin.

"That's my queue!" I grab the rifle, shotgun and ammo bag and run back to the ute. I throw all of that shit into the back seat and then rush to Natalie's open door.

"Babe, come on. We're getting out of here," I pull Natalie out of the footwell and I sit her comfortably in the passenger seat.

"Buckle up, it's going to be a bumpy ride."

"Where did he go, Dan?" Natalie twists and bops in her seat, looking back toward Keith as I try to slide her seat backwards. I frantically jiggle and pull on the lever beneath her seat to accommodate her injured ankle.

"It doesn't matter where he went, he can't go anywhere in that dump truck. He's stuck there. We're not."

Feedback from a dump truck's P.A. system pierces the air, and we hear Keith's voice again, his breathing is laboured and his speech staggered.

"You're not the only one with a trick or two up his sleeve, mate," he laughs into a handheld microphone, "Here's a little something I prepared earlier," he cackles louder into the microphone.

Natalie and I look through the compound at the yellow dump truck and see Keith standing on top of the blackened hood of the dump truck's tray. He's in a metal box that's welded to the overhang above the driver's cabin. The front panel of the box looks to be a section of tread plate and comes up to the height of his armpits. It's two metres wide has two more sheets of steel that taper off from the front panel, shielding his sides as the panels stretch behind him.

Keith holds a cabled remote high in the air and pushes a button. The whirr of a hydraulic ram arm extending signals the start of the yellow beast dumping the contents of its tray.

"Aww, get fucked!"

I close Natalie's door and race to the gate in front of the ute to remove the lock. But the exterior gates are buckled. The length of the chain between the two gates is taut, the padlock itself is open but the tension in the chain holds it in place.

"Dan, what's wrong?"

"The grenades, they buckled the fences. The gate won't open," I strain against the lock, trying to twist it free.

Bap, bap, bap.

Three bullets hit the ground in front of me.

"Fuck!"

I duck down in front of the vehicle and shuffle around to the driver's side of the ute to open my door.

"Hand me the rifle, Nat!"

Natalie quickly juts it into my hands.

The passenger side wing mirror shatters and Natalie squats back down into the footwell.

"Stay down, we're almost out of here."

"Hurry!" Natalie calls out.

I creep down the side of the vehicle and see the dump truck still tipping. It's well beyond a 45-degree angle and the tray's contents are spewing out onto the red gravel floor of the valley driveway. The heavy thuds of the bodies hitting the floor are nothing compared to the screams of the zombies that clamber to their feet and burst into sprints.

My eyes widen in fear. Confusion strikes me at how alarmingly quick the zombies explode onto their feet.

I've never seen zombies sprint like that before. How are they running so fast? A burst of automatic fire from the man in the steel box grabs my attention.

"Do you like my presents? Fast, aren't they?" Keith taunts, "It turns out that with just a little encouragement from our friend crystal meth, zombies become faster, more violent and worse than those vaccinated fuckers!"

"What?!"

I see a group of meth-crazed zombies scaling the downed front gate and three others sprinting along the outer fence. Another pack claws at the base of the dump truck, trying to get at Keith and the speaker booming his voice. It's a frenzy.

"Natalie, I need your help. Get a gun and try to pick off those bastards sprinting down the fence line, my sawn-off is under the seat if you need it!"

"Sprinting? Dan, did you say the zombies are *sprinting*?"

Natalie pushes herself up and out of the footwell to look. Her eyes confirm what I said, she sees three meth-fuelled creatures flying down the side of the outer perimeter fence at frightening speed.

"Yes, sprinting! I'll try to shoot Keith out of his lil' box, you keep those guys off our arses," I bark.

Natalie arms herself with a handgun and waits for the trio to get closer to her. I focus on the two muscular Māori zombies in orange Hi-Vis workwear in front of me. They clear the first set of concrete dividers like it's nothing, and move with such ferocity and precision, surely, they can't be zombies. I pump two pistol rounds into the bigger guy's chest, but he keeps coming.

"Well, they're definitely zombies. Fuck."

The duo clear the second set of barricades. I grab Natalie's rifle and fire a fat round into the midsection of the zombie athlete who's currently winning the 200m hurdle event through the compound. His hip shatters and putrid gore sprays out of his abdomen as he buckles forward and dives headfirst into the next concrete barrier, killing him. The second zombie surges past his downed opponent and runs toward me with white foam and stringy saliva hanging from his screaming maw. He jumps high over the final barrier and I blast a hole through his chest. He crumples into the dirt less than ten metres in front of me. The hurdler strains to his feet and lets out a guttural howl as he stands tall; his head explodes. I duck behind the vehicle quickly; I didn't fire that shot.

"Fuck. Looks like I need to work on my aim. I meant to split your head open like a melon," Keith announces. Displeased that he is helping, rather than hindering, my survival attempts.

I squint hard to see through the smoke of the drum fire and the sun's glare, Keith is perched high and comfortably sitting in his small grey box. The dump truck tray is now at full tilt, giving Keith the best seat in the house. He gets the view, the high ground and the comfort of knowing he's well out of the zombies' reach. The dump truck's undead cargo scurry around below it like pissed-off ants hunting for the kid who just kicked their anthill. Twenty zombies fill the area between me and the dump truck: most are in a pile on the ground, four are trying to clamber up the side of the truck's wheels, two more are chasing after the three zombies making their way down the side fence and a couple of zombies are trapped in the mess of chain-link fencing at the front gate. The remaining infected run aimlessly back and forth between the front gate and the dump truck; their indecision benefits me greatly.

Natalie eyes the three zombies rounding the last corner of the outer perimeter fence and she opens fire. She drops the first one with a bullet through the eye, it falls to the dirt and trips the second one, who flies face-first into a rock and caves its face in. The third zombie—an Asian woman in crisp business wear sporting a long, perfectly straight ponytail—stops midrun and claws her way along the fence line, screaming as she hunts for her prey.

"My God! Look at this crazy bitch."

The Asian lady homes in on Natalie's voice. Target acquired. She lets go of the fence and bursts into a sprint again. Natalie leans out of the open window and fires at the Asian woman, but she misses her completely. She empties the rest of her clip into the mental oriental but only manages to nick her twice in the shoulder.

"Dan, help!"

The lady tears at the buckled gates directly in front of the Hilux's bonnet as Natalie reloads her handgun. Her hands shake uncontrollably.

"Come on, come on. You stupid thing. Ay!"

Natalie urges the slippery bullets to comply. Her head snaps up and down as she tries to keep an eye on her new Asian friend and the handgun in her lap.

"Ah! Perfecto!"

She slides the magazine into the base of the handgun

and propels the gun forward with both hands ready to kill the Asian woman, but she's not there.

"Where? Where did she go? Dan!"

Natalie pushes herself up off her seat to look over the bonnet, but sees nothing, "Dan!"

I fire at Keith in his metal box and then prop my rifle against the side of the vehicle. I race to the front of the Hilux with my handgun drawn but there's nothing there.

"Nat, where'd she go?"

"I... I... I don't know. She was right there."

Natalie starts to hyperventilate. I look at the base of the buckled gates and see a tattered strip of material caught on the locking pin of the gate. I look closer at the ground and see a distinct slide mark of disturbed gravel leading under the car.

"She's under the car!" I yell.

I drop to the ground near the driver's side door and frantically look for the Asian woman. I pause, terrified, as I see two slender ankles standing on the other side of the vehicle.

"Nat!"—One glossy black slip-on shoe slowly steps onto the running board and then the other— "Nat, she's on your side! She's on the door!"

Natalie grabs the door with her left hand and leans out of the open window cautiously. Her head clears the door panel and she sees the Asian woman clinging to the side of the vehicle like some kind of rotting, acrobatic koala. The woman's head snaps up and she screams at Natalie, who panics and fires the handgun through the roof of the Hilux. The Asian woman springs up and swings herself in through the window, snapping her teeth together as she attacks. I sprint around the back of the Hilux, carelessly firing two shots toward the man in the box to keep him at bay. I slide around the side of the vehicle and see the zombie's legs kicking viciously in the air as she tries to force herself further into the car.

Inside the cab, Natalie frantically tries to block the flurry of slashing hands clawing at her. I rush up to the passenger side door and press my gun to the base of the Asian lady's spine between her hips and fire. Her legs stop kicking and I grab them. I loop my arms around her waist and slam my foot against the door and heave backwards. Natalie fends off the swipes of the meth-fuelled, undead woman with her bare hands. She grabs the door's window frame with her left hand and punches the lady in the face hard with her right. A sickening crack sounds as the Asian woman's nose breaks. I pull the lady off of Natalie and try to rip her out of the cab, but she grabs the window frame and pins Natalie's hand to it. Natalie desperately tries to free her hand.

I heave harder. I almost have her out when the woman's grey eyes snap to Natalie's pinned hand. She screeches excitedly, bares her teeth and lunges forward, sinking her teeth into the meat of Natalie's hand.

Natalie screams in horror as the small bones in her hand crunch inside the woman's fetid mouth. I finally rip the cunt out of the Hilux and roll her onto her stomach. I punch her in the back of the head with the butt of my pistol repeatedly before shooting her in the skull. Natalie wails inside the cab staring at her bloodied hand and two missing fingers.

"Dan! Dan!!"

I jump to my feet and stand at the passenger door.

"No, no, no! No!"

I'm mortified. "Nat, we have to"—a rear window shatters as gunfire hits the side of the ute.

"Shit, get down!"

I scurry to the front of the Hilux near the buckled gates and squat in front of the roo bar. Natalie holds her mangled hand out in front of her as tears course down her face.

"What do I do? What do I do?! Dan!"

"Natalie, try to stay calm. Breathe."

"Dan, am I infected?! Am I going to turn into one of those things?! What do I do?"

The gravity of the situation hits both of us.

"No, Nat. We have to act fast."

"What do you mean?"

The two zombies that were tailing the others down the fence line come hurtling around the final corner at full steam.

"Fuck me. Natalie! You're going to have to cut your hand off or something if you want to survive," I fire at the incoming zombies, "Make it quick!"

I have no idea what I just asked her to do, but it's the only idea I have, aside from shooting herself in the head.

"I have to deal with these fuckers running down the fence line!"

I try to pick off the zombie dickheads running straight for us. A skinny, ginger guy bounds over the bodies of his undead brethren and trips. He lands on all fours and rushes toward the gap under the gates where the Asian lady had crawled through moments earlier.

"Not today, you ginger cunt," I plant two slugs into his face and run for my rifle. I quickly shoulder it and pace back towards the driver's side door of the Hilux.

Natalie just stares at her hand, weeping. She rocks back and forth in her seat, holding her hand high and tight as she starts muttering something in Spanish; pleading to some unknown entity for help. A mess of bullets ting off the back doors of the vehicle. Natalie spins to look out of the back window and sees Keith standing in his grey box with his Steyr AUG rifle.

"Shit. What do I do? What do I do?" she begs herself, hoping for an answer.

Another round shatters the driver's side wing mirror and Natalie balls up into the fetal position in her chair. She covers her head with her good hand as more bullets enter the Hilux's cab through the roof. Then she sees the barrel of the sawn-off shotgun poking out from underneath the seat. She reaches for it.

I retreat to the front of the Hilux to avoid Keith's assault. I creep up the side of the vehicle and call out to Natalie as she looks for something in the cab.

"Nat. How are we doing, gorgeous?"

Natalie is holding her left hand out the window. A yellow ratchet strap is tightly wrapped around her forearm just below her wrist, and the shaking barrel of the sawn-off shotgun is pressed firmly against the base of her bloodied palm.

"I don't know if I can do it, Dan."

Natalie's hands shake as she breathes fast and shallow when a burst of rifle fire punches into the tray. Startling Natalie, she flinches and pulls the trigger.

The sharp bark from the shotgun firing deafens us momentarily and a high-pitched ringing mutes everything else. I return fire at Keith immediately and force him to duck for cover. I run up to Natalie's passenger door and fling it open. She is as white as a sheet and unable to speak. She's going into shock, she just stares into space with wide, teary eyes. I grab the open first aid kit from Natalie's lap and start unwrapping bandages and the disinfectant. She must have gotten the kit ready before fashioning a tourniquet out of a ratchet strap and blowing her hand off. Smart cookie. I hold out her bloodied stump and my stomach churns. Shattered bone fragments and fleshy gore are all that remain of her once beautiful hand.

"Natalie, you're going to be fine, just let me wrap this up and we'll go. You're going to be fine, I promise."

Natalie scrunches her eyes shut as I spray disinfectant on her open wound, she screams so hard that no sound comes out. I quickly wrap up the stump and rest it against her chest.

"Buckle up, we're out of here!"

I close her door and bolt around the backside of the four wheel drive, I unload the rest of my handgun into the compound and up at Keith in his metal box and jump into the driver's seat. I stomp the accelerator into the ground and charge through the chained gates; they spring open.

"We did it! Natalie, we fucking did it!" I celebrate.

Natalie turns her head to look at me and reaches out to touch my face, her hand falls short, so she rests it on my shoulder. I turn and lean my head onto her hand and then I kiss it; it's cold, but at least she's conscious. I take the left turn onto the narrow track leading away from Kalgoorlie along an old railway line. I look over and smile at Natalie and she smiles weakly back at me, her eyes are glossy and she looks dazed.

"Thank you, Dan," Natalie speaks very softly, "Thank you, for saving—" Natalie's sentence stops abruptly when something hot and wet splashes against my face. I squeeze my eyes shut and slam on the brakes.

I swipe at the warm, slippery fluid in a panic. It's in my eyes and mouth, and it tastes metallic. I reach down and grab a rag to wipe my face fast and hard until I can see again. I hold my hands out in front of me and stare at them, they're soaked in blood.

"What the fuck," I stare at the bloodied dash and the crimson windscreen in front of me. I quickly frisk myself, thinking that I've been shot.

"Nat, check yourself. One of us has been hit. There's so much blood!" I look to the left, "Nat?"

Natalie's body slumps forward over the centre console, it's limp and motionless.

"Natalie!"

A fist-sized crater hollows out the back of her skull; meaty, pink pulp oozes out from the fatal wound. I grab Natalie by the shoulders and pull her back into her seat.

"No, no, no! Natalie?!"

Her head falls to the side and her lifeless eyes stare through me. I run my hand through her matted, blood-drenched hair. I feel the edges of the massive hole in the back of her skull.

"No, no, no," I pull Natalie back over the centre console and hug her tightly, "No!"

I yell into the nape of her neck as my hands ball up her frizzy hair. I beg her to come back, knowing full well that she's gone. That I had failed her. That I had failed Pat.

The Hilux rocks from side to side as my helplessness

turns to anger. I shake Natalie's limp body and then throw my fists into the roof and steering wheel of the car.

"What a shot!" the dump truck's speaker announces, "I told you, mate. If I can't have her, no one can."

I grab onto the steering wheel and hold onto it like a life preserver thrown out to a man drowning at sea, my chest heaves as I struggle to catch my breath.

"If I were you, mate, I'd squeeze in a quickie while she's still warm, I know I would," Keith cackles into the microphone.

I wipe the tears from my eyes and reach into the glove box. I pull out Pat's hand cannon and hold it in my lap. I stare at it and then I glance over at Natalie's limp body, my face contorts in anger. Keith continues to taunt me from his grey box perched in the high sky, spewing vulgarities over the P.A. system, baiting me for a reaction. He fires at the stationary ute and the round punches through Natalie's door an into her leg.

"I'm so sorry, Nat."

I lean across the cab and kiss Natalie on her forehead and exit the Hilux.

BENEATH THE SALMON GUM TREE

I walk back toward the compound with Pat's pistol firmly in my right hand and the bloodied sawn-off in the other.

Two zombies come sprinting through the busted rear gates and race toward me. I keep moving forward, numb with anger. The zombies are on me in an instant, but with a point-blank shotgun blast to one's face and a pistol round to the forehead of the other, both zombies are grounded quickly. I reload and then holster the shotgun as gunfire from the Steyr rifle licks its way through the dirt by my feet. I stand still as the flurry of assault rounds whistles past my ear and pummels the boulder beside me.

"Welcome back to the party, mate. Where's your girlfriend? Still in the car?" he cackles loudly, whipping his head back as he does so.

I pull the hammer back on Pat's gun and make a tight fist with my other hand, so tight that my fingernails cut into the meat of my palm and draw blood.

"Now, listen up, mate, if you're not going to fuck that slut's dead pussy, can you at least drop her off at my place? I'd love to get up—" The radio handpiece explodes in Keith's hand and sharp plastic shrapnel sprays into his face. He curses in agony.

Keith quickly shoulders his assault rifle, but I fire again, the bullet hits the side of the rifle and it jumps out of his hands. It slides down the length of the tray and over the lip of it, landing in the twisting heap of half-crippled zombies below.

I'm making my way through the yard when another zombie squeezes through the heavy automated front gate and bolts towards me. His speed is unnatural and his face is a broken and twisted thing of nightmares. I pull out my holstered weapon and convince him to end his pursuit abruptly with shotgun blasts through his neck and the side of his face. I fire another pistol round up at Keith and it bounces off the steel tray body directly behind his head and he panics. He clambers for the crudely cut access panel above him and reaches high for it, but his large belly stunts his efforts. I aim for his head and squeeze the trigger, hoping that the bullet flies true and lands smack bang in the back of the cunt's head.

The bullet arcs a little too high and misses Keith's fat head, but luckily smashes straight into his outstretched forearm. His hand goes limp and loses its grip on the access panel's rim. Keith slides down the hood of the tray and bounces off of the side panel of his grey box. He reaches out to arrest his fall but fails and continues sliding down toward the makeshift prison cage below. He rolls over the top loops of barbed wire and lands hard in the tray and starts sliding feet first on his belly. A thin finger of his bright red blood stretches out in front of him as it traces his path of descent down the tray and through the blackened gore of the cage's previous occupants. He barrels through the twisted mess of the barbed-wire fencing at the bottom of the tray and falls the ten-plus metres to the valley floor. He lands to the side of the zombie pile with a sickening thud.

Keith Turner cries out, "Argh! My legs!" he rolls around in agony, "My legs, you bastard!"

The fall shatters his hips and breaks both of his legs. The smoke screen blocks most of my view, so I can't fully see Keith but I can bloody hear him; he screams and swears at his legs.

The sound of his suffering brings me a silent joy.

I continue through the compound toward the front gate, intent on finishing the job, when I see the attention of the zombies still climbing the gate shift to the wailing man on the ground. They leap down and descend on him instantly. His defensive screams excite the other nearby zombies and they join the massing heap of clawing, meth-fuelled undead creatures ripping Keith Turner limb-from-fucking-limb.

I look up at the tray of the dump truck above the smoke and notice an Australian Pride party logo painted on it. The six-metre-high bright white lettering stands out like dog's balls against the dark, bloodied smears around it.

"What the fuck? Another A.P. logo?"

I take one final look at the compound around me, unmoved by the destruction and mayhem, when my eyes fall upon the fuel drums burning beneath the propane tank.

The pressure relief valve releases intermittent bursts of pressurised propane as the tank's contents boil from the fires below. Flashbacks to the caravan fire bombard me.

"Ha. Nope! I know what happens next."

I jog back through the compound, eager to get very far away from the fuel fire heating the propane tank. I glance into the makeshift workshop as I pass it and spot a large white bag in the corner with a familiar yellow diamond designating the product inside as an oxidizing agent.

"No, fucking way."

I dart inside the workshop for a closer look and see a one-tonne bulk bag of ammonium nitrate sitting on a pallet with the word 'NOT' spray-painted across it.

"Ha! 'Not' ammonium nitrate my arse, Colin. This is *not* how you store this shit, if this goes bang it would,"—an idea springs to mind— "wait a minute."

I check the steering column of the parked forklift and find the keys dangling from the ignition. I quickly walk behind the containers and see that the space between the fence and the random shit in the yard will easily accommodate a forklift. If I can get that bulk bag and rig up that forklift to drive itself into that fire, the explosion would level everything in this valley.

"Better move quickly then!"

The forklift chugs to life and I hook the lifting loop of the bulk bag over the tines. The forklift struggles to lift it, but I manage to lift it high enough to move. My heart is pounding in my chest and my jaw is tight with anxiety. I drive the forklift around the back of the containers and aim it toward the burning barrels. I weave a strap through the steering wheel and ratchet it tight, this should keep it driving true and get it into the guts of the fire. I wedge a wooden glut between the accelerator and the seat and check the ratchet strap once more before I tap the gear selector into 'forward'. I jump back from the forklift as it powers down the fence line and start jogging over to the Hilux. I glimpse back at the forklift bomb intermittently, happy to see it staying on course. As I run along the outside of the rear fence, the forklift hits a pothole and jerks to the left and into the rows of barrels. I hear the thuds of barrels being knocked over and then the sound of metal scraping against metal. A loud whooshing noise pierces the air.

A massive jet of fiery vapour spews out from the side of the propane tank, the heat and force of it clear the smoke and allows me to see what fortune has smiled upon me.

The tines of the forklift had scraped down the side of the propane tank and torn a hole in its side. A concentrated jet of fire is now blowtorching the bag of ammonium nitrate.

"Time to go!"

I jump into the ute and floor it out of there.

Sixty seconds later, a towering fireball erupts into the sky, the bang is deafening and a visible shockwave pulses out from the blast. The ute rocks as dust and sand clouds the track in front of me and consumes everything beyond the windscreen.

I smirk, knowing that Keith and his mob of meth-fuelled zombies were vaporised in that blast and that there'll be no evidence that we escaped. But my smile quickly fades. We didn't escape, I did. I look over at the gorgeous Natalie slumped over in the passenger seat.

"That was for you, Natalie".

I swallow hard and continue along the sandy service

road ahead of me. I watch the plume of smoke and sand begin to shrink behind us in the smashed side mirror.

I find my way back onto the highway and drive at high speed for a couple of hours. The Hilux almost shakes to pieces as I navigate the chaos along the highway, but I want to get as far away from Kalgoorlie as possible.

Adrenaline only takes the wheel for so long before I feel my focus begin to fade. I slow the vehicle to a stop and hesitantly look at Natalie, my face runs hot with emotion. I twist the steering wheel in my hands and suck in deep breaths of fresh air, trying to keep myself from breaking down. The desert breeze gently plays with Natalie's untamed hair through the shattered window. The sun's light tinges the outer margins of her hair with a golden-brown halo. I stare at her for quite some time, caressing her cheek as I apologise a hundred times over.

I'm sorry. I'm so sorry.
We should have left when you said, you were right.
I should have driven faster out of the compound.
If only I had made you stay in the footwell.
If only I had killed Keith first.
If only…

The angelic light surrounding Natalie wanes as the thick clouds of a distant storm consume the morning sun. Natalie's lifeless form darkens and becomes a haunting silhouette.

I continue down the highway for several kilometres until I find somewhere to pull off, I take a narrow track off into the scrub and I park the Hilux out of sight. I pull a shovel out of the ute's tray and wander off into the scrub, looking for a suitable place to bury Natalie. I start digging in the softest part of the red earth under a tree. Hours and hours of painful digging eat away the day, but it must be done.

I place Natalie in a sleeping bag that she'd packed for the trip to Perth and bury her as deep as I can. I pile rocks and boulders waist-high to mark her grave and to make sure nothing else could dig her up. I return to the Hilux to fetch something of Pat's before I give Natalie the burial her father had most certainly deserved, yet circumstances had denied. A flash of Pat lying belly up in the mud attacks me, but I swat it away.

I don't know which faith Natalie held, nor did I know her father's faith, but I mark the grave with a cross made out of white plastic road markers. With a black paint marker, I pen a final message onto the horizontal cross member, lean Pat's walking stick against the cross and step back from it.

Here lies Natalie, daughter of Pat. Two souls lost too soon.
21 DEC 2018

I sit with my back against the tree near Natalie's rocky tomb and stare at the rumbling clouds rolling toward me. The humidity climbs as the smell of distant rain rides the late afternoon breeze. I push my fingers into the warm sand beside me and let handfuls of it pass through my fingers. I rest my head on the trunk of the salmon gum tree and look up. The tops of several nearby trees have grown into this tree, their limbs and foliage form a tightly packed canopy above me. I watch the wind bend and sway the massive canopy and close my eyes listening to the creaking and groaning of the branches. I convince myself that I'll get up and get back on the road in a few minutes. I just want to rest, but I know I have to push on.

The weight of the day battles against me, panic and anger are aching to consume me, but I return my focus to the rhythmic creaking and rustling of the canopy above. Within moments, the exhaustion claims me and I fall asleep in the scrub on the side of The Great Eastern Highway.

Natalie's final resting place is at my feet and this will be the last time that I pass out next to her.

DEATH BY CARAVAN

"I fell asleep, holy shit! Was I just lying here in the open this whole time? Fuck!"

I bolt upright and snap to my feet. The morning sun warms my flesh and an orchestra of cicadas and insects fills the air. I frisk myself, searching for injuries.

I'm okay. And dry? Wasn't there a storm?

"The ute!"

I jog back along the wet and sandy track to see the Hilux still parked amongst some shrubs just off the highway.

"Thank fuck for that."

I check my phone for the time, it's still early.

"I'd better get a move on, I can be home by lunchtime if I leave now."

I walk back to the tree I had fallen asleep under and find the ground dry, I look up at the dense canopy above.

"Huh, the canopy must have sheltered me from the rain."

I go to Natalie's grave and place my hand on top of her cross. I've known her for less than a day, yet it feels like I have lost someone I had known for years. It must be a family thing, because I felt a similar loss when Pat died, I don't even know their surnames for fuck's sake.

"I'm sorry, gorgeous, I have to go now," I struggle to find more words, not sure how to leave her, "Err, say hi to Pat for me, eh? Tell him, I'm sorry that I couldn't keep you safe. I'm sorry that I couldn't keep either of you safe."

My hand lingers atop her cross for a long moment before I pull myself away. I climb into the Hilux and throw one last look at Natalie's tree through the scrub before I continue to Perth. It isn't long before thoughts of Bella and Maria jump to the forefront of my mind.

How bad is it in the cities if it's this bad out here?
What if there are more men like Keith in Fremantle?
Are the girls even alive?
Yes, of course, they're alive, they have to be.
Bella and Maria have to be.

The weight of each new worry pushes my right foot harder onto the accelerator pedal; I push the Hilux to 150km/hr wherever I can. I take corners faster than I should and weave dangerously through the increasing obstacles on the road: cars, trucks, trailers, the dead and the undead. Each small town or roadhouse that I skirt around looks just like Kalgoorlie: violated. My hopes for Bella and Maria diminish as I get closer to the coastal port town of Fremantle.

Merredin, Doodlakine, Kellerberrin, Tammin and Cunderdin are all indistinguishable from each other, they are burning husks of their former selves, lost to the zombies or opportunistic survivors. Dead bodies line the roadside and the undead walk the streets, the roads themselves are choked with vehicles and almost every building is burning; the smell of death is putrid and thick in the air. The occasional screams of survivors cut through me like a knife; some plead for help, others plead for death. I see other vehicles speeding off in all directions, not many, but enough to give me hope that people are surviving.

In Meckering, a man had desperately yelled at me to pull over. I didn't know if he really needed help or if it was an ambush like the ones Keith had set in Kalgoorlie. I sped up to scare him off, but the man just threw himself onto the highway in front of the Hilux. I swerved to miss him, but it was too late, I rolled straight over the top of him. Did he actually need help or was it an ambush? I'll never know.

The Hilux itself is travelling well, it has taken one hell of a beating in the last few days. Nearly all of the windows are shattered, bullet holes riddle every panel and the engine is making some horrendous sounds and smells, yet it still just keeps powering through. I'm not sure how long it's going to keep running but I'm not stopping for anything or anyone. Every person that I had stopped for in the last few days has either died or tried to kill me. I'm fucking done. It's me versus the world now.

I look down at the instruments on my dash's display, the temperature and pressure gauges climb higher and higher as the fuel needle drops lower and lower. I have one jerry can left, which is more than enough to get me home and then some. So, I drive faster. The horizon ahead of me is filled with more towers of black smoke, as far as I can see to the south and as far as I can see to the north. I can't even fathom what I'm driving into so I drop the sun visors to block out the horizon of smoke and doubt. The visor acts like a set of blinkers on a racehorse, I try to focus on what's in front of me right now. It no longer matters what's going on around me, my only goal is the finish line, my daughter and getting home. My priority is my baby girl.

'G R E E N   V A L L E Y   3   K M S', a road sign indicates. I slow down to 80km/hr for the upcoming winding road into the small town, anticipating another choked section of road; a car park of death and inconvenience. A few abandoned cars dot the roadside, but nothing substantial. I keep my eyes peeled and both hands on the steering wheel. A massive dust cloud rising from paddocks in the distance catches my eye, it looks like it's getting closer, but it's hard to tell.

The road sinks into the undulating terrain as steep-angled, concrete revetments rise to block my view of the earthy-red dust cloud. It plumes high up into the blue and purple clouds above it. The contrast is insane. I shake my head, trying to follow the curve of the road as it dips into the town limits.

"What on earth could be kicking up that much dust?"

I flick a glance at the red tsunami of dust and then back down at the road as I round the corner; a dozen railway sleepers lie across the road in front of me.

"Shit!"

I slam the brakes on and skid right into the first sleeper, my right front wheel mounts it and the Hilux stalls.

"Fuckinelle."

An overturned flatbed truck is in the drainage ditch, most of its load of railway sleepers and steel are scattered across the road reserve, blocking it entirely. I open my door to investigate when I hear a growing rumbling sound. I listen closely and try to pinpoint where it's coming from. It seems to be coming from behind the steep banks of the drainage ditch toward the dust cloud.

"What the fuck is that?"

The rumbling gets louder and I retreat back into the cab to start the ute. but the engine struggles.

Errr-errr-errrrrrrr-er. Click. Errrr-err-eh.

Clickclickclick.

"Oh, come on!"

I shut my door and key the ignition again but it's dead. The thunderous thudding gets louder and I can physically feel the sound vibrate in the air, "Fuck!"

The dust cloud towers over the road, blocking out the sun and cloaking the landscape in an eerie red lens. I reach for the reloaded sawn-off shotgun and place Pat's handgun in the seat next to me. I jump across into the passenger seat and try to squat down into the footwell to hide. I see something down the road moving between the abandoned vehicles, a figure. It's running from one side of the road to the other and then stops. It opens the door of a white Commodore station wagon and slams it shut.

"What the fuck is going on?"

A wall of hairy tan-coloured beasts crests the embankment, loud bleats and deep throaty groans drum out of the thousand-strong caravan of dromedary camels as they pour over the angled bank and flood onto the road. The loud thumping of their heavily padded feet thunder all around me as the first line of camels barely miss the Hilux, their dusty hides only nudging the vehicle as they stampede across the road. But several camels, blinded by the dust, slam into the driver's side of the Hilux at speed and rocks it violently. The frenzy of charging camels continues to push through, even though many of them are hindered by my parked ute. The camels trample one another as wave after wave of them steamroll into the road cutting. Dense dust fills the mostly windowless cab quickly and makes it hard to breathe. I pop my head up just in time to see a beefy camel broadside the raised front of the ute. It bounces the Hilux up onto two wheels and then back down onto all four wheels. Another blow forces it back up onto two wheels and a final strike from two other camels tips the ute off of the railway sleeper and onto its side. I get thrown against the passenger side of the vehicle as the ute rolls. I tense up and accidentally fire the shotgun straight through the dashboard as all of the contents of the cab join me.

More camels strike the chassis and spin the Hilux like a Lazy Susan, nudging it toward the irrigation ditch in front of me. The vehicle teeters over the banked shoulder of the road when another blow, from what has to be the fifteenth line of camels, tips the Hilux over on its roof and into the V-shaped ditch. I lay buckled on the roof of the cab, balled up in the fetal position as the camels use the upturned ute as a ramp to cross the ditch and get into the next paddock. The Hilux's roof crumples under the immense weight of hundreds of one-tonne, desert-dwelling beasts charging across it.

Several long minutes drag on before the stampede passes. The dust cloud fills every one of my orifices with gritty sand and coarse hair; my mouth, nose, ears and eyes are caked with the shit. Even my butt crack is full of sand. I crawl out of the window and I cough hard to try to clear out my mouth and throat. I'm army crawling out of the buckled passenger door's window frame, when a heavily padded foot slams down beside me. I cover my head and shuffle backwards into the cab as the wide mouth of the camel clamps around my right shoulder and rips me out of the Hilux.

"Fuarrrk!"

The pain, and the stinking breath of the camel, is unbearable as I'm lifted a metre off the ground. Its wide mouth loses its grip on my shoulder when my foot hooks on the headrest of the passenger seat. I hit the ground hard and scurry back into the cab, crawling backwards over the clutter. I try to keep my eyes on the feet of the pissed off camel outside.

"Where's my gun?"

I search for a gun, any gun, hoping I find it before the camel attacks again. The full-sized shotgun is right in front of me but it's wedged between the roll cage and some of my baggage.

Outside the Hilux, the camel drops to its knees and forces its head into the window of the passenger door. Its long, muscular neck powers the camel's stinking, open mouth toward me. I punch it in the face repeatedly as it forces me back and almost out of the driver's side door behind me. I smash my thumb into one of its gigantic eyes and its long-lashed eyelids squeeze shut around it. I feel the eyeball pop as I push the thumb deeper through the warm jelly of its eye. The beast howls in agony.

I inch back further to avoid the thrashing beast when I find my sawn-off shotgun, I grab it and push the barrel into the camel's weeping eye socket and fire. It drops dead.

"Fuck me, what the fuck was your problem, cunt?" I spit at the lifeless beast.

I pull the barrel out of its eye and suddenly feel something bite my ankle and yank me backwards. I'm ripped out of the vehicle for a second time through the driver's side window and I drop my gun. Something big lifts me into the air and swings me out onto the road. The thick dust cloud kicked up by the stampeding camels is still settling around me, so I can barely see a metre in front of me. I see a large, silhouette stand tall and grunt at me.

It's another camel. Yay!

I scramble to my feet, but fall because of my now throbbing ankle. I crab crawl backwards away from the hairy giant as it extends its neck and runs at me. A shot rings out and the camel stumbles. Another shot follows quickly and the beast drops. I scan the dust cloud surrounding me, looking for the guy with the gun that just nailed that camel. I slide myself towards the Hilux and luckily find Pat's pistol sitting in the dry grass of the irrigation ditch. I grab it, pull the hammer back and sit up against the upturned ute. I hold the weapon out, swinging it from side to side defensively.

"Drop it!" a woman's voice instructs.

"Yeah, unlikely, mate."

The dust cloud thins out and a silhouette of a woman holding a rifle becomes clear. I pull the pistol to the right and she fires at me, the round slams into the Hilux's door.

"Drop it, I won't ask you a third time."

"For fuck's sake, yeah. Yep. I'm dropping it."

I toss Pat's pistol a short distance away from me and, as the dust clears completely, the woman steps forward with her rifle aimed at my chest.

"Are you kidding me? Where are all of you women getting these rifles? You're the second chick to hold me at gunpoint in two days."

"Hands where I can see them!"

I place my hands in my lap and slouch against the car's body. Disarmed again, what the actual fuck!

"Are you alone, mate?"

I stare at the ground and fold my arms across my chest, "Yeah, are you?"

"I'm asking the questions. What's in the car?"

"Seats, a steering wheel, a dead camel..."

"Oh, a smartarse, hey? Smartarses don't last too long out here, you know?"

Her accent is *very* Australian, eastern states for sure.

"Well," I look up at the new gun-wielding woman in my life, "I must be the exception to the rule because it's got me this far!" I say, a vaguely pissed off expression painted across my face.

The woman has a Middle Eastern appearance, maybe Lebanese. Her skin is tan, much darker than Natalie's. Her thick, shapely eyebrows crease together at her brow. A permanent wrinkle makes it evident that she is either frequently pissed off or has poor eyesight. My money is on the former, going off our first few seconds of interaction. Her curly, black, shoulder-length hair kind of looks wet, but it's not. Her dark brown eyes are piercing and intimidating, but her round cheeks and full lips soften her look. She has an athletic build with muscular arms and her strong core is visible through her tight-fitting army green tank top. Her waist is narrow and her hips are noticeably fuller, her thighs look powerful as fuck in her stoned-washed jeans. She looks to be in her late twenties to early thirties and she looks like she's done a fitness boot camp or two.

The woman laughs to herself, "Someone's a little moody, aren't they?" She brings her rifle up and rests the barrel on her shoulder.

"Someone's a little moody. A-mer-mer-mer, a-mer-mememem-me-mer," I mock.

"Alright, you sarcastic fuck. Stand up."

"No, I think I'll sit."

The woman looks me up and down and then squats in front of me. She places the stock of her rifle between her feet and holds the barrel with both hands.

"What's your name, Hank?"

I scrunch my face in confusion, "Hank? You think my name's 'Hank'? Why?"

"No," she feels a need to explain herself, "It's from a show. You're being difficult and moody. Hank Moody was... Never mind."

I ponder what she says for a second and then it hits me,

"Ha! Hank Moody, from *Californication*. I loved that show, David Duchovny for the win."

"Oh, you know it? Good, now that we're all buddy-buddy, how about you tell me your name and what's in your fucking ute? Medical supplies, guns, food, water?"

"And why do you want to know what's in my"—I look up at the woman and notice a bandage on her arm. I look back down, pretending not to notice it. I look out at the road with the railway sleepers strewn across it; well, *strewn* is the wrong word. These sleepers look like they were placed there, laid across the road and perfectly spaced in a way that someone wanting to get past in a car would have to move at least a handful of them to get by. The sleepers were a trap, an ambush, forcing people to get out of their vehicles because no car could go over them or around them. I look at the entire scene more closely. Even if I had moved some of the 60kg sleepers, I couldn't have driven through because of the steep gravel banks of the drainage ditch and the truck laid on its side across the road.

The woman snaps her fingers at me, "Oi, are you fucking deaf, mate?"

I smirk to myself before I puff up my tongue in my mouth and say, "No-ine-not-deaf, ine-jus-not-lissening-to-you," imitating how I imagine a deaf person would sound trying to say the same sentence.

The woman sucks her chin in, and continues wide-eyed, "Wow, you're going to Hell."

"Looks like I'll be meeting you there then, eh? How many people have you ambushed with your lil' railway sleeper trap here? Are you a thief or just a cunt?"

The woman stands up and shoulders her rifle, "Huh, you're not as dumb as you look, and yet, I'm still not convinced. What. Is. Your. Name?"

"I'm Dan, Daniel Forest," I shoot out my hand sarcastically as if to shake hers, "What's yours, angry lady?"

"Put that down, *Dan*. My name is woman-with-the-gun."

"What a strange name," I stand up and dust myself off.

"Oi, sit back down!" She juts out the rifle and steps back defensively.

"First, it was stand, now it's sit. Are you new to this or

something? Listen, I don't really care," I begin picking up my things that had been tossed out of the Hilux.

"I have to get back to my daughter and your little roadblock just cost me time and my ride. Do any of these cars work or do I have to walk?"

The woman fires another round at the ground near my feet and I quickly turn to rush her. Fuck it, why not? I grab her rifle and check her in the forehead with it before I grapple and spin her up against the Hilux. I press my body against hers so she can't kick or throw any punches.

"Oi, listen! I'm not a threat to you!"

The woman struggles, but I manage to keep her pinned, but only just.

"I just want to get home to my daughter and you're getting in my way, I'm just passing through, so let me. I don't want to hurt you, but—"

The woman does some fancy bullshit with her legs and sweeps mine out from under me.

I'm on the ground, again, great.

She leans over me, presses the hot muzzle of the rifle into my chest and places her right foot on my groin. She shifts her weight forward onto it, "You were saying?".

I put my hands up in surrender and sigh loudly, I turn my head to the side and look over my shoulder.

"Kill me or let me go, the choice is yours, but choose quickly, please."

The woman pauses, unsure of how to deal with me. In the silence of our stalemate I look up at her and notice that her bandage has slipped off of her arm, exposing a nasty-looking bite mark.

"Wait, you were bitten? When?"

The woman presses her boot harder onto my groin and replies, "Three weeks ago, what's it to you?"

"Three. Three weeks ago? Wait, that's unpossible, you should be dead? How—"

"Unpossible? Really? You mean *impossible*?"

Oooh, sweet fucking fuck, I hate being corrected.

"Whatever, you should be dead or a zombie by now!"

"I'm immune—I think—I was sick for a few days after the bite but other than that, I'm fine. It's just taking a while to heal," she presses her boot harder onto my groin, "Now, tell me what's in the car or I'll put this bloody bandage in your mouth, watch you turn into one of those fucking things and *then* I'll put a bullet in you."

"So, you're still infected? That's insane."

"Dan!" She lifts the rifle's barrel under my chin.

"There's a medical kit, some food and water, but not much, a few weapons, a fridge and some gadgets. You can have it, just leave me a gun and point me in the direction of a working car. Please, I need to get back to my daughter, she's eight years old and probably scared shitless."

The woman's brow twitches upwards, triggered by the last detail; she lifts her foot slightly off my groin.

"My niece… is... was about that age. What's her name?"

"It's Bella, her name's Bella. What's your niece's name?" I adjust my hips awkwardly under her boot.

"Leilah."

"And what's your name?"

The woman hesitates, "...Samira."

"Okay, Samira. I'm trying to get to my Leilah, can you help me or is your boot quite happy where it is?"

Samira's gaze softens.

"Get up, Dan. Help me empty your ute and you can be on your way."

"Thank you, Samira."

She yanks me up to my feet and adds, "Don't be dumb, or you'll be dead quicker than you can say 'unpossible'."

"I know it's *im*possible... I just. Ugh," I offer.

"I'm sure you do."

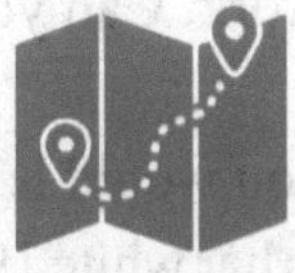

FOLLOW THE RED LINE

It takes fifteen minutes to empty the Hilux of its salvageable contents. I sneakily shoulder my backpack of goodies, telling Samira that it's just a few radios, some personal items and some ammo for the pistol. I cram some of my clothes into Russell's boredom bag and put that aside too. She confiscates both temporarily and says I'll get it back after our transaction is completed.

Samira finishes building her loot pile, which includes Natalie's rifle, my full-sized shotgun, the solar panels, some ammunition, a portable fridge and more than half of my medical supplies. I consider bartering for some of my stuff back but I have nothing to barter with.

While rummaging through the Hilux, Samira's bite wound ruptures and begins to weep. I watch her struggle to put a fresh dressing on it, so I offer to help bandage her arm properly. She allows it, and I can't help but wince at the puss-filled wound squelching as I wrap it firmly.

"Come on, we'll load up my Suzuki and then I'll get you near Northam. I have a farm out there. You won't be able to get a car into the city from here, but I have something that might work. Can you ride a motorbike?"

"Yeah, I can ride."

"Good, otherwise you would have been walking."

Samira escorts me to her white 1998 Suzuki Vitara which is parked on the other side of the drainage embankment. She drives us over to my Hilux to pick up her new belongings. As we load the Suzuki, I ask Samira if she knows anything more about the infection or what's going on in Perth and she rattles off the information like she'd rehearsed it, having heard it a million times in the week prior:

"Western Australia's borders are closed, the entire state is under quarantine and the land borders between Northern Territory and South Australia are now monitored by the Australian Army and Air Force. The waters off the coast are patrolled by the Australian Navy and the Fisheries Department. Any attempts to breach quarantine lines will be met with deadly force," she continues, "Stay indoors and store enough food and water to last four weeks. All emergency services are suspended and anyone who suspects they, or their loved ones, have been infected should be quarantined and restrained."

Samira takes a breath.

"That information was played day and night before the radio and television signals were shut off. We are on our own, Dan. Cellular and internet services were disabled a couple of days ago, too, so who knows how far this infection has spread. There were reports of an extremist arm of that Australian Pride group dumping some infected people at an immigration office in Sydney, but who knows if it happened or not."

That fucking Australian Pride party again? With members like Keith Turner, I'd believe anything!

"Far out, what is it like in the city, the southern suburbs?"

"Perth is gone. I wouldn't even try to go there. Do you see that big wall of smoke over there?" Samira points to the widest and darkest smoke plumes on the horizon, "That's Perth, the smaller grey plumes to the south are from the refineries and chemical plants in the Henderson and Rockingham area. It's toxic around that whole area."

My heart sinks and I sheepishly ask the most important question, "What about Fremantle?"

"I'm sorry, Dan, I really don't know. I was up here in Northam, but DFES, the SES and even the Army handed out quarantine kits to everyone early on in the infection, you know. The kits told you how to make your home safe from the infection, and looters, and they had first aid supplies; water purification tablets, dried food and the like. If people secured their homes quickly, and were away from the riots and infection hot spots, they could wait this out relatively safely."

I nod silently as I dutifully load the Suzuki.

"Is that where your family is, Dan? Fremantle?"

"Uh, yeah. My daughter and my, er, ex-wife are there."

Samira busies herself with loading the last of the solar panels into the Suzuki, not knowing what to say.

"Can I ask you something, Samira? How did you know you were immune? And how did you find out that you could still infect others?"

Samira pauses as she loads the last solar panel into her car, "My fiancé and I were down in Toodyay, getting some last-minute things. People were everywhere, they were fighting each other in the street, driving up on footpaths, ram-raiding shopfronts, it was mayhem. We saw some kids breaking into the Cola Café on the main street, do you know it? It's a bit of a landmark here?"

"Yeah, it's got all that Coca-Cola memorabilia and shit on the walls, right?"

"That's the one. My fiancé, Deacon, knew the owner, so he went in to try and stop them from looting his store. These kids were kicking the shit out of this younger boy, he was tiny and huddled in a corner, screaming his lungs out. Deacon started grabbing kids and throwing them out the front door. He smacked around a few of the older boys, to give them a taste of their own medicine," Samira touches her bandaged arm briefly before continuing, "Deacon ran off down the main street chasing after one of the boys who pulled a knife on him and then it was just me and the little boy. He was a little Asian boy and he was crying and twitching like he was still being kicked. I walked up behind him to help him and to tell him that the other kids had gone, that he was safe. I placed my hand on his back and, before I knew it, he bit me and then he bolted out of the door."

"Wait, wasn't Toodyay where those refugees fled to?"

"Yes, we found out later that the little boy was from a host family that was hiding one of the escaped refugees. I think I was one of the first to be bitten around Northam."

"Why didn't you go to the hospital to get help?"

"I didn't link the two things. I just thought the boy panicked and bit me out of fear."

"Did you get sick?"

"Yeah, my mother was at the farm with my sister's kids and she's a strong believer in homeopathy and healing at home, 'Hospitals only keep you sick' she used to say. I had a fever and hallucinated horrible things. I even had rage fits but I just chalked it up to the fever and when the fever broke after a couple of days, I felt fine."

"But the wound didn't heal?"

"No, I just thought it was a normal infection, so I took some antibiotics," Samira pushes on her bite wound, "but it's still tender and keeps weeping."

I pause for a moment before asking the next question.

"And, er, when did you realise you could infect others?"

"Ha. When Deacon gets, uh," Samira blushes, "Excited during foreplay, he likes to bite and draw blood; it was his kink. I didn't think anything of it, of him biting my lip, but by morning, he was very sick. So I went back into town to get him some other medication, but when I got home, it was too late, he had turned into one of those things." Samira takes in a sharp breath, "Deacon and I were living at the farm with my mother, father and my niece and nephew; they, um, didn't make it."

"Sorry to hear, Samira. I had no idea."

"We've all lost people because of this infection, Dan. Let's get you on your way so you can get to Lei… I mean, Bella," Samira closes the back of the Suzuki, "Get in."

We hop in the Suzuki and pull off the main road and drive up onto a narrow dirt track heading west into some farmland. We'll have to paddock-hop our way to Northam because of Samira's roadblock in Green Valley.

"Deacon's old dirt bike should still be at the house,"

Samira hands me my backpack. Pat's pistol and the sawn-off shotgun are unloaded, of course.

"You'll be needing these."

The dirt track takes us across the northern embankment that walls Samira's railway-sleeper-ambush. As we reach the crest of the embankment I look out over the fields and see a hundred-and-fifty-metre-wide runway of pummelled earth. It stretches out into the distance in a long curve, it's fucking massive. The path cuts through fences and many of the hedged windbreaks that skirt each paddock's boundary.

"What was up with those fucking camels back there on the road? How were there so many and why did those two want me dead? Were they infected?"

"It's quite an impressive clearing, isn't it? Those camels have created a sort of race track for themselves, it must be at least one hundred kilometres long because it takes them about three to four hours to complete a lap. They've been running it day and night for the last two days. There must be a thousand plus camels in that herd."

"Fuck, eh? Why do they keep running?"

"It must be an instinct thing? If they're moving, they can't be attacked? Or maybe they are infected and their brains are just telling them to run. I've never stopped to ask them, I just try to stay out of their way."

"Yeah, I saw you jump into a Commodore back there before they hit. I didn't know what was coming over that embankment but I did not expect camels," I laugh.

"Ha! You saw that? As I said, I stay out of their way. I have looked at a few of the dead camels, the ones that get caught in the fences or trampled, and some of them are infected, but most aren't. The ones that attacked you weren't infected, they were just pissed off that you parked in their racetrack," Samira laughs to herself.

I stretch the collar of my shirt to check the blackening camel-mouth-sized bruise on my right shoulder. I touch it tenderly, "Yep. They didn't like me one bit."

"I watched you handle the first one, but that second one caught you off guard."

"Oh, I never thanked you for saving my arse either, but I guess robbing me right after tainted that gesture. Anyway, thank you."

"No worries, I only killed it because once it had finished killing you, it was probably going to have a go at me too."

I look at Samira with a half-cocked smile, unsure of how respond, "Yeah, right…"

I curiously look around the interior of the Suzuki and see a photo strip pinned to the sun visor, the kind of strips that you get in an arcade photo booth. Two of the four photo squares have heart filters bordering the images. The photos are of Samira and two small children, her niece and nephew, I presume.

"When was this taken?"

"That was about four months ago," Samira spies the visor and quickly flips it up, hiding the photo from me, "It was a silly day at the gaming arcade on the cappuccino strip in Fremantle."

"Ah, I know it well."

"It was my niece and nephew's birthday, they're twins. They just turned six, so Aunty Sammy took them on a sugar-fuelled adventure to the arcade." Samira starts chuckling, "After we took this photo, Lachlan and Leilah went on the simulator with bellies full of candy and Lachie spewed everywhere. They had to close the ride," she laughs.

"My Bella loves that place; she beats me at air hockey every time and usually wins a major prize on the Stacker game at least once a month. Timezone is the first place we go when I get back home from my swing."

"So, you're FIFO? In the mines?"

"Yes, 2:1 and 4:1 rosters, I'm actually driving back from site now. I was on a drilling program close to the Northern Territory border when all of this shit started going down."

"Fuck, really?"

"Yeah, I've been on the roads for a few days now,"

"No, I meant the 4:1 roster. A whole month away and only one week off? How does your wife handle that?"

"Er, she didn't. Hence, ex-wife."

"Oh..." Samira focuses on the rutted paddock tracks ahead, sensing she had stumbled into a tender topic.

"Do you want to see a photo of Bella?"

"Absolutely!"

"Here, we took this photo four years ago, it's one of those Polaroid ones, it's my favourite photo of us together," I rummage through my backpack and hand her the photo.

It's of me with Bella sitting on my shoulders, I'm wearing a pair of raggedy old jeans and a dark blue singlet holding on to Bella's knees. Bella is wearing a cute floral dress and has her mother's massive, wide-brimmed straw hat on. A pink ribbon skirts the outer rim of the hat and Bella is holding it up with both hands, stopping it from consuming her whole head. The image snapped me mid-laugh and caught Bella in full hysterics. She found the oversized hat absolutely hilarious.

"Oh my god!" Samira's face lights up, "She's gorgeous!"

"Yes, she is."

Samira holds onto the picture a little longer than expected, her eyes are glued to it, so much so, she hits a pothole that snaps her out of her daze.

"Sorry," she goes to hand it back to me.

"No, no. You keep that one," I pause and wave my hand at her, rejecting the photo.

"What? No, it's yours? It's your favourite one."

"I want you to keep it," Samira retracts her arm and looks at the photo again.

"Today could have gone very differently for me, and for you, and this photo will remind you of the day when you helped a father get back to his daughter. Please, keep it. I have another one right here and multiple copies at home. I even got it blown up onto a shirt of mine," I laugh to break the tension.

Samira opens the sun visor and wedges my photo next to the photo of her niece and nephew. We share a brief smile and a nod and then Samira quickly changes the topic.

"The house is about ten minutes away. There shouldn't be too many infected around either, I've killed quite a few of them and the blocked road leading into town from Perth helps a lot too. It's a car park out there. It keeps most of them away."

"That's very nice to hear, but if the roads are so choked up, how will I get back to Freo from here?"

"Deacon worked for the rail company and has a bunch of utilities and service maps in his Range Rover. It shows fire breaks, ranger accesses, Western Power corridors and all types of active and abandoned railway maps. We used them a fair bit over the last few years for our dirt biking and camping trips during the holidays. We mainly use these tracks to avoid the speed cameras and RBTs on our return home, you know? I'm sure you can find a way back to Fremantle without having to go too close to the city, the highways are fucked and you don't want to go anywhere near a built-up area. Plus, you'll have a trail bike so you can go anywhere."

"That sounds like a plan, Samira. I'm sure I can make it work, hopefully these storms bugger off, though."

We drive through one last paddock and stop at an old rustic gate at the rear of a property; a field of long fountain grass fills an overgrown paddock. Samira takes a deep breath and exhales before she exits the vehicle.

"I haven't been here since… come on. Let's get you on your way, grab your stuff."

I throw my backpack over my shoulder and slide my sawn-off into its holster. I load Pat's pistol and keep it in my right hand, just in case something lurks in the tall grass.

"Can we expect any surprises in here, Samira?"

"I doubt there will be any infected around, I locked this place up pretty tight before I left. Squatters are the biggest worry, but it's been quiet. Knock on wood."

As we approach the old farmhouse, I notice a clearing in the long grass. I stand taller to peek over it and see five recently dug graves marked with small crosses. Three mounds of dirt are adult-sized and two are significantly smaller. Holy shit, she buried them all right here. I quicken my steps to catch up to Samira and point out something trivial on the other side of the property; a rusty old tractor sitting among some other farming equipment.

"Wow, that's an old tractor? That must be at least fifty years old, eh? Does it still run?"

Its engine is missing and a small tree is growing out of the engine bay, its narrow steel rims are buckled and its spokes have completely rusted through.

"This was my grandpa's farm. That tractor has been there since my father and his brothers were kids, they grew up here. My grandpa died three years ago, and left the house to my father. We were living over east, but he moved back to the farm. I stayed in Queensland for a few more months before moving over here with Deacon to help with some renovations. My father planned to turn the stables into some Airbnbs." Samira pulls out a bunch of keys and unlocks the garage's back door and we walk inside.

The garage is dark and dusty, Samira opens the shades on the rear window and pulls the tarp off of Deacon's old motorbike. She unveils a bright orange KTM 450, in near-new condition.

"This is Deacon's *old* bike?"

"It's a 2016, I think. So, a couple years old. Deacon likes to keep his bikes up to date."

"Jesus, I was expecting an old postie bike or farm thing. This, though," I walk up and look it over.

"This will do nicely," I smile widely.

"I'm glad you like it. The fuel is over there and there's some old riding gear in that white cupboard in the corner. You may want to shake off the jackets and check the helmet though, spiders love that cupboard. I'll go get those maps for you. Deacon's car is in the new shed with the other bikes, I'll be back, you stay in here."

"Cheers, call out if you find any trouble."

"I can handle myself. I handled you, didn't I?" Samira walks out of the garage smirking. The cheeky wench.

I drop my backpack and pistol on the workbench and start trying on the dusty, cobweb-ridden riding gear. By the time Samira returns with the maps, I'm dressed in an old brown leather cruising jacket, a pair of bright white Kevlar-lined riding pants, some orange and black gloves and a matte black helmet that had a pretty significant crack on the right-hand side of it.

"It all fits, what do you think?"

Samira stands in the doorway, "I'm glad it fits. A little mismatched, but good. Here," Samira throws me an old, canvas bag and I catch it, just.

"What's this for?"

"It's a tank bag. Strap it to the petrol tank, the maps and probably that handgun will fit in there, it's a handy little bag. I took it off one of the other bikes."

I pull my helmet and gloves off and place them on the bench with my backpack. Samira opens up the maps on a stack of old pallets as I strap the tank bag to my new bike.

"So, Dan," Samira calls.

I walk over to her by the pallets, she has two maps unfolded and a red marker pen in her hand. The first is a detailed map of the entire greater Perth region, an area covering as far north as Quinns Rocks, as far south as Mandurah and as far east as Northam.

"We are here," Samira draws a circle on the map and then hands me the pen, "Where are you?"

I take the pen and draw a circle around the area of South Fremantle, "I'm there."

"Okay then," she draws a big cross through the Perth CBD, the Crown Casino and the Perth International Airport, "These areas are either burning or thick with the infected; the fire attracts them apparently."

She draws several smaller crosses along the southern shores of the Swan River, some of the eastern suburbs and another big cross through the Kwinana Industrial Area. She points out the smaller crosses.

"These areas were affected by the riots and the infected and were barricaded off by the Army. There were checkpoints north and south of the river in the beginning, but I don't know what's left of them now. And that big cross, try to steer clear of it. As I said, the aluminium refineries and chemical plants to the south are spewing toxic shit into the air and into the ocean. The radio said it was caustic acid or something. Bad stuff."

"I bet it is, so what are my options?"

"So, from here you can take these transmission lines corridors and bounce through paddocks along the main road to Mundaring. That should be pretty easy going but once you get to Mundaring, try to stay off the roads completely. Do you remember that fire back in October, the one those dickheads lit in Beelu National Park?"

"Yeah, didn't a few hikers or mountain bikers get caught in it?"

"Yeah, that whole area was barricaded off to the public. There's a road that cuts through the park here that pops you out on the other side near Kalamunda. Try to avoid the town centre. Take this service road south and follow these ranger trails until you are south of Armadale. Avoid Armadale like the plague."

"That's standard practice, isn't it?" I joke and Samira nods knowingly.

She traces a red line along the route, "You're going to have to skirt Armadale here and try to get into the rural areas of Byford. I know this is taking you right out of your way, but believe me, avoid anywhere built up. If the infected don't get you, the people trying to survive will. Are you with me so far?"

I stare intently at the map.

"Yeah, I'm just absorbing it all. Go on."

"Okay, after you get to these paddocks past Byford, you'll have to find your own way. You'd know that area better than me, I'm sure, here."

Samira offers me the red marker.

I take it from her and lean over the map, scanning it closely, "Between this farmland and Cockburn are several land developments that I could sneak through, but after that, I'll have to try between these reserves. But then…" I stare hard at the map, "It's all built up. It's a prick to get through in peak hour traffic, let alone when it's likely a zombie-filled, grid-locked, rabbit warren of 'Fuck That!"

Samira leans over my shoulder, studying the map.

"Could you make it to the beach and ride north toward South Beach?" Samira offers, "I wouldn't try riding through the suburbs, Dan. That KTM is loud, you'll attract a lot of attention."

I consider her option, "It'll have to do, the beach looks like it is the only way in. Hopefully, the waves are crashing hard enough to drown out the sound of the bike."

"It may be your only chance, we may even get a storm later today, that'll help you out a bunch. We've had a couple in the last week, so it's possible."

"Okay, that's the plan then. Fingers crossed it's all as easy as this thin red line. What's the time?"

Samira looks at the old clock on the wall behind us.

"It's 8.45am, you'll get there before dark."

I stare at the map for a long time, retracing the route and trying to calculate how long it will take. I mutter to myself for a few minutes, weighing up my options. I swing between unrestrained confidence, doubting myself and fearing what's ahead.

"Samira, are you staying here in Northam?"

"Yes, why?"

"Do you want to come with—"

"What? No, I just met you and my family are here and," Samira steps back from the table and toward the door, "No, I'm safer here. It's not worth the risk."

"No, Samira, your family are in the paddock. You're not as safe here as you think. Not alone. I've seen some horrible things almost happen to lone women out here."

Samira's eyebrows narrow and her jaw drops slightly.

"What? How dare... Dan, you need to go. Now. Get back to your daughter while you still can."

"Hey, I didn't mean to upset you, I just—"

"Crossed the fucking line? Yes, you did. I've helped you this far and this is all I will do, Dan. I've been more than nice to you and now my patience is gone," Samira's face reddens.

"Okay, I'll go." I fold the map up and quickly gather my things, not wanting her to retract the use of the maps or the bike. I roll the fuelled-up KTM out into the backyard and Samira follows me out, locking the garage door behind us. I reach into my backpack and pull out one of Russell's long-range radios, I offer it to Samira.

"Take this, if you get into trouble or change your mind, use it. I'll be on channel eight at dawn and at dusk each day. I'll call you when I get back to my daughter. The radios have been tweaked, so they should still work."

Samira takes the radio and holds it loosely by her side, but she says nothing.

"Thank you, Samira. You're a good person, well, as good as a person can be out here. I didn't mean to..."

"Roll the bike out into the back paddock and start it out there, I don't want you attracting anyone else."

"There's an extra charger for that radio with the solar panels you took, keep that radio charged and I'll check in with you tonight."

"Goodbye, Dan."

I sigh, "Bye, Samira. Stay safe."

I slip my helmet on and push the bike out a hundred metres into the paddock. It starts up the first time and I ride southwest towards Perth.

BRAAPS THROUGH THE 'BURBS

It takes two hours of zig-zagging through fenced paddocks and navigating steep rocky outcrops before I get within spitting distance of The Lakes, a whopping seventy kilometres from Northam. A route that would normally take just thirty minutes to complete by road, but that's not an option, so I'm sticking to the sandy firebreaks. And given that I haven't ridden in a while, progress is slow, but it's coming back to me quickly. I'm on the southern side of a deep cutting that slices the highway through what was once a rolling hill. The cutting's steep angled concrete embankments allow an unrestricted glimpse at the scale of the anarchy that lay ahead of me.

Hundreds, if not thousands, of cars are crammed bumper to bumper onto the highway. The east and westbound lanes are both occupied with eastbound traffic that were trying to escape the city.

A multi-car pile-up is blocking the entirety of the highway, the burnt-out husk of a fuel tanker sits in the middle of the highway amid a sea of blackened car bodies. A fire had consumed at least a hundred vehicles and melted the road beneath them, the steep banks on either side of the highway had prevented anyone from getting around it. Bodies lay charred and mangled on the ground or sit sizzled and bloated in their vehicles. Hundreds of zombies shuffle through the maze of parked cars further down and many more fill the drain on either side of the highway. The smell of burnt rubber and the stench of the walking corpses assaults every one of my senses. I continue riding along the fire breaks, focusing on staying upright through the boggy tracks. But the scene below is like something out of a post-apocalyptic blockbuster movie, it's surreal.

The bike's loud exhaust starts getting the attention of some of the meandering zombies and they attempt to climb the embankment and come after me.

"Fuck, I've got to move further away from the road," I twist the throttle and peel off into the paddock, "This is insane."

The smell of death hangs in the air, so much so that I have to ride with my visor open. Otherwise, the helmet traps the smell and I can fucking taste those decaying bastards, it multiplies my nausea and the growing tension in my chest. I roll through the paddocks and cross shallow creeks, it would actually be enjoyable if the odd wandering undead fool didn't attempt to give chase. Luckily, each would-be pursuer gives up shortly after I disappear over a hill or pass through another paddock gate. I never realised just how many ways a gate can be hung or locked until today. There are chains and shackles, rope, wire, makeshift wood-and-rope puzzle combinations, there are spring latches, loops of wire, daisy chains of padlocks and twisted knots of metal. Some have mechanisms that baffle the mind; like a hillbilly bogan skill tester. For anything that takes longer than five seconds to unlock, a pair of wire cutters or a well-placed boot makes quick work of a fence or stubborn gate.

I get to the outskirts of Mundaring, where my fuel tank and stomach are in need of a refill. Opportunity strikes when I find a jerry can in the back of a random ute in the middle of a half-harvested wheat crop. Five muesli bars from my backpack settle my stomach's demands for sustenance. I pull out the map and find the ranger trail that I need to use to get into the Beelu National Park. Samira was right, these tracks look much easier to navigate.

The forest air of the park is a welcome relief, the smell of death is replaced by the scent of neighbouring pine plantations and eucalyptus trees. I suck in lungfuls of it and take in the refreshing change of scenery. The Beelu National Park is home to a diverse ecosystem that skirts the city's main water reservoir. It has several tourist attractions and is intersected by notable walking and mountain bike trails, like the Bibbulmun Track and Mundi Biddi trails. Grasstrees and various Banksias carpet the sandy soils of the forest floor, while wandoo and, the larger, jarrah and marri trees dominate the canopy. Screeches from black cockatoos, kookaburra chortles and magpie warbles compete with the KTM's exhaust as I coast along a pea gravel four-wheel-drive track. The dense bushland of the park's outer limits soon thins out and opens up to a barren landscape of ash, blackened tree trunks and scorched soil—scars from a trio of arsonists.

In late October—after a particularly dry winter—two troubled youths and their stepdad thought setting fire to the national park would be a great way to bond and pass the time over a hot spring weekend. The trio used motorbikes, homemade drip torches and sparkler bombs to try and make a name for themselves as infamous arsonists. The resulting fire burned for three days and nights, decimated hundreds of hectares of the park, several private properties, caused millions of dollars in damage and claimed four human lives. Investigators determined it was arson very quickly, and a manhunt was underway for those responsible. The two youths were handed in by their biological father, after he had overheard them bragging about their handiwork to their mates. This made the News instantly and the boys were placed in protective custody because scores of people wanted them dead. The two boys were tried as adults, despite being fifteen and sixteen years old, fined $250,000 each and given a ten-year prison sentence that would be served once they turned eighteen. The stepfather, however, never stood trial. He was found in his back shed hanging from an extension cord, having committed suicide after the guilt of the four hikers' deaths had sunk in.

"Fuckin' mongrels!"

I'm on the main tourist drive that I've driven many times before, it's a popular cruising route for vintage car clubs, motorcycle clubs and cyclists, especially after recent upgrades to the formerly pothole-riddled road. The park had obviously seen a few bushfires roll through each summer, but nothing on this scale, I find myself shaking my head through most of the winding road as it esses through the once beautiful national park. I'm baffled trying to comprehend what goes through an arsonist's head.

I take a gravel road that forks off the main road just before the Kalamunda town limits. The track's entry has a big yellow gate blocking public vehicle access to it. I squeeze around it and head south toward Armadale along the 'ranger only' service road. The bushland on this side of the park is alive with the sounds of lorikeets. The smell of rich earth and eucalyptus trees reminds me of the countless weekends that I'd spent camping around here with family and friends growing up.

The track ends and I pop out onto a quiet tarmac road that funnels me into a much busier Roleystone. I side-step several housing estates and finally end up in a transmission line corridor, which allows me to sneak into the southern outskirts of Byford through some bushland. I'm further south than I'd like, but it is what it is. I make my way towards Byford's town centre, and I annoyingly need another fuel stop.

"Fuck me, this bike is thirsty."

I roll my near-empty bike into the cover of some bushes across the road from a wildlife attraction, Cohunu Koala Park. I take off my helmet and hang it from the handlebars. Just down the road is a petrol station, but it's in the open and dozens of abandoned cars and infected surround it. I count thirteen shuffling fuckers loitering.

I don't want to risk being seen, not with an empty fuel tank. I look over the road, searching for any other options when I decide on the wildlife park.

"I'll try here first."

I cross the road and jump the chain link fence, hoping to find a maintenance shed and some fuel to save me the riskier option of the service station.

The wildlife park is alive with activity; the screeches of cockatiels and parrots can be heard from the front gate, and the deep drumming of the ostriches and emus contend with the howls coming from the dingo enclosures. Screaming peacocks wander freely around the property as kangaroos laze in the cool dirt under the shade of the trees, scratching themselves. The noise is both a blessing and a curse. I can move quickly around the park, but the sheer noise of the animal calls also drowns out the sounds of anyone, or anything, that could be approaching. I turn left and follow the narrow railway track that encircles the property, hoping that it leads me to a holding shed full of tools and fuel. I move fast between shrubs and bushy trees. I avoid detection until a hidden whipper snipper lying on the ground foils my super-silent-stealth attempts. I fall onto the pea gravel and quickly get to my feet to scan the vicinity.

"Well, I'm glad no one saw that," I turn around to curse the flaming whipper snipper and see a red jerry can nestled under the bushy tree.

"Oh, please, please, please." I kneel over and grab the jerry can. It's three-quarters full and has '4 stroke only' written in permanent marker on the side of the container.

I whisper-yell in celebration, "Yes!"

I pop the cap and look inside to make sure it isn't mixed

and I'm pleased to see the fuel isn't blue or purple from any oil additives. I race back to my bike undetected and fill it up as quickly as possible. I saddle the bike and whip out my map to plan the next leg of my trip home.

"Okay, so I'm here," I finger the map, "I should be able to take this side road south out of Byford and then punch it across these back roads and properties."

I look closer at the map around the Cockburn and Aubin Grove suburbs, "Fuck, why is it so built up!"

I study it closer and see a string of reserves and semi-rural areas that have the potential to get me from The Spectacles up towards Lake Coogee.

"Sick, from there I just have to skip through some scrubland into Woodman Point Regional Park and then I'm on Coogee Beach."

My finger traces up the shoreline and stops at the Port Coogee Marina, a relatively new and posh oceanside development.

"Shit, I'm sure I could peel around that estate, somehow, and then I'm home free," I convince myself.

I mark the new route on the map and fold it in a way so that only the route remaining is visible. I slip it under the strap of the tank bag for reference. It's almost 3pm and the sunny morning is long gone. The sky is overcast, once again, and the wind is starting to pick up, a storm is brewing.

"It's time to move," I start the bike and peel out.

Brraaaaaap!

The Byford to Woodman Point leg eats up three and a half hours because of detours like zombie-crowded access gates and grid-locked intersections dead-ending me. This slowed me down, yes, but each kilometre I get closer to home replenishes my energy and fuels my excitement. I confidently weave around, over or through each inconvenience and I make it all the way to Woodman Point Reserve without a hitch, thank fuck.

I'm currently squatting behind a homeless person's former shelter in the middle of the Woodman Point Reserve. I'm hiding just off of a coastal walking path with my KTM switched off and leaning against a tree. I take the opportunity to inhale a few more muesli bars and finish off the last of my water. I stretch my legs and try to crack my lower back between glugs and bites. The storm is gearing up all around me, the skies are dark grey and quickly transitioning to black. The wind is howling too, the trees sway and creak with each chilly gust. The rain appears to be holding off for now, but I can smell the wet asphalt of the carparks around me. It won't be long before it starts bucketing down; the distant rumbling of thunder gets louder as the storm comes in over the ocean.

This is the last leg of the journey, I've managed to navigate every obstacle up until now and all that stands between me and my home is a quick skip along the beach. I can do this. The beach access is only a hundred or so metres up the path ahead of me. I pick up the motorbike and rock it from side to side, listening for the sloshing of fuel in the tank.

"Hmmm, I'll make it."

I figure there's a little less than a quarter of a tank left, which is more than enough to get me along the beach, through the marina and up to South Beach. I could walk from here if I need to and still be home in time for dinner, that thought alone takes a weight off of my shoulders.

I zip and button up my riding gear and start walking my bike up along the red bitumen footpath, I grip the handlebars tightly as I wheel the bike along. My head pivots left and right with every creak and moan of the Rottnest Cypress trees that line the walking trail. Luckily, the path is long and straight enough to see all the way to the end, where it stops at a T-junction. To the left is the beach access and to the right is a large carpark for a beachside café. The trees and shrubs thrash around in the wind, the whooshing of the branches and shimmering of dry leaves are the only things I can hear. A knot tightens in my stomach as I near the end of the path. I can smell the familiar stench of death and my pulse pounds inside the helmet. Ten metres before the junction, I hop on my bike and turn the ignition to the 'on' position; my thumb hovers over the electronic start button. I tiptoe up to the T-junction and stop; I check the left path first, it looks clear, and then I look to the right and become very still.

A wall of the infected are standing right there in front of me. Hundreds of the twitching, hunched-over bastards are less than fifteen metres away—I can't even see the carpark through them. The pack is huddled together tightly with their backs to me, and the onshore wind, so there aren't any eyes on me or my exit. I slowly drop the visor of my helmet and do up the chin strap. I stab the start button and twist the accelerator hard, the braaap of the 450's motor gets every single one of the fucker's attention. The mob snap around and howl as I kick the gear selector down and pop the clutch. The KTM's impressive torque fishtails me up the sandy path toward the beach. I only just manage to maintain control as I whip down the full length of the beach access path narrowly avoiding the heavy yellow gate blocking four-wheel drive access to the beach. I power slide out onto the open stretch of Coogee Beach.

"Move, move, move!" I yell at myself.

I carve through the hard-packed sand of the popular stretch of beach and fly past the handful of oblivious beach-going zombies that are dotted along the shore. I whip under the Coogee Jetty, and in sixty seconds, I jump off the beach and onto the well-maintained lawns of a park along Socrates Parade. I have to Blitzkrieg this next leg or I'm fucked. I take a hard right and then a quick left and I'm on the main street of the marina, Orsino Boulevard.

"Fuck!"

A sea of the undead stands before me, crowded together in another foul-smelling mass of decomposing assholes. I see a road off to the left and I gun for it, it's the only exit and, of course, it's right next to the front line of the zombie horde, the KTM launches towards the only escape.

Braaapppp!

I mount the footpath and power through the closing gap between the building and the newly excited pack. One of the runners dives for me, but misses and trips in front of me. I ride straight over the top of him and the jolt from his large body almost bucks me off the bike. I weave through the shopping centre carpark and out onto Medina Parade. I jump onto the footpath and race through the estate as fast as I can toward the beach access gate at the end of the road. There are so many infected. I clear the sand dune at the end of the road and I'm back onto the beach.

"Phew-uck me! That was such a shit idea!"

The waves crash hard on the shores of CY O'Connor Beach as I speed across the wet sand. The rear wheel sends a rooster tail of sand high up into the air behind me as I travel unchecked over the old power station's drainage canal and continue across the shore.

The Old South Fremantle Power Station dominates the ocean frontage, the long concrete structure with its yawning rectangular windows stands tall and silent. Its sixty-year-old industrial skeleton—having been long abandoned—is weathered and heavily tagged with graffiti, but there's new life in the haunting landmark. On its roof, I can see the tops of different coloured tents and people with those tall garden tiki torches standing in each of its corners. At the building's base, I see caravans crammed into the fenced perimeter like Tetris.

"What the hell?"

I look again and see people, likely on look-out duty, pointing over at me, "That can't be good."

The windows on the floor level of the building are boarded up and zombies are clawing at the first of two eight-foot-high steel fences surrounding the heritage site. The people must be using it as a fort, or something, which seems strange, as the building doesn't scream 'impenetrable fortress'. Its usual inhabitants are often homeless people, junkies and graffiti artists. The smell of stale piss and the luxury of no power or running water must appeal to some.

A shot rings out from the rooftop of the building and ends my curiosity, "Fuck this!"

I twist the throttle and disappear up the beach and out of their range. I need to get out of sight and off this fucking bike fast. I continue up the beach for another couple of minutes and then ride up into the cover of the dune vegetation, I kill the bike's engine and roll it into a denser area of bushes between a few dunes. I throw off my helmet, pull out my pistol and crouch by my bike, waiting to see if anyone comes looking for me. Five very anxious, yet uneventful, minutes pass and I decide that I should move forward. I leave the bike where it is and pocket the keys, who knows, I may come back and get it later. I undo the tank bag and slide the map inside it. I consider taking off my thick leather jacket but I leave it on for protection, and warmth, it is getting cooler as the storm nears. I only have one of my gloves on and I put the other away in my bag, my gloveless hand grips Pat's pistol tightly. The shotgun holster is strapped tightly to me on the inside of my jacket and the jacket's pockets are full of shotgun and pistol ammunition. Hopefully, I don't need to use it, but I can only imagine how many zombies are in the area and how many more I would attract if I fired either of these guns.

I clear the bushes and cross the road to the high-rise apartment buildings that line the promenade. I move silently from cover to cover, trying to avoid the shattered glass and loud debris that's covering the ground. The first couple of streets are quiet and I make good progress, but when I get to the public reserve at the entrance to my street, I'm forced to hide in some bushes under a massive eucalyptus tree.

A pack of forty or so infected block the path to my house, they are crowded around a station wagon that is revving its tits off. Some poor bastard had probably tried making a run for it and got swarmed by the pack, who are now eating the poor bugger in his driver's seat. They clamber over each other in a frenzy trying to feed, unknowingly jamming their meal's foot down onto the accelerator.

"Damn it." I whisper, clenching my fist tightly, "I'm so close. Maybe I could go round... No, no," I argue with myself, "I live in a fucking cul-de-sac, that's the only way in or out".

The skies above open up and it starts to rain. Perfect. I take off my backpack and hold it above my head, although the tree shelters me from the bulk of the rain, the wind is whipping it at me sideways. Fifteen agonising minutes pass and the pack is still feeding on the poor guy in the station wagon. Fortunately, the engine had overheated and stalled out five minutes earlier, the noise was attracting way more attention than I wanted.

The storm is now in full swing as mini squalls rip through the park, dumping sheets of rain and loose branches everywhere. I'm desperate for a window of opportunity to run across the park and into the garden of the house at the entrance to my street but there are just too many infected nearby to risk it. The Coddiwomple Place street sign teases me as I ache for an opening. I bow my head in frustration, mumbling to an unknown force when my prayers are answered. A tree limb snaps off in the wild winds on the opposite side of the park, it crashes down onto a BMW parked in the street and its alarm and lights go off spectacularly. The pack's attention shifts to the BMW's blaring siren and they move toward it; some run across the park at speed and others shuffle their corpses toward the noise with laboured efforts. This is my window.

I wait until all but a few are over by the BMW, and I sprint across the park and leap into the bushes of the house on the corner of my street. I pause and scan the street for movement, it's clear. I run through the front lawns of another three houses and crouch behind a Mitsubishi Delica, careful not to trigger any alarm.

"Okay, three more houses and I'm there. I'm home."

I suddenly become very anxious, the 'what ifs' and creeping doubts multiply very quickly.

"Stop it! You're almost home! Focus."

I jump a small fence and run past the first house when the bright white beam of a security light scares the absolute shit out of me.

"Fuck!"

I dive over the next fence and hurdle over the last one, sprinting into the cover of my neighbour's tall hedges.

"Oh, fuck me," I pant hard, "That fucking security light."

I wait, watching the security light intensely, urging it to shut off and hoping like fuck nothing is attracted to its glow. It shuts off and nothing stirs in the street.

All attention remains on the BMW in the park.

"Thank fuck for that."

I push my way through the hedge and squat next to the hip-height fence that I share with my neighbour. I peer over the fence and sigh in relief.

"There it is, home. 14 Coddiwomple Place."

A cloud of emotion fogs my mind as I squat behind the fence—relief, happiness, joy—I just want to leap across the lawn and knock on the front door. But fear and hesitation rear their ugly heads and I start to think about every negative reality that could be on the other side of that door. I shake my head and try to ground myself. I look up and take in what I can see in front of me. My beautiful home.

HONEY, I'M HOME!

The front yard is untouched, no corpses or carnage litter it and the only thing on the lawn is the hose and sprinkler; this is a good sign. The roller shutters on the front windows are closed and sheets of Colorbond fencing have been screwed into the wall over them. The front door is barricaded in a similar way, heavy wooden pallets are screwed to two thick posts in the walkway and a reel of barbed wire is fixed to the base and halfway up.

"Impressive, Maria. How did you"—a thought crosses my mind, she couldn't possibly have done this by herself—"Ah."

My assumption jumps straight to the prick that Maria had cheated on me with. I look across the road and see a black, jacked-up Jeep Gladiator with ridiculous gold rims.

"Yep, just as I thought. Nik's here."

I look down the side of the house and see the side gate

swinging in the mercy of the wind. I slowly jump the hip-height fence and go to the gate. I grab it to stop it from swinging. I enter the backyard and close the gate, latching it securely. I draw my pistol, but I know I can't use it, so I wedge it in the front of my pants. I creep down the side wall of the house, pleased to see the roller shutters are fully closed here too, but there's no extra panelling protecting them like at the front of the house. I see several dents in the shutters, dirty fist-sized smears mark each dent. Someone has tried to get in or tried to attack the girls.

Maybe they're still here? I bend down and pick up one of the 6ft metal star pickets piled against the wall, it's not much in the way of a weapon, but it'll have to do. I grip the picket tightly with both hands. I get to the end of the side wall when I hear banging and other strange sounds coming from the backyard. The sounds appear to be coming from the carport door on the other side of the house.

"Shit, someone is still here," I grip the picket even tighter and cross the yard, stopping behind the pizza oven and stonewalled barbeque.

I lean around it and see someone banging on the rear door of the carport, a one-armed, surfer-looking dude wearing board shorts. He swings his remaining arm lazily at the door. His shoulder-length blonde hair hangs over his face as he leans his head against the frame, moaning and groaning intermittently. At his feet, an older man is lying face down on the concrete. He's wearing a long-sleeved purple business shirt, black dress pants and his right hand is loosely gripping an axe. I see a garish, chunky gold watch adorning his wrist, the same kind that Nik—the Eastern European prick that Maria is now seeing on the regular—

wears. I reach around the side of the barbeque wall and gently tip over the plaster garden gnome standing against it, the spare set of house keys are still inside it. I loop the keyring around my finger and grip the picket like a Civil War soldier gripping their bayonet. I run up behind the one-armed surfer and stab the star picket into the base of his skull and pin him against the door. I pull the picket out and the surfer falls to the ground. I stab him repeatedly in the throat and face, making sure that he doesn't get back up.

I place the bloodied picket against the wall and grab the surfer by his foot, I drag his body to the farthest corner of the yard and dump him there. I walk over to Nik's body and roll him onto his back. The skull of the thick-necked, barrel-chested man is caved in and his forehead is a mess of shattered bone and gore. The surfer dude must've bashed his head against the pavement until Nik stopped fighting back. Every cell in my body tells me to punch the man in his lifeless face. I raise a fist and it hovers there for a second— this man had taken my wife, ruined my family and now had the audacity to hole up in my house with *my* daughter?!

"I should drag you out into the street for those freaks to feast on, you piece of shit."

I stand up and wipe the rain away from my soaked face. I look back at the house and see that the large glass door and windows of the lounge room are barricaded with metal framing and more wooden pallets; I unclench my fist.

"But I know Maria didn't do any of this," I gesture to the reinforcements protecting my family and my home.

"So, thank you," I kick Nik in the ribs, "But fuck you."

I grab Nik by the feet and drag his heavy body over to the back fence where I dumped the surfer. Dragging Nik takes a lot more effort. I catch my breath and walk over to the back door of the carport, I slide the key into the barrel of the deadlock and knock lightly on the door.

"Maria? Bella? It's me, it's dad. I'm coming in," I whisper. I creak open the door slightly and repeat myself, "Maria? Bella? I'm coming in, I'm home."

No one responds. I struggle to push the door open because a pile of boxes, suitcases and gym equipment that are stacked up against it.

"Very smart, girls," I push hard against the door and the pile of random crap falls. Clashing and clattering as it hits the floor, then I hear whimpering.

"Maria? Bella? Girls, it's me," I squeeze through the narrow gap in the doorway and shut the door quietly, locking it behind me. I begin restacking the wall of crap.

"Girls!" I whisper-yell.

The carport is pitch black and the only sounds I hear are of the storm and the heavy rain pelting the tiled roof.

"Maria? Bella?"

I walk toward the hallway entrance door, but trip over some unseen object. I kick it across the room and it hits the wire mesh side of a large chicken coop that I'd repurposed as a dog kennel for Bones. An audible whimper makes me freeze. I don't speak or move a muscle. The muffled whimpering continues, but I can't see shit.

Is it one of the girls? The dog?

I reach into my backpack, pull out my phone and I press the torch icon. I aim the phone's torch at my feet and sweep the bright light upwards toward the kennel and move it closer to the sound. At the back of the cage, up against the walled side, a balled-up mass shakes beneath a black blanket. I draw my pistol.

"Oi, who's in there? Show yourself."

I pull the hammer back and it clicks loudly, the mass stops shaking and the blanket drops slowly, exposing a pair of dark brown, teary eyes.

"Amor? Is that really you?" a quivering voice asks.

The blanket drops and completely reveals a face.

"Maria!" I put the pistol down, "Maria! It's you. Thank fuck, where's Bella?"

I move to the kennel's door.

"What are you doing in the dog kennel?"

I go to open the cage door, but there's a padlock through the latch, as well as a large U-lock and a thick chain binding it shut. I grab a nearby battery-powered camping lamp and twist it on and the carport lights up.

"Dan, stop, stop. You don't understand!"

"Who put you in here, Maria?" My eyes scan the room, "Where's Bella?"

I reef at the locks some more.

"Amor, stop it. You can't let me out," Maria grabs the chain and pulls it tight, bracing her feet against the door.

"What? Why?!"

I try to reach through the mesh of the cage to fiddle with the lock and Maria kicks the cage door hard, I retract my hands back instantly.

"Danito! Enough! Listen to me. Mira!"—Maria holds out her arm and I shine my torch light at it— "I was bitten, Dan. That blonde piece of shit surfer boy, the one that's been banging on the door all fuckin' day."

I fall onto my arse in shock, "Wh... When? How?"

"This afternoon, before this storm. He's been banging

and banging for a whole day now, we didn't want him attracting more and... We tried to get rid of him and it... It doesn't matter."

"Where is our daughter, Maria? Where's Bella?"

Maria starts sobbing uncontrollably, "I... I..."

"Maria!" I slam the side of the cage with my hand.

"She's in the house. I told her to lock me in here and not to open the door for anyone. I'm so glad you're home, amor, I don't know what to do and..."

I leave the kennel and go to the hallway door, I knock lightly on the door as I did before, "Bella, darling. It's me, Dad. Can you open up the door, sweetie?"

I hear shuffling beyond the door, but nothing more.

"Bella! It's me," I pat myself down looking for my spare house keys as Maria calls out.

"Bella, darling. It's okay. Daddy's home, don't be rude. He's missed you, so come out."

"Daddy?" Bella's voice passes through the door.

"Oh, sweetie, you have no idea how good it is to hear your voice," tears well in my eyes.

"Daddy!" Bella twists the deadlocks and pulls the door inwards, "Daddy!!"

Bella wraps her arms around my legs and buries her head into them.

"Daddy, there were all of these sick people trying to get into the house. And you weren't here. And I was scared. And Mummy's friend is mean. And I missed you. And then Mummy got hurt and went in the dog cage. And I didn't know where you were. And you wouldn't answer your phone. Why didn't you answer your phone? And why are you so wet?" Bella starts to cry as nervous word-vomit pours out of her.

"Shhh, shh, shh, shhh. Sweetie, I'm here now and I'm never leaving again."

I pick Bella up. She wraps her legs around my waist and squeezes me even harder. I squeeze her back just as much and sway from side to side with her.

Thank you, thank you, thank you.

A long minute passes before I put Bella down. She races over to her mother and tries to hug her through the wire mesh. Maria moves away from Bella, but leaves her fingers stretched out through the mesh. Bella grabs them. And tries to squeeze and pull the rest of Maria's hand through the cage.

"Come on, Bella. Mummy's sick and I don't want you to catch my cold. Remember when we went to visit your grandma in the hospital and you couldn't get too close?"

Bella nods. "It's like that. We don't want to share our germs, do we? Eyook."

Bella mimics her mother, shaking her head, "Eyook!"

This is the girls' reaction to anything yucky; like a hairy spider or a smelly dad fart.

"Mi niña, can you go play in your room while I talk to your father? I have so much to tell him."

Bella looks up at me with wide eyes and then looks back down, knowingly. She mutters through her partly closed mouth, "Are you going to yell at Daddy? He just got here."

Bella looks at the ground as she fiddles with the kennel's wire mesh wall.

"No, honey. I'm not going to yell. We have to be quiet, remember? I just have to talk to Daddy about my… Germs."

"Mmm. okay, but I better not hear any yelling," Bella

adds as she walks off. I tussle her hair as she squeezes past me and out through the doorway.

"I'll see you soon, kiddo," I close the door behind her and walk over to Maria. I grab another battery-powered camping lamp, "Show me your arm, Maria."

Maria sits cross-legged in the kennel, her head is low and she is hunched over. She picks at the skin on the side of her thumbnail as she talks.

"You know, amor, I thought I'd never see you again."

"Well, you almost didn't, this infection is everywhere and people are going fucking crazy."

"How did you get here? Where have you been?" Maria tilts her head up for my response, tears run down her pale, clammy cheeks.

"I drove, Maria. All the way from the rig. A lot of people are dead and I almost died more than a few times trying to find a way back to you and Bella. These have been some of the hardest days of my life."

"I see..."

"And you? How have you and Bella been holding up? I saw, er, your mate in the backyard."

Maria looks off into the distance, rolling her tongue in her slightly open mouth, "His name is Nik, and if it wasn't for him, Bella and I would surely be dead. So don't start with your bullshit!"

"Stop. I saw what he did to the house. I've seen the barricades. He did good."

"Yes, well, you weren't here, as usual, so I had to get him to do *your* job," Maria casts a mean and hollow gaze at me as she finishes her sentence.

Her words are still as venomous as ever.

I pick up the lock keeping Maria in the kennel and drop it against the mesh.

"Obviously, he didn't do *too* good a job, eh? How long has it been since you were bitten?"

Maria mutters something in Spanish under her breath.

"Four hours ago, Dan."

"How do you feel?"

Maria wipes beading sweat from her brow and clenches her arm, "I'm turning into one of those fucking creatures, Dan. How do you think I feel? I'm stuck in this fuckin' cage," Maria kicks the mesh, "And I don't think a Panadol is going to make me any better!" Maria's anger quickly turns to sorrow and she weeps into her hands, "But now you are here, so you can protect Bella and get her away from this place, right?"

I sit in front of Maria with my head in my hands.

"There is no 'taking her away from this place', Maria, this infection is everywhere. I mean, between here and Port Coogee is wall to wall with the infected and if *they* aren't a big enough problem, the survivors are. I've had people try to kill me, ambush me, throw themselves in front of my ute and, you know the abandoned power station? There are people with rifles up there, they shot at me as I drove across the beach to get here!"

"What?" disbelief paints itself across her face.

"There is no escaping this, we just have to, I don't know, wait it out?"

"Wait it out?" Maria laughs, "By tomorrow morning I will be one of those... those things! You'd let our daughter see me like that? You'd keep me in this cage?"

She starts coughing violently, spitting blood into her

hand. "No, I'll tell you what we are going to do, once you put Bella to bed, you're going to take me outside and you're going to take that gun and put a bullet in my head," Maria pushes an index finger hard into the middle of her forehead, "And then you will bury me, so Bella doesn't have to see her mother become a zombie, or whatever the fuck they're calling them."

"No. I..."

"Well, give me the gun and I'll do it. Once again, it's me who has to protect this family. Where did you get that gun, uh? It's like a cowboy gun?"

I pick up the gun off the carport's cement floor and hold it in my hands, "A friend gave it to me. We were attacked and then I had to watch him die in the mud. Without this gun, I wouldn't be here. Without Pat, I wouldn't have even made it past Laverton."

"Well, you sure took your time, didn't you?"

I stand up and wedge the pistol in the waist of my pants.

"This isn't about us, Maria. Pull your fucking head in. I'm here for Bella, that's all. I'll come to check on you soon." I leave the smaller torch by the kennel and switch off the bigger lamp.

"Whatever, Dan," Maria trails off, muttering in Spanish.

I walk into the house and close the door behind me. I find Bella making sandwiches by candlelight in the kitchen.

"I'm making ham and cheese sandwiches for us, Daddy. How many do you want, four or five?"

I laugh as I walk up to the bench, "I'll have two, sweetie. How many are you having?"

"Oh, okay. I'll have one. Mummy said we have to make the food last as long as possible."

"Your mother is very smart, sweetie, so I'll just have one too."

"Oh, I thought you'd be hungry," Bella finishes the first sandwich and hands it to me, "The salt and pepper are on the table."

"Thank you, sweetie. Are you sure you don't want any help?" I pull myself up onto the bench and sit beside her as she makes her own sandwich.

"No, I'm independent," Bella announces.

"It would appear so." I smile widely at my grown-up, little girl. I bite into my sandwich and watch her quietly.

"What did you and Mummy talk about?"

"We talked about you, and how brave and grown-up you are," I lie, trying to avoid the topic.

"No, you didn't. I'm not dumb, Daddy."

"Haha okay, you got me," I throw my hands up playfully, "We talked about mummy's sickness."

"Is she going to be okay?"

"Yeah, she, ah. Tomorrow, I'll take her to see a doctor."

"I thought everywhere was closed, because of the sick people and the fires."

"Well, yes. They are closed," I struggle to keep the lie going, but I try to push through it. "This is a special doctor, he'll take Mummy away to make her feel better."

"A special doctor? What's his name? I'll Google him."

Fuck, this kid is relentless.

"Well, there are too many sick people around here, so they'll take mummy out of the city. Where it's safe. You might not see Mummy for a little while."

Bella plays with the idea in her head for a moment,

"But the doctor will fix her, right?"

"They're the best doctors in all of 'straya."

"Can we go with her? When will you go to the doctors?"

"In the morning, before you wake up, but we can't go with her, sweetie. The doctor only has room for sick people. It'll be just me and you for a while, Bella. Would you like that?"

"Yes! You've been away too long. You're always away."

"Okay then, how about you make Mummy a sandwich and we'll go hang out with her for a bit, we can drink soft drinks and eat some chocolate. It'll be like a little going-away party for Mummy."

"Yay, I'll make her some avocado and cheese sandwiches, they're her favourite!"

"Alright, sweetie. I'll get the soft drink and chocolate."

While Bella smashes up the last avocado to make Maria's sandwich, I go into the carport to tell Maria the lie I told Bella. She agrees to go along with it and we make our plan for the morning. We both agree that the gun will be too loud and that we will have to make it as quiet and painless as possible. The plan goes as follows:

After Bella goes to sleep tonight, Maria will drink a cocktail of prescription meds, sleeping pills and some muscle relaxants to knock her out. Once Maria is asleep, I'll unlock the kennel and take her outside into the backyard. Maria suggested that I hit her over the head with a hammer during her drug-induced slumber. Which I agree to, but secretly, I hope that the storm gets worse in the night, so I can use the lightning and thunder to mask a well-timed gunshot. Bludgeoning the ex-wife to death may be some ex-husband's dream, but it's not mine. That's not to say I haven't imagined it many times. I'll roll Maria up in a tarp once the task is done and place her with the other two bodies along the back fence. I'll hide them under some branches and whatever else I can find. In the following days, I would dig a grave in the neighbour's backyard and bury them all, so Bella never finds them.

A light knocking on the hallway door alerts us to Bella's presence, she's such a polite young lady.

"Come on in, Honey," Maria says, wiping away tears.

I turn away from Bella to compose myself, too.

"I brought you avocado and cheese sandwiches, Mum."

"My favourite! Ñami!" Maria exaggerates.

Although the conversation about Maria's morality was had in a strangely calm manner, the finality of it, and the lie that I'd have to keep telling Bella, weighs down on me and I have to excuse myself.

"Sweetie, I'm so sorry. I forgot to get the chocolate and soft drink. You sit with ya Mum and I'll go get it. Did you need anything, Maria?"

"The wine, please, both bottles and a glass for yourself."

"I can do that. I'll be back in a jiffy."

I gather the food and drinks and place them on the counter before walking to the ensuite to get the pills for Maria, I place them in my riding jacket's pockets with the shotgun shells and catch a glimpse of myself in the mirror. I stare hard at my reflection and question what the fuck it is that I'm looking at—a shitty husband that's about to kill and take away his child's mother as she sleeps. I frown at the man staring back at me, disgusted.

I spend the next few minutes silently arguing with myself, but no matter how I try to sugar-coat it, or how I try to justify it, I still can't bear to look myself in the mirror. I punch the mirror and walk out of the en-suite. I walk back into the carport with our food and drinks.

"Look who's got Black Forest chocolate and wine?"

I try to act like my usually animated self to bring some normality into the evening.

"Yay! Chocolate," Bella says.

"Yay! Wine." Maria follows.

I sit down next to Bella, who scoots as close as she can to the kennel with her knees resting on its frame as she reaches into the cage to get closer to her mum.

"Now, what were you two talking about? Boys? Ponies?" I jest.

"No, Daddy. Eww, boys"

Damn, right, 'Eww, boys', I think to myself.

Maria chimes in, "We were actually talking about how smelly you are, Dan. When was the last time you showered, uh?" She half laughs and coughs.

"Yeah, Dad. Shower much?"

"Well, I did have a shower the other day," I lift my arm and sniff myself, and then I sniff my hands and clothes. I can still smell the lingering scent of my night with Natalie on my fingers and in my facial hair. We didn't exactly get a chance to finish our coffees that morning, let alone shower off the filth of the evening.

"Well, I've been on the motorbike all day sweating, then it rained and this jacket was already pretty bad."

"Where did you get that jacket anyway, Dan? Did you take it off of a hobo?" Maria asks.

"Yeah, Dad. You smell like a hobo..." Bella laughs, "Wait, what's a hobo?"

Maria enjoys giving Bella ammunition to gang up on

me in situations like these. It reminds me of the good old days, before the separation.

"Never you mind, little lady. I got the jacket off a friend. After my ute, er, broke down outside of Northam. She gave me this and the motorbike I rode here on."

"Ooo, does Daddy have a girlfriend?" Bella taunts.

"Haha, not quite, sweetie. I traded her for it."

Maria starts coughing again, bloody spittle trickles down her chin. I pour her a glass of wine and go to hand it to her, forgetting about the mesh separating us.

"Er, how do I pass this to you in the kennel?"

"I got it!" Bella pulls a set of keys out of a small pocket in her dress and unlocks the first of the locks holding the kennel door closed.

Maria and I share a look of amusement.

"Sweetie, you'd better give me those keys. We'll leave the U-lock on for now. I can fit the glass between this gap."

I take the keys from Bella and pass Maria her wine.

Bella looks at the ground and fiddles with the chocolate bar wrapper, as if she's done something wrong.

"Honey," Maria reaches through the gap and places her hand on Bella's knee, "This is fine, it's much safer if I stay in here."

"Okay," Bella opens the bar of Cadbury Dairy Milk Black Forest and nibbles at it a square at a time.

I pour myself a glass of wine and a lemonade for Bella.

"A toast to us," I raise my glass in front of Bella, "The independent," I nod to her, giving her a wink.

"The brave," I nod to Maria,

"And…"—Bella interrupts—

"To the smelly!" She chuckles to herself and Maria

sends her a wink as if to say well done.

I shake my head and continue, "Okay then, to us. The independent, the brave and the smelly," I reach over and squeeze Bella's ticklish tummy.

We clink our glasses and sip our wine and lemonade.

PLEASE PICK UP

The night goes by and it truly feels like we are a family again. Just Bella with her mum and dad, having a fun night on the concrete floor of the carport. This is what I had raced back for: my daughter, her smile and moments like these. After a few hours of laughing, playing games and binging on chocolate and lemonade, young Bella passes out in my lap. I am very happy that Bella's last memories of her mother and our family being together are so warm and filled with joy. I look down at her and kiss the top of her head, whispering into her soft hair.

"I missed you so much, beautiful," I kiss her again.

I look up at Maria, who is on her fifth glass of wine, and she smiles. She stares at us with kind eyes and a heavy heart.

"For someone who said he never wanted to be a father, it suits you well, amor," Maria says, holding a half-empty wine glass to her chest.

"I'm going to put her to bed."

I stand up with Bella in my arms and nuzzle her head into my neck, she stirs but remains asleep.

Maria hums to herself and asks me, "Do you have them? The, um..."

I look down at Maria; her glazed eyes, flushed cheeks and limp hands tell me she's a little drunk.

"I assume you mean these?"

I pull out the two bottles of pills.

"Yes, amor."

I awkwardly bend down with Bella and my arms and hand the pills to her through the kennel's gate.

"I'll be back soon."

Maria nods and ushers me away with the tipsy flicking of her wrist. I walk through the hallway door and down the passageway into Bella's room. I pull back her puffy pink duvet and lay her gently in her bed. She rolls over and grabs her giant sloth plush toy and balls up around it.

I tuck her in and kiss her temple, "Goodnight, beautiful. I'll see you in the morning."

I walk to her door and linger in the doorway. I look back at her, envious of how peacefully she is sleeping, and I close the door softly. I return to Maria in the carport and sit across from her. Two empty pill bottles sit just outside the kennel door.

"I didn't even get to kiss her one last time, or feel one more of her hugs or smell her hair..." tears roll down Maria's face and her chin quivers, she silences her sobs by finishing her glass of wine, "Where were you, Danito?"

Hot guilt washes over me.

"I... I tried to get back as fast as I could, Maria. You

have no idea what is between here and there. No idea."

"No. You shouldn't have been out there. When you got sick, you should have come home to us. Your family."

"Home? You didn't want me here, fuckin' Nik was here. I'm renting some shithole apartment miles away because you didn't want me here!"

Maria smashes the wine glass in the kennel.

"We always wanted you here, so don't you dare. That's all I ever wanted. All I ever needed. Just you and Bella. And maybe that dumb dog."

The dog!

"Where is he?"

"I don't know, the stupid fuckin' thing ran off a couple of days ago. I don't know where he went."

Maria starts coughing horrendously. She cups her hands over her mouth and black, bloody spittle covers them. Dark bags sag heavily under her dulling eyes. She dabs a cloth at the corner of her mouth and I see that the flesh on her arms has become waxy and discoloured.

"Maria, I know this means very little now. but I'm sorry. I'm sorry I wasn't home and I'm sorry I chose work over my family."

"It's a bit late now, Danito. But you are here, and that says something," Maria's stomach gurgles loudly as the cocktail of wine and pills churns inside of her.

"Promise me that you will never leave her side, amor. Never. You get her through this and you stick around until she has children of her own. And then, you'll be there for her children, too."

Maria breaks down crying, "I will never see my baby grow up. Or hold my baby's babies."

"I promise, I will protect her from now until the day I die, Maria."

I hate seeing her so distraught and hopeless. I quietly hope that she passes out soon, to put an end to her suffering, but she goes on.

"You're not a bad man, Dan," Maria hiccups, "You're weird. And you work too much, but you're not so bad." Maria throws up a little in her mouth, but she forces it back down. "I'm going to lie down now. My head is…" Maria slurs a string of jumbled Spanglish and says, "Te amo, mi amor. Siempre."

Then Maria passes out, never to speak another word or to see another day again. I reach through the kennel door and squeeze her unconscious hand.

"Y tu, mi amor. I love you, too."

I feel something cold and round on her finger as I squeeze her hand, it's the engagement ring that I had given her all those years ago. I haven't seen it on her finger since the separation. Despite all of the anger, heartache and all of our mistakes, she still loved me and I still loved her. I pull her hand through the kennel and cry into it, I hold it to my face with both hands for some time.

I leave Maria in the kennel, for now, and walk back into the house. I rummage through my backpack for the radio and try to summon Samira.

"Samira, Samira, this is Dan. Do you have a copy?"

I look up at the clock on the wall, it's 10.46pm.

"Samira, Samira, this is Dan, do you read me, over?"

Only static comes through the speaker.

"Fuck, she probably turned it off already. It is a little bit later than dusk."

I leave the radio on the counter and pull a bottle of rum out of the cupboard above the fridge.

"Dan, is that you? Are you okay?"

The radio squawks to life, I grab it and reply.

"Samira, ah, it's good to hear from you. Yeah, I ran into a few problems along the way, but I got here okay."

"Glad to hear it, Dan. How's your kid, Bella?"

"Bella is fine, I just put her to bed. I would have called sooner, but yeah. How are things up there?"

"That's fantastic. Things are quiet up here. How's everything looking down there in the 'burbs?"

"It's a little crowded. Listen, Maria was bitten and she's not going to make it. It's just me and Bella now."

"Oh, no. Are you okay?"

"Yeah, I'm fine. We are going to stay put for a while. I'll call you each morning and night as I said, once all of this blows over, I owe you a beer!"

"And a 2016 KTM. But a beer's a good start. Okay, I'll try to keep this thing charged. Talk soon."

"Yeah, talk in the morning. Stay safe, Samira. Again, thank you. Over and out"

"You too. Over and out?" Samira's last transmission sounds like a question.

I turn the radio off and leave it on the bench. I grab my bottle of rum and pour myself a glass. I take a large gulp and inhale sharply, "Oh, yes. That's the ticket."

I take two more swigs and place the empty glass in the sink. I'll be needing another glass after I complete this next task. I slide the soggy riding gloves and musty leather riding jacket back on and tuck the pistol in the front of my jeans. I leave the sawn-off shotgun and its holster on the counter underneath my backpack. I walk back through the carport and out the rear door into the backyard. The rain is still hammering down and thunder rumbles loudly above. The occasional flash of lightning illuminates the entire yard. It looks like I'll be able to use the gun after all.

I check the side gate at the front of the house, thankfully, it's still closed. I wedge a branch through the latch so the wind doesn't rattle it open; I'll have to find a padlock for it later. I check the narrow side access on the other side of the house by the carport; it's clear. I check on the two bodies against the back fence, no movement there, everything seems to be in order. I drag a large blue tarp to the back of the yard and open it up, I stuff a corner under the surfer dude, so it doesn't blow away and then I head back inside to get Maria. I prop the door open so I can carry her out and then unlock the U-lock and swing open the kennel door. I remove one glove and grab Maria's wrist to feel for a pulse. I don't feel one. Maybe the concoction of pills and alcohol did one better and quietly took her life already. I crouch into the kennel awkwardly and put my hand to her mouth to check if she's still breathing.

"Damn."

She's still breathing. It's very shallow, but fuck, she's still alive. I pull out one of my keys and press it hard into her thumbnail, she doesn't move. She's not dead, but she's far from conscious. I try to get her out of the kennel as gently as I can, wary that if she wakes up, she'll either be a) a zombie or b) pissed off and groggy. Neither option is good. I sit her up against the outside of the kennel and look at her arm; it's waxy, cold and the veins beneath her skin are black.

I pick her up and shimmy her up and over my shoulder, her arms hang loose behind my back as I hold her legs steady across my chest with both arms. I carry her slowly out the back door and take short steps toward the back fence. I pass the pizza oven, the halfway mark, when a bolt of lightning strikes the tree in the neighbour's yard and scares the hell out of me. I trip over the garden gnome that hid the spare house keys and I lunge forward. I drop to one knee with a mighty thud.

"Ugh, fuck."

Pain shoots into my knee and up my thigh.

Maria's body jerks and tenses.

I remain very still, hoping that Maria does the same.

She jerks again.

I try standing up slowly and she twitches again.

"No, no. Please don't wake up," I mouth silently.

I stand fully and take a tiny step forward. Pain radiates through my knee and I stop.

Maria's limp arms become rigid and grab hold of my hips. She pushes herself upright and her head wriggles around trying to figure out what's going on.

A snarl escapes her mouth.

"No, no, no," I whisper.

I quicken my steps toward the back fence when Maria screams. She starts trying to claw up the back of my leather jacket. She exposes my lower back and just as I go to throw her off my shoulder, she buries her face into my side, chomping and ripping at the flesh around my ribs.

"Nooo! Fuck!!!"

I twist sideways at the sudden pain and my eyes burst open in horror. I try to throw her off my shoulder again, but her knees spread open and they grip under my armpits as she digs her fingers into me, trying to hold on. I fall backwards into the chimney stack of the pizza oven and Maria grunts. I lean forward and throw myself back into the chimney again trying to knock her off, but she only screams louder. My jacket slides back down and protects my back. I step forward and jump back through the air and smash her into the concrete chimney much harder. It stuns her a little, but she's trying to rip up my jacket to bite me again. I turn and face the barbeque and bounce Maria up off my shoulder to swing her body down like an axe at the hard edge of the barbeque's tiled countertop. Her skull explodes, and her limp body drops to the ground.

I fall backwards onto the lawn and crawl away from her in a hurry. It all happened so quickly. I'm shaking and I can't speak a word. I pick myself up from the wet lawn and gawk at the horrific scene in front of me. The crumpled body of Maria and the dark blood staining the rendered brick wall of the barbeque.

A stabbing pain in my back catches my full attention and I run inside. I lock the door behind me and tip the pile of suitcases and boxes against the door. I race to the cracked mirror in the en-suite. I rip off my gloves and my jacket and pull up my shirt, I twist in the mirror trying to see what Maria has done. Strips of flesh hang from my bloodied back and three ragged bite marks bleed profusely.

"Fuuck!"

I rip open the medicine cabinet and pull out the disinfectant and antiseptic bottles. I rip off each of their caps and douse my back with them. The stinging pain causes me to see stars and I almost pass out. I rip out the first aid kit from under the basin and take off my shirt. I press some gauze over my wounds as best I can and start frantically wrapping a compression bandage around my torso.

"What do I do, what do I do? Err, can I burn it? Cut off the infected parts? No, don't be stupid. I'll bleed out. No. Errr…Umm. Fuck!"

I hammer my hands down on the sink. I struggle to see any other option than to blow my brains out in the backyard. I glance down at the pistol sticking out of my jeans for a moment when one word comes screaming to the front of my mind, Samira.

I run into the kitchen and grab the radio.

"Samira, Samira. Do you have a copy?!"

"Samira, please pick up? Come on! I need you!"

The radio only returns the emptiness of static.

I look around the kitchen and living room, hoping for answers, but nothing jumps out at me. I turn to go down the hallway and I stretch my wounds open, pain stabs at me sharply.

"Argh!" I buckle forward and arrest my fall with the hallway wall. I look up and see Bella's closed bedroom door, "Bella."

I cover my mouth with my hand and slowly walk toward her door. I creak it open to see her still sleeping peacefully. I close the door again and back away from the doorway quietly, staring at it in muted horror.

My mind races. I'm infected, Maria's gone, Bella has no one, "Oh, no. Sweetie."

My options are limited, but I have to act now.

I empty my backpack onto the counter, as well as the ammunition from my pocket, and I pull out Pat's pistol. I snap open the cylinder and empty out all of the shells but one, and then snap the pistol shut. I go to my closet and slide on a dark, long-sleeve shirt, wincing as the shirt rubs across my tender flesh. I put the musty leather jacket back on, slide the radio into its pocket and calmly walk into the carport and close the door behind me. I drop onto my hands and knees and painfully crawl into the kennel. I close the mesh door behind me. I loop the chain around the gate and padlock it together. I throw the keys into the middle of the carport and slide myself to the back of the kennel, where I first saw Maria hours earlier. I have my radio and my pistol with one bullet in it. Now, I wait until dawn.

Tomorrow, I'll get a hold of Samira and try to figure out a way to get Bella to safety. I'll tell Bella I caught Mummy's flu and that someone's coming to get me and to take care of her. I'll show her how to use the shotgun and ask her to lock herself in the house and hide until someone comes to get us.

Everything's going to be okay.
Everything's going to be fine.
I can't have come all this way for nothing.

I repeat this over and over in my head, willing it to be true, hoping that the morning brings answers. It has to. For Bella's sake. I clip the radio into the wire mesh of the kennel and I tuck the pistol under the foam dog mattress that I'm sitting on. I fight to stay awake for hours, not wanting to fall asleep out of fear of never waking again, but my body surrenders and I pass out in the early hours of the morning.

A SELFISH ACT

"Daddy, wake up! Daddy?" Bella pokes at me with an old TV antenna through the mesh of the kennel.

"Huh, what's"—my head is pounding, I struggle to open my eyes and focus.

"Daddy, why are you in the kennel?" Bella sits across from me looking down at her sloth plush toy, twisting its paw back and forth.

"Uh. Oh. Good morning, sweetie. How did you sleep?" I force myself to sit up and strain, my wounds throb.

"Hmm, okay, I don't remember going to bed."

"That's because I carried you to bed and tucked you in," I smack my lips together, my mouth is dry and it tastes like the unwashed arse of a dead dingo.

"Why are you in the kennel? Where's Mummy?"

"So…" my voice cracks and I try to cough the tickle out of my throat, "The doctor came last night and took Mummy
357

away to get better, she's off getting her medicine, sweetie. I'm in the kennel because your mum, umm, threw up on me, she was very sick," I offer.

"Ewwww..." Bella scrunches up her face in disgust.

"I know, some even got in my mouth!"

"Eyook!" She sticks her tongue out and shakes her head as if it had just gotten in *her* mouth.

I laugh, "Eyook, indeed. So, the doctor said that I probably caught Mummy's flu."

"So, why didn't you go with him to get better with Mummy?"

"Who would look after you, possum?"

I poke her knee through the wire mesh.

"But I'm independent?" Bella pulls her knees away from me, giggling.

"Yes, you are, but I couldn't leave you all alone. You'd probably have a big party, stay up late, invite all your friends over and make a big mess. I had to stay."

Bella tries poking me through the cage, but I curl my fingers through the mesh to stop her.

"Now, the doctor gave me strict instructions to get inside this kennel and to wait for his nurse friend to come and get me. In fact, I have to call her now," I reach for my radio, "So, how about you go make yourself some breakfast, maybe make me some too, while I call the nurse."

"Okay, but we only have that warm cupboard milk."

"That'll be fine, sweetie. Now, go on and shut the door, there's a good girl."

Bella stands up and walks out of the carport, swinging her sloth toy by its long arm, she loves that darn thing. As soon as she closes the door my soft placating tone changes to an urgent one as I try to call Samira.

"Samira, Samira, it's Dan. Do you have a copy?"

I can see daylight seeping through the gap under the back door; it's early morning.

"Samira, Samira. It's an emergency!"

"Dan? You're an early riser," Samira replies.

"Samira, thank God. Listen. I've been bitten and Bella's here alone, I fucked up." I release the call button and the radio stays silent for a moment too long, "Samira?!"

"When were you bitten, Dan? How did this happen?"

Her response is frighteningly clinical.

"Err, last night. I was taking Maria's body into the backyard when… Ugh, it doesn't matter. She bit me and I've locked myself in the carport. I'm inside a dog kennel and I need your help."

"Dan, I'm... I'm not sure how I can help?"

"I need you to come and get Bella. I'm done for and you're the only person in the world that can help."

"Dan, I..."

The radio goes silent again.

"Samira, please. I promised I would protect Bella and now, I'm her biggest threat. I can't leave her here alone, but I can't stay in this cage either. I need your help, Bella needs your help. She's the only family I have left."

I listen to the static for twenty long seconds before Samira replies, "Do you have a plan?"

I crane my head skywards, mouthing 'thank you' to the skies above, "Samira, you're an absolute Godsend! You just saved a little girl's life."

"I haven't said yes, yet, Dan. Tell me your plan."

"Oh, right. Err… Do you have another map and a bike?

Do you remember the route we drew?"

"Yes, I do."

Bella walks into the carport with two bowls of cereal.

"Sweetie, go into the kitchen and grab Daddy's map off the counter. I need it to tell the nurse how to get here, quickly now."

Bella places the cereal on the floor and runs into the kitchen, excited to help her dad. She races back in and hands me the map, "This one, daddy?"

"Yes, that's the one. Great job, sweetie."

I bring the radio to my mouth, "Samira, are you there? Do you have your map?"

"Yes, I've got it here now."

"Okay, the route you picked for me was perfect, so we'll stick to that. Do you have a marker? I'll point out a few choke points, but stop me if I'm going too fast."

"Go ahead, Dan."

"From Northam, try to stick to the paddocks all the way until you get to the edge of Mundaring. You should be able to see the route I took. I left most of the gates open that I used and you'll see the fences I cut along the way. There's a big horde in that sunken section of highway just before The Lakes, so avoid it at all costs," I break the transmission to make sure that she's following along.

"I'm with you so far. Go on."

"Excellent. Take the 'ranger access only' tracks to get into the Beelu National Park and follow the main road until you see another ranger track, it's got a big yellow steel gate at its entrance. It's just before the big hill leading out of the park. You can't miss it. This will take you through some bushland and then you'll pop on the other side of Pickering

Brook, take that road through Roleystone and then follow the transmission line corridor south toward Byford. It gets a little thick through there but if you stay near the power lines, you'll be fine. Do you copy?"

"Yes, I see the corridor on the map."

"Good, now how big is your fuel tank? I had to fill up a few times and stopping for fuel is a bitch."

"I have a massive fuel tank and panniers, it's an enduro and I can carry fuel."

"Yes! Okay,"—Bella interrupts me, her voice transmits over the radio to Samira—"Daddy, who are you talking to?"

I put the radio down, "The nurse, sweetie. She's coming to help us. Now eat your breakfast, please, gorgeous."

I talk into the radio, "Sorry, Samira. Are you still there?"

"Yes, Dan. Was that, Bella?"

"Yes, I'll put her on once we finish with the directions. Where were we?"

"Okay, we got to Byford."

"Yes, so keep to the paddocks and head towards The Spectacles near Anketell, and then you'll skip across the bush and lake reserves. A few of the intersections were crowded, but you should be fine getting through Beeliar and into the Woodman Point Reserve. Be careful in that park, there's a zombie pack in the carpark by the café at the north end. Get onto the beach as soon as you can and head north toward Port Coogee Marina. There's another horde in there. Avoid it completely. Maybe try to take the firebreaks along Cockburn Road to get around, Samira."

"Okay, I've got it so far."

"Very good. Stay with me. Once you get onto CY O'Connor Beach, you're on the home stretch. Watch out for the abandoned power station though, some people took some potshots at me as I rode past. From there, take the beach all the way up until you see the tall white apartment building by South Beach. You'll see some large dunes just before it, that's where I ditched my bike. It's hidden under some branches. From there, you need to sneak up to a park called Mariner's Reserve. There's a cul-de-sac leading off of it called Coddiwomple Place. Do you see it on your map?"

"Yes, I see it."

"I'm seven houses down on the right-hand side, number fourteen. It has a red-tiled roof and blue Colorbond sheeting across the windows. Jump the back fence on the side of the garage roller door and we'll meet you at the back door. Do you copy?"

"Yes, Dan. This is a hell of a favour you're asking. I'll gather my things and leave as soon as I can, but, Dan, if it's too dangerous or there are too many infected, you're on your own."

I look over to Bella, "Try your best, Samira. It's all I can ask,"—Bella interrupts the transmission again, I keep the button pressed down— "Is Samara the nurse, Daddy?"

"Yes, sweetie, Sa-*mee*-ra. Do you want to talk to her?"

"Yes, please!"

"Is that okay with you, Samira?"

I release the call button.

"Sure is. Hi, Bella. How are you, beautiful?"

I hold out the radio against the mesh and press the call button for Bella. I mouth 'talk to her'.

"Are you coming to make my Daddy better?"

Bella squeezes her sloth toy to her chest.

"Yes, I am. I'm going to try my very best. Do you like horses, Bella?"

Her face lights up, "Ahuh, I have toy ones in my room."

"Well, I have real ones on my farm. Would you like to come see them?"

"Yes, please. Daddy, can I go to the nurse lady's farm?"

I answer over the radio to them both, "Of course."

"You can call me Aunty Sammy, darling. Okay then, we'll have a girl's horsey adventure while your daddy gets better, okay?"

"Yay!"

"Now, you go and pack a small bag of all of your favourite things for our horsey sleepover, okay? I'll make the arrangements with your dad."

"Yay, I will. Thank you, Sammy."

"You're most welcome."

Bella runs back into the house and closes the door behind her.

I bring the radio up to my mouth, "Thank you, Samira,"

"She sounds like a wonderful kid. I'll see you soon, if I have any dramas I'll radio you, over and out."

"Over and out."

I drop the radio into my lap and lie against the mesh of the kennel, I breathe a heavy sigh of relief.

The grogginess in my head and the burning pain in my side are intensifying. I sweat profusely and the only thing I can think about, other than the pain, is what's to come: my death and the unwanted birth of a violent, undead cunt of a thing. The thought turns my stomach and I curl into the fetal position on the foam mattress. I won't become one of those things, I can't. I look around at the kennel's structure,

363

it's only made of thin metal, chipboard and some flimsy mesh that's only tacked on with staples or wire ties. When I do turn into one of those things, this cage won't hold me for long. I lay on my side with my head on my bent elbow, using it as a pillow, and reach under the foam mattress for Pat's pistol. I grip its handle and squeeze it, finding comfort in the fact that I could end it any time before I turn but I release my grip and leave it under the foam mattress.

"No, not until after Samira gets here, not until Bella is safe and away from all of this."

My thoughts wander to the gargantuan favour I asked of Samira and all that she would have to go through just to get here. And then all she and Bella would have to do to make it back to Northam.

Bella comes through the doorway, "Okay, I'm all packed now, Daddy. When is Aunty Sammy getting here?"

Bella plonks herself down by the kennel.

I wipe my face and prop myself up to talk to her.

"She'll be here soon, probably tonight. But it's a very long journey to get here, sweetie."

"That's ages, what will we do until then?"

"Bella, I'm getting very sick and I don't want you to catch what I have. It's very contagious. So, I'm going to need you to get me a bottle of water and Mummy's pink toiletries bag from the en-suite. Then, you're going to have to go into the house and lock the door."

"But, I want to stay out here with you, you only just got home! That's not fair."

"Bella, you can't be in here and I need you to wait inside for Samira. It's the safest thing for you."

"No, you can't make me. You're stuck in the kennel,"

Bella crosses her arms and pouts.

"Bella, I can't have you getting sick and the only way to keep you safe is to keep you inside the house. I thought you were my independent little girl?"

"I am! But you only just got here and I missed you." Bella's head drops down and she starts to sulk.

"Sweetie, I'm just a little sick. We'll have plenty of time to play when I get better, okay? You don't want to be sick for your horse-riding adventure, do you? No, you don't. So, please do as I ask, sweetie."

"Okayyy," Bella walks off in a huff into the kitchen. She returns quickly with a bottle of water and the pink bag. She pushes them through the narrow gap in the gate and I take them from her.

"Thank you, sweetie. Do you know how much I love you?" I hold up my hand, pinching my thumb and index finger together, "Is it this much?"

Bella replies, "No."

I open my finger and thumb wider, "How about this. Is it this much?"

"Dad, I'm not a kid anymore. I'm big."

I ignore her and hold my two hands out a shoulder's width apart, "Is it this much?"

Bella tries to hide her growing smile and folds her arms across her chest again, "No."

I extend my arms out as far as I can, jerking a little at the stabbing pain in my side, "Is it thiiis much?"

"No, it's more than that," she answers.

"Exactly," I reach out through the gap in the gate and offer her my hand. Bella places hers inside it, "And I never want you to forget that, Bella. How much your mother and

I love you, with all of our hearts. You are my happiness and my entire world, mi el mundo!" I squeeze her hand tenderly. "Now, go inside and lock the door."

Bella pulls her hand away from mine, "But what am I going to do for like fifty hours?" she exaggerates.

"Draw. Draw a picture of me, you, Mummy and Bones. Draw your friends. Draw what you think your horsey adventure with Aunty Sammy is going to be like."

Bella's eyes widen, "I know, I'll draw a comic. I'll write a story with lots of pictures."

"And lots of colours too?" I add.

"Yeah, thanks for the idea, Daddy."

Bella stands, excited to start her comic, and before she leaves, she kisses her fingertips and presses them against my fingers holding onto the mesh

"Mwah! Love you, Daddy."

"I love you too, Bella." She skips out of the carport and closes the door, twisting the deadlock latch behind her as she was told, "Good girl."

I recline back onto the foam mattress and stare vacantly into the distance, numb with poisonous thoughts and hot with a growing fever. I pull the pink toiletries bag close and unzip it, I lazily rummage through it, picking out one bottle of pills at a time. I examine each one and discard anything that isn't pain medication or cold and flu tablets. I know they won't cure me, but hopefully, it will lessen the symptoms.

This headache is like nothing I've ever experienced before, the pressure alone is starting to distort my vision. I can still see for now, but it's getting worse. I find two bottles marked Panadeine Forte and Extra Strength Cold n' Flu. I pop two of each into my mouth and take a swig of water, hoping they kick in soon. I roll onto my stomach to take the pressure off my pulsating back. I can feel my bandages are wet with sticky blood and I can smell the coppery tang of it wafting up through my jacket as I move. I close my eyes and try to sleep.

The next eight hours pass by in a slow blur.
I toss and turn.
I cry and call out for help.
I'm a fucking mess.

I think about how fast Russell had turned and then about how slowly Maria had turned—where would I fall on that timeline? I think about how Samira didn't turn at all. I start losing track of my thoughts. Forgetting how I became locked in this cage. I can't recall anything chronologically; everything seems jumbled. I slip in and out of consciousness. I can't tell the difference between my dreams and reality, the ongoing theme for the last few days. I question everything,

I remember Bella coming in, or was it Maria? Did I dream that? She was yelling at me to shut up and then. Wait, she did come in. Bella came back into the carport.

I roll off the mattress and onto the kennel's thin metal sheeted floor. There's a blood smear, I try to focus on it, but everything's so cloudy. My head is pounding. Something hot trickles down my face, I bring my hand up to it and touch it and all I can see is red. I'm bleeding from my forehead. I touch the rough abrasion. The sensation makes me dry heave. A memory of me kneeling over and smashing my head against the ground flashes before me.

Why would I do that? I'm losing control.

"You are being too loud, princess," a voice says.

"Who, who's there?" I try to look up and out of the kennel, but my head is heavy and doesn't allow it.

"You've forgotten about me already, Dan?"

The voice seems distant, like an echo.

"Son, you have to be quiet. You're scaring Bella. Don't make me come in there."

I roll onto the mattress again and push myself into the back corner of the kennel, "I know that voice…Pat?!"

"Ah, you *do* remember me, son. Good, good. You had me worried for a minute."

The voice trails off again, becoming distant and faint.

"That's. That's not possible. You're dead. I…I left you in the mud," the visuals of Pat in the mud bludgeon me.

I start to ugly cry and force my face into the mattress.

"You had no choice, mate."

I shake my head, convincing myself that I'm imagining it, "No, you're not real. Go away."

"Oh, I'm real, son. And, yes, I am dead too, just like you will be very soon. You're sitting at the edge of two worlds; yours and mine. But if you don't shut your bloody mouth, you're going to kill little Bella too."

"No! No! You're not real. Fuck off!"

"Just like you killed my daughter, Natalie."

"No!"

"Just like you killed Russell and just like you killed your wife, Maria. You're a murderer, son. Just like Bruno. Only worse." I fold the mattress up around my ears, trying to drown Pat out, but it does nothing. "You've been slowly killing her for years. Killing her with loneliness and with your absence. That's why she's dead, Dan. Because of you. If only you had got here sooner."

A pair of hands grab my shoulders and pushes me onto my back. I open my eyes, it's Pat. His face is muddy, covered in blood and his tattered jacket is dripping onto me. I look down to see his savaged, open rib cage spilling his guts onto me. The smell is putrid. Pat's eyes scare me the most. They are black, completely black. And so big.

"All you have to do now is die quietly, son. Do it for Bella! There's a good, princess," Pat puts one hand over my mouth and then reaches under the mattress and brings his pistol up to my head and fires.

I jerk awake, "Fuck!!"

I'm covered in sweat and panting for air. My heartbeat thuds like a jackhammer in my skull, "I'm going mad, I'm losing it," I bring my hands to my head to try to stop my head from vibrating when I feel the cold steel of Pat's gun touch my forehead.

Pat's pistol is in my hand. I pull it away from me, "What the fu…When did I get Pat's gun out?"

I try to focus on the gun, but my vision is cloudy. Like I've been swimming in an over-chlorinated pool with my eyes wide open underwater. I drop my pistol hand to the side and rest it on the cold metal floor. I press my fingers firmly into my temple and massage circles into it.

"Did I try to kill myself? What's happening to me?"

I try to stay sitting up, but my body feels heavy and the room starts to spin dizzyingly. I pass out again.

My unconscious state does not bring silence or darkness, it imprisons me, as a tornado of violence, anger and regret yanks at and twists my sanity.

Scenes repeat, contort and rip at me.

Steve, Russ, Pat, Natalie…So much death.

Was I really to blame?

Guilt squeezes my chest like a vice.

Frustration pulls at my jaw.

Fatigue pins my limbs to the floor.

A rage is burning its way into my muscles, it feels like the spiked tendrils of a decaying vine are penetrating every inch of me. This invasive force is radiating out from the bites on my back and into my extremities.

It's jagged reach clawing at the base of my skull, demanding passage. The toxic thing taps and raps at the door to my mind. I resist as long as I can.

NOTHING

I'm standing outside of the kennel.

My hands are bloodied from the escape and I'm gripping Pat's pistol tightly. The kennel is now a pile of twisted mesh and chipboard. My vision is blurry, but I can see light coming from the doorway into the house, it's wide open, and something's inside. It scurries off toward the bedrooms. Something's going for Bella.

"No!" My voice cracks. It sounds muffled and foreign to me, "Arghhh!"

My head is throbbing like a bastard. The yelling only makes the pain worse, but it strangely soothes the burning sensation in my chest. I stumble towards the kitchen. I grab for its frame as I pass through the doorway, but I miss it completely and sprawl out onto the kitchen bench.

"Bella!"

My body shakes and twitches unnaturally.

I hear something fall at the end of the hallway toward Bella's room. I yell out and try to run toward the door, but my balance is way off. I have to slide myself along the hallway walls, crossing from one wall to the other as my uncoordinated legs fight to keep me upright.

"Noo, Bllaaa," my words slur together.

I get to her bedroom door and twist the handle, it's locked. I bang on it and kick at the door's base. I throw myself against the door clumsily. I hear muffled whimpers and squeals before a window breaks on the other side of the door. Something screams, Bella?

The window's roller shutter rattles and squeaks as it rolls up. Something's trying to open the shutters, something's trying to get in. I hear repeated bangs, like a hammer hitting tin and then I hear a girl's scream again.

I call out and launch myself at the door. The frame splinters and the door handle assembly separates. But it's still not opening fully, the door is partially blocked by a mound of clothes, toys and a shelving unit.

I charge into the room hunting, but the room is empty.

The thin Disney curtains flap uncontrollably by the smashed window. The wind slaps the roller shutter wildly against its frame as the storm rages on outside. I stumble toward the window. It's nighttime, a flash of lightning lets me see something run past the window toward the backyard. I fire Pat's pistol at it, but my coordination is dog shit and I miss. I shoot the wardrobe to my right.

I call out in frustration, "Aaaarghhhh!"

I barrel out of the window with the pistol in hand and hit the lawn below with a thud. I stumble to my feet quickly, but I have to hunch over and lean against the wall to keep myself upright. I've winded myself from the fall. I still have the gun and I shake my head to shake off the disorientation.

"Blaaaa! Bella! No, Pleeeeaszz.."

I slide along the wall calling out for Bella.

My vision is terribly blurry, but I see a figure coming toward me. Running straight at me.

I bring the pistol up to fire it and yell, "Nooo! Plleaz."

The fast-moving figure knocks the gun out of my hand and hits me, very fucking hard, in the face and everything goes black.

I no longer feel pain.

I'm no longer afraid for my daughter.

I feel nothing. I see nothing.

There are no more nightmares.

No bright light and there's no montage of my life.

There is only darkness.

And silence.

There is...

Nothing.

"Rise and shine, Daddy," the sound of Bella's voice wakes me. "Come on, come on, wake up! You've been asleep for like five years!"

I open my eyes to see the cheery face of Bella hovering inches from mine. I must be dreaming again, fuck off.

I convince myself that my mind is tricking me yet again, after all, it has failed me many times since fly out day. That fateful day when Steve drove the work ute into the side of the caravan and flung me out of my bunk and into this fucking nightmare.

I look at Bella's face in a haze as she reaches out toward me with her finger, "Does it still hurt?"

She pushes her finger into my forehead.

"Jesus, fu…" I hold my tongue, not wanting to swear in front of her as hot pain radiates through my forehead and into my neck.

"That's a yep! You almost said a bad word, Daddy. Aunty Sammy! He's awake!"

I'm so confused, I try to sit up, but I feel even heavier and weaker than before, my head is a cinder block and my arms are wet noodles. I try to focus my eyes on Bella; she's sitting on the side of the bed, my bed, in her pyjamas. I must be in my room. I look over at the doorway and a watercoloured blotchy blur of randomness turns into Natalie, at least I think it's Natalie. She walks into the room with a tray in her hands; a glass of juice and some are sandwiches sitting atop it. I follow the figure as it dissolves into a 4K quality image of Samira.

"Good morning, Dan. How do you feel?"

Samira places the tray on the bedside table.

I go to sit up, but Samira gently places her hand on my

shoulder, willing me to stay down.

"Slowly, Dan. You're not well."

"What? I don't understand," I reach out with my arm and it weakly trembles. Samira grabs it and helps me to sit upright.

"Hey, grab those pillows and place them behind your dad's back," Samira says to Bella, who dutifully places three pillows behind me, and Samira lowers me onto them.

"What the f... What's going on? Am I dead?"

"I'll tell you everything you need to know, as soon as you take these," Samira instructs, as she starts popping some pills out of their silver foil packaging into her hand.

I touch my forehead to find it bandaged. I look down at my arms and they're clean. I do have several new large cuts across my arms, though, all with fresh sutures. I feel the tenderness of my back jab at me and I pull at my shirt, it's a clean one that I don't remember putting on.

I see a fresh wrap of dressings around my torso.

"What's going on? My back, it was? Maria? She..."

Samira pushes the glass of juice out toward me and an open palm containing three pills, "Take these and I'll tell you everything."

I take the pills and swallow them, chasing them with a few gulps of juice, "What happened? The last thing I remember was"— The mental fog is thick— "is talking to you on the radio?"

"That was three days ago, Dan."

I strain to recall a more recent memory, but I only get obscure pieces here and there.

"No. Someone got into the house. Someone was trying to get to Bella!"

Samira looks at Bella and then at the doorway, politely gesturing for her to leave the room; nodding at her reassuringly. Bella slumps out of the room slowly and leaves the door slightly ajar.

"Dan, Dan, Dan." Samira shakes her head at me.

"What?" I snap.

"We have more in common than you know. Does anything seem strange to you?" Samira opens up her arms and looks around the room, "Do you notice how you're alive and not trying to rip me apart?"

I look at her confused, unable to decipher her bullshit riddle-me-this puzzle. Samira notices Bella hovering by the door and stands up to close it fully.

"Touch your ribs, are they sore? Like you were bitten and clawed up by your infected ex-wife?"

I stare at her, frowning "Spit it out, Samira!"

"You're immune, Dan. Do you remember the night that someone came for Bella?"

My eyes dart from side to side, trying to remember. I touch my head as it throbs, "No, it's fuzzy. I..."

Samira sits on the edge of the bed, "Let me fill you in, there was no intruder. You were hallucinating. You thought that Bella was one of those *things* trying to take her away and you chased her. She tried to keep you out of her room, but you still came for her. She smashed the window and kicked out the bottom of the roller shutters."

I shake my head in disbelief; she has to be wrong.

"No, I'd never do that to her."

"You didn't do that, Dan. It was the infection."

The image of me firing Pat's pistol flashes before me, "I shot at it though, I remember shooting at the zombie running past the window?"

"No, you shot at me, you fuck," Samira grits her teeth and punches me in the leg, "I saw Bella crawl out of her window and run off into the backyard. I followed her, grabbed her and pulled her into the bushes. I kept her quiet as you fell out of the window chasing after her. I almost shot you there and then, but I saw you holding that gun and trying to speak. The infected don't do that. I covered Bella's eyes the whole time and then I saw you coming towards us. I told her to wait behind that oven thing out the back and then I..." Samira laughs, "Knocked you out with the butt of my rifle."

Tears well in my eyes, "She must think I'm a monster," my shoulders droop and I lower my head.

"No, she only saw you trying to get out of the cage. I told her there was another man, a bad man. That's who chased her, not you. She believes me, I explained that the cuts on your head were from a seizure that you had in the kennel. She believes that too, she has no idea that you did any of these things. She thinks the bad man was imitating you, trying to trick her."

I try to piece together the well-timed madness of Samira's story, "Wait, Bella hid behind the pizza oven? Maria! She saw her mother?"

"She thinks she saw her mother. I told her she was in shock and that when you're in shock, you see the things you want most. I think she believes me, but she is still a little shaken up. But it was dark."

"Thank fuck. How, how were you sure that I wasn't infected, that I was immune?"

"I wasn't. I just hit you, kept you tied up in here until

your fever dropped. If you turned, I would have shot you and left with Bella."

"Ah. Well," I fall silent for a moment, "You saved my life again, and Bella's. I owe you everything."

"Yes, you do, now rest up. As soon as you're healthy enough to move we're heading back up to the farm in Northam. Hopefully, we are there for New Year's."

My head spins. I try to grasp everything that's happening when I hear scratching at the bedroom door. The sound of hurried clawing and nails against wood. My heart jumps up into my throat. Panic. Samira turns toward the door with curiosity, but then smiles.

Why is she smiling?

"Oh yeah, someone was hanging around in the front yard when I got here, he was scratching at the gate," Samira stands up and walks towards the door. The scratching intensifies and the door rattles against the frame, "Do you know this guy?"

In the seconds between Samira reaching for the door handle and opening it, I have visions of Horse breaking down the door and leaping through it. I see Russell crawling on his belly across the carpet holding out his family photo as Pat steps over him with his pistol raised dragging Natalie's lifeless body behind him. Samira is knocked to the ground as they pour through the door in slow motion. Maria is standing in the doorway, leaning against the frame, she's just staring at the ground shaking her head. Samira opens up the bedroom door and my hallucination vanishes. The panicked tension building in my torso melts as a hairy Australian Cattle Dog cross Siberian Husky called Bones runs into the room.

Bones excitedly jumps up onto the bed, his uncontrollable, full-body tail wags delete his coordination and he lands sideways on my legs facing back towards the door. He enthusiastically rolls and paws his way across the covers yipping and licking the air as he climbs up toward my face.

"Bones! Buddy, where have you been?!"

I half-pet and half-defend myself from his bounding display of affection. I'm ecstatic that he's alive and, apparently, he's pretty chuffed I'm okay too.

"I thought you'd be happy to see him. He's been sitting and sleeping by this door for days standing guard."

I squeeze and roughhouse the hell out of Bones, wincing and jerking through the jabs of pain from my wounds. Bella appears in the doorway next to Samira smiling, she's clenching her hands close to her chest and looking up at Aunt Sammy.

Bella nudges Samira's hip with her elbow.

"Ah. Now that you've got your Christmas present, Bella's been dying to open her gifts since yesterday."

Fuck. Christmas. I'd forgotten all about it.

"Yes, let's do that," I attempt to get up but Samira meets that with an "Uh, uh," insisting that I stay in bed.

Bones also has me pretty pinned down, too, enforcing Samira's stay command.

"I'll go get the presents, you stay put."

Bella shoots out of the doorway toward the living room and Samira starts to follow.

"Wait, Samira," she pauses by the door, "I can't thank you enough. You didn't owe me anything and you've done more for me than I could ever repay you. You came for

Bella. You've saved my arse, twice! And you found my dog! Ha! Shit, you've even saved Christmas! But, what…"

I feel incredibly vulnerable for a moment and then ask her, "What do we do now?"

Samira's head drops, "Family is all anyone has, Dan," she fiddles with the seam of her shirt, "I had to help you. I was so focused on myself and my own interests that I... I forgot..." Samira pulls out a rectangular strip of laminated card from her pocket, the photo of her niece and nephew from Timezone. She looks at it for a moment and then slides it back into her jeans.

"You're a good guy, I think, and you pretty much begged me to come. I didn't think you'd be alive when I got here, but I couldn't bear the thought of Bella being all alone, not here. Not with everything that's going on."

I look down at Bones and play with his ears, trying to avoid thinking about what would have happened to Bella if Samira didn't come when she did.

Samira continues, "As for what we do now, we do exactly what we've been doing this whole time. We survive, whatever that looks like."

She shrugs her shoulders and walks off down the hallway to help Bella with the presents. Bones jumps down and follows her with his tail high and wagging.

I look around the room, it feels familiar and foreign to me. I recognise the furniture, but it's not how I remember it. Then I see several of our old family photos back up on the dresser, in the space they used to occupy before the separation. A dusty cardboard box that had been stored away and out of sight sits open at the foot of the dresser.

My eyes drift along the floor and I see Russell's

boredom bag neatly tucked in the corner with Natalie's rifle leaning against the wall beside it. It's very surreal to see these objects existing side by side in my former home; painful reminders of what was, what is and what remains.

A yellow light shines through the ceiling's skylight into the en-suite, the warm glow reflects off the mirror and glossy tiles and touches my face. The storm has passed and the heat of a December morning sun warms the room. I feel a wave of relief as I relax into the mattress and pillows. I close my eyes and exhale a weighted breath. Samira's words replay in my head, 'we do exactly what we've been doing this whole time, we survive'.

I mumble them to myself, "We survive."

I'm unsure of the how, but I am certain of the why; I made a promise to protect Bella and I'll do everything to keep it. We will survive.

THE END.

Dan's journey is far from over.

In a world torn apart, can he honour the promises he's made—while carrying the weight of those he's lost?

Fly Out Day: Torn Apart

Coming soon.

What a wild two years it has been since *Fly Out Day* was first released on April Fool's Day in 2023. It amazed me how the initial disbelief of this book's existence soon evolved into media coverage, international sales, merchandising and then ongoing local & *global* support. *Fly Out Day* has reached Canada, South America, Germany, the United Kingdom, Japan, China, New Zealand, South Africa, Spain, Thailand and all of Australia.

I'd like to thank you, the reader. I hope this book made you laugh, think, cringe, and feel seen, sick, horny and angry!

Thanks to all my non-reading friends that supported me by other means, like spreading the word to your family and friends, promoting it with your spouse's book clubs, shouting me a beer at the wet mess or by putting my promo stickers in the most outlandish and remote places possible!

A special thank you to close friends and family that gave me the space to create and to those who guided me with unfiltered criticism—your help was invaluable.

During its creation, this book followed me through my late teens and early thirties all over Australia, up to Canada, down to Chile and across to New Zealand; on planes, trains, road trips, ski trips, diamond/RC drill rigs, test pumping units, floating resorts and in mountain cabins, caravans and all manners of staff accommodation.

I've been privileged enough to see the zombie movie genre evolve from the likes of *The Dawn of The Dead* to *The Evil Dead* to *Shaun of The Dead* to *The Walking Dead* and to the Australian *Wyrmwood*. There are so many great adaptions, niche genres and some amazing international gems out there. The zombie narrative highlights the strengths and weaknesses of humanity and it's a bloody entertaining beast to observe.

I love it, and now I get to add *Fly Out Day* to this ever-growing genre, maybe it'll become the next mini-series on your movie streaming service too.

I hope you enjoyed reading it as much as I enjoyed writing it! Share it with your friends and post your positive reviews on the websites below, and anywhere else, to help others find
Fly Out Day.

flyoutdaybook.com
goodreads.com
amazon.com.au

www.ingramcontent.com/pod-product-compliance
Lightning Source LLC
Chambersburg PA
CBHW010255100726
47904CB00011B/2603